THE SCARLET CLUB

MASON COOPER SERIES - BOOK TWO

TERENCE MITFORD

MASON COOPER SERIES

This book is a work of fiction and any resemblance to actual people, alive or dead, or real events, is purely coincidental.

Rexor Books

ISBN
978-1-8381118-9-2

BOOKS IN THE SERIES

BOOK ONE
TAKING NATASHA

BOOK TWO
THE SCARLET CLUB

BOOK THREE
INNOCENT GIRLS

THE ABDUCTION

The big man slammed the frightened girl into the large boot of the Mercedes, then leant over and placed his face near to hers. 'If you scream again, I will kill you.' He held her down while the thin man pulled her arms behind her back and tied her wrists together with heavy duty nylon cable ties. They worked with precision. As a team. They had done this before. The young girl was no match for them. She was helpless and at the mercy of three strangers, treating her not as a person with rights, but as a possession under their control. There was no escape.

MASON

Mason Cooper stepped out of his front door just after three thirty in the afternoon, and for the first time in twenty-five years, he had nothing on his mind. No thoughts of evidence gathering, or interviewing witnesses or suspects, or testing their statements for inconsistencies. He had no court case to attend, no paperwork to complete, and best of all, no senior officers on his back.

Because from today, he was an ex-cop, with just one immediate task. A ten-minute each-way car journey, and one he'd done a hundred times before. Nothing difficult or unusual. Just collect his daughter on her last day of school and bring her home.

What could go wrong?

He parked his old Ford Mondeo opposite the large iron school gates and waited. It was 4pm on the dot when Rosie walked out and jumped into the front seat beside him.

'Hi Daddy,' she said. Then she leaned across and kissed him on the cheek.

He gave her a grateful smile.

She threw her student bag onto the back seat, settled back, and snapped on her seatbelt.

'Thanks,' she said, then flicked back her ponytail.

'For what?'

'For coming, for being on time, for having a car... for being my dad.'

He laughed. 'I'm glad to be of service Madam. It's not like I had somewhere else to be.'

'Yeah, now you've got more free time I'll be able to save lots on bus and taxi fares.'

'Glad to hear it. Are you prepared for your meeting tonight?'

'I think so. I have to make a good impression on Melissa, cos she has so many contacts in the fashion industry. She said it's an informal meeting, so I need to look casual and spontaneous, but I'll be planning my outfit with meticulous precision.'

'Isn't that a contradiction?'

'You don't understand.'

Mason shook his head.

'Anyway Daddy, how was your day?'

'Great, had breakfast, read the paper, went for a run, showered, picked up a few things from the shop, and here I am.'

'Pretty boring then.'

'Uneventful maybe, boring no. Actually, I'm loving the monotony.'

'Don't you miss the excitement? Solving murders, catching criminals and all that? I know I'm going to miss being able to brag to my friends that my dad's a detective sergeant.'

'It wasn't all action and excitement, most of it was pretty routine. Anyway, the novelty wears off after twenty-five years.'

'So, you don't regret retiring early then?'

'No, but I did it for your mother. I'm not sure our marriage would have survived me doing another five years in the job.'

'Yeah, things were getting a bit strained. You were hardly ever home, and when you were, you two were always arguing.'

'I know I've neglected you both over the last few years, so now I plan to make up for it.'

'I just hope you and mum can get on better now.'

'So do I, but your mum seems a little pre-occupied lately.'

'Give it time, she'll come round.'

After a moment of silence, he said, 'Anyway, how was your last day?'

'Happy and sad at the same time. I mean I'll miss it in a way, well, not school, but my friends, and maybe some of my teachers.'

'You'll meet new friends and teachers at college in September.'

When she didn't answer, he glanced over. She was twisting her ponytail around her fingers while staring out at the blur of people, cars, and buildings flashing past.

'You okay?' he said. 'You've gone quiet.'

'Yeah fine, but I'm a bit scared. What if I'm not good enough?'

'Where's this coming from? You have a natural talent.'

She didn't answer.

'That dress you made for your mum on our last anniversary was really professional.'

'Yeah, but what if I run out of ideas? Like writers who sit staring at a blank page with no plots, or songwriters who can't think of any new tunes. What if I end up a fashion designer who can't design?'

He glanced across at her. 'Where's my confident girl gone?'

She sighed. 'Nowhere, she's still here, I think. I'm sure I'll be fine tonight.'

'Do I need to remind you of what you said a while back?'

'What's that?'

'That nothing and nobody would stop you becoming a successful, international, fashion designer.'

She sighed. 'How can I forget when you keep reminding me of it? Do I need to remind you, that when I said that I was twelve? I'm not as cocky now. I'm sixteen. I've grown up since then.'

Mason grinned.

'What's funny?'

'Nothing.'

'Don't you think I've grown up?'

'I think you are growing up, but you're a work in progress. Don't be impatient. From what I can see you're on course to be a beautiful, intelligent, successful fashion designer.'

'You forgot international.'

'A beautiful, intelligent, successful, international, fashion designer.'

Rosie sighed, 'Mm.'

'What's wrong with that?'

'Nothing, except you're my dad, it's your job to say nice things.'

'Yes, but that doesn't mean they're not true.'

She sat quietly for a moment, then unbuckled her seat belt, leant across, and kissed him on the cheek.

'Don't do that,' Mason said.

'What, kiss my dad when he says nice things about me?'

'No, undo your seat belt while I'm driving. Put it back on.'

'There you go again, worry, worry, worry.'

'I'm your dad, it's in my job description, next to the part about saying nice things. It's a lifelong clause, active from the day you were born to the day I die, so we're stuck with it I'm afraid.'

'Okay, but is trying to be funny a lifelong clause too?'

'Ouch.'

'Sorry,'

Mason glanced down at the orange light on his dashboard. 'Changing the subject, how are we for time? How long do you need to spontaneously get ready?'

'Why?'

'Because we're running on fumes, and if I don't fill up here'—he pointed to their local garage up ahead—'we're not going to make it home, never mind to your appointment tonight.'

Rosie shuffled forward and pulled out her mobile phone from the back pocket of her jeans.

'What are you doing?'

'Checking the time.'

'Where's your watch?'

'Don't need it, got my phone, nobody wears a watch these days.' She swiped the screen. 'We've got plenty of time.'

Mason glanced at his own watch. 'I didn't realise these things have become a generational thing.'

'Well, you are retired, remember?'

ROSIE

They turned onto the garage forecourt, and as Mason exited the car, Rosie reached forward and turned on the radio. She found a lively music channel, turned up the volume, and leaned back. She glanced out of her side window at a serious-looking man in a long black coat, fuelling a car at an adjacent pump. She studied him, trying to work out who he was, where he was from, and what he did for a living. Just a teenager's curiosity. She would often try to guess whole life stories of complete strangers, even though she would never know if any of it was correct. She wondered how long it had been since he had smiled. Then, due to his heavily furrowed brow, she guessed it had been a long time.

She was jolted from her daydream when the man raised his head and looked straight at her. He was tall and broad, with cropped black hair and piercing blue eyes. The kind that could burrow right into your soul. She quickly turned her head away and waited until, out of the corner of her eye, she saw him walk towards the kiosk. Then she looked back towards his car and at two people in the back seat. Closest to her was a girl, and next to her a man, like the big man, only not as large, and not as intimidating. She made eye contact with the girl and smiled. She guessed the girl would be two or three years older than her. She had pale skin and long black hair, and Rosie couldn't help noticing how pretty she was.

But something was wrong.

The girl did not return her smile, she just stared back with a wide-eyed intensity, as if silently trying to tell her something. The man in the next seat turned and said something to the girl. From the way his lips tightened across his teeth as he spoke, it was clear he was angry. The girl lowered her head.

Rosie waited for a few moments, raised an eyebrow, and turned on her phone to check her messages. There were three from her friends wishing her luck for the meeting that night. She began tapping out replies with the speed and precision honed by years of practice. Like many kids, she could text message before she could ride a bike, and lately, when her parents commented, she would tell them, that's why teenagers have thumbs.

But she couldn't concentrate. The tapping got slower and slower and eventually stopped. She turned her gaze back to the black car. If only the girl would look up, she could mime to her and ask if she was okay. But as she watched and waited, the big man returned, staring at Rosie as he threaded his way between the petrol pumps. His piercing glare prickled the back of her neck, so she lowered her gaze back down to her phone. But she wasn't reading messages or tapping replies. She was monitoring him with her periphery vision and waiting for him to get into his car.

He slammed his door shut, and Rosie looked back just in time to make eye contact with the girl as the car moved off. But there was no time to mime, and no time to gesture, only to reaffirm her first impressions.

That girl is frightened.

4

MASON

As Mason opened the car door, Rosie jumped, but then quickly told him what she'd seen and about her concern for the girl.

'I'm sure she's fine,' he said, then reeled off the different possibilities of boyfriend, husband, and father.

'No, Daddy, she's scared, something's wrong, I know it is. Please follow them.'

He'd not known her to exaggerate before, so he fastened his seat belt and accelerated away from the garage, if for no other reason than to put her mind at rest.

He recalled the car next to his on the forecourt. It was a Mercedes, top of the range, and less than two years old. He had admired the gleaming black paintwork as he walked past to pay for his fuel, but had paid little attention to its occupants. However, he did remember the large man in front of him at the counter. They had made brief eye contact, and Mason had nodded to him as he took his place, but received nothing in return.

'There it is, the black one.' Rosie pointed to the Mercedes ahead of them.

'Yes, I see it. We'll follow them to see how the girl behaves when she gets out of the car, okay?'

'Okay.'

Mason followed the Mercedes through the West London streets and eventually it turned left into a tree lined residential road. As he slowed to make the turn, he made a mental note of the name on the black and white metal sign bolted to the low wall on the corner of the street. Willow Road. He repeated it five times in his mind. It helped when committing something to memory. Although it was a tactic he normally employed when meeting someone for the first time, it worked just as well for street signs and locations.

Willow Road had little traffic on it, so Mason slowed to a crawl and stopped when the Mercedes came to a halt. They watched the big man get out of the driver's seat, glance up and down the road, then walk towards one of the houses before disappearing behind a hedgerow.

Mason glanced around. The houses were Edwardian and large and set behind small front gardens and drive-ways. The drive to his left boasted a Porsche and a BMW 7 Series, the drive to his right a new Range Rover. It was a nice area, an expensive area, the kind where stockbrokers, lawyers, and all kinds of city high-flyers would live. And maybe even celebrities. The black Mercedes fit right in.

They waited a minute, then slowly edged forward and stopped on the opposite side of the road, almost level with the Mercedes. The girl turned and looked over her left shoulder. He saw fear in her eyes.

Rosie pointed. 'Look Daddy.'

'Yes, I see.'

He turned off the engine, opened his door, and stood up. One foot on the road, one still inside the car. He paused there for a few seconds, assessing the situation and reassuring himself that he needed to do this. Not as a police officer, he'd given up that responsibility when he retired, but as a man who hated to see anyone taken advantage of, and because he hated to see anyone in trouble, and because most of all, Mason Cooper hated bullies.

So, he had just one thing on his mind. Was this girl in trouble? Was the big man and the man next to her banking on the fact that normally, the public don't get involved? They see things. They suspect things. But usually, they walk or drive on by.

But Mason was no ordinary member of the public. So he stepped out, closed his door, and approached the Mercedes. He'd done this a hundred times before in the force. But back then he'd check the registration number over the radio first, use full police powers, and call for back-up when necessary. This time he was acting as a civilian. No radio, no checks, no powers, and no back-up.

He crossed the road, grabbed the handle, and opened the car door, then crouched down to make eye contact with the girl, and said, 'Is everything all right?'

She said nothing, but appeared to fidget nervously.

The man next to her answered in a tone lacking any hint of curtesy. 'Yes, everything is all right'.

Mason waited for the girl to answer, noting the look in her eyes. He'd seen that look before. In the eyes of victims, and in the eyes of women living in fear of their own husbands or boyfriends. But this felt different. He detected no intimacy between the girl and the man sitting next to her.

The man spoke again in a strong East European accent, 'I have told you, everything is all right, now go away'.

'I would like the girl to answer, if you don't mind,' Mason said.

The man's tone escalated from unfriendly to threatening. 'If you know what is good for you, you will leave right now.'

Mason ignored the threat. This guy may be used to getting what he wants by intimidating anyone who gets in his way. But not this time, and not with him.

'What's your relationship with this girl?' he asked.

The man unfastened his seat belt. 'None of your fucking business.'

Mason studied the scene in front of him. Over the years he'd learned to trust his instincts, especially when they were screaming at him as loud as they were right then. And he had a pretty good idea what they'd stumbled across. While still in the force, he'd read National Crime Intelligence bulletins about East European sex traffickers operating in London and how they would transport girls in the back of luxury cars. They would use luxury cars to reduce attention from an overstretched police force. The girls would be forced to work in brothels and massage parlours, usually in less affluent areas than this, but would often be taken to meet wealthy clients in hotels, luxury houses, and apartments.

Some gangs would traffic the girls and sell them on to organised crime or individual pimps, and some would do it all, traffic them and force them into sexual slavery.

Although the general public would acknowledge that it happened, they would have no idea about the scale of this illegal industry.

Mason remembered the criteria in those bulletins. Two heavies in a top of the range car transporting one or more young attractive women or girls.

This fit perfectly.

If he was right, the threats would be followed by violence. These people do not back down. But he was not about to leave this girl in their clutches, so he expected trouble, and he was ready for it.

'I will teach you not to interfere,' barked the man as he threw off his seat belt and got out of the car. Then he slammed his door and stormed around the back of the vehicle. At around six feet, he was similar in height to Mason, though a little heavier.

At forty-three, Mason was fit for his age, and strong. He'd worked out all his adult life, practiced martial arts, and had been a police self-defence instructor earlier in his career. He was no stranger to confrontation.

He watched the man's approach. Chin high, chest puffed out, face grimaced. In the past, he'd taught his students to recognise this body language as a warning that violence may be imminent. Close attention to detail was vital to distinguish between mere posturing and an actual threat. And the best place to look for that detail was in the eyes.

And this man's eyes said it all. He was calm. He was confident. He was a professional. But that could be his downfall.

Mason watched him charge forward without pausing for

a second. He must have decided there was no need to assess his target. No need to consider, even for a moment, the abilities of the stranger in front of him. And Mason knew that was his first mistake. It was a common one made by so many of his kind. Hard men, even professional hard men, never stop to consider that one day, they might meet their match. And normally it wouldn't matter. Not when dealing with ordinary members of the public who could not handle the level of violence the professionals can dish out.

But Mason Cooper was no ordinary member of the public. And Mason Cooper never made the same mistake.

He never underestimated his opponent.

He stepped away from the car in a forty-five-degree stance, feet shoulder width apart, knees slightly bent, a fighter's stance, crucial for a fast response to the man's aggression. It was something he did instinctively and subconsciously. Drummed into him at an early age by his martial arts instructor. Never stand square on to an adversary, never give him a bigger target than necessary, and always stay alert and agile, ready to move and counter attack.

And watch the eyes.

Mason stepped back as the man threw his first punch, and the fist found nothing but thin air. Two more punches missed their target when Mason stepped back again and parried them away. With a look of frustration and even disbelief etched across his face, the man lunged for his third attack. But Mason moved fast, driving a powerful palm heel strike into the man's chest while giving a verbal command.

'Back off.'

It was a technique that showed he meant business without causing injury. In his police days, it would be enough to end most confrontations. The sudden jolt would usually bring people to their senses.

But not this time.

The man gasped for air, took a deep breath, and reached inside his jacket and behind his back. Mason didn't wait to see what he was reaching for. He ended the confrontation with a right hook to the man's jaw. It was quick. It was clean. It was efficient. The man was unconscious before he hit the tarmac.

Mason rolled him over and pulled his jacket aside. His fears were confirmed by the sight of a semi-automatic pistol sticking out from the man's belt. He removed it and with it a clip-on leather pouch containing spare magazines. He reached in through the open car door and took the girl's hand. 'Come with me, quickly.'

He led her to his car where Rosie was waiting, then stuffed the gun and pouch under his seat, grabbed a pen from the centre console, and scribbled the registration number of the Mercedes across the back of his hand.

Nobody spoke until they had left the area and found an empty space in a busy supermarket carpark. Surrounded by dozens of other cars belonging to the late afternoon shoppers, Mason turned off the engine and glanced back to the entrance from the main road. Satisfied they had not been followed, he turned to the girl in the back seat and again asked if she was all right.

This time she answered him with tears in her eyes. 'Yes, but you don't know what you have done.' She spoke in a similar, though softer, accent to the man they'd just left

17

unconscious in Willow Road. 'I must go back. I must work for them.'

'No, you don't, I can take you to the police station.'

'No, no, no,' she yelled. 'I cannot go to the police. They told me that if I escaped and went to the police, they would have my family killed. You don't know them, they are crazy people, they will do it.'

'Who are those men?'

'They are Albanians, they were taking me to a man who had bought me.'

Mason turned away, his hand pressed against his forehead. The full implications of the situation were becoming apparent. He knew how ruthless the traffickers could be. It was their way of keeping the girls quiet. So the possibility of them killing one or more of her family was real. They had done it before.

He glanced at Rosie, then took a moment to think. He turned back to the girl. 'Okay, come home with us and you can contact your family. Warn them and tell them to go somewhere safe. We won't involve the police until they are safe.'

The girl took a moment, then nodded.

Mason turned back toward the wheel and drove away.

'My name is Mason Cooper. This is my daughter, Rosie, and you are?'

'Natasha, my name is Natasha.'

'How old are you Natasha, and where are you from?'

'I'm twenty-two, I'm from Moldova.' She continued, as if feeling the need to explain. 'It's a small country between Romania and Ukraine.' She leant forward and placed her hand on Rosie's shoulder. 'Thank you,' she said. 'I thank you both.'

Rosie smiled back at her, no doubt too shocked by the recent events to say anything.

A few minutes later, Mason turned into the driveway of their house and parked next to his wife's car.

'Your mum's home, Rosie, explain what's happened while I take Natasha to the phone in my office. We have to act fast.'

'Okay Daddy.'

She ran to her mother in the kitchen while Mason showed Natasha to his study just off the hall. The study was a converted garage attached to the side of the house; insulated, plastered, and carpeted, and with a door knocked through from the hall. The house was a typical nineteen thirties semi-detached, with two double bedrooms and a box room big enough for a bed and not much else.

In the study, Natasha picked up the phone and dialled. Her conversation was in Moldovan. She spoke fast, cried a little, shouted a little, before eventually calming down. After the call, she replaced the receiver and turned to Mason. She seemed less tense.

'My family will leave their home and go to a relative's house in another town. Tomorrow I can ring my.... err... how do you say, my cousin and check they are safe.'

Mason nodded, then showed her to the kitchen where he introduced her to his wife, Kathy, and helped Rosie to explain.

Kathy listened intently, and then walked over and hugged Natasha. 'Don't worry, you're safe now, they won't find you here.' She looked at Mason. 'They couldn't have followed you, could they?'

'No, when we drove away, the guy was still on the ground, and the big man was nowhere in sight.'

As soon as the words had left his lips he drew a quick breath. 'I need to speak to Tom.' He turned to his daughter. 'Rosie, do you have his number?'

Tom was a year older than Rosie and had attended the same school before dropping out and getting an assistant's job at the garage they were at earlier. He was part of Rosie's extended circle of friends and knew that Mason was her father.

'Yes, I have his number, but why?'

'I approached the counter as the big guy was leaving. Tom used my name when he said, hello. I don't know if the guy heard but I can't take the chance. I have to warn Tom not to give our address away.'

Rosie searched her phone and rang Tom's number. 'It's gone to voice mail. Shall I leave a message?'

'No, hang up. We can't wait. I'll drive to the garage, it's only five minutes away.' He strode off down the hall shouting over his shoulder, 'Lock the door behind me and don't answer it to anyone while I'm gone. I'll only be ten minutes.' At the door, he paused. 'And get changed Rosie, when I get back, I'll give you a lift. You shouldn't miss your appointment tonight, it's important to you.'

A few minutes later, Mason turned onto the garage fore-court and parked next to the kiosk. It was one with a shop included which sold snacks, soft drinks, magazines, and a selection of food items. As he entered, several people were standing at the unmanned counter. He felt a surge of anxiety as he looked around the shelving displays for Tom.

'Where's the assistant?' he asked the confused-looking customers.

An elderly man at the front of the queue answered. 'We don't know, we haven't seen him, and I can't use the pump until he pushes the button.'

Fearing the worst, Mason walked around the confectionery display and behind the counter, where he found Tom lying motionless on the floor in a pool of blood. There was a small hole in the front of his blood-soaked shirt. He bent down and lifted the shirt to reveal a wound in the boy's chest. He checked for a pulse. It was faint.

'Someone call an ambulance. I think he's been stabbed.'

There were gasps from the others, and a couple of them came around the counter to look.

'Stay back,' Mason said. 'I need room, and this is a crime scene.'

'Let me by I'm a doctor,' a woman said, as she pushed her way past the others.

Mason stepped aside, allowing her to take his place. Knowing just how critical the first response can be in life and death situations, he was relieved to pass on the responsibility for administering first aid.

A man on the public side of the counter said, 'The ambulance is on its way,'

As Mason watched the doctor at work, a sudden chill ran through him. This had to be the work of the traffickers. They must have returned. But why would they attempt to kill Tom? Did he refuse to tell them what they wanted to know? Or was it to prevent him from warning Rosie they were on their way?

He had to get home fast.

As he turned to leave, he stopped and looked up at a security camera behind the counter. Whoever did this would have been caught by that camera. From experience, he knew the equipment was normally kept in the back office behind the counter. He found it on a shelf in the corner of the room. A split screen monitor displayed two views, one of the shop counter, and the other of the forecourt. Below that was an old video recorder. He pushed open the front cover. It was empty. Either no tape had been placed in the machine, or the attacker had removed it before fleeing the scene.

Less than five minutes later, his wheels locked as they skidded to a halt in his driveway. When he reached the front door and found it still locked, he breathed a sigh of relief.

But it was short-lived.

He turned his key and entered.

First, he saw the small table laying on its side in the hall, and then he saw blood on the floor. The house was quiet, too quiet.

'Kathy, Rosie, where are you?' he shouted.

He heard a strained voice from the kitchen call his name. It was Kathy.

He found her slumped on the floor, her back against the cupboards, covered in blood and barely conscious. Not knowing whether she had been stabbed or shot, he grabbed a towel and pushed it against the wound. Natasha ran down the hall and knelt by Kathy.

'What happened Natasha?'

'I am sorry,' she cried. 'It's all my fault.'

He took out his mobile phone and rang 999.

'Emergency, which service do you require?'

'Ambulance and quick, my wife has been stabbed or shot. I'm not sure which, but there's a lot of blood.

Once connected, he gave the call-taker his name and address and a brief description of his wife's condition before thinking out loud.

'I have to find my daughter.'

5

ROSIE

Only ten minutes earlier, Rosie had run up to her bedroom to get ready for her meeting. She studied garments on rails, and garments in drawers, pairing them together in her mind.

White blouse, grey trousers: Too serious.

Brown knee length dress: Too boring.

Short flowery Mini dress: Too sexy.

Finally, she pulled out a black V-necked cashmere sweater from a drawer, and a short, slightly flared denim skirt from the rail. From the bottom of her wardrobe, she chose her favourite pair of black suede ankle boots. She dressed quickly and while brushing her long coffee coloured hair in front of her full-length mirror, she heard a car pull into the driveway. Thinking her father had returned, she glanced out, only to be frozen with fear at the sight of the two Albanians getting out of the Mercedes, along with a third man she had not seen before.

As the big man looked up towards her window, she

ducked out of sight, then ran to the top of the stairs and shouted down.

'Mum, quick, they're here, we need to hide Natasha,' naively believing that if the men couldn't find Natasha, they would leave.

Kathy ushered Natasha to the stairs just as the doorbell rang. The handle turned, and the door pushed against the lock as she guided the girl up to a spare room and into a closet. 'Don't make a sound,' Kathy said.

Then Kathy and Rosie crept down to the kitchen.

'If we stay quiet, maybe they'll go away,' Rosie said.

But their hopes were shattered when the back door flew open and the big man walked in holding a semi-automatic pistol in his right hand.

He spoke slowly and menacingly through gritted teeth. 'Where is she?'

'She's not here,' Kathy said. 'My husband has taken her somewhere, now get out!'

The big man, who was now joined by the other two, looked at Rosie. 'I thought it must have been you. I saw the way you were watching us at the garage.' He turned back to Kathy. 'I will ask you one more time, where is the girl?'

'She's not here, so you are wasting your time. My husband will be back any minute and you'd better not be here then.'

He turned back towards Rosie and looked her up and down. 'Then I will take this one. She will make a good replacement. She is very beautiful.'

Rosie stood her ground and shouted at him. 'Get out now!'

Life had not yet taught her that there were times when you should stand up for yourself and give as good as you get, and then there were times like this.

He took two steps forward and slapped her across the face with the back of his left hand. She fell against the wall, then turned to run, but he grabbed her arm in a vice-like grip.

Kathy ran between them, clawing at his face and drawing blood from his cheek. 'Leave her alone, you are not taking her,' she shouted.

He pushed her away, and she clattered into a small table in the hall, knocking it over and scattering its contents across the floor. She scrambled back to her feet and ran at him again. The third man, tall, and thin, and gaunt, with long unkempt hair, pulled out a stiletto knife. He said nothing as he plunged it up to the hilt in Kathy's stomach.

She gasped and fell to the floor, clutching the wound.

As Rosie began to scream, the big man spun her around and grabbed her from behind. He placed his free hand over her mouth, wrapped his gun arm around her waist, and pulled her to him.

It was no contest. She was helpless.

He lifted her up like a rag doll and carried her out of the house, ordering the others to follow and open the car boot.

After forcing Rosie into the boot of the Mercedes and holding her down while her hands were tied behind her back, the big man growled through gritted teeth, 'Open your mouth now.' He forced a leather gag into her mouth and tied it off behind her neck. Then he tugged a black hood over her head, pulled off her boots, and slammed the lid shut.

Just as the Mercedes left the street at one end, Mason had driven in from the other.

6

MASON

The call-taker kept the line open so Mason could update her with Kathy's condition, and she could in turn update the paramedics on their way. He constantly checked her wound, then her breathing, then her pulse.

'Breathing, okay, pulse okay,' he reported every minute for five minutes. Then he turned to Natasha and asked again, 'Where's Rosie, where's my daughter?'

'I think they took her. I'm so sorry, I was upstairs. They hid me upstairs.'

'So, you weren't here. You weren't here when they took her?'

With tears streaming down her face, she shook her head. 'I'm so sorry.'

Mason looked at her and sighed. He was being unreasonable. What could she have done to stop them? He didn't need to ask. He already knew. Nothing.

'I'm sorry, Natasha, it's not your fault.' He managed a half-smile before turning his attention back to Kathy.

A siren ended mid-squeal in the road outside. As Natasha ran to open the door, flashes of neon blue streaked through the glass, along the hall, and into the kitchen.

Mason sat on the floor with Kathy's head resting against his chest. 'Stay with me Kathy,' his voice cracked, 'I need you, and Rosie needs you.'

Two paramedics wheeled a stretcher into the kitchen. Mason picked up Kathy and laid her down on it. Then they wheeled her to the ambulance where one of them kept pressure on the wound while the other attached monitoring equipment and a drip. Mason jumped into the ambulance and held her hand. But he couldn't travel with her. He needed his car to search for Rosie.

He placed his hand on the shoulder of a paramedic. 'Look after her, I'll see her at the hospital.' Then he jumped out.

The paramedic closed the door behind him and they drove away under flashing blue lights.

As Mason and Natasha rushed to his car, two police vehicles screeched to a halt on the road outside and four uniformed officers jumped out, two from each car. Mason recognised one of them as an ex-colleague.

'John, it's Kathy,' he said, pointing in the direction of the ambulance. 'I think she's been stabbed.'

He showed him the registration number written on the back of his hand. The officer took out his notebook and pen and copied it down.

Mason said. 'Black Mercedes E class, two males, white, black hair, early forties. Driver is big, six-feet-four with broad shoulders, the other is six-feet and stocky. They are traffickers, John. They have my daughter Rosie. She's only sixteen, five-two, slim, long brown hair, brown eyes, wearing jeans and a—'

'No Mason, she changed,' Natasha interrupted, then described to the officer Rosie's black sweater, denim skirt, and ankle boots.

'Thanks Natasha, did you get that, John?'

'Got it,' he said, and began relaying the information over his radio.

Mason returned to his car. As he was about to close his door, one of the other officers took hold of his arm.

'Just a minute sir, we need to establish what's happened here.'

'I understand that. I'm an ex-cop, but my wife is in that ambulance dying from a stab wound. Get someone to the hospital and I'll speak to them there.'

The officer was about to insist when his partner, John, intervened.

'It's okay, Martin, let him go, that's Mason Cooper.'

Martin released Mason's arm and stepped back, allowing him to drive away after the ambulance.

———

'So that's Mason Cooper?'

'Yeah,' John said. 'I don't know what's happened here tonight, but one thing's for sure, I wouldn't want to be the guy that stabbed his wife when Cooper catches up with him.'

7

ROSIE

In the darkness of her mobile confinement, Rosie's heart pounded above the road noise coming up through the floor of the boot. She tried twisting and pulling her wrists apart, but the cable ties were too strong and dug into her skin. The leather gag caused her to salivate, so she tried to push it out with her tongue but couldn't.

Lying on her back, she brought her knees up and pushed them against the boot lid. It didn't move. It was futile. She lay still and listened to the three men talking in their own language. Then she heard leather creaking and something moved away from her arm that was pressed up against the back of the rear seat. The voices from the car seemed louder.

She guessed that one of them had opened the armrest in the rear seat, allowing access from the cabin into the boot. She jumped when she felt a hand touch her shoulder, then move down to her wrists and tug at the cable ties. She didn't know why, but she just had a feeling it was the thin man. He moved his hand up to her face and checked the leather gag through the hood.

But it was what happened next that sent shivers through her body.

He slipped his hand inside her sweater and bra and caressed her for a few moments. Then he removed it and slid it down over her body to her legs. She tried to turn away from him, but it was impossible. There was nowhere to go. She tried to shout, 'Get off me,' but the gag made her speech illegible. His fingers touched the inside of her thigh, then briefly stroked her through her panties before he withdrew from the compartment and closed the arm rest. She heard him say something to the others, and all three laughed out loud.

That was the moment she knew why they had taken her and what they wanted from her. She thought about the times she had gone close, but never all the way with any of her boyfriends. She remembered how her friends would make fun of her because she was still a virgin, which contrasted with her mother telling her how important it was that her first time should be with someone special. Someone she loved, and who loved her.

Now all that was beyond her control. The thought of what lay ahead filled her with dread. She prayed her father would find her before anything happened. She remembered him telling her that if ever she found herself in a situation she couldn't get away from, she shouldn't do anything to antagonise her attacker. He told her to remain calm and try to gain the man's trust. Make him like her so he would find it harder to hurt her. Because of her father's profession, she'd received advice on all kinds of situations that many people wouldn't even think about. She remembered how she would mock him for being such a worrier.

The men's voices, followed by more laughter, brought her back to the present, and as she lay there in the dark confined space, new questions flooded her mind. Where were they taking her? What would they do to her? And how would this end?

8

MASON

Mason paced up and down the large open plan waiting room while Kathy underwent emergency surgery. He watched in anticipation every time a member of the medical staff walked along the corridor. The knot in his stomach was more intense than anything he had ever experienced. In less than an hour, his family had been torn apart. A happy, carefree journey home with his daughter had turned into the worst nightmare he could imagine.

'Please sit down, Mason,' Natasha said. 'I think she will be okay, she has to be.'

He turned and looked at Natasha, then sat down next to her. 'I hope you're right, I don't know what I'll do if I lose her.'

Natasha placed his hand between both of hers and squeezed. 'You are a good man,' she said. 'Rosie is lucky to have you as her father.'

He glanced at her. 'That's sweet.'

They had known each other for barely an hour, yet

already a bond was growing under the tragedy and intensity of their situation. He put an arm around her and for a moment gained comfort from having her close. But her delicate frame reminded him of Rosie. He couldn't help wondering where she was, and what would be happening to her?

He needed information.

'Tell me, Natasha, what happened to you? How did you end up with those men?'

She stared at the floor, and her eyes filled with tears. 'I was stupid. I was promised a new life, a job, somewhere to stay, and a chance to settle in England. My family begged me not to go. They were worried I was being lied to, but I wouldn't listen. I laughed. I told them they would feel different when I sent money back home to help them. Now I have put them all in danger.'

'Mr Cooper?' came a voice from across the room.

He looked up to see a Doctor in a green cotton V-necked over shirt, matching trousers, a green paper cap, and white disposable shoe covers.

Mason jumped to his feet. 'Yes, that's me.'

'I'm Doctor Mathews. I have just finished your wife's operation. I'm pleased to say that everything went as well as we hoped it would. We have stopped the bleeding, and she has had a blood transfusion. She's stable at the moment, but I must warn you she's still very poorly. The next twenty-four hours will be critical.'

Mason held his breath as the surgeon spoke. Then he exhaled long and slow.

Doctor Mathews continued. 'We will monitor her closely overnight. We have sedated her, so I suggest you go home and get some rest, and you can see her tomorrow.'

Relief spread across Mason's face. He thanked the doctor for operating so quickly.

'We had to. We don't know the extent of what we're dealing with until we go in and look. But we expect your wife to make a full recovery. She just needs to give it time.'

Mason thanked him again and asked, 'Doctor, do you know how Tom is? He's the young man who would have been brought in just before my wife. I think he'd been stabbed as well.'

Doctor Mathews glanced over to the far side of the waiting room. A group of distressed people had gathered and were comforting each other. 'I'm sorry, but I can't really discuss his condition.'

Mason nodded. 'I understand. Are those people his relatives? I think I recognise his father.'

Doctor Mathews forced a tight-lipped smile. He didn't need to confirm anything. It was obvious. Tom had not survived.

Mason shook hands with the doctor and turned towards Tom's family. He took two steps and stopped. Maybe now wouldn't be the right time to talk to them, to tell them why their son had been murdered. But he would need to at some point. He owed them an explanation. They had a right to know. He would want to know everything if it had been Rosie. So he will tell them. But not right now.

Just then, he heard a familiar voice. 'Mason, I'm pleased to hear Kathy's pulled through the operation. We need to talk.'

He'd known DS Jim Barker for over twenty years, ever

since they'd worked together as new detectives at the same sub-division.

Jim was accompanied by a woman in her late twenties, smartly dressed, in a two-piece trouser suit and a white blouse. Her hair was shoulder length and dark, with hints of highlights almost grown out that would disappear with the next trim. He introduced her as DC Kelly Taylor.

Mason shook hands with them both. Then he introduced Natasha and explained that they would need a statement from her, too.

They separated, and DC Taylor took Natasha into one interview room, while Mason went with Jim to another. It was a busy hospital, but rooms were available for police to interview witnesses.

While making his statement, Mason gave DS Jim Barker a description of the house that the big man had approached when he got out of the Mercedes. 'It's on Willow Road,' he said. 'The only one with a high hedge at the front. It must be connected somehow. Why else would they stop there?'

'We'll check it out and get back to you,' Jim said.

'Any news on the Mercedes?'

'It's on false plates.'

Mason nodded. 'Yeah, I thought so. How much do you know about these gangs?'

'Just what we get sent in the crime intelligence bulletins. I've not dealt with them before.'

'You know they are likely to be armed, don't you?'

'Of course, we'll have an armed team on standby.'

'Are you dealing with Tom, the young man brought in from the garage with a chest wound?'

'No, it's been allocated to someone else.'

'It has to be linked, it's the garage where we first saw Natasha and the traffickers.'

'I'll find out who's dealing and liaise with them.'

'Just remember, Jim, Rosie's out there somewhere with these animals.'

'We'll do our best, Mason. You know my daughter's the same age.' He handed Mason a card. 'I know you've got my personal number, but that's my police mobile number. You can call me anytime, but I'll ring you as soon as we've checked out that address.'

Mason stared into the tabletop, his hands clasped tight in front of him. 'You know Jim, for twenty-five years I followed the rules. Did everything by the book. Cracked heads when necessary, but only when necessary. But now.' He looked up from the table. 'Now, I will do whatever it takes to get my daughter back and put those bastards out of business for good. They'll find out that when they took Rosie, they took the wrong girl.'

Jim tucked his pen into his top pocket, slotted the statement into his folder, and got to his feet. As he walked around the table towards the door, he stopped and placed a hand on Mason's shoulder.

'I would feel the same. You know all the guys will do their best for you, don't you?'

'Yes, I know... thanks Jim.'

As the detectives left the hospital, Mason sat down next to Natasha in the waiting room.

'Okay Natasha, I need you to tell me everything you know about these animals, and I mean everything. I can't rely on the police. I need to track them down and find Rosie.'

She hesitated for a few moments. 'Everything?'

'Sorry, I know you don't want to relive what's happened to you, but if I'm going to find Rosie I need to know the gangs M.O. and by that, I mean the way they operate, in as much detail as you can give me.'

Her expression slowly changed to one of acceptance. 'Okay, I feel responsible for what's happened to your daughter, so I will tell you, but I must warn you, you are not going to find this easy to listen to knowing they have Rosie. But I will tell you everything. I owe you that.'

She glanced around. There was no one else close enough to hear. She breathed in and breathed out, then said, 'I met a woman in Bucharest a few weeks ago while I was visiting my grandmother. My mother is Romanian, you see. I was born there so I have a Romanian passport.'

Mason nodded.

'This woman was really friendly. She told me she was recruiting girls for well-paid jobs in Europe and America. Anything from waitressing to shop work, but for girls like me there were opportunities for modelling. She said the agencies liked East European girls because we are slim and different. She said I could earn good money. I was stupid to believe her.'

'No, you weren't. These people are skilled in what they do. They know what buttons to press, so don't blame yourself.'

She swallowed hard and continued. 'I told her I would love to work in England, so she said she would arrange it for me to meet with her representatives here. A few days later I was given my flight ticket, and I came to London.'

'Were you given an address here?'

'No, I was met at the airport by two men from Romania, and as we left the airport, they took my passport and my money and told me I owed them ten-thousand pounds and that I would have to work for them until I had paid them back. They told me my debt could take years to pay off unless I worked every day. That's when I realised that my family was right. I had been tricked.'

'Where did they take you?'

'To a house somewhere in London. There were other girls there, and three more of the trafficking gang.' She paused and took a deep breath. 'They all took turns with me.'

Mason shook his head and sighed.

She licked her lips. 'Sorry, I'm so dry.'

Mason hurried over to a water dispenser and returned with water in a plastic cup. She gulped it down and stared into the empty cup. 'I'm sorry to tell you this, but it happens to all the new girls. We are raped every day, over many days, to desensitise us, so that by the time we are ready to see clients we are numb to it all. And they treat us roughly. I think it's to make sure we prefer to see clients rather than be abused by them. When they think we are tamed, as they say, they sell us to criminal gangs who run the brothels. At first, I refused to cooperate. That's when they told me that if I resisted, or escaped, my family would be at risk. They even threatened to kidnap and traffic my younger sister. She's only twelve. I felt sick. I had no choice but to do what they wanted.'

'How did they know about your sister?'

'I'm not sure. I may have mentioned her to the woman

in Bucharest. I don't remember, but how else would they know about her?'

Tears filled her eyes. Mason walked over to a table and picked up a box of tissues. Not knowing what to say, he sat back down and handed them to her. She dabbed her eyes and took a moment to compose herself.

'After I was sold, I was taken to a house where I was made to see between five to ten clients every day for two weeks. Then I was moved again. But this time by the two Albanians you saw. They took me to a house not far from the garage where I saw you and Rosie. I knew there were other girls working there because I heard their voices, but I was kept separate. The next day I was given a dress and told to get ready for a special client. I was taken to a room where I met two men. They were Englishmen. They were wearing expensive looking suits and were well spoken, not like my usual clients. They told me to undress. I did as they said, but they weren't there for sex. They looked at me for a minute and told me to get dressed. Then they left.'

'Did you see them again?'

'No, but later that night I was told I had been sold to an organisation. An exclusive club who only bought the prettiest girls. That's where they were taking me when you stopped them.' She paused for a moment. 'That's it, that's why they took Rosie. They needed a replacement for me. They could not turn up empty-handed.' She looked up at Mason. 'I'm so sorry, I would change places with her if I could.'

Mason took her hands in his. 'Listen, Rosie knew you were in trouble and needed help. It's not your fault. Don't blame yourself.'

She was close to tears again. 'I should not have looked at Rosie the way I did at the garage, then she would never have got involved.'

'You don't know that. She always seems to know when something's wrong. Anyway, you couldn't have known what was going to happen.'

His words seemed to reassure her. She dabbed her cheeks with a tissue.

'I know this is upsetting for you, but I need to ask, can you direct me to the places where all this happened?'

'I don't know, maybe.'

'Did you tell the police about this?'

She hesitated again before answering. 'No, I couldn't. I'm worried about my family. I can't tell the police everything until I know they are safe. I told them I had just arrived in the country and that the Albanian men had taken my passport.'

'So, what can you remember about the houses you were held in?'

'They put a hood over my head when we got near, so I saw nothing of the first two. But it was dark when they took me to the third house, and the hood was stretched over my eyes, and I could see lights through the material. I remember seeing a sign, The Fountain, in big white letters above some windows. We turned left just after the sign, and the house was just along that road.'

Mason thought for a moment. 'I think I know a pub by that name. I've seen it many times. The street next to it leads to an industrial area. I need to check it out.'

'I'm coming with you.'

'No, it's too dangerous.'

'You need me to show you which house they took me to. I think I'll be able to remember how far down the road we drove before stopping. And if Rosie's there she could be traumatised. I know what she will have been through.'

Mason took a moment to think over what she'd said. 'Okay, but you'll have to wait in the car.'

She nodded.

In his car, in the hospital carpark, Mason reached under his seat and pulled out the semi-automatic pistol. 'You're not the only one who withheld information from the police.'

Natasha stared at the gun. 'Where did you get that?'

'From the Albanian guy I knocked out when I found you. It could be useful where I'm going.'

He studied the pistol. It was a Beretta nine millimetre with a standard fifteen-round magazine. He released the magazine, saw it was full, then pushed it back. It was a gun he was familiar with and one that he'd fired many times while training with a friend and colleague who was an instructor in the firearms department. Officers could attend the force shooting range as long as an instructor supervised them. Mason was a natural, and his scores would have been good enough for him to pass the shooting assessment had he wished to join the team.

He pushed the Beretta back under his seat.

'Do you know if they all carry guns?' he asked.

'I was only with them for two or three weeks, but I didn't see any guns.'

'That's good to hear.'

'But they had knives.'

9

ROSIE

The Mercedes made a sharp right-hand turn and drew to a halt. Rosie's breathing quickened and panic brewed in the pit of her stomach. She lay in anticipation of what was about to happen. The boot opened. Strong hands took hold of her and pulled her out into the cool air. She guessed from the ease with which he picked her up and threw her over his shoulder, it must be the big man. Gravel crunched beneath his feet. He stopped. A door opened. A man spoke in English. 'You're late. Come in and take her down.'

She was carried into the house and along what she guessed was a hall with a wooden floor. She tried to picture the man who spoke. He sounded well educated, posh, maybe gentry, and definitely English.

Her heart skipped a beat as she felt herself being carried down a flight of stairs and feared she was being taken into a basement. She was thrown down onto what felt like a bed and told to lie still. Adrenalin surged through her veins, but she dared not move.

The big Albanian spoke. 'Sorry, sir, we had a problem. This is not the girl you bought yesterday, but I think you'll be pleased with her.'

The Englishman sounded angry. 'But I'm paying top price for Natasha. She's beautiful, and she's the one I want.'

'One-minute sir, let me show you.'

Rosie was pulled off the bed onto her feet. There was a tug on her wrists and suddenly she was free from the restraints. She brought her hands around in front of her and massaged her wrists, one at a time. Someone pulled the hood from her head. She squinted while her eyes adjusted to the light shining from a single bulb hanging from the ceiling.

She could now see her surroundings, and it was a basement. No windows and only one door that must lead to the stairs that she'd just been carried down. One wall was bare brick, the others were plastered and painted off white, dirty, and in need of a fresh coat. The concrete floor was cold and hard beneath her bare feet. The room was large and unwelcoming. A bed and a table with one chair were the only furniture. Over in the corner there was an old-fashioned bathtub, a toilet, and a sink. A neatly folded bright white towel hung over the edge of the bath. Was that for her?

She focused on the man standing in front of her. He was tall, around fifty, well dressed in a suit and tie. He was clean shaven with neatly trimmed brown hair greying at the sides. He had an air of confidence about him. One she'd only seen in men with wealth, or power, or both, and only on television, but with one exception, her father. She had noticed from an early age that he was different from the other fathers. It was the way he carried himself and the look in his eyes. She knew nobody would ever hurt her when she was with him. If only he was here right now.

The Englishman pointed to her mouth.

The big Albanian reached around her neck and removed the leather gag. She took a few deep breaths. The Albanian stepped back. 'What do you think?'

The Englishman studied Rosie as he slowly walked around her. He returned to his starting point and brought his thumb and forefinger up to his chin in the thinker's pose.

'Mm,' he nodded. 'Very sweet.'

'So you approve then, Mr Jones?'

'Of course I approve.' He stepped closer and stroked her cheek with the back of his hand. 'Like silk,' he whispered, as if talking to himself. 'What is your name, child?'

'Rosie,' she murmured, while looking down at the floor.

'Speak up, I cannot hear you.'

She lifted her head and tried to project her voice a little louder. 'Rosie.'

'Sweet name, turn around.'

She turned.

He stepped close, and from behind, brushed her hair to one side. She heard him inhale slowly and deeply as if breathing her in, then she felt his breath on the back of her neck as he exhaled.

'Are you a virgin?' he asked.

In any other situation, she'd be shocked to be asked a question like that, especially by a total stranger. But she had no such reaction. This was no ordinary situation.

She nodded.

He released her hair and stepped back. She waited before turning around.

He said, 'From now on you speak only when spoken to, and you address me and any other man you meet as sir, do you understand?'

She nodded.

He raised his voice. 'Do you understand?'

She realised her mistake and looked up at him. 'Yes sir, I understand.'

'Good, I own you now. I am your Master. You will be looked after here as long as you do everything you are told, and I mean everything. But I must warn you that disobedience will result in consequences. Do you hear?'

'Yes, sir.'

He turned to the Albanian. 'You have done well, Artan. She is the best you have brought me so far.'

Rosie glanced at the big Albanian. Artan, she repeated to herself, and the Englishman is Jones.

'We are here to please, Mr Jones,' Artan said.

The Englishman patted him on the back. 'And to collect a big fat fee, eh?'

The big man grinned. 'Of course.'

'Come with me, I'll get you the cash and a little bonus to show my appreciation.'

As they turned to leave the room, the Englishman said, 'So, the terms are the same then, she will not be returned. You know that, don't you?'

'Yes, sir, the terms are the same. She is yours to do as you wish.'

The door closed and the lock turned.

Rosie was alone.

MASON

Mason and Natasha left the hospital car park and drove in silence for several minutes. They had plenty to occupy their minds. For him, a quiet uneventful day had turned into a living nightmare, and for her, a living nightmare had come to an end thanks to a young girl she had never met before, and her father.

As they drew to a halt at a set of traffic lights, Mason glanced at Natasha. 'Your English is very good, where did you learn?'

'I lived in England for five years, from eleven to sixteen.'

'Why was that?'

'My parents split up just before my eleventh birthday, and just after my sister was born. Then my mother met an English guy, and we moved here. She married him, but it didn't work out, so we moved back to Moldova. A year later my parents got back together.'

'Where did you live when you were here?'

'In London. Stephen, my mother's ex-husband, and my

ex-step-father, was rich, so we lived in a big house in London. He wanted me to stay with him, to carry on with my schooling. He was good to me, he bought me clothes, and was always friendly, but my mother didn't trust him.'

'It must have been hard for you, moving back to Moldova at sixteen.'

'It was, and my mother always said I'd have a better life in England, so when I was eighteen, she encouraged me to look for jobs over here. But she did not want me to accept any help from unknown people in our own country or Romania, because it is well known that girls are trafficked from Moldova to Europe. There were two girls from my country in the first house I was taken to. One of them told me she had been arrested when their brothel was raided by police. They deported her back to Moldova, but the same gang came for her and trafficked her again.'

'Yeah, I've heard about cases like that. I'm an ex-cop, so I know about the East European trafficking gangs.'

'So that's how you knew something was wrong when you opened the car door and asked me if I was okay. I'm sorry, but I couldn't answer you at the time.'

'I understand. One thing puzzles me though.'

'What's that?'

'Why didn't they put a hood on you this last time before they stopped in Willow Road?'

'Yes, I wondered about that, too.'

'It's as if they didn't care if you saw the house and its location, and that worries me even more about Rosie's safety.'

'It was the third time I'd been moved. And I had been

co-operating since they threatened to traffic my sister. So maybe they thought I would not try anything.'

'Yeah, I hope that's the reason. It would make sense for them to keep things looking normal, if possible. If they got caught with a girl in the boot, or with a hood over her head, they would be looking at long prison sentences. But if stopped with the girl sitting normally in the back seat, they'd have a better chance of talking their way out of it. Especially if the girl was intimidated into staying quiet.' He thought for a moment. 'It still worries me though.'

As they drew near to Willow Road, where Mason had rescued Natasha, he pulled over and rang DS Jim Barker.

'Jim, have you got the warrant yet? I'm in the area so I'll wait for the result.'

'Sorry, Mason, but you'll have a long wait. The Super's not convinced we have enough for a warrant.'

'What? Who's the Superintendent on tonight?'

'It's Clive Coulson.'

'Hell, he's frightened of his own shadow.'

Mason remembered Coulson well. They had locked horns a few times when Mason had been the duty detective sergeant and Coulson had been the superintendent in charge. Mason had often been frustrated, and even angered, by Coulson's cautious attitude and his refusal to take positive action. He had considered him to be the kind of senior officer who preferred to make as few decisions as possible to avoid any mistakes and criticism from above. In other words, career before duty.

'I'm coming in,' Mason said. 'I'll be there in ten minutes. Tell Coulson I need to speak to him.'

'Okay, Mason, but he wouldn't listen to you when you were in the force, so I doubt he will now.'

'My daughter wasn't being held by a gang of sex traffickers back then. He's going to listen this time.'

Mason parked in the visitor's car park at the front of the police station and turned off the engine. 'Pass me the carrier bag in the glove box please, Natasha.' He reached under his seat and pulled out the Beretta pistol and the pouch with the spare magazines.

Natasha stared at it, wide eyed. 'What are you going to do with that?'

'It depends on Coulson.'

He stuffed the gun into the bag and pushed the magazine pouch back under the seat. Just in case, he thought to himself.

'You going to shoot him if he doesn't do what you want?'

'Hope not,' he said. Then got out of the car.

The civilian on the front counter was new, so Mason didn't recognise her as he approached the desk. When he introduced himself, she lifted the desk phone and dialled.

'Mason Cooper is here to see you, sir.' She waited. 'Thank you, sir.' She replaced the handset and smiled at Mason as she pressed the door release. 'Turn right and take the stairs on your—'

'Thank you. I know the way,' Mason said as he burst through the door and made his way up to the first floor.

Coulson was waiting at his office door. 'Come in, Cooper. Good to see you. I'm just sorry it's under these circumstances.' They shook hands.

'Thanks for seeing me,' Mason said.

Coulson made his way around his desk to his chair and pointed to another in front of his desk. 'Please sit down, Mason.' He glanced at his watch. 'I know why you are here, but from what I've been told we don't have enough to apply for a warrant. We have no evidence to connect the men in the Mercedes with your daughter's abduction, and we only have the word of the East European girl that the guys were sex traffickers. Maybe they're just supplying black market workers, you know, illegal labour or something like that.' He took his mobile phone from his pocket and placed it on the desk in front of him. 'And maybe she's just scared of being deported.'

'She has a Romanian passport. She can't be deported.'

Coulson just shrugged.

'What if she's telling the truth? My daughter is only sixteen years old. She's never even had a serious boyfriend, and now she's out there somewhere in this city with those fucking animals.' He paused to compose himself. 'They sell girls, Clive. They abduct girls and sell them.'

Coulson glanced down at his phone again.

'Are you listening to me?'

'Yes, but—'

'No buts, I want that house searched, and one way or another, it will be.'

'I wish I could help, Mason, I really do.'

'All right, I have something you can't ignore.' Mason reached down and picked up the carrier bag. He stood up and took out the Beretta pistol with the barrel pointing just above Coulson's head. Coulson gasped and push backwards in his chair, banging into the wall behind him.

'Relax, Clive.' Mason released the magazine onto the

desk and placed the Beretta next to it. With both palms flat on the desk, either side of the gun, he leaned forward and locked his eyes onto Coulson. 'I took that off the Albanian I knocked out on Willow Road. What black market labour suppliers carry guns?'

'Are you crazy, Cooper? You walk in here with a loaded gun? Why didn't you hand it in?'

'I'm handing it in now,' Mason said, gaining some pleasure from the panic etched across Coulson's face.

'But you didn't tell Jim you had it. You could be done for unlawful possession.'

'Maybe I could. But my wife is fighting for her life in intensive care, and my daughter's been abducted by human traffickers and god knows what's happening to her right now. I don't think there's a jury in the land that wouldn't give me the benefit of the doubt. Do you?'

Coulson walked over to the window and seemed to contemplate Mason's explanation. Then he turned back and shrugged. 'Okay, but you and I both know that if I'd agreed to go for the warrant earlier, you wouldn't be here now, and you wouldn't be handing this gun in. Am I right?'

'Do you really expect me to answer that, Clive?'

The display of Coulson's mobile phone illuminated. He walked over to his desk and read a message. Then he sat back on his chair and seemed to relax.

'Good news?' Mason asked, irritated by Coulson's preoccupation with his phone.

'Okay Mason, you win.' He picked up the desk phone and dialled. 'It's Coulson here, go and get the warrant for Willow Road, we're going to hit the address. Mason's just brought in a handgun he took off one of the Albanians...

yes, you heard right, don't worry about that right now, I'll explain at the briefing. I'll arrange the armed response teams and we'll brief at nine. Wait, what's the latest on the black Mercedes?' He listened for a few seconds, then grunted and hung up the phone.

Mason looked at him in anticipation.

'False plates. We knew that but we've run it through all our systems and nothing. We've got nothing on it.'

Mason turned to leave. 'Jim will let me know the result of the search. I appreciate your help.'

'Just one thing.'

Mason glanced back over his shoulder.

'Leave it to us. Don't get involved, and if you hear from Rosie I want to know, okay?'

'Okay.' Mason said as he was halfway out of the door.

As he got back into his car, Natasha stared at him. 'Well, did you shoot him?'

'No need, he agreed to apply for the warrant and search the house.' He glanced at Natasha. 'When was the last time you ate anything?'

She thought for a moment. 'Yesterday, I haven't eaten since yesterday. But I would feel guilty eating before we find Rosie.'

'I know, I'm not hungry either, but we have to keep our wits about us, so we need to eat. I need you to be able to concentrate and find that last house you were at, and I'm going to need energy when I catch up with those scum. So no arguments, we'll get some fast food on the way to the Fountain Pub. We have at least an hour before the police execute their warrant.'

MASON

I t was dark by the time Mason parked on the main road in front of the Fountain Public House. It was just as he remembered, on the corner next to a residential road that led to a small industrial estate. The pub was over three hundred years old, with an exposed oak frame and whitewashed walls. Maintenance had been lacking over the years, evident by the peeling paint and cracked windows, but despite its flaws, it still oozed character.

He pointed up above the door. 'Does this look like the sign you saw?'

Natasha looked up at the brightly illuminated sign and nodded. 'Yes, that's it, so this must be the road we turned down.'

Mason drove forward and turned left. The name plate on the wall read Silver Street. 'How far down do you think they drove?'

She sat up high in her seat. 'I remember we passed two street lamps.'

Mason passed two lamps and stopped. 'Which side of the road was the house on?'

'It must be on the left. I remember getting out of the car and walking in the direction I was facing. I didn't turn and cross the road, so it must be one of those.' She pointed to the last three houses on the road. They were typical London stock. Two storeys and terraced, and in a block of three.

Mason drove forward into the industrial area, just beyond the last house. He reversed into the shadows between two units and switched off the engine.

'We can see all three houses from here. We'll sit tight and see if there's any activity.'

Just then, Mason's phone rang. He checked the display and swiped to answer. 'Yes, Jim.'

'Mason, just letting you know, we're searching the address now. We're nearly finished, but we've found nothing untoward. Some high-powered financier from the city owns the place, and he's pretty irate, threatening us with lawyers, and legal action, and all that bullshit.'

'What did he say about the big Albanian?'

'He claims the guy got the wrong address. Thought he was on Fallow Road. There isn't a Fallow Road anywhere around here.'

'What do you think, Jim? What's your gut feeling about him?'

'Honestly, I think his bluster is a smoke screen. I think he knows more than he's letting on. The place is squeaky clean, too clean. You've searched plenty of properties over the years, you know when everything just seems too organised? His desk has paper pads, notebooks, and diaries, all blank. There's no correspondence, no hand-written notes or telephone numbers, nothing. But Coulson won't let us arrest him. He's told us not to bring him in unless we find something linking him to Rosie or Natasha or any other girls. Sorry, Mason.'

'It's okay. I would have been surprised if you'd found anything. Thanks to Coulson, they had plenty of time to clear the house of evidence. But I may have another address to check out. I'm watching three houses now for any activity.'

'Okay, we've got to go back and debrief. You've got my number, right?'

'Yeah, I'll let you know.'

After the call, they watched for nearly an hour before a car pulled up outside the last house in the road, the house that was closest to them. An insignificant-looking man, losing his hair, wearing small round glasses, and carrying a little too much weight around his middle, got out and walked down the side of the house.

Mason sat up in his seat. 'Why didn't he go to the front door? Wait here. I'll take a look.'

He got out and made his way to a high wall dividing the last house from the industrial area. He peered around to see a door open at the side of the house. He could see the man outside, but he couldn't see who opened the door. He listened.

The visitor said, 'Malik sent me.'

A man inside said, 'Come in.'

The visitor stepped inside, and the door closed. Mason returned to his car.

'Well, anything?' Natasha asked.

'The guy just said, Malik sent me, and was invited in.'

'*Malik*, did you say *Malik?*'

'Yes, do you know that name?'

'There was a man called Malik at the second house I was at. I think he was the boss. He told the others what to do.'

'That's good enough.' Mason took out his mobile phone and rang D.S. Jim Barker's number. 'Jim, it's Mason. I know which house it is now. It's the last on the left along Silver Street, down from the Fountain Pub.'

'Sorry, Mason, we've been stood down. Coulson has sent everyone home. We have to report first thing in the morning. We have an operation on.'

'Hell, what for?'

'I don't know the details, but it's something to do with terrorism. We're carrying out raids all around London. It's taking priority over everything, even Rosie. Sorry, Pal.'

Mason gritted his teeth and squeezed the steering wheel with his free hand. 'Okay, Jim, but just one thing.'

'What's that?'

'This call never happened.'

'Why, what are you going to do?'

'You don't want to know. Take my word for it. You're better off not knowing.'

There was silence before Jim spoke. 'Don't do it, Mason. Not alone. It's too dangerous.'

'I have to.'

'Even you can't take on these gangs on your own.'

'If my daughter's in there, it's them who should be worried.'

'Wait for us.'

'How can I wait? What's going to happen to Rosie while I'm waiting?'

More silence. Then Mason said, 'Can I count on you, Jim, not to say anything?'

'You know me. You know you can count on me anytime. I just hope I'm not attending your funeral next week.'

'So this call never happened?'

'Yeah it happened, but it's a bad line. I haven't heard a word you've said.'

'Thanks Pal,'

'Mason.'

'Yeah.'

'Good luck.'

Mason put his phone away and turned to Natasha.

'I heard,' she said. 'We are on our own, aren't we?'

'Not we, me. You're waiting here, remember. If I'm not back in thirty minutes, go to the police station on the main road. You'll be safe there. You'll have to tell them everything so that they'll find you a safe house.'

'Be careful, Mason. For Rosie's sake, be careful.'

He leant across and kissed her on her forehead, and without another word, got out and walked to the back of his car. He opened the boot and looked through a large tool bag. He regretted having to hand over the Beretta. Not knowing what he would face in the house, or how many of them would be carrying weapons, he needed something to balance the odds. Just in case.

He picked up a hammer but discarded it. Too difficult to hide. He found a screwdriver with a long, thin shaft and quickly tucked it into the back of his belt. Just as he was about to close the boot, he remembered the bag should contain a large, sturdy carving knife. He had used it to cut insulation a few weeks back when he upgraded the levels in his loft. He left the knife in the tool bag, as he knew Kathy would not have it back in the kitchen after such use.

He emptied the bag into his boot and found the knife. He removed the screwdriver from his belt and replaced it with the knife.

Now he was ready.

MASON

Mason walked back to the wall near to the last house in Silver Street and stopped to decide his next move. Should he kick open the door like he had in the past when executing warrants? They would do that when fast entry was important to prevent evidence being destroyed. But police operations were planned, risk assessed, and resourced appropriately.

Right now, he was alone.

So, he decided to trick his way in and assess the setup from inside. His aim was not to gather evidence, and not to cause unnecessary confrontation, but to find Rosie. Because wherever she was, in the absence of police resources, he was her best chance.

He took a deep breath, approached the side door, and gave three sharp knocks. Then he stood back and brought his hand around under his olive-green hip-length jacket and checked the knife. It was there, where he placed it, just as back up. He lifted the back of his shirt over the handle, ensuring it would be hidden should he need to remove his jacket.

The door opened, and a large rugged man filled the door frame.

Mason's heart skipped a beat. At first glance, he looked just like the driver of the Mercedes, the big Albanian he'd seen face to face at the garage counter. But there were differences. The man in front of him, although similar, with a square jaw and steely blue eyes, appeared younger, and his head was shaved. As Mason studied him, he decided there were more similarities than differences. So he must be Albanian too and could even be related.

'Yes?' the man asked.

'Malik sent me.'

No need to change the words. They had worked fine for the previous visitor.

The man stared at him through narrowed eyes. Mason's adrenaline surged. He was ready to act at the first sign of trouble. He focused on the man's eyes and waited.

Eventually, the big man relaxed his expression and moved back. 'Come in.'

Mason stepped inside.

'Give me your coat,' the man said in a choppy East European accent. His tone left Mason in no doubt that it was not a question. It was an order.

Mason slipped off his jacket and handed it over. The man dropped it onto a chair in the corner of the entrance hall.

'You got money?'

This was a question, but only one answer would do.

'Yes,' Mason said, and tapped his back trouser pocket, trying to remember how much he had in his wallet and whether it would be enough to get him as far as the girls.

'What's your preference?'

'Preference?'

'Yeah, what type you go for?'

Mason liked this question. It was a good question. It would allow him to describe Rosie and find out if she was there.

'I like them young, slim, with long hair.'

The man grinned and rubbed his chin. 'I got one for you. Young and fresh. It's one hundred now and the rest later.' He winked at Mason. 'Depends on what you want the girl to do and how long you take.'

Mason took out his wallet and opened it towards himself so that the man couldn't see its contents. He counted out loud, 'Twenty, fifty, one hundred,' then pulled out the notes and handed them over, leaving just fifteen pounds in his wallet.

The man pulled open his grey suit jacket by the lapel and jammed the money into his inside pocket. 'Wait here,' he ordered. Then he turned and climbed the stairs.

Mason glanced around. The house was over one hundred years old and large. It was dated in its appearance with wood panels lining the hall and stairs. An old wooden banister had been stained dark brown, and the walls had been painted mustard yellow sometime over the last twenty to thirty years. The overall ambience was dull and dingy. He expected the house would have many bedrooms on the first floor and may even have attic rooms. He wondered just how many girls were being held there.

He stared down the hall into what looked like the kitchen. A man was sitting at a table talking to someone just out of sight. So there's at least three, he thought.

The man in the kitchen stopped talking and stared back at him. Mason looked away and lowered his head, trying to act like any regular client. He was sure the man was just about to say something to him when a voice bellowed down from upstairs.

'Come up.'

When he reached the top of the stairs, the big man pointed along the landing. 'Last room on the right.'

Mason nodded and walked along the hall. He stopped at the last door on the right and glanced back. The man motioned for him to enter, then turned and walked back down the stairs. Mason briefly closed his eyes, took a deep breath, and prayed that he would find Rosie inside.

He pushed open the door and focused on a girl sitting on a single bed in the corner of the large bedroom. She was exactly what he had asked for: Young and slim with waist-length brown hair.

But she was not Rosie.

Wearing nothing but white cotton underwear, she watched Mason cross the room and sit down on the bed next to her.

She smiled at him. 'What would you like, sir?' She reached out and began to unbutton his shirt.

Mason grabbed her hands and spoke quietly. 'Not that. I'm looking for a girl, similar age to you, same long hair, but slightly lighter. Her name is Rosie. Do you know her?'

'No, I don't. But don't worry, I can show you a good time.' She moved her face close to his and kissed his lips.

Mason took hold of her shoulders and gently pushed her back. 'I'm not here for that.'

'Why, don't you like me?' her demeanour changed. She looked nervous. 'I will be in trouble if you leave. You must fuck me, or let me pleasure you, please.'

'I'm sorry, but I've told you, I'm looking for a girl. How many girls are in this house?'

'There are three of us, but the other two do not look like the girl you described. One is black, and the other has blonde hair, and they are both older than me.'

'How old are you?'

She hesitated. 'I'm eighteen.'

She looked younger.

'Are you being held here against your will?'

She didn't answer.

He asked again.

'I can't. Please don't ask. You will put us both in danger. You don't understand these people. You will be in trouble if they knew what you were asking.'

'Don't worry. They won't hurt you. I'm not leaving you here. Where are your clothes?'

She shook her head. 'I don't know.'

Mason pulled up the top blanket from the bed and wrapped it around her. Then he walked over to the window and pulled back the curtains. He flipped the catch and tried to pull up the window, but it wouldn't budge. Several nail heads were visible around the frame.

'Bastards,' he muttered under his breath. 'They've nailed it shut.' He went back to the girl. 'What's your name?'

'Alana.'

'Alana, I'm Mason. I'm going to get you out of here, but first I need to ask you some questions. Where are the other girls?'

'In the rooms next to this one.'

'How many men are keeping you here?'

She looked at him but didn't answer.

He repeated the question. She stayed silent.

'I'm not one of the gang trying to trick you. I'm here to help. But you need to trust me.'

She looked up at him, and after a long silence she said, 'It's happened before. One of the gang pretended to be a client and asked me questions like this. I answered him, but it was a trick. They beat me and threatened that if it happened again, I would get far worse.'

'I understand, but if you want to get out of here, you'll have to trust me, I'm not one of those animals.'

She stared at him for several seconds, then nodded. 'There are usually three. The big bald one is Victor. He's always here, but the other two change every few weeks. I don't know their names.'

'Have you seen any weapons?'

'The smaller one has a big knife. He's always playing with it. He runs the point over my body, and when it cuts me he just laughs.' She turned and lowered the blanket, allowing Mason to see small fresh scars cut into her back.

He gritted his teeth and gently pulled up the blanket. 'What normally happens when clients are in here?' He quickly amended his question. 'Sorry, I don't mean between you and the client, I mean regarding the guys downstairs.'

'Victor always comes in and demands another hundred.

He waits just long enough for the client to be naked to embarrass him into paying so he'll leave. If they don't pay, he throws them out. I saw him break one man's arm when he tried to resist, and I heard he's done a lot worse.'

Mason checked his watch. 'Then we wait.'

'What for? Have you seen Victor? He's huge.'

'Let me worry about that.'

'This girl, Rosie, who is she?'

'She's my daughter.'

'Oh, and you think they have her?'

'Yes, she was taken from our home today.'

'I wish...' she paused. 'I don't think anyone is looking for me.'

'I'm sure they are.'

'No, I have been here for two years. Well, here and other places. I've had no contact with my family, so everyone will think I'm dead.'

'Two years? Since you were sixteen?'

She hesitated a moment, then shook her head. 'No, fourteen. I lied. I'm only sixteen now. I was told to lie if anyone asked.' Her eyes watered and her voice cracked a little. 'Sometimes I find it hard to remember my old life. I feel as if this is all I've ever done. But I do miss my mum.'

Mason felt the anger and disgust bubbling inside at the thought of this girl forced into prostitution at such a young age.

'I promise you Alana, you will see your mum again soon.'

Her eyes flooded with tears as she stared back at him. 'It's been a long time since anyone has been nice to me.'

Just at that moment, there were footsteps outside in the hallway. Alana jumped and scurried back across the bed to the wall, as if trying to get as far away from the door as possible.

The footsteps stopped outside the bedroom door. A brief silence followed before the door opened and Victor walked in. He closed the door behind him, then looked at them both with a puzzled expression. The sight that greeted him was clearly not what he'd expected. A fully clothed client, and the girl wrapped in a blanket.

'What's going on?' he asked.

Mason stood up. 'She's decided to resign.'

'What?'

'She's leaving with me, and so are the other girls. They're not happy with their working conditions.'

Victor stared at Mason for a few seconds, as if digesting what he had just heard. 'Oh.' He laughed out loud. 'You're a fucking comedian.'

Mason held eye contact. 'It's no joke. This girl's going home.'

Victor stopped laughing.

He shook his head and clenched his fists. 'No, she's not, and neither are you.'

Mason turned his stance forty-five degrees in readiness. When he had entered the house, he had hoped to leave without incident if Rosie was not there. But now that wasn't an option. The guy standing in front of him was huge. His heart pounded, but his adrenalin had reached a peak, and he knew what that meant. He was ready to fight, and he was ready to win. His daughter's future and maybe her life depended on it, and so did the welfare of the other three girls in the house.

'She's going nowhere,' Victor growled through clenched teeth as he stomped forward.

Mason moved with lightning speed. A low round-house kick to Victor's front knee buckled his leg, causing him to stumble. Two punches, a left and a right, to Victor's jaw sent the big man crashing to the floor.

Mason turned to Alana. 'Go and tell your friends they're leaving.'

Alana's eyes widened, and her jaw dropped as she pointed behind him and shouted, 'Look.'

Mason turned his head.

Victor, now on his feet, ran at Mason and with the force of a charging buffalo, slammed him into a tall chest of drawers, then threw him across the room. Victor took three large strides, dragged Mason to his feet, and pinned him against the wall. His large hands wrapped around Mason's throat.

Squeezing, crushing, choking.

Mason grabbed at Victor's thick forearms and pulled. But they were too rigid and too strong. The vice like grip was slowly crushing his windpipe. Unable to breathe and unable to move, time was running out. He looked into the face of his attacker. It was twisted with rage and hate. Mason's eyes watered and the room grew dim.

He had only seconds left.

He tried to reach the knife behind his back, but he was being crushed too tightly against the wall.

The room went black.

Desperate and feeling weak, he brought his hands up to Victor's face and pushed both thumbs into his attacker's eyes. As he dug his thumbs in, he felt himself stagger forward. The pressure around his throat had gone. Victor had released his grip and recoiled in pain. Mason's vision, though blurred, slowly returned. He focused on the big man in front of him. There was no time for fancy moves. So, he head-butted Victor square on the nose, then smashed his forearm into his face with every bit of strength he had left. Victor's head rocked back, and he dropped to his knees.

Mason leaned against a chest of drawers and pulled in deep, rasping breaths, filling his lungs with much needed oxygen. Victor had to be stopped or he would not get out of there alive. He staggered over and wrapped his arm around the big man's neck and applied a rear choke hold. He squeezed and held tight. He'd used this technique many times in his career to subdue violent individuals and would release the hold when the subject stopped struggling to allow them to recover.

But this time was different.

This time he maintained pressure even after Victor had gone limp, and when he finally released his grip, Victor fell face down with a thud. Mason stood over him, staring down in a trance for a few moments, coming to terms with what he'd done.

It was necessary. I had no choice. It was him or me.

'Is he dead?'

Alana's question snapped him out of it.

'I think so.' Mason bent down and flipped open Victor's jacket and from the inside pocket, pulled out a thick roll of twenty and fifty-pound notes. 'There must be two grand here,' he said.

He checked the side pockets and found a mobile phone, then he stuffed the phone and money into his own pockets and turned to Alana. 'Let's go.'

MASON

He opened the door and listened for any movement from the two men downstairs. Had they heard the fight that had just occurred?

The conversation was distant and interrupted with laughter. Confident that they had not heard anything, he shielded Alana behind him as they walked along the hall to the next room. When he placed his ear close to the door and listened, he heard muffled groans. He opened the door and ushered Alana inside.

The man who had entered the house before Mason was lying naked on top of a dark-skinned female.

Mason's voice was quiet but firm. 'Get the hell off her, now.'

He grabbed the man's clothes from a chair, and as the man stood up, Mason pushed them into his chest. 'Get dressed.'

The man scrambled into his clothes in such a panic that he pulled his shirt on inside out, then searched frantically for the hidden buttons.

Alana ran to the girl on the bed. 'Victor is dead. We are getting out of here. Do you know where our clothes are?'

The girl pointed to a cupboard in the corner of the room. Alana opened the door and found their clothes. She carried them to the bed, discarded the sheet, and began dressing.

As the man pulled on his shoes, Mason pointed at him.

'You stay here, and don't move for ten minutes, do you hear me?'

The man nodded vigorously. Sweat trickled down his face.

Mason turned to Alana. 'When you're dressed, go and get your blonde friend. Get her ready, but wait up here until I tell you it's safe to come down.'

She nodded.

Mason left the room and slowly made his way down the stairs. At the bottom, he peered around the bannister to see the same guy sitting at the table in the kitchen. As he watched him talking and laughing, he thought about what Alana had told him. How she had been held for two years since the age of fourteen. He'd never met these men before, but he hated them for how they treated young girls as their property. He had an overwhelming urge to take them out, to wipe them from existence.

But first, he needed information.

As he reached the open kitchen doorway, the man turned his head and scowled at him. 'You finished?'

'Nearly,' Mason said, and stepped into the kitchen.

He saw the second man, rocked back on one chair with his feet up on another. He was the smaller of the two, so he must be the one with the knife.

'Nearly?' the first man repeated while standing up. 'Then what the fuck have you come down here for?'

'To finish what I started upstairs,' Mason said. Then he drove his fist into the man's face, knocking him backwards over his chair and onto the kitchen floor, unconscious.

The shorter man sprang to his feet and pulled out his knife. It was big and fierce and reminded Mason of the Bowie knives he'd seen in the old western movies he'd watched as a kid.

Mason stood his ground. 'Where's my daughter?'

The shorter man pulled a sickly grin that showed a bunch of stained teeth with a double gap in the bottom row.

Mason said, 'Tell me where she is, or I'll give you a matching gap in your top teeth.'

'Are you fucking crazy?' the man said.

Waving the knife back and forward in front of him, the man shoved the table aside and lunged forward.

Mason was ready.

He drove a sidekick into the man's ribs, knocking him back several feet. Then he waited, stance forty-five-degrees. The man steadied himself and lunged again, knife first. Mason stepped aside, and the blade flashed past his face, missing him by inches. Then Mason flicked a back handed punch into the side of the man's face. It was just a distraction technique, but he followed it with a disabling punch to the man's solar plexus just below his chest. The man buckled at the waist and gasped for breath.

'That hurts, doesn't it?' Mason said. Then he grabbed the man's knife hand and jammed his arm behind his back. The knife clattered to the floor. He grabbed the back of the man's head and slammed his face down onto the table, smashing his nose. Blood flowed.

He forced the guy backwards into a chair and, as he sat dazed and disorientated, blood pouring from his broken nose, Mason pulled the kettle lead from the wall socket and wrapped it around the man's wrists, tying them behind the chair. He pulled the man's belt out from his trousers and moved behind him. Then he wrapped the belt around the guy's neck.

'Where's my daughter?'

The man spluttered and spat blood as he spoke. 'I don't know your daughter.'

'Her name is Rosie. She was taken from my home earlier today by two Albanians in a black Mercedes. They are connected to this house. Where have they taken her?'

'I don't know what you are talking about.'

Mason tightened the belt. 'This is going to get ugly for you if you don't co-operate. Now let's try again. Where have they taken her?'

He released the tension on the belt and the man sucked in air, bubbling blood from his mouth as he breathed out.

'Okay, okay. It was Victor's brother Artan and their cousin Korab. They left here today in a Mercedes with a girl, but her name was Natasha.'

'Where were they taking her?'

'I don't know.'

'Wrong answer.' Mason tightened the belt and held it for several seconds before releasing it and asking again, 'Where were they taking her?'

The man spat out more blood. His breathing was heavy, and his eyes were turning bloodshot from the bruising and lack of oxygen. 'Okay, okay,' he spluttered. 'We sold her yesterday to a client, so they delivered her today.'

'Which client?'

'I can't.'

'Which client?'

'You don't mess with them. If I tell you, I'm dead.'

Mason bent down, grabbed the chair's leg and dragged it around so that the man was facing him. He pulled out his own knife from his belt and held it close to the man's throat. He pushed the point into the man's neck enough to break the skin and draw blood.

'In case you haven't noticed, you're in a pretty fucked up predicament right now, and I'm in no mood for this bullshit. The client should be the least of your worries, because if you don't tell me, I will kill you, and I'll make it slow, and I'll make it painful. I will ask you one last time. Where did they take my daughter?'

The man raised his head and looked at Mason, and resignation spread across his face. He sighed, then took a deep breath. 'All right, she was sold to an organisation, a club. They buy our best girls. They have money, lots of money.'

'Go on.'

'You're wasting your time. You will never find her. The club is run by very powerful people.' He gulped in more air. 'They are rich and very powerful men. You don't fuck with them. That's all I know.'

'Where is this club?'

'Everywhere. I mean anywhere. We deliver the girls to different places each time. Big houses, usually in the country, in remote and isolated places.'

'Give me locations.'

'I can't. Only Artan and Korab know the addresses.'

'Give me names.'

'I don't know... Jones. I only know one uses the name Jones. He buys the girls.'

'Where can I find this Jones?'

'I've told you, I don't know.' He spat more blood onto the table. 'I really don't know.'

'How are these deals arranged?'

'I'm not involved with that. Malik deals with all that.'

'Where can I find Malik?'

'I don't know that, either. He just sends us the girls, and we put them to work. Sometimes Jones comes and buys a girl, and Artan transports her. That's it, that's all I know.'

'Are you sure?'

'Yes, I've told you everything.' He lowered his head, and the blood continued to pour from his nose down over his mouth onto his shirt, which was no longer white.

Mason released the belt and let it fall to the floor, then turned toward the first man who was starting to regain consciousness. As he looked down at him, he tried to decide what to do.

Should he just take the girls and leave? But then the gang would move to another location and carry on their business with new victims.

Should he ring the police and have them arrested? But with a body upstairs he would spend the next couple of days in custody being interviewed, and though unlikely, he could even be charged with manslaughter or worse. With Rosie still missing, he had to remain free.

But there was a third option. His preferred option.

Kill them both.

After all, they are scum. No, worse than scum. Who would miss them? And how many girls would be saved from a life of slavery if they no longer existed?

Then his rational side got in on the argument. *That would be murder, not self-defence. Victor was different. It was him or me.* He began to weigh up options one and two again when he heard a scramble behind him.

14

MASON

The bloody faced man pulled free from his restraint, leapt up from the chair, and grabbed his knife from the floor. He let out a battle cry and lunged at Mason's chest.

Mason stepped back as the tip cut through his shirt and his skin. There was no pain, but when he brought his hand up to his ribs, blood seeped between his fingers. Mason acted instinctively and rammed his own knife into the man's throat. The man dropped to the floor with blood pumping from the gaping wound in his neck.

Mason stared down at him. 'Bad move.'

He turned his attention back to the first man, who was dragging himself up from the floor with a sudden sense of urgency.

He had just seen his friend die.

The speed took Mason by surprise as the man rugby tackled him to the floor. Mason landed hard and dropped the knife. The man landed on top of him and grabbed it.

'Now it's your turn to die,' the man said through gritted

teeth, the knife grasped in both hands high above Mason's head.

Mason focused on the blade, pointing straight at him.

It can't end like this. Not now. Not before I find Rosie.

He gritted his teeth and braced himself. Ready. He'd trained for this exact scenario many times and had a defensive technique that, if done properly, would block the knife's thrust and drive its blade into his attacker. He'd practiced the move twenty or thirty times and had a hundred per cent success rate over the last five. But that was training. And like anything in training, results do not always correlate exactly in real life. Especially when the stakes are high. And right now, they couldn't be higher. Get it right and this guy ends up with a stomach full of sharp steel. Get it wrong and...

There was a dull thud.

Blood trickled down the man's forehead.

His jaw dropped open.

He fell forward on top of Mason.

He lay still.

Mason pushed him off and looked up.

Natasha was standing above them, holding a bloodied domestic clothes iron in her right hand.

'Natasha,' Mason said, 'I told you to wait in the car.' He cringed at how stupid his words sounded under the circumstances.

She stared down at him. 'Yeah, well, it is just as well I didn't, because it looked to me like you needed help.'

'I had him just where I wanted him.' He knelt up on one knee. 'But next time... hit him just a second or two sooner, eh?'

She raised an eyebrow, then stared down at the man's lifeless body. 'Is he dead? Have I killed him? I didn't mean to kill him.'

Mason searched for a pulse but found nothing. He stood up. 'It's hard to survive with a v-shaped hole in your skull.'

She gasped and flashed him a look. One that told him she was horrified at what she'd just done.

He sighed, then gently held her shoulders and smiled. 'You did great. Don't worry about him. You've just made the world a better place and helped three other girls upstairs escape this nightmare.' He softly kissed the top of her forehead, then took the iron from her hand and placed it on the table. 'Let's get out of here.'

They waited at the bottom of the stairs as the girls hurried down, and when the youngest girl approached them, Natasha gasped excitedly. 'Rosie?'

Mason shook his head. 'No, Alana. Rosie's not here.'

Alana stopped in the hallway and smiled at Natasha. Then she looked up. 'What about the client?'

Mason grunted. 'Don't worry about him. I doubt he wants to hang around for the police. He's wearing a wedding ring.'

He grabbed his jacket and led the girls out of the house and over to his car.

As Alana and the two girls slid into the backseat, Natasha turned to Mason. 'Passports. Their passports will be in the house. They always keep them with the girls.'

'Okay, wait here.'

He made his way back to the house and checked the ground-floor rooms off the hallway. They were empty apart from three mattresses and three sleeping bags in what should be the lounge. He went back into the large kitchen, glancing at the two bodies on the floor. He'd seen many before in all kinds of gruesome circumstances when attending accidents, suicides, and murder scenes, but this was different. He was directly involved in these deaths.

He tried assessing his feelings. He felt detached and almost numb to the horror that had just occurred. His lack of guilt surprised him. Including Victor, three men lay dead, but he felt nothing for them. Maybe he'd feel different later. Maybe he wouldn't. But one thing was certain. His life had changed forever. Things would never be the same again.

He snapped himself back to the task in hand and began pulling out drawers one by one, opening cupboards, and lifting lids on tins and boxes on the worktops, but nothing. Finally, he reached up and took down a large, square tin from the top of the fridge. He emptied the contents onto the kitchen table and there, besides two bundles of cash secured by elastic bands, were four passports. He stuffed the cash and the passports into his coat pocket and turned to leave.

At the kitchen door, he paused and looked back. He walked over to the sink and picked up a towel, then carefully worked his way around the kitchen, wiping everything he had touched while searching for the passports. Then he bent down and wiped the handle of the iron. He picked up his kitchen knife, wiped it, and discarded it, along with the towel. From one of the open drawers, he grabbed a first aid kit that he'd seen during his search, then headed for the door, glancing up as he reached the foot of the stairs. The client was looking down, sheepishly, from the landing.

'Go home to your wife,' Mason shouted, then threw open the door and returned to his car, where he handed the passports and first aid kit to Natasha.

She pointed to his shirt. 'Is that your blood?'

'Yes, but I'm okay, it's just a scratch.'

'Let me see.'

'Not here, we need to go, now.'

As he drove, she checked the photo of each passport in turn and handed them to their owners. As she checked the last one, she gasped.

'It's mine. You found mine. Thank you.'

Twenty minutes later, he pulled up in front of a tall block of apartments.

'Where are you going?' Natasha asked.

'Follow me. You'll be safe here. No one knows about this apartment.' He led them into the lobby, where they took an elevator to the ninth floor.

They entered apartment 906, and Mason opened a cupboard door in the hall and flicked on the electricity.

'I have just bought this apartment to rent out, but it's not on the market yet. It has two bedrooms and it's fully furnished with everything you need. Except food. There's no food in the fridge.'

Natasha pointed to the blood on his shirt. 'Let me see that now.'

Mason sat at the kitchen table while she cleaned his wound with antiseptic wipes and covered it with a lint pad and medical sticky tape.

'I have pulled it together with the tape,' she said. 'But it really needs stitching.'

'It'll be fine, thank you, Natasha.'

He fastened his bloodied shirt and closed his jacket to hide the bloodstains. He pulled out the bundles of cash and handed them to Natasha. 'Here, share this out. There must be ten thousand there. I have another two I took from Victor, but I'll use it to buy your flight tickets home later, then I'll share what's left between the four of you.' He checked his watch. 'Make yourselves comfortable. I'll go to the twenty-four-hour shop down the road and get some food and toiletries and stuff. I won't be long. I hate to say this after you've all been held against your will, but please stay here, don't go out.'

At the local store, Mason grabbed toothbrushes, toothpaste, soap, shampoo, a selection of sandwiches, cereals, milk, coffee, and sugar. When he returned, the girls showered one by one and ate the food. Then they headed off to the bedrooms, two in each, while Mason stretched out on the sofa for the night. With Kathy and Rosie dominating his thoughts, it was several hours before he fell asleep.

15

ROSIE

osie sat on the edge of the bed and looked around the room. It was nothing like her bedroom at home. No soft carpet or pretty curtains, pink pillow cases and duvet cover. No photographs of her friends dancing, pulling faces, and kissing boys. No posters of her favourite boy bands on the wall. No dressing table stocked with hair brushes, makeup, and shiny accessories, and nothing to gauge time. No clocks, and no view of the outside world. Just grey and hardness everywhere. And silence. Complete and utter silence.

Loneliness gripped her like never before. She laid back, closed her eyes, and thought of home. She pictured her mother in the kitchen, cooking, chatting, and asking her about her day, interested in whatever she had to say. Her father interrupting whenever she mentioned a boy's name. Who was he? Where did he live? What does he do? What does he want to do? For a few moments, she felt the warmth inside as she remembered the affection of her family and the love that she felt for them. What she wouldn't give to be back at home with them right now.

Her thoughts were interrupted by footsteps on the other side of the locked door. They grew louder and closer, then stopped. The lock clunked as it turned and the door opened.

It was Jones, carrying a glass of water in one hand and a pill in the other. 'Take this, it will help you sleep.'

She stared at the pill in the palm of his hand. It was big and round and blue. 'What is it?' she asked.

He glared at her.

'What is it, sir?'

'It is just a mild sedative. It won't hurt you.'

She continued to stare at the pill.

'Don't worry, girl. Do you think if I were going to kill you I would give you this? Hell no, I can think of much better ways, much more enjoyable for me, than poisoning you. So do as I say and take it.'

Reluctantly, she popped the pill into her mouth and flushed it down with the water.

'Good girl. Now go to sleep.' He stared down at her as she lay on the bed.

Her heart began to pound. What was he waiting for? Was he waiting for her to pass out? Was he going to rape her while she slept? She stared back at him, looking for any sign of his intentions.

He gave nothing away. But, after a minute or so, he turned and left the room, locking the door behind him.

She gave out a long, slow sigh of relief and rested her head on the pillow. She tried to gauge how she felt while searching within her for any feelings of drowsiness. She wanted to sleep, because then she could escape this reality, if only for a few hours.

Her thoughts turned to her father, knowing that he would do everything possible to find her. But how? How would he know where to look? She had no idea where she was, so how could he?

She yawned as drowsiness swept through her body. Her limbs felt heavy. She closed her eyes.

The Black Mercedes pulled up outside the last house in Silver Street. Artan and Korab approached the side door and gave the coded signal. Two knocks, a pause, two more knocks. They waited only a few seconds before repeating the sequence. There was no reply.

Growing agitated, Artan tried the handle, and the door opened. 'It should be locked, it's always locked.' He flung open the door. 'Victor... where are you?'

There was still no reply, so he shouted louder. 'Victor, are you there?'

More silence.

He stepped inside and looked down the hall to the kitchen. An overturned chair was in full view, along with tins and boxes scattered around the floor.

He drew the semi-automatic pistol from his belt and moved slowly to the kitchen, where he discovered the full aftermath of the men's encounter with Mason. He stood between the bodies, glancing from one to the other. Their fate was obvious. No need to look for a pulse or check for breathing. The pools of blood and the injuries said it all.

He turned to Korab. 'Where's Victor? Where's my brother?'

Korab shrugged.

Artan stormed past his cousin and charged up the stairs. One by one he flung open the bedroom doors. 'The girls are gone,' he shouted.

Then he reached the last room on the right.

He flung open the door and let out a long, laboured groan as he instantly recognised the large man lying face down on the floor in front of him. He dropped to his knees next to Victor and rolled him over onto his back. The left side of Victor's face was a reddish brown where the blood had settled and his skin was cold to the touch. Artan knelt next to his dead brother for a few minutes, and Korab appeared in the doorway. Slowly, he got to his feet and stood rigid, fists clenched by his sides.

'Whoever did this is dead. I will tear them apart, piece by piece, every last one of them.'

He stormed out and returned to the kitchen. Korab followed. He picked up the tin that had earlier contained the money and the girl's passports, looked inside, then flung it across the kitchen. Breathing hard, with sweat trickling down his face, he took out his mobile phone and made a call.

'Malik, it's Artan. They are dead, all dead.' He choked with emotion and rage.

Malik waited for Artan to compose himself, then asked. 'Who's dead? Where are you?'

'Silver Street, all dead, my brother is dead.'

'Victor's dead? Are you sure?'

'I'm sure.'

'And the girls?'

'No, the girls are gone. Someone has been here. The girls could not have done this.'

Malik said. 'Okay Artan, I'm sorry about Victor, but I need to arrange three collections from that house. For your own sanity, get out of there before the cleaners arrive. I will call you back later.' He hung up.

16

MASON

Mason woke to the sounds of female conversation, voices talking over one another, trying to be heard. But the tone was light, even playful. The tension that had been ever present the previous night had gone. They were still far from home, but they sounded more relaxed, free from their ordeal. They were safe. Except Natasha, she was not part of the conversation, which wasn't too surprising after the previous night's events.

He stretched and pulled on his shoes, then sat on the edge of the sofa, hands clasped over his face. He'd managed a few short hours of sleep, three at the most, and woke with a headache. His nightmare was far from over. He had to get to the hospital to see Kathy, and then start his search for Rosie.

After freshening up in the bathroom, he found Natasha in the kitchen. 'Can you take care of the girls? I need to check on Kathy.'

'Of course. I hope she's okay.'

Mason paused and looked back from the kitchen doorway. 'Thank you, Natasha.'

She nodded. 'I'm just glad I could do something to help, even if it meant crushing a man's skull with an iron.' She frowned. 'Did that sound as bad as I think it did?'

He walked over to her. 'Look, after stressful situations like last night, it helps to use a little humour or sarcasm. It distracts from the horror of what happened. That's how police officers get over traumatic incidents.'

She nodded, as if grateful for his explanation. 'That man,' she said. 'The one I killed.'

'Yeah.'

'He was one of them... he was one of the men that raped me.'

Mason sighed and nodded. 'He was evil. He's no loss. Don't give him a moment's thought.'

'I'll try not to.'

'Are you going to be okay?'

'Yes, go... you need to go. I'll be fine.'

He gave her a hug, and she managed a smile before he left for the hospital.

As Mason turned the ignition key in his car in front of the apartment block, Victor's phone rang in his jacket pocket. It was what he had been waiting for and why he had taken the phone. He checked the display. Malik calling. He accepted the call and brought the handset to his ear.

A voice on the other end said, 'Whoever you are, you will know from the phone's display who I am. So tell me, who am I speaking to, and who are you working for?'

Mason's heart beat faster. It took all his willpower not to shout abuse down the phone. If the dead knife-man at

Silver Street had been telling the truth, he was now listening to the main man in this trafficking organisation, or at least one higher up the chain.

'I'm just a father looking for his daughter,' Mason said.

'Just a father, what's that supposed to mean?'

'It's pretty self-explanatory, isn't it?'

'Are you telling me you're working alone?'

'That's right.'

'Impossible. You could not have taken out three of my best on your own. You are obviously not the fucking police, so who are you? And who are you working for?'

'I've told you. Now let's get to the point. Your animals took my daughter. She's only sixteen, and I want her back.'

There was a long moment of silence before the voice spoke again. 'If we had your daughter, why would I give her back to you after what you did?'

'Because you want the ten grand I took from the house. And because if you don't, I will hunt you down, and I will kill you and the rest of the scum you have working for you.'

'Big words. But you obviously don't know where to look, because if you did, you would not be talking to me on this phone. You would be here, wouldn't you?'

'You already know what I'm capable of, so just return my daughter now, or tell me where I can find her, and that will be the end of it. I will take my daughter and go, and you will not hear from me again. But I promise you this. If you don't, I will not stop until every one of you is dead.'

Malik let out a roaring laugh. 'Then I shall look forward to meeting you. Oh, and just so you know, your daughter fetched a high price. But I'm sure she'll prove to be a good investment for her new owner.'

'You are sick, Malik, but every scumbag like you eventually makes a mistake that brings them down. When you took my daughter, you made yours. Think about my offer. Because it's the only way you will survive this.'

Mason ended the call, then punched the steering wheel. He couldn't show his emotion during the call, and he had resisted the temptation to plead for Rosie's return because Malik would have been seen it as weakness. But Mason knew that despite Malik's bravado, his threats would have sown seeds of doubt in Malik's mind. And maybe just a hint of fear. Fear that comes from the unknown, and fear that comes from a lack of control. And despite all the bluster, Malik had no control over where and when this girl's father would strike. So deep down, he would be wary, and that's exactly what Mason wanted. Wary enough to keep Rosie alive if they still had her, and if not, then wary enough for him to pass on the threats to whoever did.

Malik made another call. 'Artan, it's me. I think I know who killed Victor.'

Artan snapped back, 'Who?'

'The father of the girl you took yesterday. The one you delivered to Jones.'

'But how could he know where to go?'

'Didn't you say he has Natasha? She must have told him or shown him.'

'But she was hooded when we took her to Silver Street.'

'Look, all I know is, that when I spoke to him on

Victor's phone a few minutes ago, he ranted about wanting his daughter back. It must be him.'

'Victor's phone, he has Victor's phone?'

'Forget about that. You need to get around to his house again. If he's there, you know what to do.'

'If he's there, I will tear him apart.'

'Okay, but take Korab and Skinny. If he's telling the truth, he's not your usual family man. He's got skills.'

'Right. But I'll still tear him apart.'

'One more thing. If you see the girl, Natasha, you know what to do. You can have your fun with her first but get rid of her, do you understand?'

'I understand.'

17

MASON

The enquiry desk at the hospital was busy. Even with two receptionists, the queue moved slow. Mason found it hard waiting his turn, but finally, the little old lady in front of him thanked the staff and moved away.

'Cooper, I'm here to see Kathy Cooper. She's in intensive care.'

The receptionist tapped away on her keyboard. 'Yes, she's in recovery. Follow the corridor on your right to the end, turn left, and have a seat. I'll get someone to you as quick as I can.'

'Thank you,' Mason said, already heading for the corridor.

He reached the waiting area but couldn't sit down. He paced back and forward until a nurse came through the double doors in front of him.

'Mr Cooper?'

'Yes.'

'Follow me.'

Kathy was in the third bed on the left and as he approached, he sighed with relief to see she was awake and looking at him.

'They took her, Mason. I tried to stop them but they took her. I couldn't protect her.'

Mason sat in the seat next to the bed and took hold of her hand. 'I know, don't blame yourself. It's not your fault.'

She tried to sit up. 'I need to get out of here, we need to find her.'

'Don't move. You had surgery last night. I will find her. I promise you, I will find her.'

'But how, where will you look?'

'You must relax. You must get better. Rosie will need you when I bring her home, and no matter how long it takes, I will bring her home.' Mason spoke with more confidence than he felt, but he needed to reassure Kathy. 'Have the doctors told you anything yet?'

'I was lucky. The knife went deep, but missed my major organs. They say I'll be here for a few days, but I should make a full recovery.'

'Then do nothing to jeopardise that. I love you and Rosie loves you. Just remember that.'

Kathy smiled and nodded.

Mason asked, 'Can you remember what happened, who stabbed you?'

'A few minutes after you left, Rosie went up to get changed. I stayed down in the kitchen with Natasha. We heard a car pull on to the drive and thought it was you, but Rosie shouted down from upstairs that they were here, so she must have recognised them. We hid Natasha in the spare room and went back to the kitchen. There were three of them. They kicked open the back door and came looking for Natasha. I told them she wasn't there, so the big one took Rosie instead. The guy who stabbed me was tall and thin, with long scruffy hair. That's all I remember.'

'Well, that's a lot. It sounds like it was the same men from the Mercedes plus the thin man.'

A nurse approached. 'Excuse me Mrs Cooper, It's time for our checks again.'

Mason moved aside. 'Should I leave?'

The nurse shrugged. 'You don't have to, but it might be better for your wife if you come back tomorrow.'

Mason nodded, kissed Kathy, and turned to go.

'Mason,' Kathy said.

He looked back.

'Tell me once more. You will find her, won't you?'

He forced a smile and nodded. 'I will find her. Now rest.'

Mason got back into his car and stared out at the London skyline. He thought about Rosie. *Where is she? Where do I start?* Then he remembered Silver Street and the bodies they left behind. After the call from Malik, he was sure they would have been disposed of and the house cleaned of all evidence. They certainly would not have called in the police.

With that lead dead, in more ways than one, he had just one more. If D.S. Jim Barker was right, the owner of Willow Road had some explaining to do.

He decided to check on the girls on his way to Willow Road so he could divide the remaining two thousand pounds he'd taken from Victor's jacket. And he intended to suggest they book their flights home.

When he entered his apartment, he was surprised at how quiet it was. Four girls, yet no noise? He checked each room. The lounge, the kitchen, two bedrooms, and the bathroom. No one there. He sat on the edge of the sofa in the lounge, trying to think. He took the roll of money from his pocket and dropped it onto the coffee table in front of him. He was angry with himself for not sharing it out before he left that morning. He should have known they would not want to hang around the apartment all day. It's only natural they would want to get home as soon as possible, and although they had already divided the ten thousand he took from the kitchen at Silver Street, he wanted them to have the remaining two thousand as well.

But there was one positive about this. He could now turn his full attention to finding Rosie without worrying about the girls. So it was best this way, wasn't it?

But he had to admit, he would miss Natasha.

MASON

He pulled up a few houses short of the target house on Willow Road and stared at the empty space where the black Mercedes had parked the previous day. It was less than twenty-four hours since he'd stopped on the opposite curb and saw Natasha for the first time. And in the hour that followed, his world had been turned upside down. How could things change so quickly, so abruptly? Should he have shown more gratitude for what he had? Should he have thanked God or the universe for his wife, his daughter, and everything they had? Was this payback for taking it all for granted? He turned off the engine and took a couple of deep breaths. His headache had cleared, but he felt a heaviness inside. A dull ache, buried so deep it was woven into his soul, and the only cure was to get Rosie and Kathy home safe.

A delivery truck thundered past and snapped him back to the present. After the truck left the road, the area was quiet. No doubt most residents were already at their high-powered jobs in the city. Jobs necessary to pay the bills in such an affluent suburb in one of the most expensive cities on earth. It was easy to see how a high-ranking criminal could blend in unnoticed amongst those with such busy life styles. A polite nod to the neighbours and the occasional conversation across the driveway is all it would take.

He got out and approached the house on foot, and as he turned onto the driveway between high hedges on each side he was disappointed, but not surprised, to see it was empty. No cars.

He looked towards the house and the large bay windows up and down that dominated the front. Leaded lights in the modern double glazing maintained a sense of character. In front, the small, neatly trimmed lawn butted up against the block paved driveway. High foliage around the property's border suggested the resident preferred a degree of privacy. There was evidence of recent mainte-nance in the form of grass cuttings and leaf trimmings visible along the edge of the path that curved from the drive to the front door.

He followed the path to the end, grabbed the silver door knocker in the centre of a black panelled door, and gave three sharp knocks. He got no reply, so he knocked again. Still nothing. The curtains were pulled back, but there was no sign of life inside. He turned and looked over his shoulder but couldn't see the houses opposite due to the high hedges. Which meant they couldn't see him. He peered through the front bay window into the lounge, and as he scanned the tastefully decorated room, he considered his next move. He had to find out what, if anything, this guy had to do with the Albanians. He went back to the door and knocked again, louder. Still nothing.

He knew what he had to do.

He made his way around the side to a tall wooden gate blocking access to the back of the house. One more glance back confirmed there was nobody around, then he pulled himself up and over the gate and found what he was looking for around the back. A small window, probably the bathroom window, on the upper floor was cracked open just a few inches. He stood back, clicked his phone onto silent, and planned his route.

The climb up a drainpipe to the pitched roof over a ground floor extension brought back memories nearly twenty-five years old. As a young police officer, one of his first jobs on his own was the report of an elderly man who had not been seen for several weeks. He remembered making house to house enquiries before climbing a drain-pipe, much like this one, and entering through an upper bedroom window. He found the old man lying in the kitchen with a rug on top of him. It was the first time he had seen a dead body, and it was a call he would never forget. He guessed the old man had collapsed and pulled the rug over himself to keep warm before eventually passing away. When he lifted the rug, the rancid smell of decomposing flesh sent him running for the door. He couldn't get out into the fresh air fast enough.

It was what police term a sudden death, and an investigation was needed whenever a death occurred without a doctor being able to certify a cause. A detective, who had been in the area, had turned up and mocked him for remaining outside. But karma struck a few seconds later when the detective ran from the house, retching.

. . .

Mason reached in through the small bathroom window and opened a larger window below it. He climbed through onto the edge of the bath and listened for any movement in the house. When he heard nothing, he made his way onto the landing and listened again. Still nothing.

One by one he worked his way around the five doors on the landing. Four bedrooms and a bathroom, with standard fixings for a house of its period. Panel doors, coving around the ceilings of the bedrooms, and seven inch moulded skirting board around the walls. Two of the bedrooms were empty apart from a few boxes stacked around, as if the owner had either not bothered to unpack from a previous move, or had packed for a future move. Two rooms had double beds, drawers, and wardrobes. Not expensive, not cheap, not new, not too old. After confirming no residents were present, he made his way down the stairs to a long narrow hall stretching from the front door to a kitchen at the rear of the house.

He stopped and picked up two letters from the doormat addressed to Mr N. Buckingham. He dropped them back onto the mat and headed down the hall. Just before the kitchen there was a panelled door which led to the through-lounge. Originally, there would have been two doors close together, giving access to a lounge at the front and a dining room to the rear. But like most houses of this era, the dividing wall between the lounge and dining room had long since been removed and the lounge door bricked up.

He began his search at a desk in the corner of the dining room. While sitting in the leather-bound office chair in front of a walnut veneered desk, he carefully rummaged through drawers, not sure what he was hoping to find. He flicked through notebooks, diaries, and loose papers for anything which could link the resident to illegal activity with girls. If Buckingham had hidden evidence before the police attended, maybe he had returned it after they left.

He was careful to replace everything just as it was, and after a thorough search of the desk's contents, he found nothing incriminating. But he had learned, from paperwork, letterheads, and business cards, that Buckingham worked in the city as a senior finance broker, and that he owned at least two more properties, one in Kent, and another in Cornwall. Mason scribbled the addresses onto a blank piece of paper, took one of the business cards, and left the room, mulling over the fact that only the day before, when Jim had searched the house, none of this paperwork had been present. Maybe Jim's gut feeling was right, and Buckingham knew more than he was letting on.

In the hall, he opened a closet door below the stairs and rummaged through pockets of the coats and jackets hanging on the rail. From the last pocket of the last jacket, he pulled out a small card. It was the size of a standard business card but without the usual professionally printed text. Instead, there was just a name, Mr C, and a phone number, handwritten in red ink. He flipped the card over to see Mr S, and another number written in the same red ink. He flipped the card back and forward, looking at each side as if somehow the information would suddenly make sense. Why only an initial and not the full name?

Its mysterious simplicity pricked Mason's curiosity just enough that he popped the card into his own pocket. Then he reached up and pulled down a cardboard box from a high shelf above the rail. From its light weight, he thought it was going to be empty, but when he looked inside, he found a stack of black eye-masks. The kind worn at fancy dress balls. He pulled out the masks and dropped the box onto the floor, then counted through them. There were twelve, all with thick white elastic to hold them in place, and all looked new. But why so many? Was he an organiser of events? Ordinarily they would not be too significant, but Mason wondered if Buckingham was involved in arranging parties or gatherings where the guests wanted to conceal their identities. He took one mask and returned the others to the box, then put the box back on the shelf and headed upstairs for a quick search of the bedrooms.

After failing to find anything else of interest, he made his way back to the bathroom window, but paused as he pulled himself up. Something he'd seen in the master bedroom had stuck in his mind. He had to take a second look at a painting on the wall above the king-size bed. It was dark and moody and initially appeared abstract, but as he studied its shapes for the second time, he saw the silhouette of a girl laying on a bed. She appeared to have her hands tied behind her back. It was subtle and easy to miss with a mere moment's attention, but the longer he looked, the more he was certain that it was some kind of sadomasochistic artwork. Though not condemning in itself, like the masks, it was another small indicator into Buckingham's Psyche.

Artan entered the Cooper's family home the same way he had the previous day. A Beretta semi-automatic drawn, cocked, and ready. Korab and Skinny followed. They worked their way through the house, room by room, and by the time they had finished, Artan was raging.

He kicked over the TV, swept vases from tables, and flung chairs across the room. He knocked photo frames to the floor and stamped on them, stopping only when interrupted by the phone ringing on the kitchen wall.

After six rings, the answer machine clicked in.

Hi, this is Kathy, sorry we're not home, but leave a message and we'll get back to you.

A long beep followed, then came the same voice. 'Mason, if you're there, pick up... Mason, are you there? Okay, when you get this message, can you bring me some clothes in? The doctor says I should be able to go home the day after tomorrow. I tried your mobile but it's switched off. Any news on Rosie yet? Bye.'

Artan looked at Korab. 'His wife survived, she's in hospital. Let's go.'

On the drive to the hospital, Artan pulled over. 'If we go in there, she will recognise us.' He pulled out his mobile phone, selected a number and when it was answered, he said. 'It's Artan. Are you on duty . . . good, we need your help. Meet us in the car park near to Emergency and I'll explain.'

———

Forty-five minutes later...

'Mrs Cooper, I'm Doctor Black. How are you feeling?'

'Good, I feel okay to go home.'

'It's too soon today, but maybe in a couple of days. In the meantime, I just need to give you another antibiotic injection and then we should be able to move onto pills tomorrow.' He drew the curtain around her bed, then opened a medication kit and prepared the syringe. 'Give me your arm… there now, hope that didn't hurt.'

'No, it was fine. Thanks, Doctor.'

He left the ward and returned a few minutes later with a wheelchair. 'Now, Mrs Cooper, I need to take you for some tests.'

Kathy tried to speak but couldn't move her mouth, nor her face, nor her arms, nor her legs.

He leant over and put his mouth close to her ear. 'If you are wondering why you can't move, it's because the injection I gave you was not antibiotics. It is a muscle relaxant, a paralysing drug given to patients before operations. You see, you are fully conscious, but you can't move or talk. Clever, don't you think? And in case you are wondering, I am a real doctor so don't worry, you're in safe hands.'

The curtain parted and Artan entered wearing an orderly's jacket. He lowered his voice. 'We meet again, Mrs Cooper.' Then picked her off the bed and placed her in the wheelchair. He nodded once at Black, then pushed Kathy out of the ward, along the main corridor, past the reception desk, and into the car park. Korab helped to place her into the back of the Mercedes before they left the hospital grounds.

19

ROSIE

Mr Jones unlocked the cellar door and clapped his hands together twice. 'Up you get.' Then he picked up a carrier bag from outside the door and entered.

Rosie jumped off the bed and stood in front of him, her heart pounding, her mouth dry in nervous anticipation.

He turned back towards the door as a woman entered the room. She was tall, probably in her early forties, with shoulder length auburn hair brushed back from her face. Black-rimmed spectacles gave her an air of sophistication, as did the white blouse, grey tweed pencil skirt, and matching waistcoat. Jones motioned to the woman with an open palm and spoke to Rosie. 'This is Danielle, but you will call her madam, and you will do what she says.'

Rosie bowed her head. 'Yes, sir.'

Danielle moved closer to Rosie. 'Pretty little thing, isn't she?'

Jones nodded. 'She's not the youngest we've had, but I think she'll be the most popular.' He threw the carrier bag onto the floor next to Rosie, and pointed at it. 'There's your boots.' Then he turned back to Danielle. 'When you're finished, tell her about the club.'

He left the room and locked the door behind him.

Rosie looked up at Danielle but said nothing.

'Do you know why I'm here?' Danielle said.

Rosie shook her head. 'No, madam.'

She studied the woman for signs. Why is she here? What does she want? Is she a lesbian?

'Remove your underwear.' Danielle said, then turned and placed a large leather bag onto the table.

Rosie swallowed hard. *Oh god, is she a lesbian?* She remembered two of her friends who were openly gay and had often tried to persuade her to *give it a try*, but she'd always laughed off their advances, telling them she preferred boys. She had a feeling she would not be able to laugh off this situation. And as she watched the woman, she knew resisting would be futile. So she unbuttoned the front of her cashmere sweater and slipped it off. Then did the same with her bra. Then she unzipped her skirt and let it fall to the floor. Naked, except for her panties. She waited while Danielle removed items from inside the bag and placed them on the table. She couldn't see what they were, but she heard the sound as they made contact with the wooden surface.

The suspense became too much to bear. 'What are you going to do, madam?'

Danielle turned and stared at her. 'What are you doing, girl?'

'You told me to undress.'

'I told you to remove your underwear. I meant your knickers.'

'Oh, I'm sorry, I thought...'

'Mm, I think I know what you thought, and I must admit, looking at you standing there like that, I am tempted. But I need to establish your sexual status. I need to confirm your virginity. Now do you understand my instruction?'

Rosie sighed with relief, and her face flushed and prickled with the heat of the blood flooding her cheeks. 'Yes, I see.' She quickly picked up her skirt from the floor.

'Not now, girl, just take off your pants and lie on the bed.'

Reluctantly, Rosie dropped her skirt and did as she was ordered.

The examination was over in a few seconds, and Danielle smiled. 'Good girl, Mr Jones will be pleased.'

Danielle sat down on the bed and stroked the side of Rosie's face with her fingertips. Then continued down over her breast and stomach and with the back of her fingers she gently stroked up and down Rosie's silky soft skin just below her navel. Then she leant forward and kissed her on her lips. Rosie instinctively flinched and pulled away.

Danielle laughed and returned to the table. 'You can get dressed now,' she said.

Rosie pulled on her clothes. 'What's going to happen to me?'

Danielle went to the sink and began washing her hands. 'You must know why you are here. You can't be that naïve.'

'I think I know, but I haven't been told anything. Am I here just for Mr Jones, or will there be others?'

'Oh, there will be others all right. All the members will want you.'

'Members? What do you mean?'

Danielle finished at the sink and walked back to the table. 'You are now the property of The Scarlet Club. It's very exclusive. There are two grades of membership, standard and VIP. You won't meet the standard members for a while. We usually provide them with voluntary girls. But VIP members are different. They get free access to all the girls owned by the club. They can attend normal member's nights and special events.'

'Is Mr Jones a VIP?'

'No, he's one of the founders.'

'How can a club own girls? It's not legal to own a person.'

Danielle laughed. 'You are in a different world now to what you are used to. Normal laws do not apply to you anymore.'

'Where are the other girls?'

'Not here. They are kept at different locations. You will meet them at the VIP special event tomorrow evening.'

'What happens at the special event?'

'Whatever the members want to happen.'

'When can I go home?'

Danielle stared at Rosie for a few seconds, as if deciding how to answer. She snapped closed her bag and sat on the edge of the table.

'I'm sorry, sweetheart, but you need to forget about home, your family, and friends. You have a different purpose now. You will be here for as long as you are of use to the club, unless...'

'Unless what?'

'Unless you cause problems.'

'Then what?'

'Do I need to spell it out?'

Rosie gasped, and a tear trickled down her face.

'Can you help me?'

'Why would I do that?'

'Because you're a woman.'

Danielle laughed again. 'Women's solidarity, is that what you mean?'

'Well, yes.'

'But for that I would have to have a heart, compassion, empathy, and all that soppy stuff. I've got none, I'm afraid, so you're out of luck.'

Rosie's stomach sank as the hope drained from her. 'Have they ever let any of the girls go home?'

Danielle did not answer.

Rosie sobbed. 'Please tell me.'

Danielle's voice stiffened. 'Just concentrate on doing what they want, and do it well, that's the best way. From now on you exist to please Mr Jones, your Master, and the club members. When you understand and accept that, it will be easier for you, and maybe you'll learn to enjoy it.'

'Never,' Rosie snapped. 'I will do what I'm told, but I'll never enjoy it. One day my father will find me and then you'll wish you'd helped.'

Danielle smirked and shook her head. 'Your father will not find you, and even if he did, there's nothing he could do.'

'You don't know him, but you will, you'll see.'

Danielle gestured to the room with her hand. 'This is your home for now, so get used to it.'

Rosie looked around. Other girls must have been held in the basement before her. She needed to know what had happened to them.

'The last girl that was kept here, is she dead?'

Danielle picked up her bag from the table and headed for the door. 'No more questions. I have to go.'

'Wait,' Rosie pleaded. 'Why are you doing this? Why are you helping them?'

Danielle knocked hard on the door, then turned back to Rosie. 'I'm your master's wife.'

The door opened long enough for her to leave and then slammed shut again. Disheartened, Rosie slumped down onto the bed, her mind racing with everything that she'd heard. Any hope of this woman helping her to escape had been shattered. Her loyalties were clearly with Jones and the other members. This woman had called her sweetheart, but really, she was cold and uncaring, and talked as if it were perfectly normal to hold girls captive to be used by men.

A few minutes later Jones entered the room with food and a drink, which he set down on the table. He looked down at Rosie.

'Because of my rank, I normally try out the new girls before I offer them to the other members. However, my wife has confirmed to me that you are virgin, so you will be preserved until tomorrow night.'

'Tomorrow night... sir?'

'I will auction you off to the highest bidder.'

'You're going to sell me again?'

'I'm not selling *you*, just your virginity, and I must warn you that my members are very important people. Many hold powerful positions in government, justice, business, and some are even celebrities. That's why they will be wearing masks. But whoever wins you tomorrow must be satisfied with his purchase, do you understand?'

Rosie nodded reluctantly. 'Yes sir, I understand.' She was resigned to the fact that whatever was going to happen would happen, and there was nothing she could do about it. So her best chance was to try to gain their trust, no matter how long it took. Then maybe one day they would trust her enough to keep her upstairs, where she might get an opportunity to escape.

After Jones left the basement, she sat at the table and began to eat and tried to understand why anyone would treat her this way. Do they have no conscience, no guilt? She knew from documentaries, news items, and articles in magazines that such people existed, but could never have imagined ever falling prey to them.

20

MASON

It was just before mid-day when Mason returned to the hospital. When he entered Kathy's ward, he froze. A doctor and a nurse were having a heated argument beside Kathy's empty bed.

Mason interrupted. 'Where's my wife?'

The Doctor turned and looked startled. 'I'm sorry, Mr Cooper, but she's not here. Someone has taken your wife out of the hospital.'

'What?'

'Your wife is missing, and other patients told us they saw a man push her out of the ward in a wheelchair.'

'What did this man look like?'

'Apparently, he was a large man with short black hair and spoke with a strong accent.'

Mason's blood pressure surged. 'How could this happen? Where were your staff?'

'I'm sorry, Mr Cooper. We have called the police and they are on the way.'

'Then you explain to them. I have to get out of here.'

Mason barged through the ward doors and hurried along the corridor. When he reached the reception area, he stopped and looked around. There was a camera behind the desk and another just above the entrance. No need to see the footage. It must have been Artan, but maybe the police could get stills and circulate his image.

Just then, a man walked past him and approached the desk. Although he spoke quietly, Mason heard what he said to the receptionist.

'Excuse me, can you tell me which ward Mrs Cooper is on? Mrs Kathy Cooper.'

Mason moved closer and studied the man. He was in his mid-forties, tall, with thick dark hair brushed back. He was smartly dressed in jacket and trousers and an open-neck shirt. He could be a detective.

The receptionist said, 'Can I ask who you are?'

The man said, 'I'm her brother.'

Mason froze. This man was not her brother, she doesn't have a brother. Why would he lie?

The receptionist picked up the receiver of the desk phone. 'Just a minute, sir,' she said, then made a call. 'I have a gentleman asking for Mrs Cooper. He's her brother.'

As the man nervously glanced around, Mason picked up a newsletter from the counter and pretended to read it.

The receptionist replaced the receiver. 'I'm sorry, but Mrs Cooper is not available to see anyone right now. Can I take a message?'

The man fidgeted. 'No, it's okay, I'll come back another time.' Then he turned and walked quickly out through the double doors to the carpark.

Mason followed closely behind as he threaded his way

through several rows of parked cars. When he stopped and unlocked a car door with a key fob, Mason grabbed him and spun him around.

'Who are you?' Mason said.

The man tried to push him away. 'What the hell?'

Mason tightened his grip on the man's jacket lapels and pushed him back against the car. 'Who are you, and why were you claiming to be my wife's brother?'

'Your wife? Are you Mason?'

'Yes, I am. Who are you?'

The man's expression changed from confusion to fear. 'I... I'm just a friend.'

'Why pretend to be her brother?'

The man leaned back at the shoulders, as if trying to get as far away from Mason as he could, but his back was pinned against his car. 'I just said that because I thought they wouldn't let a friend in to see her.'

'How do you know my wife?'

'Err, I just work with her, I'm a colleague.'

'How did you know she was here?'

The man hesitated. His voice lowered in tone. 'She... she rang me this morning.'

Mason released his grip and stepped away. He stared at the ground for a few seconds, processing the situation, then turned and glared at the man.

'No more lies, what's your name?'

The man thought for a moment, no doubt trying to decide whether to tell the truth or continue to lie to an ex-cop.

'Peter,' he said.

Mason stepped closer. 'How long have you been seeing her?'

The man stared at Mason like a rabbit caught in headlights. Then he sighed and said, 'A few months.'

Mason stared back at him for a moment, then without saying another word, turned and walked away. He sat in his car, trying to assess his feelings. Under normal circumstances, he would be devastated to learn Kathy was seeing someone else. He may even have knocked the guy out. But these were not normal circumstances. And he had other priorities. She was still Rosie's mother, so regardless of her deceit, he had to find her. He would deal with it later, when they were both safe.

He turned his thoughts back to the traffickers. Why would they take Kathy, and where would they take her? What could they hope to gain if they had access to Rosie? They already have their hostage, their bargaining chip, if he got too close.

Or did they?

He remembered the information he got from the knife man at Silver Street. The club that had bought Natasha, and may now be holding Rosie, was run by rich and powerful men. Maybe they're more powerful than Malik's gang. If they were, then it would be difficult, if not impossible, for Malik to get Rosie back, even if he wanted to. And he had shown no signs of wanting to. So they would need a new insurance policy, and that was Kathy. If they had taken her for that reason, at least they would keep her alive.

But there was another, more sinister possibility. Maybe Artan had taken Kathy to get even for the death of his brother. If he had, her life was in danger.

Mason pulled out Victor's Mobile phone and switched it on. No pass-code was requested, so he could go straight into the previous calls list, select Malik's number, and ring it.

Malik answered, 'Hello my friend, I'm still waiting for you.'

Mason needed to find out if Malik had ordered his wife's kidnap. 'Why my wife, Malik?'

'Your wife, what are you talking about?'

'Why did your goons take my wife?'

There was silence for a few seconds. 'I thought your wife was dead. Skinny stuck her when they took your daughter.'

Mason had his answer. Kathy was not taken on Malik's orders. There would be no reason for him to deny it, and he would surely have delighted in piling on the pain if he had ordered Kathy's abduction.

'My wife survived, but was taken out of hospital today by a man I believe to be Artan, and I know he works for you.'

More silence before Malik laughed down the phone. 'So you're worried that Artan will take his revenge on your wife. Well, if he has taken her, you are right to be worried. But I cannot take the credit for it. Artan is hurting and needs his revenge.'

'That may be the case, but I will hold you personally responsible for what happens to her.'

Malik's tone became serious. 'I don't know if Artan has your wife.'

'Then find out.'

Another silent moment followed, then Malik said, 'I will

find out, just for the fun of hearing you squirm when I tell you.'

'You'd better make it fast.'

'Or what, you have no control here. You have no bargaining power.'

'You won't be saying that when I have my arm wrapped around your throat and you are about to take your last breath.'

'I will find out. However, if Artan has her, and if you want to get her back unharmed, you must agree to back off. That means you stop searching for your daughter.'

'I will never stop searching for my daughter.'

'If Artan has your wife, that's the only way you will ever see her alive again. You need to accept that your daughter's gone, she's been sold. It was just business, and there's nothing I can do about it now.'

'Get her back. Give them their money back.'

'It's not that simple. The organisation that bought your daughter doesn't care about the money. They have their own motives, and they never return girls, never.'

Mason gritted his teeth. 'If my daughter was just business, you should have no reason to hurt my wife. There is no money in it for you.'

'That's true, but some things are necessary to keep my staff happy. Artan is my best man. He and his brother were my top enforcers, but thanks to you I no longer have Victor. But here's what I'll do. I will speak to Artan and I will call you back. But I warn you. We will want something in return.'

Before Mason could speak, the line went dead.

Mason remained in the hospital carpark waiting for

Malik's call. The minutes felt like hours. But when the phone sprang to life, Mason answered on the first ring.

'Malik?'

'Mr Mason Cooper.'

'Congratulations on finding out my name.'

'You were right. Artan has your wife. If you had rung me five minutes later, it would have been too late. But I have managed to delay him taking his revenge for a while. Now I need to know what you are offering in return.'

Mason gritted his teeth as he searched for an answer. 'Listen, Malik, I owe you nothing. My wife is innocent in all this, and you know it. But if you let her go, and get my daughter back, I will meet Artan anywhere he chooses, and on his terms. It's me he wants, not my wife.'

'You, for your wife, interesting. I think Artan will accept that offer, but not for your daughter. There is nothing I can do about her now.'

'I suggest you speak to whoever has her. Do they really want me tracking them down? Do they need this aggro? Do you?'

'I have spoken to them to let them know about you. I have a message from them. If they see you or police anywhere near them, they will slit your daughter's throat. I can tell you, they mean what they say. So, if you want your daughter to remain alive, you should back off. Even if you find them, you won't have a chance. You would need an army to breach their security.'

'I will not be involving the police, this is personal.'

Malik laughed. 'Let's get back to business. You for your wife seems a fair swap, on that we could have a deal.'

Mason thought for a moment. He had to accept that

however he was going to find Rosie, it would not be with the help of Malik. But this was his best chance of saving Kathy. 'You have a deal. Let my wife go and I'll meet Artan.'

'Wait for our instructions.' There was a sense of victory in Malik's voice.

After the call, it was time to think. How would a meeting take place, and where would it happen? How could he ensure that Kathy would be released in the exchange, and would he get a chance to take out Artan and whoever was with him?

21

MASON

He drove to his house to pick up a few things, including a change of clothes, and when he entered, he found the chaos left by Artan, Korab, and Skinny. He stood in the lounge and surveyed the damage, but there was no emotional reaction. It was just property and could be replaced. His wife and daughter were what mattered. So he had no time or energy to waste on a few items of broken furniture.

He bent down and picked up a photo frame. The glass was cracked across a picture of Rosie on a day out by the seaside when she was a little girl. He studied her smiling face and remembered how happy she was on the day it was taken.

Would he ever see that smile again?

Then he picked up another, more recent photo of her, brushed away the splinters of broken glass, and affection-ately touched her image with his hand. *Wherever you are, Rosie, I will find you and bring you home. Be strong, Darling, and remember everything I told you about staying safe.* He removed the photo from the frame and slipped it into the inside pocket of his jacket.

He grabbed a holdall bag and ran up to his bedroom, where he pulled out a blue long-sleeve button-up shirt and a pair of black cotton jeans from a wardrobe. Then he grabbed a few more essentials before going back downstairs.

He went to his workshop in the back garden where, under the bench in a white plastic storage box, he found what he was looking for: an old ballistic vest that he'd kept from his days as a police self-defence instructor. It had been issued for him to trial while carrying out normal duties and to provide feedback on its suitability in terms of comfort and practicality. He had recommended it because it was one of the thinnest vests they had trialled, and it was the only one that could be worn covertly. Which was ideal for detectives working under cover. The tradeoff was that it was rated only for protection against hand guns up to .38 calibre or nine millimetre ammunition.

Before he left his house, he picked up his laptop computer, his phone charger, and an old charger for Victor's phone.

It was late afternoon by the time he got back to his apartment. He dropped his bag in the lounge and collapsed onto the sofa. He pulled out Victor's phone and checked the display. No messages and no missed calls, but the battery symbol was flashing, so he pulled out the old charger and plugged it in.

He sat back and closed his eyes while running through

different scenarios in his mind regarding the meeting with Artan.

A sudden noise from one of the bedrooms behind him snapped his eyes open, and he jumped to his feet. He moved swiftly to the kitchen and quietly opened a drawer. He selected the largest kitchen knife and moved back to the wall next to the open doorway. Another sound confirmed that someone was in the apartment and was now walking along the hall towards the kitchen. He pressed himself up against the wall, out of sight of the intruder. If it was Artan, or an accomplice, he would almost certainly be armed. But he reckoned that if he acted as soon as they drew level with the kitchen door, he should be able to plunge the knife into the intruder's neck before he could fire his gun.

The footsteps drew closer, almost level with the door frame. Mason held his breath, ready to pounce. Two more steps and it would be time to act.

He counted.

One-two.

Then sprang from the doorway into the hall, with his knife raised and ready to kill. As he came face to face with the intruder, he froze.

Natasha screamed and jumped back. 'It's me,' she shrieked.

Mason dropped the knife. 'Natasha, my god, I thought you were one of them. They've trashed my house, so I thought they must have found this place as well.'

Her breathing was short and shallow. 'I'm sorry to give you a scare,' she said. 'But I didn't hear you come in.'

'I thought you'd gone home,' he said. 'When I came back this morning and you weren't here, I guessed you'd all bought tickets and flew home.'

Natasha nodded. 'I did buy us all tickets with the money you left us, but I couldn't go. I couldn't leave while Rosie is still missing. So, I shared out the money with the other girls and came back. How is Kathy?'

Mason sighed. 'Well, it's good to see you again. Come and sit down and I'll tell you what's happened.'

Natasha followed him to the lounge and sat on the sofa. Mason sat on a chair opposite and brought her up to date with that day's events, except for the encounter with Peter. No need to go into that with Natasha.

She listened intently while Mason told her about his deal with Malik to meet Artan and exchange himself for his wife.

Then she said, 'I understand why you are doing that, but I wouldn't trust them. They won't keep their promise. They will kill you both.'

'I know that, but it's my best chance to get Kathy back.'

'How? They will have guns and you don't.'

'I don't know yet. I'm waiting for their call. Once I have the details, I can make a plan.'

'But it would be suicide to try it on your own.'

'Yeah, I hear you. But I've been told that if I get the police involved, they will kill Rosie and Kathy. Also, I'll have to act fast, so there won't be time for the police to plan an operation.'

'Maybe so, but I still think it's too dangerous.'

'I'd better have you on standby with a clothe's iron then.'

She smiled and got to her feet. 'I bought some food, so if I can't talk you out of it, I'll cook you something while you're waiting.'

'That would be great,' Mason said as he leaned back in his chair.

It was only the second day of this nightmare, but it felt longer, much longer. He remembered the last meal he'd eaten with his family, and how it had ended in a heated argument with Kathy after Rosie had left the house to go to her friends. He hadn't understood why Kathy seemed so stressed and on edge recently, but since speaking with Peter in the carpark, it was starting to make sense. The long hours he had worked in the force had driven a wedge between them. His decision to retire after twenty-five years' service was based purely on trying to save his marriage. Initially, their relationship had improved, but only a few days later, the cracks reappeared. Kathy had drifted away from him, and now he knew why.

Natasha brought two plates of steak and chips through and handed one to Mason.

'That looks good.' He took a bite. 'Tastes good too.'

Natasha sat back down on the sofa, a deep frown shaping her delicate features. 'I've been thinking.'

'What about?'

'The exchange. You for Kathy.'

'What about it?'

'You know they plan to kill you, whether they release Kathy or not, don't you?'

'Well, I'm not expecting them to take me to dinner.'

'There's another way.'

'Yeah, tell the police. I told you it's not an option.'

'No, there's another way, apart from the police.'

'I'm listening.'

'Exchange me.'

'What?'

'When they ring back, tell them you'll exchange me. I'm worth money to them, and although they want to kill you, their reason for breathing is to make money. They will do anything for money.'

'I'm not giving you back to them. I'd never do that.'

'They won't kill me. That would be like flushing thousands down the drain. They won't do it.'

'Maybe not, but they'd sell you back into the sex trade, so forget it. It's not going to happen. And the fact that you're serious and would actually go through with it is all the more reason they are not getting their hands on you again. You're a sweet girl.'

'At least think about it. All this happened because of me. You could get your wife back.'

'I did think about it. For a nano-second when you suggested it, and even that was longer than I needed to decide.' He got up and sat next to her on the sofa and gave her a hug. 'Don't think for one-second that I regret getting you away from them. I regret what's happened to Rosie and Kathy, but not rescuing you. I wouldn't change that even if I could put the clock back. I would do it again. I might do some things differently after that, but I would do it again.'

Just then, Victor's phone rang. Mason quickly jumped up and went back to his chair, disconnected the phone from the charger, and answered. 'Yeah.'

'You will meet Artan tomorrow.' Malik said.

'Where and when?'

'I will contact you tomorrow with the details, but I must warn you not to involve the police. We will give you a location and you must attend alone. Do you agree to that?'

'Yes, I agree.'

The phone went dead.

Mason placed the phone on the table and picked up his knife and fork. 'Tomorrow, no other details yet.'

They spent the evening exchanging life stories. Mason told her about his career, how he met Kathy, and why he decided to retire early, and Natasha told him about her childhood growing up in Romania, then Moldova, then England, and then back to Moldova.

Then she said, 'I do have regrets about leaving London when my mother moved back to Moldova. If I had stayed with my stepfather, I would not have met that woman in Romania and none of this would have happened.'

'If only we could see into the future, we could do a lot of things differently.' He thought for a moment. 'But you said that your mother didn't trust him?'

'Yes, she thought he had an unhealthy interest in me. He would often come into my room when I had come home from school and would sit on the bed talking to me, asking me about school, and boys and things, but he never did anything to me. I think my mother was just being overly protective.'

'I can understand that. All parents are. I worry about Rosie all the time. About where she goes, who's she with. I don't relax until she comes home.'

He drifted off, deep in thought.

Natasha picked up the dirty plates and carried them to the kitchen, leaving him with his thoughts.

When she returned, he looked up. 'We'd better get some sleep.'

Natasha nodded. 'Which bedroom do you want?'

'You take the big room. It's got the softest mattress.'

She smiled and headed off to bed.

22

MASON

Saturday Morning...

Mason had managed to grab five or six hours sleep. Not enough, but better than the previous night. However, the sinking feeling in his stomach remained and would be there until he held Rosie tight in his arms again.

The smell of fresh coffee drifted into the lounge, and as he placed his feet on the floor, Natasha shouted from the kitchen.

'How do you take your coffee, black or white?'

'White, thanks.'

He pulled on his jeans and the blue button-up shirt, and joined her in the kitchen. 'You are an angel,' he said.

She smiled and handed him a mug with a spoon sticking up from it. 'Do you take sugar?'

'No, that's fine, thank you.'

She reached over and removed the spoon. 'Sit down and I'll bring you some bacon.'

'I won't be able to let you go if you carry on like this.'

She laughed. 'I think Kathy may have something to say about that, don't you?'

She turned and poured vegetable oil into the frying pan, but glanced over her shoulder when Mason didn't answer. 'Sorry I shouldn't joke.'

Mason looked up from his seat at the kitchen table. 'No, don't worry, I was just thinking.'

'I know. You must really miss them. You don't have to explain.'

'Maybe I do, but...'

She looked at him. 'You okay?'

'Yeah, but just when you think things couldn't get any worse.'

'What now?'

He told her about his encounter with Peter in the hospital carpark and the implications.

'Maybe there is a normal explanation,' she said. 'Don't think about that until you get a chance to speak to Kathy.'

'You didn't see his reaction. He had guilt written all over his face. I don't think there's anything normal about his relationship with Kathy. He virtually admitted it. But I shouldn't be bothering you with this. It's just that I feel as if I'm going crazy with everything that's happened over the last couple of days. But I need to concentrate on getting them back to safety and I'll take it from there.'

'Yes, that's best.'

Mason's phone rang. It was DS Barker. 'Jim,' Mason said. 'Have you heard about Kathy?'

'Yeah, this morning. I'm sorry, Mason.'

'I should have expected something like this but I was too focused on finding Rosie.'

'Any news about Rosie? Last time we spoke you were going to check out an address in Silver Street.'

Jim was a good friend and could be trusted, but there was no need to burden him with the details of what happened at Silver Street. He was a serving police officer and would be in a difficult position if he knew the facts.

'Yeah, I checked it out. It was being used as a brothel, but Rosie wasn't there. I got hold of one of their mobile phones and I've spoken with the head of the crew running the brothel. He admitted they took Kathy.'

'Why would they take her?'

'As leverage to get me to back off. That's how they operate. But I've agreed to meet them and make an exchange for Kathy.'

'What are you going to exchange?'

'Me.'

'What? Are you crazy?'

'I don't have a choice, It's the only way to get Kathy back.'

'When and where?'

'I'm waiting to hear.'

'If you can delay the meeting until tomorrow I could get you some help.'

'I'll have to go it alone, Jim. I won't get much time to act, and if they get a sniff of police activity, Kathy will be in trouble. I need to get her back and then concentrate on Rosie.'

'Just one day, Mason.'

'No time, but thanks for the offer.'

'You're one stubborn bastard, Mason. I can't talk you out of it, can I?'

'No, I have to do this. But I need to ask you something.'

'What's that?'

'If you don't hear from me by ten tomorrow night, I need you to promise me you'll do everything you can to find Rosie and Kathy.'

'Of course I will.'

'Thanks Jim. I am going to write down everything that's happened so far, and everything I know about the traffickers and the syndicates running the brothels, and I'm going to seal it in an envelope. I'll give the envelope to Natasha. But it's only in case I don't make it.'

'Okay.'

'One more thing,'

'Yeah?'

'If I don't make it, I need you to see that Natasha gets home safe.'

'You have my word, Mason. But just make sure you're around to ring me tomorrow.'

'I'll do my best.'

Mason ended the call and began writing down the information he wanted Jim to know if he didn't return from the meeting with Artan.

Natasha watched in silence as he wrote before asking. 'Are you going to tell him everything?'

'Almost, except for your part. I'm not going to involve you inside the Silver Street house. It would make things difficult for you, so I've written that you stayed in the car.'

'But that means you take all the responsibility.'

He waved the paper. 'This is just in case I don't return, in which case none of that will matter. What will matter is that you get home safely and as quickly as possible. You don't want to be held here over murder or manslaughter investigations.'

He sealed the paper inside a long white envelope, then folded it and tucked it into his jacket pocket.

Just then, Victor's mobile phone rang. Mason answered and waited.

Malik said, 'Cooper, I will send you a South London post code. Follow the road until you see a large building with boarded-up windows. It's a disused warehouse and the front doors will be open. You must come alone and bring the money you stole from Silver Street.'

'What time?'

'Twelve. Don't be late.'

The call ended, and Mason checked his watch. He had less than two hours. His phone pinged. It was the text with the postcode and he immediately punched it into the map on his smart phone. He knew the area and believed he knew the building. It had been a furniture warehouse but had been empty for several years. An illegal rave had been held there a couple of years back and reported on the news. It had no close neighbours, but it was an industrial estate, so any gunshots would be heard by other business users in the area. Maybe this was a mistake for Artan, but good news for Mason. It could mean no guns.

'Right, I have just over an hour to plan this.' Mason said.

'How can I help?' Natasha asked.

Mason turned on his laptop and again punched in the postcode for a better view of the map. He chose satellite view and zoomed in as much as it would allow.

He pointed to the map. 'Just as I thought, access to the

front of the site is down this road and only this road. But from the rear of the site there are many options. It would make sense for them to have their vehicle waiting at the back because it would be easier for them to make a quick getaway.'

'How does that help you?'

'I need to get Kathy out of the front door.' He looked across at Natasha. 'Can you drive?'

'Yes, I drove at home, but I've not driven here.'

'My car's automatic, so you won't have any confusion with the gears being on the wrong side. Do you think you could handle it?'

'Yes, I am sure I can. Why?'

'Well, there's nothing certain about this, but I think I can get Kathy out of the front doors. So if you are waiting in my car you can get her out of there.'

'What about you?'

'I hope to be joining you, but I have to get Kathy out first. The rest will depend on whether they are armed.'

'What will you do if they have guns?'

'I'm still working things out. We need to go to my house, there's something I need to do.'

Thirty minutes later, they entered his house and Natasha gasped. 'I forgot you told me they had been back.'

'It looks worse than it is. You go up and grab a change of clothes from Rosie's room while I get what I need from my workshop. And don't worry, she has lots of clothes so she won't mind.'

'Thanks, I will.'

Mason searched the drawers and cupboards in his workshop until he found what he was looking for. Then he grabbed some tools and went to work under the bonnet of his car. He dropped the lid down just as Natasha came out from the house wearing a pair of black leggings and a blue fitted V-neck sweater. Mason couldn't help but stare at her for a few seconds.

'Rosie has good taste in clothes,' she said.

'She should have, she's going to be a fashion designer.'

'I'm ready when you are.'

'I need to show you something.'

Inside the car, he picked up two wires from the floor beneath the dashboard.

'You see these,' he said. Then with a pair of pliers he quickly stripped back the insulation of both wires and touched them together.

Natasha jumped as a police siren blasted out from under the car bonnet. 'Where did you get that from?'

He broke the circuit and it was silent. 'Years ago, I wrote off a patrol car in a crash. It was a complete mess, and the siren was just about the only thing that still worked. So my old shift presented it to me as a joke. I never thought I'd ever use it.' He checked his watch. 'I just need a couple of things from the house.'

He went back into the house and into his study. He grabbed a paperback novel from a bookshelf and a cloth shoe bag from a drawer. The kind that protects clothes when travelling with shoes in a suitcase. Then he went back to his car.

'It's time to go.'

23

ROSIE

osie sat at the table in the middle of the room with her hands clasped nervously together and tried to guess the time. She'd been in the basement for two nights, and it had probably been a couple of hours since Danielle had brought her breakfast. So it must be late Saturday morning.

She wanted time to stop. Then she wouldn't have to be sold to some stranger that evening. She closed her eyes and pictured a clock stuck on eleven, the second hand frozen just past the hour.

If only she had the power.

Familiar footsteps interrupted her concentration, and she jumped to her feet. Danielle entered the room carrying the same large leather bag. She placed it on the table and pulled out a white lace dress, white lace panties, and high heel shoes.

'This is what you'll wear tonight,' she said.

Then she emptied the rest of the contents of the bag onto the table.

'There's shampoo here, a brush, and makeup. There's lipstick, mascara, foundation, and blusher. Everything you need to look beautiful. However, you have such clear young skin'—she pointed to the foundation and powder blusher —'you don't need very much of these. In fact, you must apply the make-up very lightly. And don't cover up your freckles. It's important that you look your age and no older, do you understand?'

Rosie nodded, 'Yes madam.'

'I will bring you food in a few hours, and then you should get ready. Do you normally use a hairdryer?'

'Yes madam.'

'Then I will bring you one later. You must look your best tonight.' Danielle then turned and left the room.

Rosie slumped back down onto the chair and stared at the items on the table. She ran her hand over the lace dress. It looked expensive and quite fashionable. It was beautifully made and something she would normally be proud to wear. She checked the label, size small, her size.

Then more footsteps. But this time they were not Danielle's. Too heavy and loud for Danielle. The door opened again and a man she had not seen before entered. He was short and stocky with cold eyes and a face with at least fifty years' worth of lines across it. He was carrying a large mirror, which he hung on a hook on the far wall in-between the bath and the bed. Then he turned and walked out without saying a word.

Rosie stood in front of the mirror and studied her reflection. She moved closer and looked into her own eyes. They were different. There was a dullness and a sadness she'd not seen before. For the first time, she looked at herself and wished she was ugly. If she was plain, they would not have taken her. If she was plain, no man would pay for her and she would be of no value to the traffickers.

She looked behind her. I could break the mirror with the chair and cut my face with the glass. Then they wouldn't want me. She picked up the chair and held it above her head. She stepped toward the mirror. It would be so easy. She didn't even care about the pain. It would be worth it. She could show them. She could spoil their VIP function. As she urged herself to do it, she remembered Danielle's words the first time they met and the warnings she had been given. She would be there as long as she was of use to them and disposed of if not. These people were not playing games.

It would be certain death for her.

Images of her mother and father, miserable, flooded her thoughts. They would never see her again, nor her them. Was it worth it? Her vision blurred as tears filled her eyes. Whatever was going to happen to her that night could not be worse than never seeing her parents again. Never hugging them, laughing with them, loving and being loved by them. She lowered the chair and wiped her eyes. She must remain strong... whatever happens.

24

MASON

They pulled up in front of the warehouse with ten minutes to spare. The site was large and unloved and must have been that way for some time. The wide concrete forecourt was cracked and strewn with tufts of grass and weeds, consistent with years of neglect. A dozen windows were covered in boards and painted green, as if it were some attempt to minimise the environmental impact of such a large abandoned building. Double wrought-iron gates were open and pulled back, allowing access to the site, and large double doors in the centre of the property were open wide, giving a partial view into the darkened foyer. No doubt Artan and others were already inside and may even be watching him right now.

He turned off the engine. 'Once they release Kathy, I will send her out through those front doors. As soon as you see her, start the car and twist the two wires together, just like I showed you. If anyone other than me comes out after her, take off as soon as she's in the car. Have you got all that?'

She nodded.

He took Victor's mobile phone from his pocket and handed it to her.

'If everything goes to plan, I won't need to ring you. But if it doesn't I will ring this number, and that'll be the signal for you to touch the wires together immediately, okay?'

Natasha's face showed confusion, but she nodded. 'Yes, I can do that, but when they hear the sirens, they'll probably shoot you and run.'

'That's what I'm counting on.'

Natasha stared, open-mouthed. But before she could speak, a figure appeared in the shadows of the foyer. Mason peered hard but could not make out his face, only that he was big and wide.

'Okay, that must be Artan.' He unfastened his seat belt and opened the car door.

'What's in the black bag?'

Mason opened the cloth shoe bag and pulled out the paperback novel. 'Hopefully, in the bag it'll look like ten thousand pounds.'

Natasha looked at the cover and read the title out loud: 'Double Cross, by James Patterson.'

'Don't worry, if things go to plan they will be long gone before they find out it's not the money.'

'What if things don't go to plan?'

'Then I'll have to hope they are James Patterson fans.'

Natasha placed her hand on his arm. 'I know I've said this before, but be careful.'

Mason pushed the book back into the bag and tucked the bag into the inside pocket of his jacket. Then he smiled at her and got out of the car.

He closed the car door, walked a few paces, and looked back over his left shoulder. He nodded, then turned back to the warehouse.

The air was crisp and cool for early summer despite the sun being high in the sky and not a cloud in sight. A faint breeze carried the distant sounds of the surrounding streets. An occasional car horn, a heavy goods vehicle straining under acceleration, no doubt as it pulled away from one of hundreds of traffic lights around the capital, the high-pitched whine of a small-bore motorcycle, and the low hum created by everything else in a city of just under nine million people.

But the business park was quiet. As he glanced around the nearby units, he guessed most of them were empty or abandoned. No doubt the area had been marked for redevelopment. Not what he'd hoped for, but there was no turning back now.

As he approached the open doors of the warehouse, the large figure melted back into the shadows. With his heart pounding and adrenalin pumping, he walked through the doorway into the foyer. Another door in front of him was wedged open, and beyond that was complete darkness.

His lack of control concerned him. The beating of his heart grew faster. His mouth was dry, his palms sweating. There was more riding on the outcome of this encounter than just his safety. Had it just been about him, he would not have felt so worried. He had been in life-and-death situations on many occasions during his police service. He was used to danger, and he was used to making decisions, sometimes split-second decisions, under pressure.

But this wasn't just about him.

The lives of his wife and daughter were on the line. So the stakes were as high as they could get.

And that made him nervous.

Had he judged this right? Would it play out the way he had planned?

He took two deep breaths and walked through the single door into the darkness.

Slowly, his eyes began to adjust to the lack of light, and the blackness faded to grey, revealing two shadowy figures on the far side of the warehouse. As he strained to focus, double doors sprang open on the wall behind them and a thin shaft of bright light flooded through the centre of the building, lighting up Mason as if he were an actor on a stage. There were now three silhouettes framed in the open doorway, casting elongated shadows along the concrete floor towards him. The shadows slowly crept past his feet as the silhouettes walked forward, then stopped twenty yards away. His vision continued to improve, and he focused on Kathy standing between Korab and a taller, thinner man. He thought how vulnerable she looked in her white hospital robe and slippers.

'Kathy,' Mason said. 'Are you okay?'

'Yes, I'm okay,' she said.

A voice spoke from the deep shadows to his right.

'So, Cooper, we meet at last.'

Mason recognised the voice. He peered into the darkness. 'Malik?'

Malik slowly moved from the blackness into the grey middle-ground. 'Have you got the money?'

Mason patted his jacket chest high. Then partially

pulled out the black shoe bag to show them. 'It's here, but first release my wife.'

The lie was irrelevant to his chances of success. Either his plan was going to work or it wasn't, and the money, or lack of it, should make no difference to the outcome.

Malik laughed. 'You are not in a position to make demands.'

Mason locked his eyes onto Malik's grey outline. He was wearing a long overcoat, which even for a cool day seemed excessive. Mason hoped it wasn't concealing some serious hardware. At around five-nine he was shorter than the others and not as broad. But if he's the brains of the organisation, he doesn't need muscle. He can hire it.

'The deal was me and the money for my wife,' Mason said. 'So the quicker you release her, the quicker you get what you want.'

This was a gamble, a calculated guess that they would act exactly as he needed them to. If they did, Kathy would be out of there within minutes. But if they didn't, it's likely neither of them would get out of this warehouse alive. But he trusted his judgement. He was good at guessing criminals' actions. It was an ability that had brought him a great deal of success in the past. So he must have confidence in his plan. It had to work. Failure was not an option.

Malik stopped laughing.

Mason held his breath.

Malik turned towards Kathy and the men on either side of her. 'Let her go,' he said.

They hesitated.

He said it again, 'Korab, Skinny, let her go.'

Korab put a hand on Kathy's back and pushed her forward with a jolt. 'Go,' he said.

Kathy walked quickly towards Mason, confusion on her face. As she got close to him she spoke in whispered tones, 'What are you doing?'

Mason said, 'Keep walking, my car is out front.'

She opened her mouth to speak but Mason interrupted. 'Trust me and keep walking.'

She passed him and continued to the front doors.

Another figure stepped out from the shadows and stood next to Malik. It was Artan. 'Now you are mine, Cooper.'

Mason glanced over his shoulder and through the inner door to see Kathy walk out into the sunshine. He released his hold on the phone in his pocket. Part one of his plan had worked. She was free.

Now for part two.

The hard part.

When he looked back, Artan was walking towards him, fists clenched tight by his sides. He was twenty paces away.

Mason stood his ground, waiting and listening. He wanted nothing more than to take him on, but it was not part of the plan. Rosie was still missing, so he needed to stay focused. No unnecessary risks.

Artan was now fifteen paces away and only a matter of seconds from reaping his revenge for his brother's death.

Mason waited and listened.

It had been several seconds since Kathy had left the warehouse. Natasha must have seen her by now. He listened. No siren.

Now only ten paces away, Artan's face was clearly visible. His lips pulled tight across his teeth, his eyes narrow slits of pure hatred.

Still no siren.

He'd shown Natasha the wires and how to touch them together. How hard could it be? Had she remembered to turn on the ignition?

It was now or never.

Artan's breathing was deep, the veins were bulging on the side of his neck.

Mason braced himself for combat.

Then at last, there it was, loud and clear.

Never before had he appreciated the sound of a police siren as much as he did right then.

Artan froze a few feet in front of him.

Malik ran forward. 'Bastard,' he shouted at Mason, then said, 'Artan, let's go.'

Artan stood fast, staring at Mason. Clearly unwilling to give up his prize so easily.

Malik shouted again. 'Artan, not now, let's go!'

Mason pulled out the shoe bag and threw it towards the open doors at the back of the building.

'Take it and go,' he said. Then walked slowly backwards, putting distance between them.

Artan shook his head. 'No, you don't.' He put his hand into his coat pocket and pulled out a semi-automatic pistol. He raised it shoulder high, pointed straight at Mason and fired. Bang-Bang. He couldn't miss.

Two bullets smashed into Mason's chest, knocking him off his feet. He crashed to the floor, gasping for breath.

Artan walked forward and pointed the gun again. 'Time to die.'

Mason focused on the barrel, waiting for the flash and the inevitable pain that would follow.

Malik stepped up next to Artan. He looked down at the holes in the front of Mason's jacket. 'It's done Artan, you got him, we must leave now.'

Malik ran to the cloth bag, picked it up, and ran out of the back doors.

While Artan's attention was on Malik, Mason pedalled his feet on the smooth concrete, pushing himself along the floor on his back. When Artan looked back, his gun was no longer pointed at Mason. But he raised it, took aim, and fired two more shots. Both bullets found their target, and Mason rolled over, holding his ribs.

Artan turned and ran out of the back doors.

The sound of screeching tyres echoed around the empty building followed by silence as the siren cut out, then footsteps as Kathy and Natasha ran into the warehouse. Mason lay doubled up with his arms wrapped around his middle.

'Oh my god, they shot you,' Kathy cried.

Mason looked up as she knelt beside him. He gasped for breath and had to force out the words, 'It's okay, it was expected, and as it happens, necessary.' He drew more breaths, each one just a little easier than the last. 'It was the only way to get you out and for me to survive as well.'

'What?' Kathy said.

Mason lay flat on the floor, opened his jacket, pulled up his shirt, and slapped the ballistic vest. 'Bullet proof.'

Kathy stared at him, speechless.

Mason said, 'It stops the bullets, but they still hurt like hell.'

He unbuttoned his shirt and pulled at the velcro

fasteners over his shoulders and on the sides, then sat up and pulled off the vest.

Kathy touched the red marks where the bullets had impacted, as if she couldn't believe her own eyes. 'Are you okay?'

Mason winced. 'Well, I'm alive, I think.'

Natasha gave a sympathetic gasp as Mason winced, then knelt down next to him. 'So that was your plan, to get shot?'

'It's the best I could come up with in the time I had.'

'Why didn't you tell me?' Natasha asked.

'What would you have said if I had?'

'I would have said you're crazy, of course.'

'That's why I didn't tell you. I needed you to concentrate on those wires and not be worrying about whether or not the bullets would bounce off me.'

'You're still crazy.'

'I've heard that before.'

He looked at Kathy. She studied Natasha for a moment, then took hold of his right arm. Natasha took his left, and they helped him to his feet. He groaned as he straightened up. 'Let's get out of here.'

25

MASON

They helped Mason into the front passenger seat, and Kathy took the driver's seat.

'I think you need to see a doctor,' Kathy said.

'No, I'm fine. Just take me to the apartment,'

'But you might have cracked ribs.'

'They're just bruised. Anyway, I can't go to a doctor or hospital, they'll ask too many questions and I still have to find Rosie.'

'Then I'll take you to Jan's and she can check you over.'

Jan was Janice, Kathy's sister, and a general practitioner at their local doctor's surgery. Mason got on well with her husband Mike, and the four of them often got together for drinks and meals at weekends.

He shuffled in his seat and glanced at Kathy. 'Okay, let's go to your sister's and she can check on you as well. It's too risky for you to go back to hospital, so you should stay with her until this is over.'

'I don't know about that,' Kathy said.

'Look, I made a deal with those bastards back there that

150

I would give them the ten grand I took from them and exchange myself for you. They got neither. Do you think they won't come looking for us?'

'Can't you get us police protection, and what's this about ten grand?'

'I think we'd better go to the apartment first. I need to explain a few things to you.'

Kathy nodded. 'I think you do.'

They pulled up outside the apartment block and Natasha jumped from the back seat, ready to help Mason from the car.

He smiled at her. 'Thank you Natasha, but I can manage.'

When they entered the apartment, Natasha pointed to the sofa. 'You two sit down, and I'll make some refreshments.'

Kathy watched her walk from the lounge into the kitchen, then whispered to Mason, 'I thought she would have gone home by now. Why is she still here?'

'She feels responsible, so she wants to help in any way she can, and she was a big help today.' He flopped down onto the sofa. 'If it wasn't for that siren I doubt I would be sitting here now.'

Mason began explaining to Kathy everything that had happened since he had left the hospital the first time, but when he described the events at the house in Silver Street, he hesitated. Should he tell her how Natasha had saved his life by killing the man that was just about to stab him? Should he tell her about the two he killed? He was beginning to suspect that Kathy wasn't too happy about Natasha still being around. And he was unsure how she would react when he told her that he knew about Peter. Would their marriage survive this? Did he want it to? He decided to hold back some details about Natasha's involvement. For now, at least. Then she would be free to return home whenever she wanted to.

So he told her about the fight with Victor and the two in the kitchen and that all three had been killed, and he told her about the money he had taken and shared between the girls.

Kathy listened intently, her eyes wide and her mouth open as he spoke. She waited until he finished, then said. 'So that's why they took me from the hospital. It makes sense now. This Artan wanted revenge for you killing his brother.'

'Yes.'

Kathy sat forward in her chair. She looked stunned by what she'd heard.

Natasha carried a tray of sandwiches and coffees into the lounge and set it down on the low table in front of them. 'I Hope you all like cheese.'

Kathy studied her closely before turning back to Mason. 'After all that you must have got a shock when you went to the hospital and found me missing.'

Mason sighed and nodded. 'I did, but that wasn't the only shock I got at the hospital.'

Natasha fidgeted nervously. 'Err, I'll just be in the other room,' she said, and quickly left the lounge.

Kathy picked up a sandwich. 'What happened?' She took a bite.

Mason paused to think. Should he tell her now? Or should he hold back until he found Rosie?

He weighed up the choices, and said, 'I ran into Peter.' He watched her reaction.

She stopped chewing and stared at him as if trying to decide if she'd heard him right. She swallowed hard. 'Who?'

'Your boyfriend. I heard him at the desk pretending to be your brother so he could get in to see you.'

'But... but how—'

'I followed him into the carpark and confronted him.'

Kathy's face flushed. 'What did he say?'

'At first he claimed he was just your friend—'

'He is.'

Mason shook his head. 'Eventually he admitted he'd been seeing you for months.'

She looked at him with wide eyes. 'Oh my god, what did you do to him?'

'Nothing, don't worry. I felt numb. I just walked away.'

Kathy put down her sandwich and stared at the floor. After several seconds of silence, she looked at Mason. 'So what now?'

'Right now, my priority is Rosie, so this will have to wait. But what happens after that, to be honest, I don't know. But you need to tell me the truth about what's been going on. No lies.'

Kathy got up from her chair and sat next to him on the sofa. She put her arm around him. 'I'm so sorry, I was so lonely with all the hours you were working in the police.'

Mason pushed her arm away. 'That I can understand, after all, it's why I've just retired early. I knew you weren't happy. But you've known I was going to retire for months now and yet you're obviously still seeing him. That I can't understand.'

'I'm sorry.'

Mason studied her. 'Is that all you have to say? Did I give up my career for nothing?'

'No, I don't know. I don't think so, but why did you risk your life to save me when you knew what I'd done?'

'Do you really need to ask me that? I can't just switch off my feelings for you. And I wouldn't have left you with those animals no matter what you'd done.' He shook his head. 'Finish eating. We need to go to your sister's.'

'I'm not hungry now.' She remained silent for a few moments. Then said, 'If I stay at Jan's, what about Natasha?'

'What about her?'

'Is she going to stay here?'

'I'm taking that one day at a time. I told you she wants to help.'

'Is she the reason you want me to stay at Jan's?'

Mason's jaw dropped. 'What are you saying?'

Kathy nodded her head towards the bedroom where Natasha had gone a few minutes earlier. 'She's very pretty.'

'Good god, Kathy, she's half my age. Just a few years older than Rosie, how could you think that?'

'Because I've seen the way she looks at you. I know that look. Whether you know it or not, she wants you.'

Mason jumped up. 'You're crazy. She just wants to help get Rosie back, and she was worried about you. She told me not to jump to conclusions over Peter until I'd spoken to you about it. She's a good kid.'

'That kid is twenty-two years old and knows how to entertain men.'

'That's enough, Kathy. Stop right now.'

Kathy sighed, 'I'm sorry, I shouldn't have said that.'

'No, you shouldn't. She's just as much a victim in this as Rosie is. You wouldn't say that about Rosie when I get her back, would you?'

'No.'

'You don't know this yet, but she even offered to be exchanged for you back there today.' He paused and shook his head. 'No, it was more than an offer, she insisted. But I refused. You know the rest.'

Kathy looked guilty but said nothing.

Mason said, 'Look, we all want the same thing here. That's find Rosie and put this nightmare behind us. Now, I'm going to call Natasha in here and I want you to be nice to her.'

Kathy nodded. 'Okay.'

They finished the sandwiches in silence, then Natasha cleared away the plates and mugs.

Kathy looked at Mason as Natasha disappeared into the kitchen. 'Is she wearing Rosie's clothes?'

Mason glared at her.

'It's okay, I just recognised them, that's all.'

'You know Rosie, so you know she wouldn't have a problem with it.'

'No, I guess not.'

Natasha returned to the lounge and gave Kathy a half smile. 'When you two go to your sister's, I will stay here if that's all right. I will only be in the way.'

'Yes, that's fine,' Kathy said without looking at her.

'No, Natasha,' Mason said. 'You should come with us.'

Natasha shook her head. 'No, after everything that has happened, I think you both need some time together. I will stay here.'

Mason looked at Kathy and said one word, 'See.'

Kathy looked away.

26

MASON

Jan's house was just fifteen minutes away by car, and as usual she was pleased to see them.

'Come in, you two. Kathy, I've been trying to ring you for two days, but you've not answered your mobile or your home phone. Where have you been?'

'It's a long story Jan, let's go inside and we'll tell you.'

They sat at the kitchen table, and Mason explained most of what had occurred over the past two days, but not everything. He did not mention the three deaths at Silver Street. The fewer people who knew about that, the better.

When he finished, Jan jumped up and grabbed her medical bag.

'See to Kathy first Jan,' Mason said. 'She should still be in hospital, really.'

Jan checked Kathy's blood pressure, then carefully removed the dressing from her stomach. 'Everything looks good here,' she said, then tore open a new dressing and applied it to the wound.

Jan turned to Mason. He opened his shirt, and when

Kathy saw that the red marks were turning blue, she gasped.

'Don't worry, Kathy,' Jan said. 'It's just the bruising coming out.' She carefully examined each mark with her fingertips, pushing, prodding, and massaging. As she applied pressure, Mason winced and drew a breath.

Jan nodded. 'I can see they're painful, but I don't think your ribs are broken or cracked, they're just badly bruised and they're going to be sore for a few days.' She pointed to the dressing on his ribs. 'What happened here?'

'It's just a scratch, nothing serious.' He buttoned up his shirt and got to his feet. 'Jan, I need to ask you not to discuss any of this with anyone accept Mike. Obviously, he needs to know, because I'm going to ask you to look after Kathy for a few days. Or until I find Rosie.'

Jan looked at Kathy. 'Of course she should stay here. But why did they take Kathy from the hospital?'

'It was revenge. I freed some girls from the house they were being held in, and I took ten grand from the house, and gave it to the girls.'

Jan looked puzzled. 'But why—'

'Sorry Jan,' Mason interrupted. 'I need to get on with my search for Rosie.'

'Yes, of course.' Jan said.

Mason gave Jan a hug then bent down and kissed Kathy. 'If I get the chance, I'll pick up your mobile phone from home and drop it off.'

'Yes, I should have it just in case Rosie tries to contact me.'

Mason entered the apartment and dropped his keys onto the table in the lounge.

Natasha looked up from the sofa. 'How is Kathy now?'

'Medically she's fine, she's going to stay there. Jan changed her dressing and she will take good care of her.'

'That's good.' Natasha said. Then she shuffled forward to the edge of her seat. 'Do you want me to go?'

'What?'

'I'm sorry, but I heard what Kathy said about me earlier. I wasn't trying to listen, but I couldn't help but hear. If you want me to go, I'll understand.'

'I'm sorry you heard that. If you're asking me if you should go, I'd have to say yes. Your family must be worried about you, and it's not safe for you here. But you should stay with your relatives for a while. It would be too risky to go home just yet.'

She nodded slowly, a look of acceptance on her face, but said nothing.

'But if you're asking me if I want you to go, I'd have to say no.'

'Do you think of me as a kid?'

Mason sighed. 'So you heard that, too. It's just a figure of speech. You're not a kid, you're a beautiful young woman. I was just responding to what my wife said. She gets crazy ideas sometimes.'

Natasha smiled. 'It's okay, I understand. But Kathy was, err... well, what she said...' There was a long pause. 'She might be right.'

Mason looked at Natasha, and he studied her, and for the first time, he really saw her. He saw dark shiny hair contrasted against pale skin. He saw delicate, angelic features and a slender, elegant figure. He saw eyes that were dark pools of pure seduction. He saw her breathtaking beauty.

With everything that had happened, he hadn't really looked at her before. And now, as he did, he was beginning to understand why Kathy was feeling so uneasy about having such an alluring young woman around. But he had to clear his head and not think like that. He had a job to do, and it was the most important job of his life.

'Look,' he said. 'You've been a great help. You've saved my life once, if not twice, and I know you would be a great help to Rosie when I find her and get her away from those bastards. But you've suffered too, and in my determination to find my daughter I lost sight of that. I'm sure you need the support of your family right now. So I don't want you to feel obligated. None of this is your fault. You don't owe me, or Kathy, or Rosie, anything. In fact, it's important to me that you recover from this ordeal and go on to have a happy life. You deserve it.'

'So what you are saying is that you think I should go home for my own welfare?'

'Well, yes.'

'Are you telling me to go?'

'No, I'm not insisting.'

'So it's my decision to make?'

'It's your decision.'

'And you'll respect my decision?'

'I'll respect your decision.'

She got up from the sofa and looked up into his eyes. 'Then I'm staying until you find Rosie. So, if you do want rid of me you'd better get on with it.'

He returned her gaze and smiled. He couldn't help but feel pleased.

'Right then,' he said. 'Let's go over what we know. I think you're right about Malik's gang passing Rosie on to the people who bought you. So what do we know about them?'

Natasha shrugged. 'Not very much.'

'If the guy at Silver Street was telling the truth, they're rich and powerful. Rich is self-explanatory, but what did he mean by powerful?'

Natasha shook her head.

'I need to take a closer look at Mr N Buckingham, the owner of the house on Willow Road. He works in the city and owns at least three properties. I would say he certainly qualifies as rich. Then there's this'—he pulled out the eye mask from his jacket pocket—'I took this from his house. He had a dozen of them in a cupboard.'

Natasha studied the mask. 'It's like fancy dress.'

'Yes, and the fact that he had so many of them suggests he must be some kind of organiser. But they can't be normal fancy dress parties. Not if everyone is wearing the same mask.' He held it up to his face. 'It covers everything from the forehead to the nose and from the style I'd say it's designed for men.'

Natasha nodded. 'It doesn't make a lot of sense.'

'Unless they're for hiding their identity. Why would a dozen men meet all wearing these masks?'

'A club,' Natasha said. 'I was told that the Englishmen who bought me belonged to an exclusive club.'

Mason nodded. 'The guy at Silver Street mentioned a club. If they were rich and powerful men, I suppose they would have reason to want to hide their identity from the girls. Especially in this age of kiss and tell.'

'Yes.'

'So, Buckingham is the best lead we've got. Let's try Willow Road again. It's Saturday, he may be home.'

27

MASON

I t was late Saturday afternoon when they turned into Willow Road. Mason parked in the same spot as the previous day when he had searched Buckingham's house. 'Wait here. I'll see if he's home.'

He opened the car door, and just as he placed one foot on the ground, a silver BMW 7 Series emerged from Buckingham's driveway. The male driver looked left, then right, then pulled out and drove towards the end of the road.

'Is that him?' Natasha asked.

Mason pulled his foot back inside and closed the door. 'I think so. He looks like the guy I saw in some of the photos in his lounge.' He started the car and followed the BMW.

The roads were busy, even for a Saturday, and when Mason turned onto the main road, there were two cars between him and the BMW.

'Can you pass them?' Natasha asked.

'Not yet, but having them in front helps. When he looks in his mirror, he won't see us. It looks like he's heading into the city.'

Twenty-five long minutes later they were four cars behind as they filtered around Piccadilly Circus and onto Shaftesbury Avenue, in the heart of London's West End.

They ground to a halt at a red traffic light on Shaftesbury Avenue and the BMW continued out of sight. Mason's fingers tightened around the steering wheel. He waited, squeezing the wheel, until the lights changed to green and he could go again.

'Can you see him?' Natasha asked.

Mason studied the row of cars in front of them and pointed to a Silver BMW turning right about fifty yards ahead.

'There, I think that's him.'

He followed into Chinatown and just caught sight of the back of the BMW before it disappeared down the entrance ramp into an underground carpark. He pulled up to the barrier, pushed the button for a ticket, then he drove down into the carpark. He turned onto the first level with a row of parking bays on each side, but there was no sign of Buckingham or the BMW. All the bays were full, so he drove to the end and turned down onto a lower level. He was greeted by two more full rows of cars. When he turned onto the third level, he was rewarded by the sight of the BMW edging into a space halfway along the left-hand row. Mason crawled passed and got a clear enough look at the driver to confirm it was Buckingham, or at least the guy they had followed from Willow Road. But there were no other free bays, so he had to descend another level, where he found several empty spaces.

He squeezed into the nearest spot and jumped out. 'Quick, before we lose him.'

Natasha followed Mason to the stairwell to exit the car park. While he held open the door for her, the sound of footsteps echoed down from above.

He whispered, 'I think that's him.'

They climbed several short flights of stairs, each one doubling back on itself, until they reached the ground floor corridor leading to the outside world. They emerged into the daylight just in time to see Buckingham threading his way through the crowds.

Mason tapped Natasha's arm and pointed. 'This way,'

They followed, past casinos and numerous bars, all with customers standing around outside with a drink in one hand and a cigarette in the other. They passed buskers and street performers and crowds of onlookers, then watched Buckingham turn toward a doorway. He nodded and appeared to speak briefly to a large, suited doorman, then he disappeared into the building. They were too far away to hear what was said, but as they approached, Mason drew Natasha's attention to pictures of scantily clad girls in a glass display next to the venue's door. 'It's a lap dancing club.'

'Yes, I see.'

Mason watched a group of six young men flash what he guessed was ID as they filed past the same doorman.

He checked his watch. 'Why would he drive into London and attend a strip joint at five-thirty in the evening?'

Natasha shrugged. 'Are we going in?'

'Yes, do you mind pretending to be my partner? It might help to prevent me getting pestered by the girls inside.'

Natasha smiled. 'Of course not.' She linked her arm through his. 'Come on, then.'

Mason nodded to the doorman as they approached. 'Is there an entrance fee?'

The doorman glanced from Mason to Natasha, then back to Mason with just the hint of a smile. 'No, you're just in time, it's free to enter. Welcome to Lady Blue.'

Mason nodded again and thanked him as they passed.

Inside, he leant close to Natasha. 'Did you see that?'

'What?'

'The smirk on his face. That doorman thinks I'm punching above my weight.'

Natasha laughed and nudged him with her elbow.

They walked through two sets of double doors into the main club. A long bar spanned the width of the large, glamorous, and seductively lit room. Deep red velvet was the predominant theme, with drapes, half-moon open booths, and even sections of the walls covered in it. A semi naked dancer slithered seductively around a pole in the centre of a small stage surrounded by tables and chairs and lone men studying her every move. At the far end of the club, red velvet drapes hung down from the ceiling and must conceal individual booths where the girls dance intimately for their clients.

The group of six young men had found the bar and already each one had a beautiful girl draped around him. The girls must have closed in on their prey the second the men entered. Mason smiled to himself. The men were clearly enjoying the attention from the scantily clad women.

He scanned the tables and found his target. Buckingham sat at a corner table opposite a beautiful dark-haired female wearing a white string dress that left little to the imagination. She leant forward, elbows on the table, staring seductively into Buckingham's eyes. They appeared to know each other, but that could be misleading. These girls were skilled at making men feel special. Because when men felt special, they were more easily parted from their money.

Mason had no strong views on strip clubs. Why should he? They were providing a service and seemed harmless fun. Men get to feel wanted while enjoying the attention of a beautiful girl, and the dancers made a good living. He'd heard the arguments about exploitation, but watching them at work, it seemed that if anyone was being exploited here, it wasn't the girls. As long as they were there voluntarily, with no pressure, no threats, and no intimidation, he saw no harm in it.

A tall blonde dancer, in high heels and a black lace basque, slinked towards them. Mason instinctively moved closer to Natasha.

'Hello,' the blonde said as she reached them. 'Are you together?'

Mason glanced at Natasha, then back to the blonde. 'Yes, we are.'

'Are you looking for a dance? I can dance for both of you.'

Mason shuffled his weight from one foot to the other. 'Thank you, maybe later, we're just going to have a drink first.'

The blonde smiled and lightly stroked her long fingernails down his chest. 'I'll hold you to that,' she purred, then blew him a kiss and walked away.

Mason's gaze dropped to the blonde's rounded bottom that swayed as she walked. Clearly a deliberate tactic to get his attention. Frustrated at his lack of willpower to avoid the blonde's bait, he turned back to Natasha. 'Let's get a drink.'

'Okay, but put your eyes back in first.'

'Was it that obvious?'

Natasha raised one eyebrow and smirked. 'I'll watch Buckingham,'

'Sorry,' he said sheepishly. 'What do you drink?'

'What are you having?'

'I'll get a Jack Daniels and coke.'

'I'll have the same, please.'

Mason paid the barman and handed Natasha her drink. 'Let's grab a table.'

They sat four tables away from Buckingham and discretely monitored him. The dancer leant over and whispered in Buckingham's ear while running her fingers up the back of his head. He nodded. She stood up, took his hand, and led him toward the private booths. They walked past the front row and disappeared around a corner.

'Must be a VIP booth around there,' Mason said.

'Have you been here before?' Natasha asked.

He threw her a sideways glance. 'Of course not, I'm married.'

'That would not stop a lot of men.'

He shrugged. 'Maybe not, but no, I haven't been here before. Though if I'm honest, I've nothing against these places.' He looked towards the bar where the dancers were flirting with the young men, and then at the girl gliding around the pole on the small stage. 'I can see the attraction.'

Natasha grinned. 'Yes, it is like a sweet shop for grown men.'

A few minutes later, the dancer in the white dress reappeared alone and made her way to the stage. The music finished, and a voice blared out over the speaker system. 'Thank you Candy, and now for your continued entertainment, please welcome Lucy to the stage.' Candy stepped down from the platform and the girl in white, introduced as Lucy, jumped up and began to gyrate to a new track.

Mason looked at Natasha. 'Where is he?'

Natasha shrugged. 'I don't know.'

They waited and watched, but after a few minutes, Buckingham was still nowhere to be seen. Soon it was time to change dancers again, and one of the girls from the bar area swapped places with Lucy.

Mason jumped to his feet. 'I need to talk to that girl.' He moved quickly to intercept her as she approached the men at the bar. 'Hello Lucy, I enjoyed your dance, can I buy you a drink?'

Her eyes sparkled, and her lips pouted ever so slightly. 'Of course you can. Gin and tonic, please.' She rested her hand on his shoulder and glanced over to a few unattached dancers at the bar. A clear signal informing them this one's taken.

Mason bought her drink and handed it to her. 'Will you join us over there?' He pointed to Natasha waiting at the table.

Lucy looked at Natasha, then turned back to him. 'Is she with you?'

'Yes, do you mind?'

'Why would I? She's very pretty.'

They made their way to Natasha's table.

'Hello Darling,' Lucy said. Then bent over and kissed Natasha's cheek.

'Hello err, Lucy is it?'

'In here it is. Can't use my real name, but I'm sure you understand.'

Natasha smiled. 'Yes, of course.'

Mason pulled out a chair from the table for Lucy to sit down.

'A gentleman,' she said, as she accepted the offer.

Mason sat next to her and got straight to the point. 'Lucy, I saw my friend with you a few minutes ago. Where did he go?'

'Your friend?'

'Yes, Mr Buckingham, you were at that table, then you took him for a dance, I think.' He tried to sound casual.

'Oh, you must mean Nigel, how do you know him?'

'He was a colleague in the city, we were in finance together.' He lied, but in this case, the end certainly justified the means.

Lucy's expression changed. Her smile evaporated, and she began to bite her lower lip.

Curiosity or worry? Mason wondered. 'What's wrong, Lucy?'

The music stopped, and the dancers around the pole swapped again. Mason waited for the new girl's introduction to finish so he could continue. 'Do you know Nigel?'

Lucy hesitated and looked around. 'Not here. If you want information, you'll have to pay me to dance for you in there.' She pointed to the booths.

Mason glanced at Natasha. 'Will you be okay?'

'Of course, go on, I'll wait here.' She gently pushed his arm, then she smirked at him. 'Tough job, eh?'

He gave a short, nervous cough and turned back to Lucy. 'Okay, let's go.'

28

MASON

Lucy took his hand, led him to a booth, and motioned for him to sit on a bench seat. Then she pulled the curtain across, shielding them from the rest of the club.

'It's private in here, but security often look inside to make sure we're behaving ourselves. So you're not allowed to touch, okay?'

'Okay, but you don't need to dance, I just want to talk to you.'

She held out her hand. 'You need to pay me now, it's twenty for three minutes, or you can pay for longer.'

Mason took out the role of money from his jacket pocket and handed her two fifty-pound notes.

Her eyes widened as she took the money and slipped it into a small, sequined pouch. She started grinding her hips from side to side while giving him a long, smouldering look.

'Forget that,' Mason said. 'I need to ask you some questions.'

She moved close to him and straddled his thighs and put her mouth close to his ear. 'I have to dance for you, because if the security guy looks in and sees us just talking, he might think I'm negotiating extras with you, and that's forbidden. I could be banned. So I'll dance, and you can ask me what you want to ask me.'

Mason relented. 'Okay, I can think of worse ways to have a conversation.'

She slid off him, and pulled down the zip on the back of her dress, then slowly slipped off each shoulder strap, one at a time.

'I asked if you knew Buckingham.' Mason said.

She let her dress fall to the floor. She was now naked except for her shoes and a small pair of pink lace panties, which she began to tease down, one side at a time, hips swaying to her right, and then to her left.

Mason's eyes widened. Under normal circumstances, he would sit back and enjoy the show, and it was some show. The girl's body was flawless. But unfortunately, this was not the time. He had to stay focused.

'Stop,' he said, holding up a hand.

It was too late. Her panties were around her knees. Then a shimmy, and they fell to the floor. She kicked them to the side before stepping forward and straddling him again. This time, totally naked, and with her breasts towards his face.

'This is becoming a habit,' he mumbled under his breath, then gently held her shoulders and eased her back. 'Listen to me, this is great, and any other time I'd be in heaven, but right now, I need information. I need to know about Buckingham.'

She stopped her seductive grinding, stepped back, and crouched down, shielding her body as if suddenly embarrassed by her nakedness. She grabbed her dress and slipped it back on.

Mason stood up. 'I'm sorry, but this is really important.'

'All right, I've danced for him before and so has a friend of mine.' She bit her bottom lip again.

Mason studied her face. Now he was sure it was a sign of worry and not curiosity. Did she know something? If she did, would she talk? It was time to take a chance and be honest.

'Lucy, I'm not Nigel's friend. I don't know him at all, I just followed him here. You see, my daughter's missing. She was abducted two days ago, and I think he knows something about it. He may even be involved.'

Lucy's eyes widened, but she stayed quiet.

'What is it? What do you know?'

'I don't know anything about your daughter, but my friend danced for him, then she told me he'd offered her a lot of money to dance privately at a party he was organising. She agreed and seemed excited about it, said the money would help her family back home. That was six months ago, and I haven't seen her since.'

'Did you report her missing?'

'No, he came in here a few days later and told me she never showed up at his party. He said he gave her the money and thinks she must have gone home to Lithuania with it.'

'What do you think?'

'She wouldn't have gone without telling me. We've been

dancing here together for a year. She wouldn't just leave like that.'

'So what did he want with you tonight?'

'He offered me the same deal as my friend. A thousand pounds to dance for him at a party tonight.'

'Tonight? What did you tell him?'

'I refused. I don't trust him. I mean, I don't know if he had anything to do with my friend going missing, but I'm not going to take any chances. And now you tell me you think he's connected to your daughter's disappearance, I'm glad I didn't accept his offer.'

'Did he tell you where this party was tonight?'

'No, only that it was somewhere in Kent, so if I was interested, he would have to take me straight there.'

'Kent,' Mason repeated. Another small piece of the puzzle.

Lucy picked up her panties and stepped into them. She shimmied as she pulled them up under her dress. Then she pulled back the curtain.

'Where did he go?' Mason asked.

'After I'd finished dancing for him, he went through the staff door to see the manager. He's trying to buy this club.'

Mason thought about what she'd said. If Buckingham was the mastermind of an organisation that abducted young women, a strip club would be very convenient for him, but very dangerous for the girls. It was time to confront him face to face.

'What's the manager's name?'

'Benny Grant, he's one of the good guys, and I should know. I've worked in enough of these places to know a good'n when I see one. He looks after us.'

Mason wasn't overly impressed. So he's a good boss. So he should be. Girls in this industry deal with enough crap from the punters without having to take it from the boss as well.

'Is the staff door locked?'

'No, they always leave it open before ten.'

Mason got to his feet. 'Thank you, Lucy, or whatever your real name is.' He smiled. 'You've been a big help. Before I go, what's your friend's name?'

'Her dance name is Sandy, but her real name is Ellie. She's blonde and has a flower tattoo on the top of her left shoulder at the back.' She stretched her hand over her own shoulder and pointed. 'A red rose, just there.' Then she took a business card from her purse and handed it to him. 'As you can see from my card, I do private dancing, but only for select clients. Please ring me if you find Ellie, even if it's bad news.'

'Okay, I'll look out for her.'

MASON

H e stepped out of the booth and glanced around, checking for any security men. There were none, so he looked over to Natasha and mimed, *One minute,* while pointing behind him.

Natasha nodded and mimed back, *Okay.*

It was time to confront Buckingham and see his reaction. He would know by his face if he was involved, and if he was, then evidence was irrelevant. He wouldn't be arresting him and trying to prove a case against him. He would get the information he needed from him one way or another, and god help anyone who tried to stop him.

He made his way around the booths, noting another row behind, half the number, but double the size. He was right, VIP. Then he pulled open the unlocked staff door and stepped in to a small hallway leading to the stairs. A door to his right was marked toilet, and from the tapping sound coming through the door on his left, it was almost certainly an office, which held little or no interest for him. He took the stairs in front of him two at a time to the top where he found a door marked Benny Grant - Manager. He knocked twice and entered without waiting for a response.

A man jumped to his feet behind a large desk. 'Who the hell are you?' he shouted. He was in his mid-fifties, clean shaven, with thick silver hair, brushed back and parted on the left. His charcoal black suit had seen better days, and his white shirt was greying from too many washes.

Mason stepped inside and closed the door. 'Mr Grant I presume, no need to be alarmed, I'm just looking for Mr Buckingham?'

Grant grabbed a walkie-talkie radio on his desk.

'Wait,' Mason said. 'I'm not here to cause trouble, I'm just looking for Buckingham.'

Grant held down the button on the top of his radio. 'I need security in my office now. There's a guy in here and I want him out.'

His radio crackled back at him. Then a voice surrounded by static said, 'Yes Boss.'

He glared at Mason. 'If you're with Buckingham, you are trouble.'

Mason shook his head. 'I'm not with him, I'm looking for him.'

'Why?'

'Let's just say he has some questions to answer.'

Before Grant could speak, the door burst open and a burly man in a black suit rushed in, puffing hard. He glanced from Mason to Grant and back to Mason, then charged forward.

Mason side stepped and used the man's own momentum to bounce him off the wall. The security guy spun around with a look of both surprise and embarrassment in equal measures. After a moment's hesitation, he headed back to try again.

'Tony, wait!' Grant shouted.

The security man froze. 'You want him out, Boss?'

'Maybe, but wait a minute.' Grant studied Mason. 'You're fast on your feet.'

'I've had plenty of practice.'

'Are you the law?'

'No.'

'Private?'

'Detective? No.'

'Do you work for Buckingham?'

'No.'

'Why are you here?'

'I just want to talk to you, that's all.'

'Who are you?'

'Mason Cooper.'

Grant studied Mason for a long silent moment, then sighed and relaxed his shoulders. 'It's okay, Tony, you can go.'

'Are you sure?'

'Yes, you can leave us.'

'Okay Boss, I'll be outside if you need me.'

Grant pointed to a chair in front of his desk. 'Have a seat.'

Mason glanced around the office. The furniture was pretty standard, not expensive, but functional. A desk, four chairs including Grant's, which was the only one that looked comfortable, filing cabinets, one with a table fan perched on top, letter trays on the others. A laptop computer sat on the desk, pushed to the side to make way for a glossy magazine that Grant must have been reading before being interrupted. But what set the office apart from any other were the large framed photographs of partially dressed dancers in seductive poses hung around three of the walls. Certainly not standard office fixings.

Mason nodded to Tony as he passed, then sat down when the door closed. 'He's a bit out of shape, don't you think?'

Grant sat behind his desk, opened a drawer, and pulled out a whiskey bottle. He reached back in and pulled out two shot glasses. Without a word, he filled them both and pushed one across the desk to Mason. 'I suppose he is, but he doesn't usually have to run up the stairs in such a hurry. Most of our trouble happens down on the door, or on the floor. And in the case of the latter it usually involves too much alcohol, or wandering hands, or both.'

'Yeah, I suppose it would. I'm sorry to burst in like that.'

Mason watched him place the top back onto the bottle, but he didn't screw it down. Must be planning on refills.

'So is he pressuring you as well?' Grant said.

Mason leant forward, picked up the glass, and took a swig. 'Not exactly.'

Grant took a swig and nodded. 'But you got issues with him?'

'You could say that. What about you?'

Grant flashed his eyes around the room. 'He wants to buy this place. Made me a good offer too.'

'And?'

'Turned him down. It's not for sale. I opened this club ten years ago. Started it from scratch, on my own.' He raised his chin and a look of pride spread over his face. 'Worked hard to make it the best club in the West End. We treat the girls good here, with respect, you can ask em. That's why they stay, well most of em. Not like the other clubs.'

Mason let him talk.

'This line of business has the fastest turnaround of staff than any other.' He shrugged. 'That's if you call em staff. They're self-employed really, and they make good money here.' He took another swig of whiskey. 'Don't need to sell, don't want to sell.'

'So where's the problem?'

'He won't take no for an answer. Seems desperate to get his hands on this place.'

'What can he do? If you don't want to sell, he can't buy.'

'It's not that simple. Mr Buckingham is connected.'

'Connected?'

'Yeah, he carries quite a bit of influence in the City. From what I hear, what he wants, he gets, and he can call on some pretty mean people to make it happen.'

'Where did he go after leaving your office?'

'He left by the rear exit, down the fire escape. He didn't want to go back through the club. Maybe he knew you were following him.'

Mason studied Grant. He seemed a straight up sort of guy, no nonsense, but fair. Worth trying to get as much information as he could.

'Do you know anything about his other business interests?'

Grant's face straightened. 'All I know is he's been in

here a few times. Takes some of my best girls for a dance and a couple of them have left with him. Never see em again. Lost two of my best like that.'

Mason shifted in his seat. It was clear Grant was no fan of Buckingham. So it was probably safe to tell him why he was looking for him.

'I think I need to explain something to you.'

Grant looked interested. 'Yeah?'

'I think he's running some kind of brothel.'

'A brothel?'

'Yeah, but not an ordinary brothel. The kind where some, or all of the girls, have been abducted or tricked, held against their will and not allowed to leave.'

Grant shook his head. 'I'd know if he had a brothel in London. I hear about most things. You know how it is. In this business word gets around.'

'Maybe it's out of town, and maybe the clients aren't your usual clients.'

'What do you mean?'

'I think he runs some sort of club for a select group of rich clients. Probably not in London, so your usual sources wouldn't apply. They'd be out of the loop.'

'What makes you think he's got a brothel?'

'Because I think he's got my daughter, or at least his club has her. She was abducted from our home on Thursday. Her mother... my wife, was stabbed.'

Grant's eyes widened as he drew breath.

'She's okay. She survived. But they still have my daughter.'

'What makes you think Buckingham's involved?'

'Just piecing everything together.'

Grant leaned back in his chair, shaking his head. 'I've heard about those gangs who trade in that shit, you know, tricking girls from Europe to come here and forcing them into prostitution.'

'Yeah, I've had a run in with them, that's how this all started. But I don't think they have my daughter now, they've passed her on.'

Grant slowly shook his head. 'I'm not into that. My girls are here cos they wanna be here.' He gulped down his whiskey, grabbed the bottle, and filled his glass. Then he reached over and filled Mason's glass.

'Is there any more you can tell me about Buckingham,' Mason asked.

Grant shrugged and shook his head. 'No, that's it.'

Mason stood up and reached over to a pad of paper on the desk. 'Do you mind?'

'Go ahead.'

Mason picked up a pen and wrote his name and mobile number on the pad. 'I'd appreciate a call if you hear anything.'

Grant got to his feet and nodded. 'Of course. I hope you find her.'

'Thanks for the drink.'

'Any time.'

Mason pointed to his full glass on the desk. 'I'll pass on that one if you don't mind, I need to keep a clear head.'

'No problem.'

Mason turned to leave.

Grant said, 'Remember what I told you, he knows some bad people.' Then he gulped down the contents of both glasses.

As Mason he closed the door behind him, he came face to face with Tony in the corridor. They held eye contact for a few long seconds, then Mason held out his hand. 'Sorry about earlier.'

Tony stared down at Mason's outstretched hand, then wrapped his own around it and squeezed. 'That's okay,' he said, then let go and stepped aside, allowing Mason to pass.

As he descended the stairs, Mason flexed his hand and smiled to himself. Obviously, Tony's ego was still bruised.

When Mason entered the main room, he stopped in his tracks. The table where he'd left Natasha was empty. Even their drinks had gone. As he scanned the room, the sound of a disturbance came from a nearby booth. He pulled back the curtain and found Natasha pinned against the wall by one of the drunk young men from the bar. 'What's going on here?' he snapped.

Natasha looked at him, eyes wide. 'Mason,' she mumbled through the fingers of the man's hand pressed over her mouth.

The drunk glanced over his shoulder at Mason, rolled his eyes, then turned back to Natasha. 'Come on, get them off, I've paid you.'

Mason stepped into the booth and grabbed the man's throat with one hand. 'Get away from her now, or I'll snap your scrawny little neck. Do you hear me?'

The drunk stared at him through glazed eyes, pupils rolling side to side, unable to focus. He took his hand away from Natasha's mouth. 'Yes sir, sorry sir, I just wanted the bitch to dance, that's all. I paid her to dance.'

In one smooth movement, Mason pushed him out of the booth, sending him clattering into a table.

He turned back to Natasha. 'Are you okay? Did he hurt you?'

'Yes-no, I'm fine, he just pulled me in here and told me to dance for him.' She put her hand down the front of her top and pulled out a twenty-pound note from her bra. 'This is his.'

Mason scanned the club. The other men and the dancers at the bar seemed oblivious to what was going on. Too many distractions for them to notice.

'Where the hell is the security in here?' he said.

'I don't know, but one ran past earlier just after you left.'

'Yeah, I met him upstairs. So they must only have one guy on.'

Mason took the twenty-pound note from Natasha, then guided her out of the booth. 'Come on, let's get out of here.'

He stopped next to the drunk, who was steadying himself against the table, grabbed the man's jaw and pulled it down. 'I think this is yours.' He stuffed the note into the man's mouth. 'Careful you don't swallow it. Use it to buy a self-help book on how to treat women.' Then he took Natasha's hand and led her out of the club.

There was a buzz in the London air. It was a pleasant Saturday evening in the West End and people were out for fun. Day trippers, some with children in tow, mingled with tourists and early party goers. Groups of women in fancy dress, guys in silly hats carrying bottles of beer and singing arm in arm. Just good clean fun. All oblivious to the seedier side of London's criminal underworld. To the suffering, fear, and intimidation of women and young girls being held for the gratification of men looking for a quick thrill. Secret encounters, evidence of which would be washed away as soon as they got home, hidden from wives and girlfriends and family members alike. Did they care whether the girls who entertained them did so voluntarily? Most had read articles and seen documentaries on the subject. If asked, most would acknowledge that it happens, somewhere. But none would admit to seeing it first-hand. None would admit to using these girls, intimidated and threatened to perform against their will. Oh no, not them. If they bragged to their friends, they would never mention the pain in the girls' eyes, the blank expressions born from drugs or boredom or fear. Not the girl they paid for. She was not a sex slave. It must be happening somewhere else... to some other girl.

ROSIE

S he lay in the bath submerged in the warm, comforting water, her eyes closed tight. She could be anywhere. Back in her family bathroom, or at her friend's house on a sleepover, or in a luxury hotel on holiday washing off sand and suntan lotion after a day in the sun. Her imagination had whisked her away, far away. For just a few precious moments, she was free, peaceful, and happy. But not for long. The second she opened her eyes, the stark reality was back.

Her inner clock suggested it must have been at least an hour since Danielle had brought her food and ordered her to eat and get ready. Not knowing how long it would be before they come for her, she grabbed the towel and stepped out from the bath onto the unforgiving concrete floor.

Standing in front of the long mirror, she dried her body and towelled her hair until nearly dry. She let the towel drop and studied her reflection. Her teenage body had been slower to develop than her friends. There was a time when she'd feared she would never fill out and become a woman. That the taunts she'd received from the boys in school would continue into adulthood. That she'd struggle to attract boyfriends, and would forever envy her friends' popularity.

But no longer.

In a few short months, she'd caught up, and how quickly the change had occurred. She'd even become the focus of the boys who once mocked her, but although flattered, she wasn't interested. Not in them. They were too immature. She would wait until she found a young man worthy of her attention. One who would respect her, and enjoy her company, and not just her body.

But what of her plans now? Would she ever laugh with her friends again, compare stories, and share photos of their latest admirers? Would she ever be free to choose her dates? Everything was so uncertain. She was in a different world now, and the people in her new world didn't care about her. Not like her family and friends. They only cared about what she could do for them.

She pulled on the white lace dress, reached behind, and pulled up the zip. It was a perfect fit, as if made especially for her. She stepped into the white lace panties and hitched them up under the dress. Then she slipped into the high heel shoes. They too fit perfectly, taller than she would normally wear, but surprisingly comfortable. She scanned the items of makeup scattered across the table where Danielle had left them and remembered her words. Everything you need to make yourself beautiful. She remembered being told to apply the makeup lightly to maintain her young looks.

She dragged the table over to the mirror, and as she stared down at the makeup, she had an overwhelming urge to use it all, to spread as much of it on her face as she could. If she made herself ugly, the men would not pick her, they would not be interested, and if they were not interested, she would remain a virgin.

Then she sighed. Who was she kidding? She'd been warned. Do as they say, or there would be consequences. Her world was scary enough without making them angry. Why start a war she couldn't win? If she refused to cooperate, they wouldn't simply open the front door and allow her to leave. She'd seen their faces, knew their names. If they were their real names, though probably not. What could she hope to gain by being difficult? She had no choice, not really. Not if she wanted to gain their trust and find a way to escape.

She picked up the makeup and began to apply it sparingly. Just a hint of mascara, a dab of blusher, and a thin layer of the reddish-brown lipstick. Then she stood back to judge the result. It was hard to be objective, but she was satisfied that she still looked her age, maybe younger.

If only she were going on a date with a new boyfriend, someone she liked and wanted to impress. This outfit would surely do the job. He would be blown away, wouldn't he?

But she was not going on an exciting new date, or out dancing with friends, and her efforts were not for a good-looking young man. They were for some stranger, who would no doubt be fat, bald, and ugly, and probably old too.

Danielle entered the basement and smiled. 'Turn around girl, and let me look at you.'

Rosie complied.

'Wow, you look good enough to eat.' She stepped closer to Rosie and inspected her face. 'Perfect. You did as you were told. Mr Jones will be pleased.'

For just a moment, Rosie's mood was lifted. The compliments felt good, just for a second. But the feeling faded fast as she began to wonder. . . what would the night bring?

'Turn around, my sweet,' Danielle said.

Hesitantly, Rosie turned.

'Now put your hands behind your back.'

'What?' Rosie spun back around to face Danielle.

Danielle's mood changed. As quickly as the smile had appeared, it vanished, and she scowled at Rosie. 'Now, we're not going to have a problem, are we?'

'No, madam, but you're not going to tie my hands, are you?'

'Of course I am,' snapped Danielle.

Rosie's breathing increased as her heart raced. 'But you don't need to, I won't try anything, honest I won't.'

'I know you won't, little one, because you won't be able to. Now do as I say and turn around.'

Rosie studied Danielle's face. No softness, no femininity, just hard lines and a look made of stone. Best do as she said. She was bigger and stronger and could force her if she needed to. Rosie turned around and placed her hands behind her. She felt metal around her wrists and heard the clicking of the ratchet as the handcuffs were adjusted to fit.

Something tightened around her neck. It was hard and uncomfortable. Her heart pounded louder than ever. 'What's that?'

'Nothing to worry about, it's just a collar and lead.'

The collar was close against her skin, but not so that it interfered with her breathing. Rosie sighed. At least she wasn't being strangled.

'There now, well done. Now come with me.'

Rosie turned and followed Danielle, staying close to maintain slack on the lead. The stairs were steep, narrow, and dark, but a rectangle of light at the top showed the way.

As they stepped out through the basement door, Rosie's eyes widened at the sheer decadence of the entrance hall, large enough to swallow an average size house, maybe two. From its centre, a double width oak staircase curved gently up to a galleried landing. Directly opposite, double doors made from oak and stained glass would impress any visitor.

She'd been wrong about the floor. It wasn't wood, but an exquisite cream marble with golden brown veins twisting and stretching in every direction and must have cost a fortune to lay.

Two antique side tables, etched in gold, and set ten feet apart, were each centred beneath large gilt-framed mirrors along one wall, with panelled doors on either side. A crystal chandelier hung from the high ceiling, bathing everything in soft light.

It was so different to the way she had pictured it in her mind while being carried in with the hood over her head. She had thought posh, just not this posh.

How could anything bad happen in such a grand and beautiful setting? Surely anyone who could afford such luxury must have high morals. They must know right from wrong. Or was she just being naïve?

As she glanced at her reflection in a mirror and at the collar around her neck, she had her answer. These people were not typical well-to-do people. They were warped, and perverted, and cruel.

She gasped as the lead jerked, pulling her forward through an open door displaying a bronze nameplate on which the words, Drawing Room, were engraved. The door closed before she had a chance to look past Danielle at the room's contents. They were in complete darkness. It was only a moment or two, but seemed much longer before a light was switched on and she could see again. The room was large enough for a banquet, except there were no tables and no chairs, just open space. But the room was not empty, and its contents turned her blood cold.

In front of her, were a row of figures. Human figures. All wearing hooded robes that reached down to their ankles and were tied around the waist with braided rope. They appeared to be made from deep red silk, and all had the hoods pulled over their heads like something from a devil-worshipping cult movie.

She tried to focus on their faces, but no features were visible. Then she saw why. They wore shaped black masks, each one identical, with holes for their eyes and cut away above their mouths. Each figure had a small coloured badge pinned to the left breast, and each badge was a different colour with the name of the colour printed across and prefixed with Mr as if it were the man's name.

She began counting them from left to right, but as she reached six, they parted, and another figure in a similar robe stepped forward and took his place in the middle of the row. His face was shadowed by the hood, but he was different to the rest, taller and no black mask. The letter J was embroidered where the others had badges, and his robe wasn't red, it was jet black.

Danielle turned and unclipped the lead from the collar around her neck. Rosie lowered her gaze to the foreground between her and the robes. In front of her, on the polished wooden floor, was a circle about six feet in diameter that appeared to be laid down with black tape. As she stared at the circle, her legs began to tremble, and adrenalin surged through her body. Her stomach churned. It was hard to breathe, and her mouth was so dry she hoped she wouldn't have to speak.

ROSIE

The figure in black stepped forward and slowly lowered his hood to reveal his face. It was Mr Jones. She couldn't decide if she was glad it was him or not. But at least she could see his face, unlike the others who remained intimidating in their disguises.

Jones clapped his hands together twice, the sound echoing off the walls. 'Gentlemen, this beautiful creature is Rosie. I have brought her here tonight especially for your enjoyment. She is sweet sixteen and a virgin.'

A few of the figures mumbled among themselves and then fell silent. Jones walked up to the front of the circle and pointed down.

'Come here, my dear and stand in the circle.'

Rosie hesitated and found herself re-assessing her plan to co-operate. She tried pulling her wrists apart, but the steel handcuffs bit into her skin. She thought about running out and down the stairs, but wondered how she would open the front door with her hands behind her back. And even if she could, where would she run to? She glanced over her shoulder at the door to the room. It was closed, and another red-robed figure was guarding it.

There was no escape.

But maybe she should try one more time appealing to Danielle. She glanced around. But Danielle was nowhere to be seen.

So she walked forward into the centre of the circle.

Jones lifted her chin with his hand. 'If it's the circle that's bothering you, don't worry, we are not devil worshippers, and the robes are only for anonymity.'

Rosie said nothing.

He turned to face the row of hooded robes. 'You are all VIP members, so no payment is necessary to enjoy her. Except...' He paused and turned back to Rosie. 'Because she is a virgin, the first to take her will pay ten-thousand. As you know, that is the rule.'

He held out his arm and pointed to Rosie. 'I'm sure you'll agree. She is the cutest we've had, so I have raised the termination fee to fifty-thousand.'

The fourth robe in the line raised his hand like a pupil in a class volunteering to answer a question. 'Master, it's usually twenty-thousand.'

Jones nodded. 'I know, but the extra cost reflects the quality of the girl, and it's my way of saying that I don't want her terminated.'

The robe, displaying the name Mr Brown on his badge, nodded and lowered his hand.

That word echoed in Rosie's mind. Terminated. She became light-headed and disorientated. The figures in front of her all blurred into one. Her legs buckled and she fell to the floor.

When she opened her eyes, she was surrounded by the robes. She looked up at their masks, all tilted down towards her, all watching her in silence.

A glass of water was held up to her lips. 'Drink,' Jones said.

She parted her lips and took a sip, then another, and another. Her breathing slowed, and her heart was no longer racing and beating out of her chest. 'What happened?' she asked.

Jones pulled the glass away. 'You fainted.'

Then she remembered why. This is a death cult. They kill the girls when they are finished with them. Terminate them for a price and entertainment. Now it made sense why Jones and Danielle didn't cover their faces. It didn't matter. They could never be identified if the girls were terminated.

A strange calm came over her.

Was she beginning to accept her fate? Was there no fight left? She thought about her parents again and wondered if they'd ever find her body. She prayed they would so that she could be buried. Somewhere for my parents to visit and grieve.

Hands gripped her arms and lifted her up onto her feet, her wrists still restrained behind her back. She felt small and helpless in the middle of the robes. All of them standing just outside the circle, but close enough for her to see their eyes. Not one of them appeared to care. Not one showed her pity. They just waited, ready to pounce. Ready to use her for their gratification.

But what then?

Would any of them be willing to pay fifty-thousand to

watch her die? It was a lot of money, but what if they all clubbed together? It would cost them less than five thousand each, and these were rich men.

She looked at each one in turn. Mr Brown, Mr Green, Mr White, Mr Grey and the others with colours for names. Who are they? Where do they live? What do they do for a living? Do they have wives and children? Maybe some have daughters her age. How would they feel if their daughters were here now, ready to be consumed by the perverted, sadistic members stood next to them?

She'd read articles on the pack mentality and how it can minimise individual responsibility. Some people do things as part of a pack that they'd never do if acting alone. It's as if their conscience evaporates when in a group.

Now the lead was back on and pulling her forward. The robes moved aside, and she followed Jones to the end of the room, to a small platform standing three feet high. At the back, three steps led to the top.

Jones unclipped the lead, then removed the collar. 'Up you go,' he said.

Still a little unsteady on her feet, she carefully negotiated the steps and stopped in the middle of the platform. Jones was behind her.

'Gentlemen, it's time. You know the price if you want to be the first.'

The robes gathered in front of the platform like hungry wolves waiting to be fed. Mr Brown raised his hand again. 'I'll pay to go first.'

Jones pointed to him. 'As it stands, she's yours.'

Mr Brown nodded.

Then Mr White spoke. 'I'll pay to be first.'

Jones stepped to the front of the platform. 'It seems we have an auction underway. Mr White, what is your bid?'

Mr White raised a hand. 'Twelve-thousand,'

Mr Brown raised his chin. 'Fifteen-thousand.'

Rosie looked from one to the other. Brown was the member who'd shown an interest in the fee to terminate. She found herself rooting for Mr White.

'We have fifteen-thousand from Mr Brown.' Jones said.

Rosie looked at Mr White and listened, but he remained silent.

'The bid is fifteen-thousand,' Jones repeated.

White raised his hand. 'Sixteen-thousand.'

Rosie held her breath as she focused on Mr Brown, willing him to remain silent.

But Brown spoke with slow determination, 'Twenty-thousand.'

Mr White shook his head and stepped back, indicating his surrender.

Rosie sighed. She was now at the mercy of Brown.

Jones pointed to Brown. 'Endorse the book with your IOU for twenty-thousand and go to the red room. She will be there waiting for you.'

Mr Brown turned and left the room. Jones tapped Rosie on her shoulder. 'Follow me.'

She stepped off the platform.

As she passed the row of red robes, she looked at each one in turn, hoping to see a spark of humanity in just one pair of eyes, just a hint of concern. But there was none.

They reached the door, and Jones stopped and shouted back. 'Gentlemen, go to the clubroom, there are a few treats there for you.'

32

ROSIE

Rosie followed Jones out of the drawing room, up the sweeping stairs to the first floor, and into a large bedroom. The focal point was a high four-poster bed with carved oak posts on each corner. The dark red velvet valance that framed the base below crisp white bedding oozed elegance.

Rosie walked into the centre of the room and faced the foot of the bed. Her heels sank into the deep pile of the beige carpet. It was the kind of bedroom her mother would love. She'd spend hours scanning home and garden magazines that were full of exquisite luxury décor, just like this.

Jones stepped up behind her and in a second released her from the handcuffs. 'There now. That should make you more comfortable. Now wait here for your guest and remember what I told you. You must make him happy, very happy.'

She remained silent.

'Look at me.'

She turned, but hesitated before raising her eyes to his.

'Let me hear you say what I've just told you.'

'I must make him happy, sir.'

'Good.' He turned to leave.

'Sir.'

He paused.

'Can I ask you a question?'

He turned and stared at her as if deciding whether to allow her a question. Then shrugged. 'What is it?'

'Are they going to kill me?'

He sighed. 'So you picked up on the comments about termination?'

She nodded.

'The members here tonight are VIP members. They have the authority to do anything they wish to the girls I provide. Most of the time it's sex, and sometimes there's sadomasochism. It's rare, but occasionally things go further. But don't worry, I doubt they will go that far tonight. They are very rich people, but fifty-thousand is probably beyond what they would be willing to pay.'

'Can they pay as a group?'

He laughed. 'Lateral thinking, I like that. But no, whoever does the deed, pays the fee. Or should I change the rules?'

Rosie shook her head.

'Then don't worry about it. Tonight is not your night to die.'

Rosie sighed. Her galloping heart slowed to a canter. 'Sir, why do you do this? You're rich. You could be anywhere, doing anything you want. Why are you doing this to me?'

'Because I can. As you say, I'm rich, but not as rich as

the Members. They are some of the wealthiest men in the Country. A few of them earn more in a day than most men earn in a year. Many of the others hold prominent positions in multinational companies, or in government, or in the medical, or legal professions. We even have celebrities. And some fly in from abroad. They have high-pressure jobs, high-pressure lives, and need to let off steam. This is how they choose to do it.'

'So raping and killing girls is just letting off steam?'

'That's four questions. You asked for one.' He paused for a moment. 'I don't usually talk to the girls like this, but you're brighter than most, so I'll explain. It wasn't always like this. It started out innocently enough. I began throwing parties for wealthy and powerful men who wanted to spend time with beautiful young women without any complications. And it worked well for a time. But I had to step it up. Even though I provided the best girls in the business, it wasn't enough. Some wanted more. They wanted to take it to a whole new level, and they were willing to pay for it. But most of them had wives and reputations to maintain, so they needed someone discrete. Someone they could trust. I gave them what they wanted. I thinned the members down to a select group with alternative appetites and formed this club with a partner. We were financed by the sickest of all of us. He is the Grand Master. We call him Mr Scarlet. I hope for your sake you don't meet him yet. Not until you've acclimatised to what goes on here.'

She stared at him for a long moment, processing what she'd heard.

'Can't you stop it?' she said.

'Probably not, even if I wanted to, which I don't. It is all about the money for me. If they are willing to pay, I will provide them with any service they require. Everything is available for a price. You are just unfortunate to be here. But now that you are, you will be used whenever and for whatever we wish. But you will learn to accept it. They all do eventually. At least those who last do. Then it will be easier.'

'Easier for who?' she mumbled, but not loud enough for him to hear. No need to push her luck. She sighed, deflated by his response. Any glimmer of hope she had of finding compassion had gone.

She tried a different approach.

'Isn't it risky? What if one of the members reports you to the police?'

'That will not happen. This is a closed club. Members are vetted thoroughly before they join. They must be sponsored by an existing member and they must have extreme tendencies. In other words, anyone who would find our activities shocking will not be allowed to join. Many of our members met through encrypted sites on the dark-web. Although, we have stopped using it now because the authorities are starting to figure it out.'

'I would have thought all men would find this place shocking.'

'You would be surprised at how wealth and power corrupts. These men have no shame.'

Just then the door opened, and Mr Brown entered. Without another word Jones turned and walked out of the room, and as they passed each other the two men bowed their heads as a sign of mutual respect.

Rosie tutted to herself under her breath. If it wasn't so serious it would be laughable. Mutual respect between the twisted club member who enjoys abusing girls, and the facilitator who makes it happen.

Now she was alone with him, the buyer, the successful purchaser of her innocence. She didn't know him, nor would she recognise him if they were to pass on the street in the future, that's if she has a future, yet soon they would be engaged in what she considered the most intimate act known to humanity. An act she had been saving for someone special. And whoever that person was, it was not the man in front of her hiding behind the mask and hooded robe.

He moved close and cupped her face in his hands. She looked away. There was nothing romantic about this. She didn't know him, but already she hated him. It was an emotion she'd never experienced before, at least not this strong. She'd thought that she had hated some of the boys in her school. The ones who teased her and made fun of her, who'd sneak up behind and lift up her skirt, just for laughs. She'd hated them, hadn't she? Well, not really, not like she hated Mr Brown, the man who was about to take her virginity as if it were nothing special. Just his for the taking. All for a few moments of pleasure.

His pleasure, not hers.

He lowered his head and kissed her full on the lips. The cut away in the mask allowed for contact between them. She closed her eyes to avoid looking at him, but it seemed to encourage him even more, and he kissed her again.

He slipped the dress off her shoulders, then reached behind and pulled down the zip. He tugged the dress down below her hips and let it fall to the floor. He stepped back to look at her for a moment, then pulled her to him and kissed her again. He pressed his lips against hers and forced his tongue inside her mouth. She wanted to heave, but resisted the urge to pull away, even though he repulsed her. She didn't know his name, his age, or his occupation, but there were two things about him she did know. He wore a wedding ring, and he had no respect for his wife. Because if he did, he would not be here doing this to her. After all, how could he rape her and then go home to his wife and family and act as if nothing had happened? It didn't seem compatible. He must be a good actor. Maybe he kissed his wife before leaving home today. Maybe he took her flowers on her birthday and on special occasions. Almost certainly his wife had no idea what he got up to on the evenings he wasn't at home. She almost felt sorry for his wife, living with a man with a secret. Especially one like this.

He held the top of her arms, then pushed her down onto the bed. The satin quilt was soft under her skin, softer than the bedding in the basement. He lay on top of her, hooked his thumb into the top of her panties, and pulled them down. Now she was naked, but he was fully clothed in his robe. His hands were all over her, touching and stroking, his body heavy, pinning her to the bed. She kept her eyes shut tight. It was as close to hell as she could imagine. What could be worse? Then his weight lifted off her. The moment she'd feared had arrived. He opened his robe and pulled it off. The sound of a zip opening filled her with dread. He lowered himself down onto her. Her eyes remained closed. She didn't want visual memories, not of this, the worst moment of her life. She knew he'd opened his shirt because the hair on his chest scraped against her breasts like sandpaper. She kept her hands by her side. She couldn't bear to touch him. She gasped as a sharp pain shot through her groin. He was inside her, and it hurt. Tears filled her eyes, then trickled down her face. She stifled the cries in her throat and prayed it would be over soon. She longed for the solace of the basement.

He moved faster, his breathing increased, he groaned and tensed his body. She opened her eyes. His face contorted, his mouth open, only inches from hers. He moaned, sighed, and relaxed, his body now limp on top of her.

It was hard to breathe. He seemed heavier now. She waited for him to move, but he just lay there, crushing her. She brought her hands up and pushed as hard as she could. He rolled off onto his back and lay with his eyes closed, a smile of sick satisfaction across his face.

She sat up and looked down between her legs. No blood. How could that be? How could there be so much pain without blood? She sat next to him on the bed, not knowing what to do. He lay still, his breathing deep and rhythmic. Was he asleep?

She thought about the stark contrast in their emotions. He was satisfied, gratified, and relaxed. She was violated, humiliated, and distraught.

But at least it was over. The deed was done.

She watched his chest rise and fall for a few moments. This could be her opportunity, the one she'd hoped for. She held her breath and eased herself off the bed, pausing when her feet touched the floor. He grunted, drew in a deep breath, and exhaled long and slow. She picked up her underwear and dress and slowly pulled them on, then carried her shoes to the door. It would be easier to run in her bare feet. She glanced back, still no movement. Carefully, she opened the door...

Then jumped back.

Jones was right there in the doorway.

Her heart sank.

Her chance had gone.

Jones pointed up to the corner of the room, to a camera aimed straight at the bed. He'd been watching her. Maybe filming her, too.

Her stomach rose to her throat. She felt dirty and used.

'I think I'm going to throw up,' she said.

Jones casually walked over to a sideboard and returned with a large porcelain bowl. 'It's only for decoration, but you can use it if you need to.' His voice was cold and uncaring.

She took the bowl and placed it on a chair, then bent over it. She retched, but nothing came out. She retched again and again, but still nothing. Minutes passed and the feeling subsided.

'I think I'm okay now,' she said.

Jones returned the bowl to its place and glanced at the man sleeping on the bed. 'So far so good, but you haven't finished yet, you need to come with me.'

33

ROSIE

osie put her hand to her forehead. It was cold and clammy. Her insides were numb and her mouth dry. She followed Jones down the stairs to a door marked The Club Room. As she entered, the sound of male voices echoed around her. It was the robes, talking in twos and threes, some next to attractive girls, dressed to impress, in short skirts and heels. They must be the girls that Danielle had mentioned. The men were laughing and rambling excitedly. They seemed happy. The girls did not, but they were quiet and respectful, nodding when spoken to, and submissive in their posture with hands clasped tightly around a glass held in front of them. Their heads slightly bowed.

The room was laid out to entertain. Tables and chairs and curved booths gave it the air of a luxury hotel lounge. A bar spanned one end of the room in front of a long row of bottles. Just about any spirit you could want, all lined up, all full. From a lower shelf, rows of glasses hung upside down, perfectly organised in descending sizes. Ice buckets and plates of neatly cut sandwiches covered the bar top.

She counted seven girls. Each one chosen for her beauty, and all would stand out in any gathering of young women.

Jones escorted Rosie to the centre of the room and introduced her to one of the other girls. 'Rosie, this is Ellie. Ellie, this is Rosie. It is her first time tonight. She has just had her first encounter, so I would like you to explain to her what happens now.'

Ellie nodded.

Rosie sighed. Her ordeal wasn't over.

When Jones moved away, Ellie took hold of Rosie's hand and led her to a quiet spot over by a window.

She said, 'Now you've been broken in.' She paused. 'Sorry to use that term, but that's what they call it. You must entertain the others. They will want you, too.'

Rosie stared at her, open-mouthed. 'All of them?'

'They're all entitled, but no. Some are with the other girls, so you'll probably only go with five or six tonight.'

Rosie's knees buckled, she almost collapsed. 'I can't, I just can't go through that another five times.'

Ellie held her hand. 'You can and you must. It's the only way to survive here. You must do what they want, believe me, you must. I was brought here six months ago and already I've seen three or four girls disappear after refusing to co-operate. Mr Scarlet came and took them. I never saw them again. You're young, you must think about your future. If you do what they want, maybe you'll get away from them one day.'

Rosie's eyes widened. 'Have you seen any girls get released? Or heard about any going home?'

Ellie's expression dropped. She didn't answer.

'Ellie, have you?'

'No, I haven't. But that doesn't mean they don't or that you won't. So you must not give up. Just think of your family and you'll get through this. It gets easier after a while.'

'That's what Jones said. Have they brainwashed you?'

Ellie shook her head. 'No, they haven't. It's about being smart. We can't fight them, so we must do whatever it takes to survive. You'll see.' She turned to look at Jones, and he beckoned her to him. 'I have to go, but just one thing.'

'What?'

'I think Jones likes you.'

'Why do you say that?'

'Because he asked me to talk to you. While you were... you know, upstairs, he spoke to me. I think he wanted to make sure you co-operated so it would go easier for you.'

'And you think that means he likes me?'

'Well, look at it this way. I've seen many girls on their first time here, but he's never asked me or the other girls to speak to them and warn them before.' She turned to walk away.

The flower tattoo on Ellie's shoulder caught Rosie's attention. Then she saw Ellie's back, through her low-cut dress, and gasped. 'Ellie, wait.'

Ellie stopped and glanced back. 'What?'

'Those marks on your back, what happened?'

Ellie moved to Rosie's side. 'You don't know?'

'Know what?'

Ellie glanced around. Jones was pouring himself a drink at the bar, so she continued. 'They have S and M nights here.'

'What's that?'

'Sadomasochism, but the emphasis is very much on the sadistic side. They get their kicks inflicting pain on us.'

Rosie slumped. 'Jones mentioned it, but I didn't understand what he meant.'

'There are events every weekend and others in the week. Some are like this where they just fuck us, but some are in the dungeon in the basement. It's kitted out for pain, our pain, and their pleasure.'

'I've been in the basement since Thursday. There's nothing like that down there.'

Ellie smirked. 'You've been held in what they call the holding room. It's in the basement, but it's not the only room down there. Have you seen the size of this place? It's a mansion, and it's huge. There's another basement much bigger than yours where they do that kind of stuff.'

Rosie said nothing. Just when she thought it couldn't get any worse, she discovered there was more to come, much more.

Ellie said, 'I think that's why Jones told me to talk to you. Normally if girls cause problems they are taken down there, and sometimes they don't come back.'

'But you came back.'

'Yes, but that was different. I was whipped on a normal S and M night, as we all are.' She motioned with her hand to the other girls.

Rosie raised an eyebrow. 'Normal?'

Two of the robes approached her. They stood either side and stared at her in silence. She glanced from one to the other. Her heart raced and her throat tightened, making it hard to swallow.

Ellie reached out, squeezed Rosie's hand, and gave her a warm smile. 'You need to go with them,' she said. 'Be strong, you can do this.' Then she let go and walked away.

The robes moved closer. They held her arms and silently escorted her back to the red room. Back to where Mr Brown had raped her. She looked over at the bed. Empty, and the quilt had been straightened. She would never have known what had occurred there only minutes before had she not lived through it herself.

'Take it off,' one of them said.

She looked at the badge on his chest. It was Mr White. He'd lost the auction to be first, but he got the consolation prize of being second. Ellie's words were still echoing in her mind. We must do whatever it takes to survive. She remembered Ellie's expression and those of the other girls. They weren't happy, but they seemed resigned, as if they had accepted their situation and learned to deal with it. And more importantly, they were alive.

She pulled down the zip and slipped off the dress. Without further instruction, she pushed down her panties and kicked them away. Then she waited, naked except for her shoes.

Mr White bent down and pulled them off one at a time, then pushed her face down onto the bed. Before she could turn, he was on top of her, his hot breath on her neck, his hands all over her. Then came the same shuffling and adjustment of clothing as before.

Then he was inside her.

This time, she didn't have to close her eyes. She couldn't see him. She stared into the white satin beneath her. But he was different from Mr Brown. He was rough, very rough. His hand pushed down on the back of her head, forcing her face into the bed. He moved up and down on her as if possessed. He was bigger and heavier than the first, and it hurt even more. But worse, he took much longer to finish. It seemed like forever before he finally tensed, groaned, and collapsed onto the bed next to her.

Before she could take a breath, the other man pinned her down again.

She began to sob.

When he finished, both men adjusted their robes and left the room.

She was alone.

But unlike before, escape was not on her mind. She looked up at the camera and wondered who was watching her. Was it just Jones? Was it Jones and Danielle? Or was it all of them?

She burned between her legs. She put her hand down and felt wetness. She wasn't surprised. None of them had used a condom. But when she pulled her hand away, it was covered in blood.

She jumped off the bed and stared back at the bright red patch on the white bedding. Her hands were shaking. What would Danielle say or do? And what about Jones? She looked around for something to clean up the blood. Two white fluffy towels lay neatly folded on a chest of drawers. She grabbed one and rubbed at the stain on the bed, but then slumped down in despair. It was hopeless. Now she'd ruined a towel as well.

Now she was in trouble.

The door opened and Danielle entered. Rosie scurried backwards into the corner of the room, her body trembling, one arm across her chest, the other down between her legs, trying to cover herself. Trying to preserve what little dignity she had left.

She watched Danielle, but there was no anger on her face. No shouting or aggressive posture, and nothing to justify the panic brewing inside.

Danielle pointed to the blood-stained bedding. 'Don't worry, my dear. This was expected.' Then she picked up the towel. 'But this was not. What were you thinking?'

'I'm sorry, madam, I didn't think. I just grabbed it and tried to—'

'Forget it, it's done. Come with me and we'll get you cleaned up.'

Danielle dropped the towel.

Rosie breathed more easily. Where was the domineering mistress she'd expected to see? Was she human, after all? Did she care, just a little bit?

Rosie picked up her dress.

'Leave that. You won't need it again tonight.' Danielle said. Then she took a pink bathrobe from the back of the door in the nearby on-suite bathroom and handed it to Rosie. 'Here, put this on.'

Rosie gladly wrapped the robe around herself and followed Danielle down the stairs and back down into the basement. She stood in the centre of her underground cell and stared at the bed. Is this where she would be sleeping again tonight? Had she not earned an upgrade to a room above ground with the other girls? She turned back to Danielle.

'How long will I be kept here?'

'That's for Mr Jones to decide.'

'It's just that I thought I might be able to stay with the other girls, with Ellie.'

Danielle's face straightened. All hint of compassion gone. 'Clean yourself up, and I'll check on you tomorrow.'

Rosie walked to the bath and turned on the taps, then flicked the lever to change the flow over to the shower attachment. She let the robe slip from her shoulders and stepped under the water.

The door slammed shut.

Danielle had gone.

As the warm water trickled down over her body, she closed her eyes, relieved that the day was over.

But what would tomorrow bring?

34

MASON

When they returned to the underground carpark, Mason exited the stairs on the level above his own car. 'Let's see if his BMW's still here.'

Natasha followed in silence.

The space where Buckingham had parked was empty. Mason sighed.

Natasha sighed. 'Now what do we do?'

He turned and hurried back to the stairs and then down to the lower level. He clicked off the alarm on his Mondeo and slumped into the driver's seat. Natasha got in beside him and waited for his answer.

He pulled out a piece of paper from his pocket and unfolded it. 'We check his properties. He has three. Willow Road is clean, but he has one in Kent and one in Cornwall.'

'Are they not a long way away?'

'Yes, but it's all we've got. He tried to recruit the dancer, Lucy, for a party tonight and told her it was in Kent, so we'll start there.'

'I've never been to Kent.'

'It won't be a sightseeing trip. At least not the kind you'd find in any travel guide.'

'The only sight I want to see is you hugging Rosie in your arms, safe and well.'

Mason looked at her, touched by the warmth of what she'd said. She gazed back at him through big brown eyes with just the hint of a smile.

His stomach flipped over.

What was happening?

Was he losing control of his emotions? Was he losing his ability to remain detached, to stay focused on the task at hand? A stirring in his stomach reminded him of his youth. The first time he felt it was on a date with Kathy many years ago. A kind of excited anticipation deep down inside. And now he was experiencing those same emotions again.

Powerful, uncontrollable, and scary.

He was married. She was half his age. And his daughter was still missing. Any one of those facts should have been enough to snap him from this starry-eyed moment.

He willed himself to look away, to turn his head, but he couldn't. His iron willpower had deserted him and left him at the mercy of his newfound emotions. As he gazed into her eyes, his desire for her overwhelmed him.

Was this real?

Was he falling for a girl he hardly knew?

But then that wasn't true. Though he'd only known her for two days, they had not been ordinary days. They had experienced enough drama, tragedy, and heartache to last a lifetime. And because of that, he'd learnt things about her that would normally take many months, or even years, to learn.

They drifted closer to each other as if a magnetic force was at work. They were just inches apart. He inhaled her breath. It was intoxicating. His heart thumped and his breathing shortened.

Her silky red lips gently touched his. They were soft and warm and felt good, too good. The tender caressing became a full-blown kiss, hot and fiery, and passionate.

His heart thumped against his chest. It was going to explode any second. It had to. How could it endure this amount of sheer emotion without blowing? But how would it be explained? How would they know that the only weapon involved was a kiss from a gorgeous young woman?

Right then, the phone rang in his pocket. He sprang back into his seat, breathing hard, his pulse racing as if he'd just ran a marathon. 'I'm sorry Natasha. I don't know what came over me. I really shouldn't have done that. I—'

'It's okay,' she interrupted. 'I wanted you to. I have since the first day.'

He took a deep breath and tried to compose himself. He nodded, grateful for her honesty. At least he didn't imagine it, she'd felt the same.

Natasha pointed to his jacket pocket. 'You had better answer that. It might be important.'

He fished around and pulled out his phone. It was still ringing. Normally after four rings it would go to answer machine, but he had recently disabled the voice mail to give him more time to answer his calls. It used to frustrate him when he wasn't quick enough to reach his phone and answer within the four rings. Then he would have to wait to see if a message had been left before calling back.

He swiped the screen without looking at the caller ID. 'Hello, Cooper here.' He'd answered formally. A habit from his police days that would be hard to shake off. Especially if stressed or distracted, and right then he was both.

'Mason, it's Jim. I had a few minutes so I'm just checking in. How did things go? You're still alive at least.'

'Jim, sorry for the delay, I dropped the phone.' It was the first excuse he could think of. But why worry? How could Jim know what had just happened?

'No problem, any news?'

'Yes, it went well, I got Kathy back.'

'Is she okay?'

'She's fine, or as well as she can be until I find Rosie. I'll tell you all about it when I've got more time.'

'Any news on Rosie yet?'

'Shouldn't I be asking you that? Have you heard anything from the guys in Crime Intelligence?'

'Sorry Pal, I've not had a spare minute. Been tucked up on this terrorism job. Been hitting houses all over the place. You must have seen it on the news.'

'No, I've been a little pre-occupied myself lately. Not seen any news. Tell me.'

'Nothing much to tell, really. We hit addresses early in the mornings, make arrests, supervise the searches, interview, you know, that kind of stuff.'

'I thought the Counter Terrorism Unit would take over all that.'

'Yeah, they do, but you know what it's like, they need help with this number of hits.'

'Yeah, I suppose so.'

Mason kept his answers short. Didn't want to give anything away. Too much had happened. Too risky to bring Jim up to date. With three dead bodies out there somewhere with his DNA signature all over them, he didn't need Jim asking too many questions. Even though he would trust him over almost anyone else he knew, it was better for Jim if he didn't know the details. Then he wouldn't be in a compromising situation of having to choose between a friend in need and upholding the law.

Jim said, 'Coulson was asking about you.'

'What did you tell him?'

'That I hadn't spoken to you for a couple of days.'

'He's not exactly my biggest fan, is he?'

'Not really. You two are just so different. Opposite ends of the spectrum.'

'Glad to hear it. Don't know what I'd do if I was likened to him. Shoot myself I suppose.'

'You holding out on us?'

Mason laughed. 'Don't worry. Coulson got the only gun I had.'

'Yeah, and he nearly crapped himself from what I can gather.'

'He told you that?'

'He didn't have to. I saw it in his eyes at the briefing when he told us you pointed the gun at him.'

'Well, not really, but he was pissing me off stalling on getting that warrant.'

'Yeah . . .but . . .think ...'

'Jim, you're breaking up. Must be my end, I'm in an underground carpark so my signal's next to nothing.'

Only crackle came back at him.

'Jim, I think I'm losing you. If you can hear me, I'll call you when I've got something. Take care Pal.'

Mason clicked off the call and dropped the phone into his pocket. He glanced at Natasha only briefly. His cheeks flushed. He couldn't remember the last time he felt this embarrassed. He thought those days were behind him. He'd done it all, seen it all, so nothing would embarrass him ever again, not at his age, or so he'd thought. He pulled his seat belt across.

'Better go.'

As he spiralled his way up through the car park, he remembered his last conversation with Kathy.

She'd been right.

She had told him, but he didn't believe her. How could he? Both he and Natasha had been through such traumatic events. How could such a beautiful young girl be attracted to a man like him? Especially after everything that had happened. And even if she was, how could he possibly return her interest with Rosie still missing? But then emotions are strange unpredictable entities. They don't conform to expectations or follow any protocol. They are totally maverick in their interaction with their host.

Sadistic little B's really.

They threaded their way through the London traffic and eventually picked up the M25 and followed it to the M20. Mason pulled out a sat-nav from the glove box and plugged it in. 'Have you used one of these before?'

'No, never.'

He passed her the paper with the Kent address scribbled on it. 'Just select a new route and punch in the postcode.'

Several attempts later, the route finally popped up on to the screen.

She clapped her hands together once. 'Got it.'

'That was quick,' he said with a straight face.

She slapped his leg. 'Not funny, I told you I've not used one before.'

He grinned.

The voice from the sat-nav piped up. 'Take the next exit and follow the signs for Maidstone.'

He obeyed. 'I think it's on the outskirts of the town. The South side.'

He slapped his forehead with his open palm. 'Natasha, I forgot to ask. Did you contact your family?'

'Yes, I rang them from the airport yesterday. Everything is good. They are safe.'

'I'm pleased to hear it. Hell, was it only yesterday you took the girls to the airport? So much has happened over the last few days, it's crazy.'

'I know.' She tilted her head to look at him. 'And just so you know, I don't normally go weak at the knees over some guy I only met two days ago.'

He grinned. 'Same here, trauma does strange things to people, doesn't it?'

She tilted her head again and raised an eyebrow. 'So kissing me was strange, was it?'

He fought to keep a straight face. 'Strangest thing I've done for a long time.'

'Stranger than beating two guys to death? Stranger than allowing yourself to get shot? Stranger than visiting a strip club?'

'Okay, I get the message. But yes, it was stranger than

all those... because kissing you made me feel twenty-five again.'

She unbuckled her seat belt and leant across and kissed him on his lips.

His expression dropped, and he stared past her at the road ahead.

'What's wrong?' she asked.

'Sorry, it's not you, but what you just did then by leaning across and kissing me like that, well... it was one of the last things Rosie did just before we saw you and before she was taken. Except she kissed my cheek, of course.'

Natasha brought her hand up to her mouth. 'I'm so sorry, I didn't know.'

'Of course not. How could you? But it must be a warning, or a message, or something, reminding me of the job in hand.'

Natasha shuffled back into her seat and clicked her seat belt into place. 'You're right, we need to stay focused.'

Mason said nothing. He just placed his hand on her arm and gently squeezed. No words were necessary.

35

MASON

The instructions from the sat-nav guided them to a country road on the south side of Maidstone, and eventually to a large house, surrounded by fields, and set back one hundred yards or more from the road. The light was fading. But Mason could still make out a scattering of outbuildings stretching along the back of the large plot, with several top-of-the-range cars lined up along the front courtyard.

He pulled over onto a gravelled area near to the single-track lane that dissected the wheat fields as it meandered its way to the property. A few small trees lined the approach road but were too sparsely spaced to offer them cover or any element of surprise. Vehicles approaching would be visible from the main house. At first glance, he thought farmhouse. But as he looked more closely, he decided it was more of a grand manor-house with out-buildings that were more likely to house luxury cars and rich boys' toys than tractors and straw.

He glanced at his watch. 'It'll be dark soon. We should wait. But we're a bit conspicuous here. Best go back to that cafe-diner we just passed next to the service station back there.'

Natasha nodded.

Inside the diner, Mason chose a booth in the window that gave a clear view of the forecourt. Three other tables were occupied. A family of four tucked into their meals a few feet away. A young couple sat in a booth behind him, and a man, probably a trucker, took up a corner table. A counter displaying snacks and soft drinks separated the public from the kitchen area, and a man and woman in their forties, both wearing aprons, were busy cooking and serving, with the woman taking the role of waitress.

'Looks like a family business.' Mason said.

Natasha looked around and nodded.

He pulled out the roll of notes from his jacket and slid two twenty-pound notes and a ten across the table.

'There's fifty there. You should order some food.'

'What about you?'

'It's nearly dark. I'll be leaving in a few minutes.'

'Formica tables and paper napkins. I don't think I'll need fifty.'

'I don't know how long I'll be. You may need to keep ordering coffee so they don't throw you out. Take it just in case.'

'So you don't want my help?'

'Don't take this the wrong way, but no. I'm not sure what I'll find over there, and I can move faster alone.'

She slid the money back towards him. 'I've still got my share of the money you gave us yesterday.'

He slid it back. 'I know, save it, it'll help you get back on your feet when this is over, and you'll be getting the rest of it then, anyway.'

The waitress approached with a pad and pen. 'What can I get you?' she asked, then flashed him a smile full of lipstick and false eyelashes.

Mason motioned to Natasha with his open palm.

'Oh, just a coffee for now,' Natasha said. 'I'll look at the menu later, thank you.'

'And you, sir?' The waitress maintained her smile while tapping her pen repeatedly against the pad. Evidence of impatience and insincerity, he thought.

'I'll have the same, white, no sugar, thank you.'

Natasha waited for the waitress to leave, then asked, 'How will you get into the big house over there?'

'I don't know yet. I'll try to get close enough to look inside and see what's going on.'

'I hate to remind you, but Rosie's been with them since Thursday. That's a long time with those pigs. Have you prepared yourself for what you might see?'

'Not counting you, I know better than most how these gangs treat the girls under their control, and what they demand from them.'

Natasha nodded. 'Yes, of course.'

'I was in charge of the Sexual Offences Department for two years. We dealt with rape, domestic violence and child abuse.'

Natasha gasped, 'Oh, that must have been difficult.'

He nodded. 'Awful, I had to block it out at the time to maintain my sanity. But to see just how some people treat fellow human beings is mind blowing, and it certainly opened my eyes to what goes on behind closed doors in some families.'

She frowned. 'There are some evil people in this world.'

'You're right, and my job meant that I got to meet more than my fair share of them.'

Natasha nodded and leaned back as the waitress placed the coffees down in front of them. She took a sip, licked her top lip, and looked across at him. 'What happened earlier, in the car. I want you to know, I won't say anything. I won't make things any harder for you, you know, with Kathy.'

Mason considered what she'd said before answering. 'Thank you. I don't know what the future holds for me and Kathy. I can't even think about it yet. Not while Rosie's still out there. But I do know that I don't regret that kiss. Not from my point of view, anyway.'

Natasha smiled. 'Neither do I.'

Headlamps from a car flashed across the window. An elderly man got out of a shabby-looking hatch back and sauntered inside and up to the counter.

Mason got to his feet. 'It's dark now, I'll leave my car here and walk over.'

Natasha's expression dropped. 'At the risk of becoming boring, be careful.'

Mason smiled. 'You could never be boring.'

He approached the counter and asked the waitress, 'Excuse me, what time do you close?'

She answered without turning around from her task of preparing a drink for the elderly customer. 'We don't, we're twenty-four hours during the spring and summer months.'

Mason thanked her, and walked outside, and crossed

the forecourt to the main road, and glanced back to the diner. Natasha watched him through the window. He waved, and she waved back, then he turned and crossed the road.

MASON

I t was a short walk back to the gravel access road where Mason stopped to plan. The front of the large house was lit up by floodlights on the ground. Two men, dressed in suits and ties, stood in front of the tall double doors. He studied them long enough to be sure they were security. It was something about their demeanour and the way they had their backs to the door, looking out over the luxury cars. The same way police officers guard a crime scene.

He considered his approach route. The driveway was not an option. Too open. They would spot him before he could reach the house, and the gravel would be an audible giveaway. So Plan B it was then. He vaulted over the waist-high fence and scurried through the knee-high wheat, arcing his way around to the fence at the side of the house.

Just as he placed his hands on the top rail to pull himself up, a floodlight on the side of the house lit up the whole area. He dropped to the ground and lay prone. A figure, dressed similar to the men out front, walked from the back of the house along the side carrying a torch which was rendered redundant by the millions of candle power emitted by the floodlight.

Mason tracked him as he turned and walked along the front of the property, exchanging a few words with the others as he passed. When the flood light switched off, plunging the side of the house back into darkness, Mason began counting. He needed to know how long it would take for the man to lap the building and activate the light again.

On the count of fifty-five, the area was again flooded with light, and the same sentry passed by. The second it went dark again, Mason vaulted the fence and dashed to the house, counting as he ran. It took just eleven-seconds to cross the no-man's-land between the field and the house. His approach didn't activate the flood light. He glanced up. There were two PIR detectors, one aimed to the front, the other to the back of the house. He had approached on their blind side. He checked the ground-floor windows, hoping to find one unsecured. But they were all tight and locked down.

The count was twenty-six.

He looked around for cover, but there was none. The whole side of the house was exposed. He thought about taking out the sentry as soon as he appeared around the corner, but quickly dismissed that option. The two goons at the front would know something was wrong when he failed to show and all hell would break loose. That's not what he wanted right now.

The count was thirty-eight.

He looked up and found a better option. A flat roof over

a single-storey ran most of the way along the side of the house. It was the perfect place to hide.

The count was forty-five.

He took three steps back, then ran and jumped and grabbed a drain pipe as high as he could. His left foot found a window ledge, giving him leverage to push and then pull himself up and over onto the roof in one fluid motion. He rolled over and lay flat.

The count was fifty-three.

The security light clicked on a few feet from his head, throwing its wide beam downwards. He lay still as the footsteps of the sentry crunched along the gravel path below. As they faded and the light clicked off, he jumped up and checked the nearest window. It was secure. The curtains were drawn and illuminated from inside, as if occupied. He placed his ear to the glass. The muffled talking was too low to decipher. He moved to the next window. Like the first, it was closed tight and illuminated from inside. He listened, but heard nothing.

He moved along to the next window, and his last chance for entry. The room was in darkness. He hooked his fingers under the sash frame and pulled up. It moved an inch. The security light on the roof activated, and he dropped to his stomach. The sentry below could not see him, but silence was critical until he passed by.

When the light clicked off, he jumped up and pulled at the window again. It was stiff and difficult to move. He pulled harder. Inch by inch, he edged up the sash frame until there was a gap wide enough to squeeze through. He wiggled in head first and lay motionless below the window. All was quiet.

In the darkness, he felt his way along the grey outline of the bed to the side table, then fumbled for the switch on the bedside lamp. He clicked on the light and stared at the heavily blood-stained bedspread, then at a bloodied towel on the floor.

Whatever had happened there had been recent. His experience attending crimes scenes had taught him that blood stains turn dark red with time and eventually black as they age. These were bright red and fresh.

He searched around the bed and underneath it. There were no bodies, so he cracked open the bedroom door an inch and peered into the wide hall. Nothing moved. He stepped out and closed the door behind him. He crept up to the bannister and looked down over the grand foyer below. Two figures dressed in dark red robes were deep in conversation at the foot of the stairs. Then another walked into view, accompanied by a young female wearing a short dress and high heels. They began to climb the stairs toward him.

A man shouted out from below, just out of sight. 'Use another room. The red room is out of action for the rest of the night.'

The man on the stairs with the girl shouted back. 'Okay.' He wore a black face mask.

Mason reached into his pocket and pulled out the identical mask. He'd been right. Buckingham's house was the venue for some kind of a club, and no ordinary club, but one where the men wore masks and long red robes. Was it a cult? Or was the disguise merely hiding their identity? And who were these men?

He turned and hurried back into the bedroom he'd just

left and quietly closed the door. He scanned the room. Red curtains, red valance around the bed, red shades on the bedside lamps, red trim around the ornate chairs on either side of a small table. This had to be the red room. Appropriately named. Red in décor, and red with blood.

He didn't know who's blood it was or what had occurred in that room only minutes before. So in ignorance, he waited until the couple passed by before he cracked open the door just in time to catch a glimpse of the girl and see which room they went into.

She was young, barely developed, certainly no older than Rosie, but probably younger. He had his evidence. Buckingham and this place had to be connected to his daughter's disappearance. His muscles tensed. He fought to control an urge to charge down the stairs and take out every one of them with his bare fists. He took deep breaths to calm himself down.

He moved back to the balcony. The men in robes were no longer in view, but voices echoed up from the foyer below. They were just out of sight. He needed a red robe so he could move among them. He had the mask, so he was halfway there. Maybe they kept spare robes in the bedrooms.

It was worth a look.

He went back to the red room and opened cupboards and drawers, but found nothing. He left to try the next room along, when a muffled scream stopped him dead in his tracks. It came from the door opposite where the man had taken the girl. Then another scream, and another.

A desperate cry for help that turned his blood cold.

He clenched his fists tight, his nails dug into his palms,

and his adrenalin surged through his veins like an out of control tidal wave. He fought to dismiss the sound and block it out. He had to find Rosie. He couldn't be side-tracked now, not when he was so close. She could be in another bedroom, or downstairs with the men in robes.

He stepped past the door.

There it was again, a muffled scream filled with pain.

He froze.

Then a slap, and another slap. The screaming stopped abruptly, cut off by the second slap. Then sobbing. A man's voice, 'Open your mouth or I'll hit you again.'

Another slap, louder than the first two. He knew that sound. It was unmistakable. An open palm contacting skin, hard. He sighed. He had no choice. He couldn't walk past and leave her at the mercy of that man.

He burst through the door.

37

MASON

The man stood at the foot of the bed, his robe parted, and his trousers around his thighs. The girl was naked on her knees in front of him. The left side of her face was bright red, finger marks clearly defined. Tears streamed down her cheeks.

The man turned towards Mason. 'Who the hell are you?'

It was over in a flash. The man fell to the floor, unconscious.

The girl screamed.

Mason bent down in front of her and brought his finger up to his lips. 'Shh, It's okay, I'm not one of them.' He pulled off a faux fur throw draped across the foot of the bed and wrapped it around her. 'I need to ask you how many girls are here besides you?'

The girl wiped her eyes. 'I don't know, maybe six. I just got here. They brought me in the boot of a car and told me to put that dress on.' She pointed to a pink dress discarded on the bedroom floor. 'Then they gave me to him . . . I want to go home.'

Mason held her hand in his. 'What's your name?'

'Carly,'

'How old are you Carly?'

'Thirteen.'

Mason's eyes narrowed. He took a deep breath and shook his head.

'I'm sorry Carly, I'm sorry this has happened to you, but he's not going to touch you again. None of them are. Come with me.'

He led her by the hand to the red room. She followed, clutching the throw tightly around her. He quickly pulled off the blood-stained bedding and threw it on the floor, covering the bloodied towel. Then he grabbed a clean towel from the chest of drawers and went to the on-suite bathroom, where he soaked it in cold water. He returned and gave it to Carly.

'Hold this on your cheek. It'll cool it down and help stop the bruising.'

She did as he said.

He went back to the bathroom and returned with a blue bathrobe. 'Put this on. I think it's a man's robe, but it's better than the throw because you'll be able to move easier in this.' He turned away while she changed into the robe.

'You can turn around now,' she said. She looked tiny in the large bathrobe.

'Where are your own clothes?'

'They took them off me in a bedroom up here before taking me downstairs in that dress.'

'Can you remember which room?'

She stared silently at the floor for a few moments before lifting her head. 'I think it was the room opposite the top of the stairs.'

'That's next to this one then.'

She nodded.

He led her to the ensuite. 'Wait in here and lock the door and don't open it to anyone but me. My name's Mason. I'll be back in one minute, okay?'

'Okay.' She gave him a half smile, then closed and locked the door.

Mason picked up the throw and went back to the other bedroom. The man lay where he left him, on his back and unconscious. Mason pulled him around into a seated position on the floor with his back against the foot of the bed. He propped his head up against the footboard and pulled off his mask. There was no blood. He had taken him out with one punch to the temple. The man looked surprisingly normal. He could be anyone's husband, father, brother, or friend. There was no label across his forehead reading Pervert or Paedophile.

Mason took out his mobile phone and snapped a photo of him. Then he found the man's wallet in his trouser pocket, opened it, and pulled out a driving license. Martin Joseph Pankhurst, his address read Mayfair, London. The edge of a photograph was just visible in one of the wallet's compartments, so Mason slid it out, then shook his head in disgust. Pankhurst was pictured with one arm around a woman, and the other around a young girl, similar in age to Carly. He pushed the photo back into place and dropped the wallet into the man's lap. 'What would your wife and daughter think about your dirty little hobby then, eh?' Mason didn't expect a response. Pankhurst was still unconscious.

He went to the room opposite the top of the stairs. Scattered across the bed, he found a pair of skinny jeans, a red sweater, and a pair of purple knickers. He gathered them up with a pair of pink sports shoes next to the bed, returned to the red room, and knocked softly on the bathroom door. 'Carly, it's Mason.'

The door opened, and she smiled, clearly relieved to see him back.

He handed over her clothes and pulled the door shut. 'Be as quick as you can.'

When she appeared a few minutes later in her own clothes, he led her to a chair near to the open window, then turned off the bedside lamp plunging the room into darkness.

'You okay, Carly?'

She answered in a timid voice. 'Yes.'

He crouched down next to her and explained about the floodlight, and that they would have just over fifty seconds to climb down and run to the field.

She stared out of the window. The flat roof and the field were just visible in the moonlight.

Mason went to the bed, pulled off the bottom sheet, and twisted it around several times until it resembled a rope. 'If you hold on tight to this, I'll lower you down off the roof.'

'Yes, I can do that,' she said. 'I've climbed ropes in the school gym.'

The flood light activated, and Carly gasped.

'It's okay,' Mason said. 'As soon as it shuts off, I need you to squeeze through and lay down on the roof and be as quiet as you can.'

They waited. The light cut out.

'Go,' Mason said.

She was through the narrow gap in a few seconds, and Mason quickly followed with the sheet. They lay side by side on the roof and waited for the light to come back on and off again. When it did, Mason jumped up and Carly followed him to the edge of the roof. He lowered her to the ground, then pulled up the sheet and quickly pushed it back through the window into the red room. Then he lowered himself over the edge of the roof and tried to locate the drainpipe with his feet. He felt nothing but the wall of the house. He edged further along and tried again. Still no pipe. The count was thirty-four. He turned and whispered down, 'Move away Carly, I'm going to have to jump.'

'Okay,' came the little voice from below.

He pushed back and dropped to the ground, landing on his feet, but then fell onto his back with a thud. He stood up on the count of forty-two and took hold of Carly's hand. 'Run as fast as you can.'

They reached the fence at the edge of the field and he lifted her over in one quick movement, then he vaulted over and pushed her to the ground. Moments later, the floodlight lit up the whole area. They lay flat in the long wheat and waited. When the light clicked off again, he stood up and looked to the front of the house. The two security men were in the same place, standing tall and looking official. Mason glanced to the driveway. A shadowy figure of a man was walking towards the house. His size and build reminded him of Artan. When the man turned toward the house, Mason tapped Carly on the shoulder. 'Now.'

38

MASON

As they crossed the carpark in front of the diner, Mason's heart skipped a beat. The booth where he had left Natasha was empty. Then, as he glanced at the car nearest to the diner's entrance, his blood ran cold. He recognised the plate; it was the black Mercedes.

He turned and clicked his key fob to unlock his car. 'Carly, I need you to wait in my car while I get my friend, Natasha.'

'Okay,' she said, without questioning why.

He opened the rear door and she got in. 'If anyone comes near this car, duck down out of sight. Don't let anyone but me and my friend Natasha see you, okay?'

'Yes, okay.'

The fear had returned to her eyes.

'Don't worry, it's just that we're still close to the house, so I don't want anyone to see you.'

She nodded.

Mason entered the diner and scanned the tables. Only

two were occupied, and Natasha was nowhere in sight. He approached the counter. 'Excuse me, but did you see where my friend went?'

The waitress gave him a blank look.

'You remember, the pretty girl sitting in the window seat over there about thirty minutes ago. We ordered coffee before I left.'

Another blank look before something clicked. 'Oh yes, the foreign girl, nice girl, she went—'

'I'm here.' Came a voice behind him.

The waitress glanced over Mason's shoulder, then turned away. Her services clearly no longer needed.

He spun around to see Natasha staring at him. 'Thank god for that,' he said. 'I was thinking the worst for a moment when I didn't see you.'

Her face was deathly white, her eyes wide and staring. 'We need to get out of here.'

'Okay, I saw the Mercedes out front. Where are they? Did they see you?'

She turned and headed for the door. 'We need to leave. Now.'

He followed and caught up with her in the car park, where she froze in front of his car and turned to him excitedly. 'You found her, you found Rosie.'

Mason shook his head. 'No, that's not Rosie, it's Carly, she's thirteen.'

Her tone dropped. 'So Rosie's not there?'

'I don't know, maybe, but I had to get this kid out of there in a hurry.'

'Is it what you thought? Are they keeping girls over there?'

'Yes, that's why I had to get her out.'

'So she was in that house?'

'Yes.'

Natasha turned back to the car and stared at the girl, then opened the rear door. 'Hello Carly, I'm Natasha. Can I sit next to you?'

Carly nodded and moved over to the next seat.

Natasha got into the back and closed the door. Mason got in behind the wheel.

'I've been through the same thing,' Natasha said. 'Mason rescued me a few days ago.'

Carly's mouth dropped open. 'So they took you as well?'

'Yes, they did, but I'm good now. How are you?'

Carly's eyes filled with tears. 'I'm okay, but it was scary, so scary, I thought I was going to die.'

Natasha opened her arms. 'Can I have a hug?'

Carly nodded and moved into Natasha's arms. They hugged each other tightly for a full, silent minute.

Then Natasha turned to Mason. 'We need to go.'

Mason knew from the look in Natasha's eyes that something was wrong. He started the car, reversed out of the space, and drove onto the main road. 'You okay, Natasha?'

'Just keep driving, please.'

He drove for a few miles then turned into the car park of a hotel. He found a space and reversed into it, ready for a speedy getaway if necessary. He turned off the engine.

'What happened back there?'

Natasha took her arms from around Carly, but held her shoulders with her hands and looked into her eyes. 'I just need to speak with Mason, okay?'

'Okay,' Carly said.

Natasha opened the door and stepped out. Mason did the same, and they walked a few feet from the car.

'What is it?' Mason asked.

'I was sitting in the window when the Mercedes pulled up outside. I froze as soon as I saw it. I began to shake. The two Albanians came in—'

'Artan and Korab?'

'Yes, the two who drove me to Willow Road.'

'Did they see you?'

'Yes, they came to my table and told me that if I screamed or called out for help, they would kill me and everyone else in the cafe. The big one opened his jacket. He had a gun. I was terrified.'

'What happened?'

'The big one—'

'Artan?'

She nodded. 'Told the other one to watch me while he went outside. He said something about selling me again and getting a good price for me. I think he walked over to the house because he went in the same direction as you.'

'I thought I saw him approaching along the driveway.'

'The other one stayed with me. He said I was in trouble for escaping and that I would suffer, but I could make things better if I went with him to the men's toilet.'

'And?'

'I went with him… but I took a knife from the table with me. He pulled me into a cubicle and opened his trousers. He pushed my head down, and that's when I did it.'

'You didn't…?'

'No, not that. I stabbed him in the balls and then in his neck. He's still in there, slumped over the toilet. I think I killed him, but I didn't stay to find out. That's when you came in.'

Mason thought for a moment. 'Well, that's two all then.'

'Mason!' She slapped his arm.

'Sorry but I can't help being pleased if another one of them animals is dead, the more the better.'

'So what now?'

'We have to get this kid somewhere safe.'

Natasha looked past Mason to the car and to Carly, who was watching them. 'Okay,' she said, then got back into the rear seat and Mason got back in behind the wheel. 'Where do you live, Carly?'

'Maidstone, it's not far. It can't be. I was only in the boot about twenty minutes.'

Natasha flashed Mason a look without saying a word.

He nodded. 'Let's get you home then.'

39

MASON

They drove into Maidstone, and Carly directed them to her house. They pulled up in a street of modest 1960 semi's and Mason killed the engine. 'Carly, what happened, how did they take you?'

'I went to meet a boy I'd been chatting to online. He said he'd meet me at the park, but he wasn't there. Then when I left the park, a black car pulled up next to me. A man got out and grabbed me from behind and pushed me into the boot of the car. He tied my hands and put a hood over my head. It was really frightening. They took me to that big house. I thought they were going to kill me.'

Mason and Natasha shared a glance. 'Did you give the boy your address?' Mason asked.

'Who, the boy on-line? No, I didn't. I didn't want him coming to my house, cos my mum and step-dad would go mad. But the boy wasn't in the black car, he's only sixteen. The man who grabbed me was much older.'

'Carly, I don't think the boy exists. I think they tricked

you to get you to meet them. Whatever you do don't communicate with him again. Don't respond if he contacts you. Tell your parents what happened and tell the police, okay?'

'So he pretended to be sixteen? Are you sure?'

'No, I'm not sure, but you can't take any chances. It's a hell of a coincidence that you go to meet a boy who doesn't show and then you're bundled into a car. The men who took you are very devious. They're professionals, they've done it before many times using different methods. Promise me you won't talk to any strangers online again, and never arrange to meet anyone you don't already know.'

'I promise, I won't ever again. From now on I'll stick with my friends.'

'Good girl, let's get you inside.'

As the three of them approached Carly's front door, it sprang open and a woman in her late-thirties folded her arms across her chest. 'What's going on here, Carly? Who are these people?'

Mason answered. 'I'm sorry if we worried you. My name's Mason Cooper, this is Natasha, can we come in and talk to you?'

The woman scowled at him, shifted her gaze to Natasha, then back to Mason. 'Are you coppers?'

'No,' Mason said.

'Social Services, she's called you again, hasn't she?'

'No, we're not Social Services. Can we do this inside?'

'I need to know who you are before I let you in,' the woman said.

Carly spoke up. 'Mum, it's okay, they helped me.'

The woman paused for a moment, then stepped aside and waved them through the hall into the lounge. 'Sorry, but you can't be too careful these days, can you?'

'It's okay. We can explain,' Mason said.

They stood in the middle of the lounge for a few moments before the woman spoke. 'Sorry, I'm Carol, Carly's mum, and that lazy lump fast asleep over there is Bobby, her Da'—she hesitated—'her step-dad.' She kicked Bobby's foot, and his eyes sprang open. 'Wake up, we got visitors.'

Bobby stretched, yawned, and shuffled himself up in his chair while rubbing his eyes.

Carol motioned to the sofa with an open hand. 'Where are my manners? Please sit down.'

Mason perched on the end of the sofa, and Natasha sat next to him in the middle seat and patted the cushion next to her for Carly to sit down. Carly glanced at her mum, then sat down next to Natasha. Carol sat in a chair opposite them.

Mason spoke first. 'I don't want to shock you, but your daughter was abducted today.'

Carol gasped. 'What did you say?'

'Carly has been chatting with someone online for a while, and today she went to meet him. But I don't think the boy she was chatting to on social media was quite who he claimed to be. A man dragged her into a car and took her to a house a few miles away.'

Carol's brow lowered even more, and her eyes narrowed as she scowled at Carly. 'What have I told you about that bloody computer?'

Natasha shifted in her seat and placed her hand on Carly's hand. 'It wasn't her fault, she thought she was meeting a boy her age, or similar.'

After a short awkward silence, Carol switched her gaze to Natasha and lifted her expression, as if suddenly conscious of being judged. 'Of course it wasn't her fault.'

Mason said. 'The men who took your daughter are professional traffickers. They sold her to another group of sick individuals.'

Carol gasped.

'It's okay. I got her out of there before anything happened. But she's had a traumatic time, so she needs you to go easy and not judge her.' He was pulling no punches. He wasn't falling for the sudden change in Carol's demeanour, He'd seen it before. Parents who blame their kids for everything and anything, but wait until they are alone to let rip. It may be appropriate on some occasions, but not this one. Not after everything Carly had been through. She needed love and support, not a lecture saying I told you so. He glanced over to Bobby, who sat expressionless, staring at the floor.

Natasha nudged Mason's leg with hers. She must have picked up on the same vibes.

A photograph in a frame on the end of the mantelpiece caught Mason's eye. It was of two girls arm in arm looking similar, except there appeared to be about five or six years' difference in their age. The younger girl looked like Carly, and he guessed it had been taken within the last couple of years.

He picked up the photo. 'Carol, Carly will need to speak

to the police about what happened. Does she have an older sister that could go with her?'

A puzzled look crossed Carol's face. 'Yes, that's her sister, she's nineteen, but I can go with her.'

'Of course you can, it's just that sometimes it's easier for kids to speak to the police if their parents are not present. Also, her sister may understand the social media thing better, I know my daughter does.'

Carol seemed to mull over his words for a few seconds. Then she kicked Bobby's foot again. 'Go and get Katie, and tell her it's urgent.'

Bobby pulled himself up and stretched again. Then without a word, he turned and ambled out of the front door.

'Be quick!' Carol shouted, then went to the window. 'She lives down the road with her boyfriend, so she won't be long.'

Mason put back the photo and took the opportunity to glance around the room. The contents were basic but clean. They could do with updating, but he saw nothing to worry him. An overweight dog with wiry hair and grey muzzle ambled in from the kitchen and collapsed at his feet. Within seconds, it was breathing deeply and snoring every time it inhaled. He wished he could fall asleep so easily. It had been days since his last good night's sleep.

'That's Duke,' Carol said. 'Lazy just like his dad.'

'Carol, the men that took Carly also took my daughter. I think she's in the same house. They know I'm onto them, and they've threatened to kill her if they see police. Can I ask you to delay contacting the police until tomorrow, to give me time to go back and get her out of there?'

Carol thought for a moment while staring at her daughter, then she said, 'Okay, I suppose we owe you that for bringing Carly home.'

'Thank you, Carol.'

Mason's concerns faded a little. Maybe he'd been too quick to judge Carol. However, the lack of interest shown by Bobby was worrying.

But his thoughts were pulled back to Rosie. Whatever the situation was in this family, Carly was in a safer place than his own daughter. Now he needed to get back to the house and finish what he'd started.

He sprang to his feet. 'Carly, I need to go now. My daughter's still missing so I have to find her. Are you going to be okay?'

Carly jumped up. 'Yes, I'm okay. Go and find her. Katie will be here soon.' She flung her arms around his waist and squeezed. 'Thank you for saving me.'

He stroked the back of her hair. 'Just remember what I told you. No more meetings with strangers online, right?'

'Right,' she said.

Mason glanced at Carol. 'Look after her.'

Carol nodded and put her arm around her daughter. Natasha got up and gave Carly a long hug before they left the house.

Back in the car, Natasha sat biting her lower lip. Mason squeezed her hand. 'She'll be okay, you know, she'll get support from the police, and I'm sure her mum's not the tyrant we think she is.'

Natasha nodded thoughtfully. 'I hope so. She reminds me of my little sister back home. I don't know what I'd do if anything like this happened to her.'

'I thought so. I saw your protective instincts kick in and it was heartwarming to watch.'

Mason accelerated hard as they left the town limits. 'I need to get back there fast.'

40

MASON

Fifteen minutes later, they were back at the diner, but Mason pulled up on the road outside. A police officer sat in the driver's seat of a patrol car parked in front of the main doors. Another was visible through the diner window, talking to the waitress.

'They must have found the body,' Natasha said.

'I'm not so sure,' Mason said. 'There's only one car, so probably only two officers, one inside, one out, no ambulance, no scenes of crime van, and no CID by the look of it. If they'd reported finding a body, both officers would be inside, with one preserving the scene. And the Mercedes has gone.'

'Why would the police be here then?'

'If your man staggered out of there and drove off, he probably left a trail of blood, which would have freaked out the owners.'

'If that's right then I didn't kill him.'

'No, so it's still two-one to me.'

'Well, this is one contest I'm happy to lose.'

Mason shifted the gear stick into drive and pulled away. He passed the lane to the big house and drove for two hundred yards before turning around and driving back again. 'Everything looks the same at the house. The cars are still out front. In fact, there's a few more there now.'

He drove back past the diner and pulled into the garage forecourt next door. He reversed into a parking bay for customers visiting the attached shop and switched off the engine. 'You've still got Victor's phone, right?'

'Yes, it's here.'

'Good, give it to me.'

She handed him the phone. He tapped away, then handed it back. 'I've programmed my number into it so you'll know if I ring you. Don't answer it to anyone else.'

She nodded.

'I'll leave the keys in the ignition. Any problems, just drive away, and if I'm not back in two hours, drive back to the apartment. The address is programmed into the satnav. Just select it from the menu.'

'They may be waiting for you over there. Why don't you tell the police?'

'Malik said that the organisation who has Rosie threatened to kill her if they see police. And we're not in London now. This isn't covered by the Met Police. Here, they will put on a cordon, call for backup, call out senior officers who'll hold briefings, plan an operation, call for more resources to implement the operation... do I need to go on?'

'No, I get it.'

'I should be back within the hour. With Rosie, I hope.' He pulled out the envelope from his jacket pocket and popped it into the glove box in front of Natasha. 'Just in case.'

He got out and headed back across the road and into the same wheat field. When he reached the fence near to the side of the house, he paused to scan the cars. Just as before, there were Rolls-Royce, Jaguar, Ferrari, Mercedes, and BMWs. In fact, most top brands were represented. He couldn't read the number plates from his viewpoint, but he thought it likely that one of the BMWs belonged to Buckingham, and that the black Mercedes on the end could well be Artan and Korab's vehicle.

As the flood light clicked off, he made the dash to the side of the house and without stopping he jumped and climbed onto the flat roof. He went directly to the window of the red room and was thankful to find it open, just as he had left it an hour earlier. Once inside, he scanned the room. Everything seemed the same, the bedding on the floor, and the sheet, still twisted, lay just inside the window. He pushed the sheet under the bed. He may need it again soon.

As before, he opened the bedroom door and waited. A gaggle of voices echoed up from the foyer. He went to the room where he had left Pankhurst. He had gone, but the room was undisturbed. Carly's dress lay where she'd left it, so he stuffed it into the nearest of two large walnut fronted wardrobes. If the men downstairs didn't already know she'd escaped, they may come looking for her.

Hanging neatly on a coat hanger in the same wardrobe was exactly what he was looking for, a long red robe. Maybe Pankhurst left it there before leaving, or maybe it was intended for a member of the club who hadn't turned up. It didn't matter. It was his now.

He removed his jacket and put on the robe. Then he took out the mask and covered his face. He hung his jacket on the hanger in the wardrobe and left the room.

As he walked down the stairs into the foyer, his heart beat like a drum. Would the other members see through his disguise? Would they know he was an imposter? Would there any kind of special handshakes or code words he would need to maintain his cover? He didn't have the answers to these questions, but he guessed he wouldn't have to wait long to find out. He was now among other robed members and they seemed agitated about something. But it wasn't about him. Not yet, anyway. None had even looked in his direction.

Something else was distracting them. Five or six of the members had gathered around a door marked Study. He moved closer to hear their conversation, and that's when he saw the blood on the floor. Star-shaped splashes every few inches led from the front doors to the study door, with a cluster somewhere in between. It must have been where the injured person, probably Korab, had stopped briefly. Maybe Natasha didn't kill him after all. Maybe he staggered out to the Mercedes, drove over here and staggered inside. Maybe the members held him in the foyer until someone in charge took him into the study.

The study door opened. A woman walked out carrying a blood-soaked towel. He moved closer to the open door. Several figures in red robes surrounded a long table. The lower half of a pair of legs were visible, horizontal on the table. At least two of the men were holding the man down, while another was up by his head, bent over like a surgeon in an operating theatre.

Mason turned to the men close to him and asked, almost in a whisper, 'What's going on?'

A man in a robe said, 'He's one of the suppliers. He's been stabbed. Doctor Black is working on him now.'

Mason gave a nod of gratitude. He recognised the name Doctor Black, but it took a few moments for him to recall where from. Then he remembered. Kathy had told him that the man who'd injected her at the hospital was a Doctor Black.

Coincidence or the same man?

He didn't believe in coincidence.

His thoughts turned back to the injured man on the table. It had to be Korab. He would certainly describe him as a supplier, and he'd been stabbed only a few hundred yards from there. Case closed. But Mason was unsure whether he wanted him to die. Not that he felt any concern or compassion for Korab, but he worried about Natasha having to deal with being responsible for another death. *So maybe on balance the bastard should pull through.*

One of the robed men around the table approached the door. Mason hadn't noticed until now that he was taller than the rest and was the only one in black. It must be significant. He was not wearing a mask, but his face was shrouded by the hood. He placed one hand on the open door. 'Gentlemen, there is nothing here for you to concern yourselves with. Please return to the clubroom and enjoy your evening.' He closed the door.

41

MASON

Mason followed the others into the Club Room where he mingled with more red robed members who had not been curious enough to leave the scantily dressed girls of various descriptions, but all qualifying as beautiful. He counted around ten or eleven men dressed in robes, all wearing identical masks, and seven or eight girls.

He looked around at the other men and saw that he was the only one not wearing a coloured badge with a name on it. Then he remembered Pankhurst had been wearing a badge too. He was concerned that if asked about his lack of a badge, he wouldn't have an answer. Just then, the door opened and two more members entered the Club Room. Neither wore a badge. They walked to a cabinet on the wall near to the bar, and one of them pulled out a key from his robe pocket and opened the cabinet door. He appeared to scan the contents before selecting a badge and pinning it to his robe. The second man did the same.

Mason waited for them to move away before casually

walking over to the cabinet and trying the door. It was locked. He put his hand deep into the right-hand pocket of his own robe. It was empty. He put his left hand into the left pocket and felt something down in the pocket's crease. He pulled out the object and stared down at a small key. He popped the key into the lock and opened the cabinet. He studied four rows of hooks, some empty, and some with name badges. Which one should he take? Would it matter? There must be some logic to the names, but he had no idea what it might be. But what if he chose the wrong one, and another member yet to arrive discovered his badge missing, or worse, Mason wearing it?

Then something caught his eye. Above each hook there was a small sticker bearing either two or three initials. He checked along the top row, then the second row, and halfway along the third he found what he was looking for. A sticker with the initials M. J. P. and on the hook below hung a badge displaying the name Mr Gold. Mason pinned it to his robe, then closed the cabinet, thankful that Mr Martin Joseph Pankhurst must have put his badge back and left.

The door opened again, and three more girls entered, followed by the man in the black robe. As the man in black moved to the middle of the room, Mason focused on the letter J embroidered on the robe. He recalled how, just before he died, the trafficker at Silver Street had told him that the man who bought the girls uses the name Jones. This must be him. He must be Jones.

The men in robes took it in turn to go behind the bar and pour their drinks before returning to the girls. Jones did the same. Mason waited for him to exit the bar, then he helped himself to a Jack Daniels. He sipped it while slowly moving closer to Jones in an attempt to overhear his conversation with some of the other members.

Jones addressed a group of three men who seemed keen to converse with him. 'Gentlemen, glad you could all make it tonight. Have any of you sampled the new merchandise yet?'

All three shook their heads, and one answered. 'Not yet, Master, but there's plenty of time.'

Mason almost choked on his drink. *They call him Master. What the hell?* He had to find out what was going on. He took the opportunity to approach another member at the bar, who was filling his glass from a spirit dispenser.

'Hi,' Mason said, as he refilled his own glass from the JD bottle he'd left on the bar.

'Hi,' the man said.

'Been a member long?' Mason asked.

The man turned to him and paused before answering. 'A few months, you?'

'Second visit, but I forgot to ask last time, why do we call him Master?'

'It's to maintain respect and discipline. It's based on the Free Masons. They have Master and Grand Master and all sorts of other titles. But here, VIP members tend to call him Jones. Didn't your sponsor explain things to you?'

Mason took a drink, giving himself a few seconds to think. Of course, a sponsor made sense. They couldn't simply advertise a club like this and randomly sign up new members. They would have to be ridiculously selective.

Mason said, 'He was supposed to, but he got distracted last time.'

'Yes, well, that can easily happen here.' The man held out his right hand and with his left he took hold of his name badge and lifted it slightly. 'Mr White, nice to meet you Mr Gold.'

Mason shook his hand. 'You too.'

'You do know about the code though, don't you?'

Mason raised his glass to his lips and sipped slowly. *Code?* Before he could answer, the man continued.

'The code. What happens in the club stays in the club.'

Mason swallowed. 'Of course. Wouldn't be here otherwise.'

'That's good. Sampled the goods yet?'

'Not yet, have you?'

'Yes, about an hour ago. I'm taking a time-out before trying another one. I heard they brought a young girl in earlier.' His voice lowered in tone. 'Only thirteen.' He sipped his drink then said, 'That reminds me, did you see what happened to the supplier?'

'Who, the guy in the study?'

'Yes, apparently, he and his partner brought in the girl and then left. About ten minutes later, the big one returned and spoke to Jones. Then the other one staggered back in bleeding from the neck. Mumbled something about someone stabbing him nearby. I think they must have had a fall out or something, what do you think?'

Mason took another sip. 'Probably, it's how that sort settle differences, with a blade or a gun.'

He was desperate to ask the man about the girl he'd been with earlier, but didn't want to appear too inquisitive. So he said, 'The girls are a very high standard here.'

'Absolutely, that's why membership is worth every penny. I'd have paid double if they'd asked me to.'

'Me too.' Mason glanced over at some of the girls. 'Which one's next for you then?'

'I was waiting for the young one, but no one's seen her since she went upstairs with a member earlier. Come on, let's ask Mr Jones where she is.'

Mason followed behind Mr White. He thought it strange that no one had discovered that Carly had escaped. And what about Pankhurst? Where had he got to?

Jones turned to Mr White to answer his question. 'She went upstairs with a member earlier and I haven't seen her since.'

Mr White asked, 'Do you know which member took her up?'

Jones shook his head. 'No, I didn't see, and there's no need to sign the book if she's not a virgin. Although she was only thirteen, I was informed by the suppliers that she was not a virgin. So she was free to all.'

White nodded. 'Thank you, I'll wait a little longer.'

From what Jones said, Mason was now sure that Artan or Korab, or somebody on their behalf, had pretended to be the sixteen-year-old talking to Carly on-line, and she must have been quite frank with them during their chats.

As Mr White turned back towards the bar, Jones said, 'Let me check the register, just in case.'

In case of what? Mason wondered.

Jones went to a small side table against the wall between two windows and opened a black ledger. It reminded Mason of the kind of register newlyweds sign after their ceremony.

Jones examined the register, then lifted his head and walked back to Mr White. 'Bad news I'm afraid. It looks like the member had his fun then took her to the dungeon. He's written an IOU for twenty-thousand so you know what that means.'

White sighed. 'So he's terminated her?'

'It looks like it. No other reason to write that in the right-hand column.' Jones patted White's shoulder, then turned and approached other members at the bar.

Mason tried to make sense of what he was hearing. 'Terminated,' he said in a tone that could be considered a statement or a question. He hoped it would prompt White to say something, and it did.

'That's a shame, I was looking forward to her.'

'I know what he meant by terminated, but what did he mean about the twenty-thousand?' Mason asked.

'Weren't you here earlier when Jones auctioned the virgin?'

Mason shook his head. 'No, I was late.'

'You know about the dungeon, right?'

'Of course.' He lied.

'If we take things to the ultimate conclusion in the dungeon, even by accident, we pay twenty-grand, the price for a replacement girl. Only right, I suppose, otherwise they'd need even more new girls every club night.'

Mason swallowed hard. It was worse than he'd imagined. Not only are the girls raped here, but they are also beaten and tortured, and sometimes killed. He was shocked at the casual way this member was talking about it, as if it were perfectly normal.

'What about the body?' Mason asked.

'They go into the pit.'

'The pit?'

'In the dungeon, there's access to an old mining shaft. It leads down to a disused mine. They dump the bodies down there and one of the goons goes down and drags them into the mine. Clever eh, no risk of being stopped with a body in the boot.'

Mason's stomach turned over. He thought he'd seen it all, but this was something else. This was right out of a Stephen King novel.

But unless two thirteen-year-old girls had been brought in that night, Pankhurst must have lied in the ledger. Mason slowly pieced it together. When Pankhurst regained consciousness and discovered the girl missing, he must have panicked. Maybe he worried about being held responsible for her escaping. In this club, the punishment could be death. So maybe he decided to sign the ledger and pay the twenty-thousand, the price for termination, so that it appeared he'd taken her down to the dungeon. That way, no one would go looking for her. Mason took a sharp intake of breath, because if he was right, then Pankhurst must have written his badge name in the ledger, the badge he was now wearing.

Before he could say anything, Mr White piped up. 'I'll check the ledger to see which member terminated her.'

'Do you think you should? Maybe . . .'

White didn't stop to hear Mason finish. He went straight to the ledger and opened the book. His reaction confirmed to Mason he'd been right. The look on White's face said it all. He headed straight for Mason.

'It was you. Why didn't you say?'

'What?' Mason was searching for an answer.

'Mr Gold, that's you, you signed the book.'

Mason looked down at his name badge. 'I must have picked up the wrong badge. It was on my hook. I'll be back in a minute.' He turned and quickly walked away before Mr White could respond. He went to the cabinet, opened it, and grabbed another name, then casually made his way back.

'My mistake,' Mason said. 'I should have been more careful. I'm Bronze, not Gold.' He tried to laugh casually and waited for the response. It was the one he'd hoped for.

'Okay, I thought you were holding out on me. Never mind, let's get another drink.'

42

MASON

Mason followed Mr White to the bar, and they both filled their glasses. It was time to ask.

'Which girl did you have earlier?'

'Oh, none of these, she's not here now.'

'Was she good?'

'Yes, very cute. Only sixteen and a virgin until tonight. Unfortunately, I wasn't the first. I lost the bidding to Mr Brown. But I went second, and she was still worth it.'

Mason fought hard not to react. This man was almost certainly talking about Rosie, and now she was nowhere in sight. He tried to maintain a casual tone in his voice. 'Where is she now, in the dungeon?'

'I don't think so. Me and Mr Fawn had her after Mr Brown. We left her up in the red room for anyone else who wanted her. Chances are she's still there. Also, Jones put the price of termination up to fifty grand, so I doubt anyone has paid it. Mind you, if you'd seen the amount of blood on the bed when we'd finished, you'd think we'd slit her throat.'

Mason's heart missed a beat. 'What was her name?'

'Rose, Rosie, or something like that.'

Mason's stomach turned over. The blood in the red room was Rosie's. He couldn't speak. His mind whirled as he gritted his teeth and clenched his fists in his pockets. Every muscle fibre in his body tensed, and it took all his willpower not to rip out this man's throat with his bare hands. He had resigned himself to the fact that his daughter had probably been raped by now, but standing next to one of the offenders, without taking him out, was the hardest thing he'd ever done.

He studied the man. He couldn't see his hair or his face other than his mouth, but he could see that he had brown eyes and a small scar on his top lip. He would remember him.

Eventually, he managed to speak. 'I think I'll try to find her.'

Mr White said. 'You best ask Jones. He'll know where she is.'

Mason nodded and made his way to the bar. He waited for his opportunity and then said to Jones. 'I heard what you told Mr White about the thirteen-year-old, but he said there's a sixteen-year-old here as well. Is she available?'

Jones smiled and shook his head. 'I'm afraid you'll have to wait for another night. She's been removed.'

'Removed?'

'She was a mess, so Danielle took her back to her room.'

Mason wanted to ask him where the room was, but couldn't. It would seem too suspicious. 'So she'll be available another night then?'

'Certainly, and I can tell you she's worth waiting for. But why don't you choose another.' Before Mason could speak, Jones called over one of the girls.

'Ellie my darling, take Mr'—he looked down at the badge on Mason's robe—'Mr Bronze upstairs to the blue room and show him a good time.'

Mason opened his mouth to decline the offer but stopped himself just in time. Ellie, he repeated to himself. Maybe she's Lucy's friend from the Lady Blue Club.

'Yes, I'd like that,' he said.

Ellie closed the door to the blue room and pointed to the bed. 'Sit down, sir and I'll dance for you.'

Mason noted the flower tattoo on her left shoulder. He sat on the edge of the bed and patted the space next to him. 'Before you dance, come and sit next to me. I'd like to talk first.'

'Whatever you say, sir.'

Mason took a deep breath and asked. 'Do you know a girl here called Rosie?'

Ellie gave him a curious look. 'Yes, I met her tonight. She's new here.'

'Ellie, are you Lucy's friend?'

Her jaw dropped open, and she gasped. 'How do you know Lucy?'

'I saw her today at the Lady Blue Club. She told me about you, and that she hadn't seen or heard from you for several months. Ellie, are you here against your will?'

She stared at him through watery eyes and nodded. 'I miss Lucy. I can't ring her. They took my phone from me, and we are not allowed to leave this place, but who are you, and why are you here?'

He raised his mask. 'My name's Mason. I'm Rosie's father.'

'Oh my god,' Ellie said. 'How did you find her?'

'It's a long story. I'll get you out of here but I need to find Rosie first.'

Ellie looked up at him. 'She was brought upstairs. . .'

She paused.

'It's okay Ellie, I know what happened earlier. But they've taken her somewhere. Do you know where they are holding her?'

'If she's not upstairs, she's either in the dungeon or the holding room. Oh god, I hope she's not in the dungeon.'

'Where's the dungeon?'

'It's in the basement. There are two hidden doors under the stairs, one on each side. The one on the right leads to the dungeon. The one on the left leads down to the holding room. None of the members ever go down to the holding room, but they go to the dungeon. All you need is. . .' she hesitated for a few moments, nodded slowly, and said, 'You need to take a girl down there for punishment. You can take me.'

'No Ellie, I'll find another way.'

'You'll need the master or his wife to open the entrance, and they will only do that if you have a girl with you. You have no choice. If you want to go down to the dungeon, you'll have to take me.'

'What's the procedure down there?'

'You take the girl down and choose the punishment. Madam is usually there and will often administer the punishment herself. It seems to excite the members watching her do it.'

'Who is madam?'

'Her name is Danielle, she's the master's wife.'

'Hell, this place just keeps on surprising. What does she look like?'

'She's tall with brushed back shoulder length hair. Usually smartly dressed as if she works for a city firm.'

'I think I've seen her. A woman like that walked out of the study with bloodied towels when the injured guy was in there.'

'She's cruel to the girls. I think that's why the members like her.'

Mason raised an eyebrow.

Ellie continued. 'You've probably guessed by now this is no ordinary brothel. The members here don't want just normal sex, well sometimes they do, but they want other services too that they can't get in a normal brothel or massage parlour.'

'How do they keep this place secret?'

'From what I've heard, it's very select. It's not open for anyone to join even if they can afford the fees. I think there are less than thirty members in total.'

'And is Jones the head of this sick group?'

'It's called The Scarlet Club and I think he set it up in the beginning, but I've heard there's someone higher. The top man, I don't know his name, they just call him Mr Scarlet. I've only seen him a few times but when he comes here, the girls are terrified in case he picks them.' She paused.

'Why?'

'Because he's not interested in just sex. Most of the girls he takes down to the dungeon don't come back.'

'Is he here tonight?'

'I haven't seen him.'

'How do you know? They all wear masks.'

'He wears a bright red robe, brighter than the rest. You can't miss him.'

'Okay, I think it's time I call in reinforcements.' He glanced around the room. 'Is there any recording equipment in here, like cameras or audio, that you know of?'

'No, that's only in the red room.'

'The red room. That's where they took Rosie.'

'How do you know?'

'I saw the blood.'

Ellie gasped, 'Blood?'

'Yes, on the bed, you know. . .' He hesitated.

'Oh, I see, I'm sorry. I spoke to her earlier. She's a sweet girl.'

Mason nodded, took out his mobile phone, and rang Jim.

'Hi Mason.' Jim said.

'Jim, I need backup.'

'Where are you?'

'I'm in a big manor house south of Maidstone, in Kent.'

'That's not the Met's area.'

'I know, but I need you to contact Kent Police. I don't have the time to go into the necessary detail with the Kent control room.'

Mason gave Jim a quick outline of the situation, including what was going on at the house, and explained the need for immediate police action.

'Okay, but I'm under orders. I'll have to ring Coulson

first. He's made it clear that he wants to know when you ring in with any concrete information.'

'Well, I suppose it will be better if the request for action comes from a senior officer. I just wish it wasn't Coulson.'

'I'll ring him now.'

'Okay but text me his number so I can ring him direct if things get out of hand here.'

'Will do. Stay safe.'

Mason ended the call, then pulled down his mask as they left the bedroom and made their way down the stairs to the foyer, where another member tapped Ellie on the arm. 'Come with me, young lady.'

Mason stepped back to Ellie's side. 'Sorry, she's with me.'

'Excuse me, but she's available to all of us. You are welcome to join us if you want, and you can even go first, I don't mind.'

The man gripped Ellie's arm above her elbow and pushed her back toward the stairs. Mason stepped in front of them and put a hand on the man's chest, but Ellie looked at him and shook her head. Then whispered, 'It's okay, this is what happens here. Don't make a scene, I'll see you afterwards.'

Against all of his instincts, Mason stepped aside and let them pass. He noted the man's name badge. It was Mr Ruby.

Mason returned to the club room as his phone vibrated in his pocket, informing him of an incoming message. He went back to the bar and poured himself another drink, but couldn't help thinking of Ellie, and what she must be going through right then.

43

MASON

Mason overheard Jones talking to a member at the bar. 'Welcome to VIP status.'

The man grinned back at him. 'Thank you, this is my first special event.'

Jones said, 'Would you like to see what happens in the dungeon?'

The man nodded. 'Yes I would, it's why I joined.'

'Come with me then, there are a couple of punishments about to happen that you might like.'

This opportunity was too good to miss. It was Mason's chance to get into the dungeon to see if Rosie was there. As Jones passed by, Mason said. 'I'll come down too, if that's okay.'

Jones turned and glanced down at Mason's badge. 'Of course, Mr Bronze, you are a regular down there.'

Whoever the real Mr Bronze was, he obviously had a taste for punishing the girls, or at least watching someone else do it.

Mason followed Jones and the other member out of the

clubroom and over to the wall under the wide staircase. As if by magic, a large panel opened, allowing access to a steep and narrow staircase. As they reached the bottom, another door opened, giving access to a large dungeon.

There was no mistaking its purpose. Chains hung from walls, chains hung from the ceiling, and chains lay on the concrete floor bolted down through iron rings. Spread around the underground room were wooden benches and tables in all shapes and sizes, with leather straps in various positions ready to secure any victims unfortunate enough to be taken down there.

Bolted to one wall were two seven-feet high wooden crosses with straps to secure spread-eagled victims. Another wall displayed whips, canes, and steel cables organised in wooden racks.

Footsteps echoed from the stairs and two girls entered the dungeon surrounded by four robed men. They were taken to the two crosses, stripped naked, and securely strapped into place, one facing the wall, and the other with her back to the wall.

It was then that Mason noticed a woman standing in the shadows close to the girls. She stepped forward and selected a short whip from a nearby rack.

Mason shuffled uncomfortably, concerned over what was about to happen. *This must be Danielle, the bitch who likes to hurt the girls. Maybe she'll get some of her own medicine before the night's out.*

He checked his watch. Coulson should have spoken to the local police by now. But it was hard to guess how long it would take them to mobilise an armed response team.

The other men in robes moved closer for a better view

of the proceedings. Jones raised a hand. 'When you're ready, my dear.'

Danielle shifted her feet into position, then raised the whip high above and behind her head. She whipped it forward and the thin leather cracked as it tore into the girl's back. A red line raised across her bare skin. She screamed.

Danielle took two steps to her right and unleashed a similar strike across the breasts of the second girl, and she screamed.

Danielle continued to strike each girl repeatedly. Mason couldn't watch. He had to do something. He scanned the room and counted the men present. Including Jones, there were six. He doubted the members would get involved if he acted decisively. But he would need to move fast. He would need to end it with minimal techniques to avoid any of them finding the courage to join the fray.

He moved closer to Jones. He would dispatch him first. A powerful strike to the jaw should put his lights out, allowing him to focus on any member with the courage or stupidity to challenge him. There would be no hesitation, no soft play, it would be fast, and it would be hard.

But before he could act, two security men in suits appeared at the door and called out to Jones.

Jones raised his hand, and Danielle stopped the sadistic punishment.

The girls sobbed.

The security men beckoned Jones over and one handed him a mobile phone. Jones took the phone and left the dungeon. When he returned a few minutes later, he studied the members one at a time, including Mason, then nodded and said. 'Gentlemen, I have just learned that one of you is an imposter. It seems we have been infiltrated.'

The members looked at each other, as if by some means they'd be able to tell who it was.

Jones said, 'Danielle, release the girls and take them back up to the clubroom.'

Danielle freed both girls and escorted them out.

Jones took a small book from his robe pocket, unclipped a pen that was attached, and studied inside.

No one spoke.

Mason began to plan.

The security men were almost certainly armed, so they would have to be his first targets. He would need to eliminate them with one strike each. It would be too dangerous to enter into a full-blown brawl.

He pulled out his mobile phone, and while shielding it from Jones, he selected the text message with Coulson's number. He intended to ring it and let Coulson overhear what was happening. Then, if he didn't make it out of there, at least they might have some evidence of what was going on at this place.

He highlighted the number and drew a deep breath. The main part of the number seemed familiar, especially the three sevens at the end. He'd seen it somewhere recently, but where? He searched his memory. Then he reached into his back pocket and pulled out the card he'd taken from the jacket hanging in the closet at Buckingham's house. He stared at the number written in red ink on the card after Mr S. It was not a match. He turned the card over and stared at the number after Mr C. It was an exact match with the number in the text message. He slipped the card back into his pocket. What did it mean? Why would Buckingham have Coulson's number?

Then he recalled his conversation at the police station, and how reluctant Coulson had been to search Buckingham's house, and how he had changed his mind after receiving a text message on his phone.

It began to make sense.

Coulson delayed the search until he was given the all clear from Buckingham. That would explain why, when Jim and his team had searched Buckingham's house, they found no paperwork in the desk, yet when Mason had gone back the next day he'd found the headed notepaper, business cards, and paperwork relating to three properties.

Mason watched Jones. He appeared to study each member in turn before making a mark in the book. From the movement of the pen, he must have been ticking off each name on a list.

'Right, gentlemen,' Jones said. 'It will be easy to establish who it is.' He walked back to the door and his security men followed.

Now the gap between Mason and the three of them was too big. He would be picked off before he could reach them. If only he'd worn his ballistic vest.

Jones said, 'Gentlemen, when I call your name please come over here. I will ask you for the codeword you were given when you joined. The one you give at the front door when you arrive. I will start with Mr Coral.'

The man next to Mason flinched as he heard his name called. He walked over to Jones and mumbled something. Jones pointed to the stairs, and the man left. Jones called another name, then another, until only one other member and Mason remained.

He was being saved until last. Jones must know it was him and was ensuring there would be no witnesses by the time he called out Mr Bronze.

A chill ran through him. If Coulson was involved in this, it was doubtful he made the call to Kent Police. So that meant he was on his own.

He made a new plan.

When called, he would go and stand close to the security men. When Jones asked for his codeword, he would strike the first man in the throat, and take out the second with an elbow strike to the jaw. It should take no longer than a couple of seconds.

But it was risky.

It could easily go wrong.

He had to let Natasha know about Coulson. If he failed to make it out of there, she needed to know he could not be trusted. His phone was still in his hand next to his thigh, shielded from Jones by his body and the loose robe. He glanced down and selected the number for Victor's mobile, pressed to call, then dropped the phone back into his pocket and hoped Natasha would keep the line open.

44

MASON

Jones called for Mr Ruby, the last remaining member, and Mason prepared himself for what he had to do. Adrenalin pumped through his veins, and adrenalin was his friend. It gave him a tremendous increase in strength and had over the years given him the ability to overpower men far bigger and stronger than him. After all, it was the entire basis on which the character The Hulk in the Marvel comics could dispatch his enemy. Only with Mason there was no turning green and no ripped clothes as he doubled in size. It was just a pure increase in speed, strength, and agility.

But things changed course. The man next to him didn't move. Jones called out again, 'Mr Ruby.'

Then Jones turned to the security guys. 'I think we have our man. Mr Ruby, remove your mask.'

Mason was baffled by this. Mr Ruby was the man who took Ellie upstairs. He was one of them. He had to be.

A security man pointed a semi-automatic pistol at

Ruby's head. He slowly removed his mask. Mason glanced to his left.

It was Buckingham.

Jones walked over to Mason. 'Well, Mr Bronze, we have our man.' Then he turned to face Buckingham.

Mason stood rigid and confused. How could it be Buckingham? He was one of them. This made no sense.

But now he had a decision to make and not much time to make it.

A few seconds ago, he was ready to fight for his life and for Rosie, and although his plan was by no means certain to succeed, he had thought he had nothing to lose. Because to do nothing would be certain death.

But now he had the opportunity to walk away. To leave the dungeon and maintain his cover. He found himself thinking, *What about Buckingham? What if he is innocent? I can't just leave him to his fate.* It was his conscience talking. And he always followed his conscience, no matter what he did. Even the law and police procedure would take second place to it. But then he thought of Rosie being so close, and of what she'd been through, and how terrified she must be alone with these monsters. So he made his decision. For the first time in his life, he would have to ignore his conscience and walk away from someone in danger.

For the sake of his daughter.

And he couldn't dismiss the rational thoughts that this made no sense. It was Buckingham's house, so he had to be up to his neck in this organisation.

As he slowly made his way to the door, he heard a distinctive metallic sound. It was the cocking of a semi-automatic pistol, the sliding action which loads the first round into the chamber.

Instinctively, he glanced behind him and stared straight down the barrel of a gun pointed at his head. It was in Jones's right hand. The distance between them was around eight feet.

Jones grinned. 'Mr Cooper, did you think we'd fallen for your little undercover jolly?'

Mason sighed, threw back the hood of his robe, and removed his mask. 'Tell me, where did I go wrong?'

'That phone call. It was quite enlightening.'

'Oh, really.' He raised his voice, hoping Natasha would hear. 'Who was it, Superintendent Coulson?'

Jones raised an eyebrow. 'Superintendent? What makes you say that?'

Mason glanced at Buckingham. 'Just a hunch.'

'You will need to explain that remark, but no, it was your friend, Artan. Earlier tonight he saw Natasha, the girl I had arranged to buy, and who you so gallantly rescued. Apparently, she was at the nearby diner. He left his cousin, Korab, with her and came here to arrange a new purchase price.' He smirked. 'Because as you know we had already bought a replacement after you stole her from us.'

Mason gritted his teeth at the indirect referral to Rosie.

Jones continued. 'I agreed a price, but then Korab staggered in here with a knife sticking out of his neck. I wonder how that got there. By the time Artan got back to the diner, the girl had gone.'

'Now, Artan is a little slow. It took him a while to put two and two together and realise, that if Natasha had been there, you must be close by. When he rang here to warn us, my men were trying to locate the name badge for one of our members. You see it was missing from his hook.'

Mason glanced down at the badge on his own robe. 'Pity the real Mr Bronze couldn't take a night off.'

Jones grinned. 'For you maybe, but for us it was very fortunate. It saved us a lot of trouble trying to work out who the intruder was. Oh, and Artan told me you two have some unfinished business.'

'Does he work for you?'

'Let's just say he's in acquisitions and transportation, and we do a lot of business with him. So in the interest of our future relationship, I have agreed to his request.'

'And what would that be?'

'To hold you until he gets here. And he's asked me to prepare a little entertainment for you. However, I don't think you are going to like it.' He turned to a security guy. 'Billy, bring me little Rosie. Artan has plans for her.'

The security guy smirked and left the dungeon.

Mason focused on Jones. 'If you're planning on bringing my daughter in here and strapping her onto one of these things, you'd better think again.'

Jones waved the pistol. 'Is that right? And just what do you propose to do about it?'

Mason took a deep breath and narrowed his eyes. The gun was now aimed at his chest and at that distance Jones couldn't miss. He had to get Jones to raise his aim.

'There are not enough bullets in that gun to stop me from ripping out your throat with my bare hands.'

'Is that so? Do you think you could do that with a bullet between the eyes?'

'That's the only way you'll stop me.'

Jones raised the gun. 'Then that's what you'll get if you take one step towards me. Thank you for the warning.'

Mason got what he wanted. He knew that if Jones opened fire at his chest from short range, his chances of surviving were virtually nil. It would be almost impossible for Jones to miss. But Jones probably didn't realise that it's not easy to shoot someone in the head who's running at you from close range.

Mason's training had taught him just how fast someone can close a gap. It's something American police officers know only too well. An assailant can close an eight-foot gap before an officer can react and draw his weapon.

This situation was a little different, as the gun was already pointed at Mason, so Jones would only have to pull the trigger. But even so, Jones would probably only have enough time to fire one shot. So Mason only needed him to miss with that first shot, and the chances of that would be higher if he was aiming for the head. Especially for an untrained and unskilled marksman. If Jones was trained, he would have stepped back, giving himself a better reactionary gap. So Mason calculated that he'd just increased his chances from almost nil to around thirty per cent.

Better than certain death.

He had a plan, and for the sake of his daughter, he was ready to act on it.

Mason looked at Buckingham. 'So I guess Coulson rang you to warn you about the search of your house?'

Buckingham just grinned.

Jones motioned for Buckingham to move away from Mason's side.

Mason focused on Jones's trigger finger, then on his eyes.

A phone rang out from Jones's robe. He used his left hand to reach over and pull it from his pocket while his right held the gun levelled at Mason's head.

'Jones here.' His eyebrows raised as he listened. 'That's unfortunate, but from what you say they haven't got enough evidence.' He thanked the caller and slid the phone back into his pocket. He looked at Buckingham. 'Something's come up.'

'What is it?' Buckingham asked.

'That was Malik. Artan was arrested at the diner near here. They were speaking on the phone when the police grabbed him. Malik overheard the conversation. They think Artan may have assaulted someone. He was seen in the diner with Korab and shortly afterwards Korab staggered out bleeding from the neck.'

Buckingham nodded. 'So what now?'

Jones took out his mobile phone again. 'The police don't know that Korab came here.' He made a call. 'Charlie, it's me. Move the Mercedes into a garage at the back of the house. Make sure it's out of sight.' He ended the call and looked at Mason. 'We must postpone our little game, Cooper. We will wait until Artan is released by the police.'

'That could be a long time, and he might talk. He might tell them about this place. Let me take my daughter and go.'

'He won't talk and if they don't have a victim, they can't hold him for long.'

'I'm impressed. You know the law and the procedures. Not strictly true about the lack of a victim if they think a crime has been committed. But it would be fair to say it's unlikely they would charge him without a body or a victim being found. Is Korab dead?'

'Not yet.' Jones turned to the remaining security guy. 'Search him and lock him in the cell, but stay sharp. If he gives you any trouble, shoot him. I'll tell Billy to leave the girl where she is for now. The father-daughter reunion will have to wait.' He turned to Buckingham. 'Nigel, come with me, we need to hide the girls in case the law comes sniffing around here.'

Jones and Buckingham left the dungeon.

MASON

The security guy led Mason at gunpoint to a cell at the far end of the dungeon. He'd seen many cells in his time, but this one was different. Four brick walls, no bench, no mattress, no blanket, and no Police and Criminal Evidence Act to protect his rights.

'Take off the robe and face the wall.' The guy in the suit said.

Mason turned to the side, removed his mobile phone, and slid it into his trouser pocket, then slipped off the robe. The security guy moved closer and patted Mason's side pockets. 'What's that?'

'My phone.'

'Take it out slowly and hand it to me.'

Mason pulled out the phone and glanced at the display. The line was still open. He brought the phone to his mouth and shouted, 'Natasha get out of there now and do what I told you to do.'

The security guy knocked the phone from his hand and as it clattered to the floor, he raised his boot to stamp on it.

That was Mason's chance. He grabbed the barrel of the gun and drove his shoulder into the guy's chest. They bounced off the wall, locked in a struggle for the weapon. Pulling, pushing, twisting, in a game of life and death. Finally, Mason drew a deep breath and pushed the guy back against the wall, then drove his elbow into his ribs, causing him to buckle and release the gun. While still locked together, Mason shoved the barrel into the man's chest and fired one shot at point blank range.

The man crumpled to the floor.

The struggle was over.

Mason grabbed his phone. 'Natasha, are you still there?'

'Yes, what's going on?'

'Just a little disagreement with the security guy showing me to my room. I didn't like the view.'

'I heard a shot.'

'Don't worry. The bullet is in the security guard.'

'What was that about a superintendent?'

'I think Buckingham has been in contact with Coulson. He had Coulson's number on a card I found in his house. I'm not sure what it means, but until I am, we can't trust Coulson. You need to remember that if I don't get out of here.'

'Make sure you do.'

'Rosie's in this house. I'm going to find her. Drive away from the garage and go to where we stopped earlier with Carly.'

'I'm scared, Mason. Leave the call open so I can hear what's happening.'

'I will, don't worry.'

He dropped the phone into a button down breast pocket

286

on his shirt and searched the dead man for spare magazines. He found one, then glanced down at the pistol in his hand. Another Beretta. At least they have good taste in weaponry. The Beretta nine millimetre was a popular handgun in America and Europe, renowned for its solid build and reliability.

He tucked the spare magazine into his back pocket, and as he left the cell, a man in a black suit appeared from the stairway and fired. Bullets slammed into the cell door frame next to Mason's head, and one clipped its target. He felt a stinging in his left ear, as if someone had just sliced it open with a knife. When he pulled his hand away, there was blood on his fingers. He ducked down behind a heavy table with pulleys and levers and chains and iron loops, and raised the Beretta, ready.

Three more bullets slammed into the table in front of him. Then silence. Then the sound of a magazine being ejected. Then the sound of Mason's Beretta firing a volley of four shots.

The man in the black suit staggered back and fell.

Mason held his breath as he approached, Beretta raised and ready, but exhaled as he reached the man's body.

He was dead.

He waited and listened for any reaction to the gun battle, then slowly made his way up the narrow stairs to the foyer. Several figures in long red robes had gathered there and seemed agitated. When they saw him, they scattered, running in different directions.

Two security men in black suits near the front door drew their weapons. Mason took aim and fired two shots at each. They fell dead. A girl screamed and ran up the wide staircase.

He threw open the door to the clubroom and entered. Beretta raised and ready.

Several of the men in robes cowered behind tables. 'Where's Jones?' Mason asked.

No one answered.

He raised the volume. 'Where's Jones?'

One of the men picked up a bottle and stepped out from behind the bar. He smashed it against the edge of a table and pointed the jagged glass towards Mason.

Mason adjusted his grip on the pistol and pointed it at the man's head. 'Are you crazy? Stop where you are.'

The man paused a few feet away.

Mason stepped back, creating a reactionary gap, and focused on the man's eyes through the mask. Then a shiver ran down his spine as he glanced at the name badge: Mr Brown.

According to Mr White, Brown had been the first one to rape Rosie.

'You don't know who I am, do you?' Mason asked.

'Why, should I?' Mr Brown replied.

'You raped my daughter.'

'What?'

'Tonight, in the red room, Rosie is my daughter.'

Brown's mouth fell open as he drew breath. Then he stammered, 'Yo-your daughter.'

Mason nodded once. 'Take off the mask.'

Brown slowly removed his mask, revealing the fear in his eyes and the panic etched across his face. They stood-fast, staring each other down with Mason fighting the urge to blow a hole in Brown's face and Brown clearly shocked to be facing the father of the girl he'd raped.

The stand-off was broken when Brown's eyes narrowed and determination replaced the panic. Maybe he'd decided his only chance was to fight. He raised the broken bottle and lunged forward.

Mason squeezed the trigger.

A single bullet smashed into Brown's forehead, killing him before he hit the floor. Mason stared down at his lifeless body. This was no time for soft play. No time to wound him or knock him out. This man lost his rights when he joined a club for raping, abusing, and killing girls. And he lost any chance of mercy from Mason when he raped his daughter.

Mason left the Club Room and the cowering men in robes to search for the door under the stairs to the holding room. But in the foyer he came face to face with a member in a robe. He glanced down at the badge. It was Mr White. Mason thought about putting a bullet between his eyes. He raised the Beretta to White's head but stopped when he heard running water. He glanced down to see a wet patch growing down White's left leg and a stream of yellow liquid pouring out from the bottom of his left trouser leg. Mason pulled back the pistol. Then smashed the butt into White's mouth, knocking out two teeth.

'That's something to remember me by.' Mason said. 'Consider yourself lucky I didn't put a hole in your head.'

Mason walked away, leaving him bleeding and soaked in his own urine. But he took a few steps and turned back to look at Mr White. Then pointed the Beretta and fired one shot into the man's leg. Mr White screamed out as the bullet tore through his right thigh, knocking him off his feet.

Mason said, 'That should slow you down and ensure you don't get away. Now crawl back into the clubroom and stay there. If you try to leave, I will kill you.'

Mr White dragged himself through the clubroom doorway.

Mason walked to the left side of the stairs and searched for the secret door that Ellie had told him led to the holding room. But there was no handle, no lock, and no visible means of entry.

He needed to find Jones.

Behind the staircase, a long, wide hallway stretched back away from the foyer and led to a large conservatory at the end. With the Beretta raised and ready, Mason walked along the hall and straight into an ambush. Bullets smashed into the wall on both sides, sending him diving for cover in a recessed doorway. He counted three men in black suits firing from open doors and around corners. One was even brave enough or stupid enough to run at him, gun blazing.

Mason pointed the Beretta, took aim, and fired three bursts of four shots each. When it was over, three more men in black suits lay dead. In the eerie silence that followed, and amongst the lingering smell of gunpowder, Mason checked himself. But the only blood on him was from his left ear, which still stung like hell.

He checked the rooms off the hall and then the conservatory, before returning to the foyer. He was alone, apart from the two bodies near the front doors.

He paused and listened, heard nothing, so began to climb the stairs. He stopped on the third stair and listened again. Still nothing, so he took another three. Then the silence was shattered by shots from Jones's semi-automatic pistol on the landing above. Mason dived for cover behind a pillar at the foot of the stairs, rolled over and returned fire. He'd been right about Jones's skill level. Not one bullet had found its target. Mason ejected his empty magazine and slid home the spare and let off several rounds at the bannister where he last saw Jones. But there was no reply and no sign of Jones. Cautiously, he climbed the stairs again, pistol at the ready.

As he reached halfway, a force from behind knocked him flat. A burning ripped through his left shoulder. He rolled over to see a security guy near to the front doors firing more shots. The bullets smashed into the stairs next to his head, showering him in marble fragments. He raised his gun and fired. He didn't know how many times, but kept firing until the man in the foyer fell back.

He looked down at a red patch forming on the front of his own shirt. A bullet had gone clean through his left shoulder just below his collarbone. A warm trickle of blood ran down his chest. It was like someone was holding a red-hot poker to his skin. It was hard to move. He took deep breaths and fought to overcome the agony sweeping through his upper body. He remembered how the heroes in movies always seemed to fight on, even with many bullets in them. If it hadn't been for the pain, he would have laughed. He'd taken a bullet through the shoulder and he couldn't move. His arms seemed limp and useless. The movies got it wrong.

Footsteps plodded down the stairs behind him. He glanced over his shoulder.

It was Jones.

Mason waited for the bullet in the back of the head and wondered if he would hear the shot. Probably not. There was an old saying from the trenches: You don't hear the shot that kills you.

'It seems you are empty, Mr Cooper. Now that's a shame.' Jones walked past him and over to the three dead security men. He picked up their guns one at a time and ejected the magazines. He dropped each magazine into the pockets of his robe and checked the dead men for more. Then he turned back to Mason.

Mason managed to raise his right hand and point the Beretta at Jones. Then he sighed. The last bullet casing had been ejected, and the gun's slide had recoiled. Jones was right. He'd fired the last shot.

'You are losing a lot of blood, Mr Cooper, so I will talk fast. I'm going down to the holding room. You might want to follow me. That is, if you want to see your daughter one more time before you bleed to death.'

Jones walked to the left side of the staircase, and Mason heard a door open. 'See you down there.' Jones said.

46

MASON

The burning in his shoulder raged like an out-of-control furnace, but Jones's words had motivated him to overcome the pain. *If you want to see your daughter one more time.* He forced himself to stand, then staggered to the open door. Still clutching the empty Beretta, he rested against the door frame and stared down the narrow staircase to a shaft of light at the bottom.

His body was telling him to sit down. To rest. To give up.

But he couldn't.

Not yet.

Rosie was down there.

So close.

If he could just get the strength to walk down the stairs, he would see her again. He closed his eyes and took several deep breaths, and with each breath he summonsed that strength, and for the first time in his life, he prayed. *Give me the strength I need to finish this. Let me get my daughter out of here and I'll never ask for anything again. And I'll pay any price you ask of me.* He opened his eyes.

Not knowing whether it was divine intervention, adrenalin surge, or sheer willpower, he found himself standing unsupported and focused on the door at the foot of the stairs.

He had no plan, and no idea who, apart from Jones and Rosie, was down there. And he had no idea if he would win. But he had to try.

He took a deep breath and made his way down the stairs, and as he pushed open the door, he saw her standing by the bed next to Jones. She was wearing her black sweater, denim skirt, and suede ankle boots, exactly as Natasha had described the night she was taken.

She shrieked, 'Daddy!'

Mason stepped into the room. 'Rosie, are you all right?'

She tried to run to him, but Jones grabbed her arm. 'Stay here,' he ordered.

Mason straightened up. 'I'm okay, Rosie.'

'I knew you'd find me, I knew it.'

Jones pulled Rosie back. 'Very touching.'

Footsteps echoed down from the stairs, and Buckingham entered the basement holding a revolver. He walked over to Jones. 'The security guys are all dead.'

Jones said, 'I know, it's inconvenient, but not a major problem, we can replace them. What about the girls?'

'I've locked them in the attic room. I can watch these two while you get the car.'

'I think we need to deal with them before we leave here. This place is finished now.'

Buckingham shook his head. 'We should take the girl

with us.'

Jones looked at Rosie. 'Yes, you are right.'

More footsteps rang out from the stairs. Jones and Buckingham pointed their guns at the doorway.

Mason turned as Natasha entered the room, with Danielle behind, prodding her forward. 'Look what I found,' Danielle said, gloating with each word spoken.

Natasha looked at Mason with wide eyes as he put his arms around her. 'Are you okay?'

She nodded. 'Yes, are you?'

'I think I'm going to need your patching up skills again.'

Jones stepped forward within touching distance of Mason and scowled at Natasha. 'Do you remember me?'

Natasha nodded.

'It's a shame I'm not going to get my chance to enjoy you. But after all the trouble you've caused, you leave me with no choice but to deal with you once and for all.'

Jones was close. This could be Mason's chance. He could grab the gun and put a bullet in Jones's head before he would know what hit him. But when he glanced over his shoulder, he had to rethink. Buckingham was holding the revolver to Rosie's head with the barrel touching her temple.

He couldn't risk it, not yet.

The phone in Jones's pocket rang out again.

He answered. 'Jones here.'

He listened, then said, 'Artan, good to hear you are free. We have Cooper here. How long will you be?'

He listened again before replying. 'You'll find him in the holding room in the basement, and as a bonus, Natasha will be with him. They're all yours.'

Jones closed the call and walked over to Danielle at the door. 'My Darling, go and get anything you need, we'll be leaving here soon.'

Danielle walked over to Mason and stared into his eyes. 'I would have enjoyed torturing you,' she said.

Then she turned and left the room.

Jones pointed his gun at Natasha's heart. 'Cooper, go and stand by your daughter and don't try anything unless you want to watch these sweet young things die in front of you.'

Mason crossed the room to Rosie and hugged her. She flung her arms around him and burst into tears. 'How's Mum?'

'She's okay, Rosie, don't worry.'

Jones laughed. 'There's nothing like a father-daughter re-union to melt the heart, is there Nigel?'

Buckingham stayed silent as he walked over and stood next to Jones near the door.

Jones grinned at Natasha. 'Artan has plans for you after he's finished with Cooper. It's a shame I can't stay to enjoy the show.'

He flicked the gun barrel twice from left to right, motioning for Natasha to join Mason and Rosie by the wall. She walked over and stood in front of Mason, and as she turned back to face Jones, she put one hand behind her back and lifted the hem of her sweater.

Mason glanced down at an ammunition magazine sticking up from the waistband of her leggings. With a quick intake of breath, he glanced down at his right hand. For some unexplained reason, he was still holding the empty Beretta pistol as if it was glued to his palm.

He raised his gaze back to Natasha. *This girl is amazing. She must have remembered the spare magazines I left under the seat.*

Jones placed his hand on Buckingham's shoulder. 'I'll get the car. Bring the girl and lock the other two in, and leave them for Artan and Skinny. They'll deal with them.'

Buckingham nodded.

Jones paused in the doorway. 'Keep your distance. He's a tricky bastard. If he tries anything, shoot his daughter first.'

While Buckingham had been distracted, Mason took his left arm from around Rosie and grabbed the magazine from Natasha's waist band. He brought both hands around behind his back, ejected the empty magazine, and tucked it into his back pocket. But entering the new magazine and cocking the gun by pulling back the slide would be trickier. The sound would be distinctive. Anyone who had ever used a semi-automatic pistol, or watched a gangster movie, would recognise it.

As Jones's footsteps faded, Buckingham turned back to face them. 'Rosie, come here.'

Mason moved closer to her, hoping she'd seen the magazine and knew he was about to act.

She remained by his side.

He ran through the procedure in his mind. Bring both hands in front of him, push the magazine home, and pull the slide to cock the gun, all in one fast motion. He rotated the magazine in his left hand to locate the open end, the end with the bullets, and the end that needed to enter the handle of the pistol. There must be no fumbling. No mistakes. He had to get it right first time.

Buckingham pointed the revolver at Rosie. 'I won't tell you again.'

Mason stepped in front of her, blocking Buckingham's sight. His hands still behind his back, Beretta and magazine at the ready. 'Tell me, Nigel, how do you know Superintendent Coulson?'

Buckingham paused a moment, then laughed. 'You don't know?'

'Should I?'

'Look closely.'

Mason studied Buckingham through squinted eyes. 'Oh my god, you're not . . .'

Buckingham nodded and grinned proudly. 'I think you've just got it. Shame there's no prize. But yes, I am. I'm Clive's older brother.' He pursed his lips. 'Well, half-brother, to be accurate. Different fathers. His was weak,' he smirked. 'Mine taught me to take what I want and crush anyone who gets in my way. If he were alive today I think he'd be proud of me, don't you?'

'Maybe, if he was a twisted bastard like you. But it looks like he failed to teach you a vital lesson.'

'What's that?'

'That sooner or later you'll pick on the wrong person, and instead of crushing, you'll get crushed.'

'What are you going to do, throw that empty gun at me?' Buckingham tipped his head back and laughed aloud.

It was now or never. Mason moved fast. He stepped forward in front of Natasha, shielding both her and Rosie. He slid home the magazine, pulled back the slide, raised the gun, and fired two shots, all in a split second.

He was surprised at how well it went, but probably not

as surprised as Buckingham, as both bullets found their target and he slammed back against the open door, a red patch spreading around two closely grouped holes in his white shirt just below his neck. He spluttered and slid down the door into a seated position.

Mason walked over, crouched down in front of him, and pulled the revolver from his limp hand. 'Well, it looks like you picked on the wrong person when your goons took my daughter. But there's a bright side to this.'

Buckingham just stared back, blood seeping from the wounds in his chest.

'At least now you'll get to ask your father if he's proud of his raping, murdering son.' He raised the gun to Buckingham's forehead and began to squeeze the trigger.

'Daddy,' Rosie shouted.

He glanced over his shoulder.

She shook her head. Her eyes wide. 'Don't.'

As he studied the fear and panic in her eyes, he sighed. After everything she'd been through, she still didn't want him to end this monster's life. It was impossible not to feel a sense of pride.

He relaxed his trigger finger and turned back to Buckingham to tell him how lucky he was.

But he wouldn't hear those words, or any others. Not in this life, anyway.

Mason placed two fingers on Buckingham's neck and confirmed what the glazed eyes and still chest had suggested.

He was dead.

47

MASON

Mason straightened up, and Rosie ran into his arms. As he held her tight, his gaze fell upon Natasha. She remained where she was, and he knew why. It was Rosie's time.

She smiled at him.

He smiled back.

This is what the last few days had been about. Why she had stayed with him instead of flying back to Moldova to be with her family. He pushed the Beretta into his waistband and held out his arm. Rosie turned and held out an arm. Natasha moved to them and for a few moments, they hugged each other in silence.

Then Mason pulled back and looked at them both. 'We're not safe yet, we need to get out of here.'

Natasha nodded.

He bent down, picked up Buckingham's revolver, then removed the empty magazine from his back pocket and pushed the revolver into its place. Slowly and carefully, they made their way up to the foyer.

It was silent.

As they stepped over the bodies of the security men, the front door opened and Skinny entered. He closed the door behind him and stood face to face with Mason.

Rosie gasped, 'That's him, that's who stabbed Mum.'

They stood still, as if frozen, a few feet apart. In Skinny's right hand, a long-bladed knife glinted in the light from the chandelier.

Mason pulled the Beretta from his waistband and pointed at Skinny's head. 'I would like to tear you apart with my bare hands, but as you can see I'm a little disadvantaged right now.'

Skinny's focus dropped to Mason's bloodied shirt, but he remained silent.

There was a familiar sound behind them. The sliding action of a semi-automatic pistol.

'Stay where you are.'

It was a woman's voice. The same one he'd heard a few minutes earlier in the basement. Mason turned to see Danielle pointing the gun at Rosie.

'Try anything and she dies first,' she said.

His heart sank. The pain from his wounds had been returning, but as he stared at this woman, threatening to kill his daughter, his adrenalin surged and the pain receded.

'Throw down your gun, Cooper.' Danielle said.

Mason noted the determination on her face. He knew she would do it. He'd seen how brutally she had whipped the two girls in the dungeon and how she seemed to enjoy inflicting pain. So he didn't doubt she would pull the trigger if she wanted to.

'Okay, just relax.' He dropped the Beretta onto the marble floor and kicked it away.

'So this is your father, Rosie?'

Rosie nodded. 'Yes, I told you he would find me.'

Mason stepped to the side, putting space between Rosie and Natasha and himself. 'Danielle, it's over. The police are on the way. Let them go, let the girls leave.'

Danielle shook her head. 'You shouldn't have come here. Then she would have lived.'

Skinny spoke from behind. 'Let me have him.'

Danielle stared at Skinny for a moment, then studied Mason. 'Okay, but make it quick.'

Mason turned to face Skinny and focused on the knife. Would he have time to draw the revolver from his back pocket, kill Skinny, and then shoot Danielle before she could shoot Rosie? It would depend on Danielle's first action once she saw his revolver. Would she shoot Rosie first or turn her gun towards him? If she did the latter, he could move fast enough to make it difficult for her, and would bet his life on winning that exchange.

But the risk was too great. He wasn't prepared to bet Rosie's life on the outcome. Danielle was just evil enough to shoot Rosie first, so he decided to deal with this situation another way. By taking out Skinny with his bare hands, so Danielle wouldn't know he had the revolver until it was too late.

Skinny waved the knife back and forward in front of him, then made his move. Mason stepped back as the knife flashed in front of him.

Rosie shrieked, 'Daddy.'

'Stay there, Rosie.' Mason said.

Skinny lunged again. Mason kicked skinny's legs from under him.

The adrenalin had taken care of the pain in his shoulder, and although stiff, he still had some function in his left arm. He readied himself as Skinny scrambled to his feet and lunged forward again. Mason feigned another kick, and as Skinny reacted instinctively by pulling back his front leg, Mason stepped in and drove his fist into the man's face. Skinny's head rocked back, and he staggered and dropped onto his knees. Mason grabbed a handful of hair and pulled back Skinny's head.

'This is for Kathy,' he said through gritted teeth, then smashed the edge of his right hand into Skinny's neck, instantly crushing his windpipe. When he let go, Skinny fell face down, dead.

Mason turned back to Danielle. While watching the fight, she had relaxed her aim, but as she stared at Skinny's lifeless body, she began to raise her weapon.

Mason shouted, 'Danielle.'

It was a distraction technique. To give him the split second he needed to draw the revolver from his back pocket and fire two shots. The first missed, but the second thudded into Danielle's left breast and through her heart. She dropped the gun, clutched her chest, and fell back onto the floor.

Rosie walked over to her as she writhed on the cream marble.

'I told you,' she said. 'I told you he would find me. You should have helped me when I asked.'

Danielle stared up at Rosie, her face frozen with fear. Then her pupils dilated as she took her last breath.

Mason opened one of the double doors. 'Wait here girls while I check out front.'

As he walked out onto the front forecourt, he was suddenly blinded by two huge spot lights. An amplified voice rang out in the distance. 'Drop the gun and keep your hands visible'. He recognised the sound. It was a police address system. He bent down and placed the revolver on the gravel drive, then raised his hands and stepped away from it. *Did Coulson make the call after all?*

'Daddy,' Rosie shouted from the doorway.

'Stay there Rosie and don't worry, it's the police, it's over, you're safe.'

As police officers moved in, rifles raised and trained on him, he began to relax.

He'd done it.

With Natasha's help, he'd found Rosie and rescued her from a living nightmare. But now the pain swept over him like a steamroller. His strength drained away and he dropped to his knees. Was God collecting his debt. Was it time to pay the price for Rosie's freedom? If it was, it was okay. A deal's a deal. He couldn't complain. He'd got his daughter out of there, and she was safe. So if his death was the price for his daughter's life, then so be it. He would pay his debt.

The last thing he felt was the gravel on his face as he hit the ground.

48

MASON

He heard clanging, shuffling, and voices, all jumbled up and punctuated by a rhythmic beeping. Then breathing, but not normal breathing. It was deep, and loud, and kind of mechanical. It seemed familiar. He'd heard it before, in hospital, when he'd visited his grandmother. She'd been admitted for an operation to fix a broken hip after a fall. When he went to see her, she was hooked up to various pieces of apparatus to monitor her breathing and heart rate. Her oxygen mask made her breathing sound mechanical. Exactly like this sound.

But that was years ago, so why was he hearing it again? And why was it so dark? Why doesn't someone turn on a light?

Who's voices are they?

One male, well educated and with an air of authority. The other female, softer tones, agreeable and obliging. But what were they saying?

Someone touched his arm, and something tightened

around his bicep. The beeping increased in frequency, as did the mechanical breathing.

Okay, now I remember. I was shot. I must be in hospital.

He tried to open his eyes, but they felt welded shut. At least his senses were returning, slowly. He could feel a heaviness in his back and left shoulder. Not pain exactly, and not even discomfort. Just a numbness throughout his body. Must be the drugs, probably morphine, keeping it under control.

The female voice spoke again, and this time he heard the words. 'Everything's fine, blood pressure normal.'

The male voice answered, 'Good, maybe the increased heart rate means he's regaining consciousness. Keep an eye on him and call me if there are any developments.'

'Yes, Doctor.'

As the footsteps faded, he felt himself sinking, falling back into sleep. But wait, what about Rosie, and Kathy, and Natasha? Now wasn't the time to sleep. There were too many unanswered questions.

He tried again, and this time managed to force open his eyes and gradually focus on his surroundings. He was in a room with three other beds, one empty, stripped back, awaiting fresh bedding and its next occupant. Two occupied. The two patients were either sleeping or unconscious, and like him, they were lying almost flat and seemed to be hooked up to every monitoring device known to medical science.

'Mr Cooper, you're awake.'

He pulled off the oxygen mask and turned his head to

see a nurse smiling at him. She took a pen from her top pocket and wrote onto a clipboard.

It took a few seconds to get his first words out. 'How long have I been here?'

'Three days. How are you feeling?'

'Three days? Did I lose that much blood from one bullet hole?'

'One? Mr Cooper, you were shot three times. One went straight through, but the surgeon dug two more out of your back. You've been a topic of conversation among the surgeons and theatre staff. They couldn't believe you were still alive.' As soon as the words left her lips, her face flushed, and she brought her hand up to her mouth. 'Oh, I'm sorry, I shouldn't have said anything before you see the doctor.'

'Don't worry, I won't let on. Where's my wife and daughter?'

'They're along in the cafeteria getting something to eat. Your daughters have been here since you were brought in. They'll be so happy to see you awake. They should be back soon.'

'Daughters? You mean my wife and daughter?'

'No, your daughters, Rosie and Natasha, beautiful girls might I add, and your wife'—she paused for a moment and glanced up to the ceiling as if searching her memory —'Kathy.'

He hesitated before answering. Maybe they only allow close family to remain on the ward outside normal visiting hours. He didn't want Natasha to be excluded, so he decided not to correct her mistake.

'Oh, yes of course,' he said.

The nurse straightened his bedding and checked the equipment. 'I'll let the doctor know you're awake.' She hurried out of the ward and returned a few minutes later with Doctor Mathews.

'Mr Cooper, it's good to see you awake. How are you feeling?'

'A little numb, but other than that, I'm okay. Please don't take this the wrong way, Doc, but it's not good to see you again. Not like this I mean.'

Doctor Mathews grinned. 'The numbness is normal. You have a morphine drip in your back. We have reduced the dose, so if you feel no pain, we could think about removing it and using oral medication. But there's no rush.'

'Thanks Doc, did you do my operation?'

Doctor Mathews took the clipboard from the young nurse and began his own entry. 'Yes I did, and I'll tell you about it later when you've had a chance to come around properly.'

Mason glanced at the nurse and winked. She smiled, tipped her head to one side, and hurried across to the patient in the opposite bed.

'How's my wife's injury?' Mason asked.

Doctor Mathews stopped writing and lifted his head. 'Thankfully, she's healing well.'

'That's good to hear.'

'Let me apologise on behalf of the hospital for what happened.'

Mason shook his head. 'No need Doc. I'm as much to blame as anyone. I should have known that could happen. I should have foreseen it. I normally pride myself on being able to see the bigger picture, but this time I was wearing blinkers. I was focused only on Rosie and failed to protect Kathy.'

'Don't be hard on yourself. From what I've heard you made up for it.'

'Thanks Doc, but you don't know all the details.'

'All I know is you're a bit of a celebrity around here. We had the press camped outside in the carpark for three days and a police officer outside the ward doors since you were brought in. Not the same one of course.'

Mason laughed, then raised his head off the pillow and listened. 'That's them, I recognise my daughter's voice.' He listened again. 'Yes, that's Rosie.'

Doctor Mathews said, 'I am pleased to tell you that the doctor who administered the injection to your wife has been arrested.'

'You must mean Doctor Black.'

'Yes, that's not his real name, but yes, I do mean him.'

'That's good to hear Doc.'

The voices grew louder until Kathy, Rosie, and Natasha walked onto the ward. Their faces lit up when they saw Mason smiling at them.

Rosie ran to his bedside and hugged him. 'Daddy, you're awake.'

Kathy sat in the chair on the other side of the bed and held his hand. Natasha stood at the foot of the bed.

Kathy said, 'It's good to see you awake. We thought we were going to lose you. It was touch and go for a while.' She leant over the bed and kissed his cheek.

Mason nodded and held out his arms. 'It's good to see you all.'

Doctor Mathews said, 'I'll leave you all to catch up, and I'll speak to you later, Mr Cooper.'

Mason nodded, 'Thanks Doc.'

Then he hugged Rosie and Kathy for a full minute before he moved his head and looked past them to Natasha. She smiled at him as she watched the family reunion.

Kathy and Rosie glanced back at her and Rosie said, 'She's been here with me since you were brought in.'

Mason smiled again and held eye contact with Natasha, and said, 'You were brilliant.'

Natasha lowered her head, as if embarrassed. 'It's the least I could do after what you did for me.'

'That spare magazine you brought me made all the difference. You remembered me putting some under my driver's seat?'

'Yes, and over the phone I heard a man say that your gun was empty. So it was the obvious thing to do. As I walked in through the front door, I ran straight into that woman. I wanted her to take me to you and she did.'

'I'll say it again. You were brilliant. Not many could have done what you did. I mean that, Natasha.'

Rosie said, 'The Detectives who interviewed Natasha told her not to return to her own country just yet. They said it would be too dangerous. They've had cases where girls have escaped and gone home only to find the traffickers waiting for them. Some have been trafficked again, and some killed.'

Mason nodded at Natasha. 'Yes, it's wise for you to wait awhile. Have you been staying at our house?'

Rosie answered, 'I told you, she's been here with me

since you were brought in. But we've been home to shower and change.'

Mason glanced at Kathy. She said nothing, but he didn't detect any atmosphere. Not like he did back in their apartment.

The silence was broken when the nurse appeared on the ward again, followed by DS Jim Barker dressed in his usual slightly creased, dark grey, two-piece suit.

'Are you okay to speak to the police?' the nurse asked.

'Of course. Hi Jim.' Mason held out his right hand.

The nurse smiled at Jim and motioned for him to move closer to the bed, then spun on her heels and left the ward.

Jim swapped places with Rosie and shook Mason's hand. 'All the guys and gals send their best wishes,' he said.

'Thanks, Jim.'

Jim grimaced. 'Coulson's on his way.'

'What, he's coming here?'

'Yeah, he should be here any minute.'

Natasha stepped forward. 'Mason, I need to tell you something.'

'What is it, Natasha?'

'They have the letter. The one you wrote for Jim. They took it from your car.'

Mason glanced at Jim. 'Who's got it?'

'Coulson,' Jim said. 'The Kent Police gave it to him, unopened.'

'How?'

He attended the scene in Kent. He was there when they searched your car, and he took it from them.

'Well, he's got what he needs now.'

'Why, what's in that letter?'

'Enough to put me away for a long time.'

'But you wrote it.'

'Yeah, but it was only supposed to be read if I didn't make it, so I wasn't too careful choosing my words. I wrote what happened at Silver Street, but worse than that, I wrote what I was thinking at the time. It won't look good. It could blow a hole in any claim of self-defence, and as you know, vigilantes are not viewed in a good light in this country.'

Jim looked puzzled. 'Self-defence, vigilantes, what are you talking about?'

'Have you not seen the letter?'

'No, what's in it?'

'When I told you about Silver Street being a brothel and that I got hold of one of their mobile phones, I didn't tell you everything. So you don't know what I did. But stick around, you will soon if Coulson has that letter.'

MASON

Coulson walked onto the ward wearing a brown checked sports jacket, open-necked shirt, and fawn trousers. He stopped at the foot of the bed. 'How are you, Mason?'

'I'm okay, I'm going to live, anyway.'

Coulson nodded to Kathy. 'You must be Mrs Cooper.'

She smiled, 'Yes, I'm Kathy.'

He then glanced at Rosie. 'So you must be Rosie.'

Rosie nodded.

'And that's Natasha,' Mason said.

Coulson acknowledged her with a smile and turned back to Mason. 'We need to talk.'

'Yeah, I've just heard, you've got the letter I left for Jim.'

Coulson put his hand inside his jacket and pulled out a white envelope. 'You mean this one?'

Mason recognised his writing. 'That looks like it.'

Coulson nodded.

'So you've got what you want then, Clive.'

'What I want?'

'No need to play dumb, you've spent the last fifteen years hoping to get something on me. Now you've got it, written in my own handwriting. It doesn't get any better than that. Maybe we'll be sharing a cell.'

Coulson moved closer, a look of resignation on his face. 'I don't think so.'

'No? How do you explain Nigel Buckingham away?'

'I don't. He's my brother.'

Jim gasped. 'What?'

Coulson glanced across to him. 'I'm sorry you have to hear this, Jim, but it's right that you do.'

Mason exchanged glances with Jim before locking eyes on Coulson. 'How deep are you involved, Clive?'

Coulson glanced at everyone gathered around the bed.

Kathy got to her feet. 'Should we leave?'

Coulson shook his head. 'No, you can stay.' He turned back to Mason and sighed. 'Nigel was the one everyone looked up to in our family. The hero, the role model. He splashed money around like he'd discovered a never-ending supply. He'd made a fortune in finance, and stock trading, and business, but the money wasn't enough. Not for him. He had a dark side.'

Mason winced as he shuffled himself up on the bed. 'He certainly did.'

Coulson said, 'I knew about some of it. The dodgy business deals. His cocaine habit. I even helped him find a way out when he lost it with an ex-girlfriend of his. I mediated, and he paid her off so she didn't press charges. Oh, I knew what he was like all right. But I never gave up. I thought I could change him, if I just stuck by him. So I did, year after year, through one problem after another.' He lowered his gaze and slowly shook his head.

Nobody spoke.

He lifted his head and looked at Mason. 'But I didn't know about this. I didn't know about The Scarlet Club.'

'But what about that day in your office when I asked you to get the warrant to search his house? You were reluctant until you received a text message. Then it was all systems go. I thought you were just being your usual reluctant self, but when I discovered you and him were brothers, it suddenly made sense. Was that message from him? From Buckingham?'

Coulson nodded and shrugged. 'I know what it looks like and you're right. I was stalling. But not because I thought he had anything to do with Rosie.' He glanced over to Rosie with an apologetic smile.

'Why then?'

'It was to give him a chance to get rid of the drugs and some paper work referring to business deals. At least that's what he told me, and I believed him. I mean, I knew he'd gone bad, but I had no idea just how bad. I never would have supported him if I'd known about this, you know... if I'd known about the girls. That's fucked up. Completely fucked up.' He glanced across from Kathy to Rosie. 'Sorry for the language.'

'When did you find out?' Mason asked.

'When Jim told me where you were and what was going on over there at his house in Kent. That's when I realised he hadn't told me everything. It's one thing turning a blind eye to drugs and business deals, but it's completely different when we're talking about abduction, rape, and murder of young women and girls. I'll have no part of that.' He was breathing heavily, and beads of sweat gathered on his forehead.

'So what now?' Mason asked.

'I've already reported myself to Professional Standards and will accept whatever happens. The main thing is you've got your family back. I just hope someday you can understand why I did what I did.'

Nobody spoke as Mason stared at Coulson for a full minute. Then he shrugged and pointed to the envelope. 'I would be a bit of a hypocrite if I couldn't. As you'll have seen from the contents of that letter, I've done worse. At least you didn't kill anyone.'

Coulson thumbed the envelope. 'You'll be fine, Mason. It was all in self-defence.'

Mason raised his eyebrows. 'Maybe it was. But if you've read what's in there, you'll know it might be hard to convince a jury of that in relation to Silver Street. The prosecution lawyer is going to have a field day.'

Coulson raised the envelope in his right hand. Mason saw the torn edge and knew Coulson must have opened it and read its contents.

Coulson said, 'So the only real evidence of what happened in Silver Street is in this envelope?'

Mason nodded. 'That's right, as good as any you're ever likely to get.'

'Evidence that could convict you of murder or manslaughter.'

'I'll go for manslaughter on the grounds of diminished responsibility.'

Coulson stared at Mason, and another long silence followed. Then he grunted and gripped the envelope with both hands.

Then he ripped it in half.

He placed the pieces together, and ripped them again, and again, using more effort with each rip. 'Well, I guess the prosecution just lost a vital piece of evidence then.'

Mason's jaw dropped open. 'But—'

'Listen to me, Cooper. You never did a damn thing I asked you to do when you were in the job. But you're going to do this. You're going to think long and hard about what you say when you are interviewed about all this, and what you put in your statement. You did what any father and husband would want to do in the same circumstances, but very few, if any, would have the balls or the ability to do it. So some evil scum died, organised criminals, armed criminals, and I include my brother in that. But so what. I can't think of any situation where that could be anything other than self-defence. No one back in the office is saying anything different. And I'm sure your memory must be quite hazy about Silver Street after three days in a coma. So leave your pride back in that dungeon and do what's right for your family. What do you say?'

The tension in the air was thick as nobody said a word. Mason didn't even blink as he stared at Coulson and processed what he'd just heard. Finally, he took a deep breath and nodded.

'Yes, sir.'

Coulson sighed, and turned to Jim. 'It took fifteen years, but I finally got him to say those two words.'

Everyone laughed as the tension drained from the room. Coulson lifted the lid of a waste bin next to the bed and scattered the torn shreds of the letter into it. Then he turned, nodded at Kathy and Rosie, and walked out.

Nobody spoke as they stared at each other for what seemed like several minutes, but was probably only a few seconds before Rosie flung her arms around Mason.

'I knew you'd come for me Daddy, I would just lie on my bed and pray for you to come.'

Mason cuddled her as he stroked her hair and kissed her forehead. 'I would never have stopped looking, no matter how long it took.'

Tears filled her eyes. 'I know that.'

He looked up at Jim. 'I guess a leopard can change its spots.'

Jim nodded, his expression blank, as if still in shock from the recent developments.

'What about Jones, did you get him?' Mason asked.

'He was arrested as he tried to drive away from the house.' Jim said.

'And Ellie, and the other girls, what about them?'

Rosie lifted her head. 'Ellie's safe. I spoke to her at the police station when we were giving our statements. She helped me in that house. I might not be here now if it wasn't for her.' She sniffed and wiped her eyes. 'I wasn't going to co-operate and I probably would have been killed. But she told me to think of home and my future and helped me to cope.'

Mason kissed her forehead again. 'I spoke to her in the

house. She helped me too.' He looked over at Natasha. 'One day I'll have to tell you just how incredible Natasha was. I really couldn't have done it without her.'

Rosie nodded. 'I do know. She's my best friend now. We'll stay in touch.'

50

MASON

The morning routine woke Mason, just as it had done every day since he regained consciousness. The clattering of the breakfast trolley and the clanging of utensils as the barely edible food was dished up. Nurses hustling from bed to bed with too much to do and not enough time to do it. Peace and quiet shattered in a matter of seconds. If his ward was anything to go by, the hospital was certainly in need of some tender loving care, or even a cheap makeover. Like fresh paint on the walls, maybe a new floor in place of the worn out cracked tiles, pounded by feet and trollies for probably twenty-years or more. Curtains sagging, rings missing, worn out from thousands of journeys back and forward along the same rails around the beds, and always ending up back where they started.

But this was the National Health Service at its best, and Mason couldn't complain. He couldn't have been looked after better if he'd been in a private hospital costing hundreds a night. And for him, that's what mattered.

He lay awake with his eyes closed and thought about the day ahead. Because this day was different. This was the day he got to check out and go home. And it was three days short of three weeks, and over a week sooner than expected or planned by the medical staff. According to Doctor Mathews, his faster than average recovery must be attributed to his higher than normal fitness level at the time he was wounded. With maybe just a sprinkling of magic thrown in from somewhere, the doctor had joked.

But there had been a serious tone to Doctor Mathews' voice when he explained that if one of the bullets had struck him just five millimetres to the right, he would have been paralysed for life. But then the doctor had joked, that if he'd been a cat, he'd have just lost three of his lives, to which Mason had explained, if he'd been a cat, he would have been dead already, because he'd lost many more lives over the course of his police service.

He opened his eyes, stretched, and pulled himself up in the bed. One of his regular nurses, a girl called Keya, rushed over to help. Originally from India, she'd been with the NHS for just over a year, and a few days earlier, while changing his dressings, she'd entertained him with tales from Mumbai. And she'd told him that Indian names had meanings, and that Keya meant flower. He'd told her that it suited her perfectly.

'How are you feeling today, Mr Cooper?' she asked with her usual bright smile.

'Morning, Keya. I feel good. I go home today.'

'We'll miss you,' she said playfully.

'I'll miss you, too,' he said. Then glanced both ways and lowered his voice to a whisper, 'My favourite nurse.'

Her smile widened, and she whispered back, 'My favourite patient.'

They both laughed.

After finishing breakfast, nurse Keya pulled the curtain so he could get dressed in private. The rest of the morning was spent chatting with the other patients while waiting to be discharged. And that happened just before lunch, and just as Kathy, Rosie, and Natasha came to collect him. They met in the corridor outside his ward.

Rosie flung her arms out wide for a hug. 'I'm glad you're coming home, Daddy. So things can get back to normal.'

Mason hugged her tight. 'So am I, Rosie. But I'm not sure things will be back to normal for a while.'

Rosie stared up at him with questioning eyes.

'There are unresolved issues,' he said. We still don't know the identity of the top man, Mr Scarlet. Artan and Malik are still out there, Artan's brother is still dead, and their trafficking and slavery operation has been seriously damaged. I doubt they'll let things go just yet.'

'But nothing's happened over the past three weeks.' Rosie said.

'That's because you've had police parked out front twenty-four-seven while I've been in here. That won't last forever. Priorities change and resources get redirected.'

As they walked through the carpark, Mason dropped back a few paces next to Natasha. 'How is your family? Are they back home yet?'

'No, they are going to stay with my cousin a while longer, but I speak to them every day and they are okay.

They understand the situation and think it is better to be safe.'

'Do they understand why you haven't gone home yet?'

'Yes, and they agree I should wait. They don't want me to take any risks.'

'That's good. You know you've got a room at our house for as long as you want, don't you?'

'Thank you, I appreciate that, and Kathy has said the same. But now you're out of hospital I'll be moving out.'

Mason glanced over, but didn't speak.

She glanced back at him. 'You know it is for the best after…' Her voice trailed away.

Mason thought for a moment. 'Where will you go?'

'Stephen, my ex-stepfather, has been in touch. He's asked me to go and stay with him until I'm ready to return home.'

'What does your Mother think about that?'

'She is not pleased about it. But she prefers it to me returning home just yet. It was my mum who passed me his number after he rang her to find out where I was.'

Mason looked at her, puzzled. 'How did he know you were involved?'

'It was all over the news three weeks ago. He rang my mum to see if it was me.'

'But they didn't release your name. At least not on the bulletins I saw, and Jim Barker promised your name would be withheld.'

'But they did say a twenty-two-year-old girl from Moldova had been rescued from a trafficking gang by you. Your name and picture were all over the news.'

'I know. They used a ten-year-old photo. Made me look a lot younger. But there must be thousands of twenty-two-year-old Moldovan girls. How could he narrow it down to you?'

'He said he was worried when he saw the news, so he rang just to make sure it wasn't me. When he found out it was, and once he knew the situation, he asked my mum to pass on his number to me. She did, reluctantly, and when I rang him he invited me over. I told him I would go when you got out of hospital.' She paused for a few seconds and said, 'I liked your photo.'

The journey home was short and taken up mainly with Kathy explaining how good her sister Jan had been at looking after her, and how Mike, her husband, had helped to straighten up the house after the mess left by the Albanian's.

As they pulled into the driveway of their house, Mason had a flash-back to when he'd arrived home to find Kathy bleeding on the kitchen floor and Rosie missing.

'Who fixed the back door?' he asked.

'Mike,' Kathy said. 'And he's fit extra bolts so it'll be impossible to kick it open now.'

'I owe him,' Mason said.

51

MASON

They entered the house, and Kathy and Rosie went straight to the kitchen to prepare some food. Natasha went with Mason into the lounge. She sat in an armchair, and Mason sat on the sofa opposite.

'It looks better than the last time I saw it,' he said.

Natasha glanced around and nodded. 'I'll ring Stephen later, and he can pick me up tomorrow.'

'That's fast.'

'It's better that I go soon. Kathy apologised for what she said at your apartment, and she has been great these past three weeks, but I think she is happy for me to go now that you are home.'

'Did she say that?'

'No, it is just a feeling I have, and when I suggested going, she agreed.'

'I'll talk to her.'

'No, don't, I will go. You two need time and space to sort things out. I will be fine at Stephen's house.'

'Where is it?'

'He lives in Surrey now. It's a house he has owned for many years, but it was rented out when we lived with him in London. He moved into it two years ago.'

Mason thought for a moment, and said, 'I'll take you.'

'What?'

'I'll take you to Stephen's next week. Stay with Rosie over the next few days. I know she'll love that.'

Natasha stared at him through narrowed eyes. 'What are you up to, Mason?'

'Okay, I want to get him checked out before you go over there. I'll speak to Jim.'

'You are as bad as my mum. She doesn't trust him either.'

'It's not that I don't trust him. I don't know him. I just want to be sure, that's all.'

She stared at him with just the hint of a smile, but said nothing. Her expression said it all. She was pleased he cared.

'What's his last name?'

'Harrington-Webb'

'Double-barrelled?'

'Yes, isn't it considered posh in the west to have a double-barrelled name?'

'I don't think like that. A name's a name and that's it. Is Stephen spelt with a v or a ph?'

She took a moment to answer. 'Ph.'

'Are you sure? You had to think about it.'

'I had to remember it in written form. They both sound the same when you speak them.' She took another moment. 'Yes, I'm sure. It's with a ph, but I don't think you'll find anything. He does not seem the type to have a. . . how do say—'

'A criminal record?'

'Yes, I don't think he's been arrested for anything.'

'You're probably right, and it's no guarantee of his character either way, but I'd still like to check.'

She smiled and gave a nod. 'Then I'll wait until you get the answer.'

The lounge door swung open, and Kathy and Rosie carried in plates of wedge-shaped sandwiches, two types of cake, and four mugs of coffee. They placed them down on the glass topped coffee table and Kathy pointed to a crack running across its width.

'That's what our uninvited visitors left us with,' she said. 'That and a broken television, and broken photo frames, and chipped dining chairs, and—'

'Forget it,' Mason said. 'None of that's important. We got our baby back, and that's all that matters.'

'I'm not a baby, I'm sixteen,' Rosie said.

He grinned. 'You'll always be my baby girl, no matter how old you get.'

She sighed. 'I feel a lot older than sixteen after everything that's happened.'

'I know, Darling, and I'm so proud of you.' He glanced at Kathy. 'We both are.'

Kathy nodded.

Natasha put down her coffee cup. 'I've only known you for a few weeks, but I'm proud of you, too, Rosie. I could not have dealt with it like you when I was your age.'

Rosie smiled at Natasha.

Mason turned to Kathy. 'Natasha will be going to stay with her ex-step-father in a couple of days.'

Kathy glanced from Natasha to Mason. 'Yes, she told me she would go after you were discharged from hospital. She's been a big help with Rosie. I couldn't have gone back to work if she hadn't been here. I couldn't have left Rosie on her own.'

'Mum,' Rosie said. 'Not you as well.'

Just then, the doorbell chimed, and Kathy and Rosie jumped.

Mason sprung up from his seat. 'I've just remembered. I didn't see the police out front when we came home. When did they leave?'

Kathy answered, 'They were here yesterday, but they said it was their last day because they would be standing down when you came home. They said they wouldn't be needed if you were here.'

'I half expected that, but I'm not exactly back to full fitness just yet.'

He walked to the front window and glanced out just as the bell chimed for the second time. 'It's Jim,' he said as he tapped on the glass. One minute, he mimed. Then went to the door and showed Jim into the lounge to say hello to the girls. After a few minutes, Mason suggested they talk in his study.

Mason sat on his office chair and ran his hand across the laminated wood effect desk. Then he looked at the dust on his fingertips. 'Last time I sat at this desk, my only concern was what I was going to have for dinner, and what

328

I was going to do for the rest of my life. It's only been three weeks but feels like a hundred years.'

Jim sat back on one half of a two-seater sofa. 'From what I heard, it could have been a lot longer than three weeks.' Should have been a funeral according to the incident report. As if your reputation amongst the guys wasn't big enough. You're bordering on superhero right now.'

'I don't think that's justified. I just got lucky, that's all.'

'Lucky?'

'Yeah, I had Natasha on my side.'

Jim just looked at him.

'One day, I'll tell you all about it.'

Jim shrugged.

Mason asked, 'What's the latest with Jones?'

'He's not said a word since they took him in. No comment all the way and always with a high-powered lawyer by his side. No duty solicitor for him.'

'What's his real name?'

'Gregory Carlton Bartholomew.'

Mason shrugged. 'I can see why he uses Jones.'

Jim nodded.

Mason lowered his voice. 'I need to ask you to do something for me.'

Jim raised an eyebrow, but said nothing.

'What's that face for?'

'What? Why am I apprehensive? Why am I worried? Could it have anything to do with the fact, that recently, people in contact with you have either ended up with a bullet between their eyes, or their windpipe crushed?' He grinned out of one side of his mouth. 'Am I over reacting when you suddenly lower your voice and ask me to do something for you?'

Mason laughed and nodded. 'Putting it like that, I guess not. But don't worry, I'm not asking you to kill anyone. Just run some checks on a name for me and before you say anything, I know what I'm asking. It's against regulations to do PNC checks for someone outside the force. I'll have to get used to being a powerless civilian.'

'Powerless. If ever an adjective didn't apply to somebody, it's that one with you.'

'Okay, but what I mean is, you can justify this check.'

'How?'

'Because the check is relevant to a witness living on your patch.'

Jim stayed quiet, but looked puzzled.

'I want you to run the name Stephen Harrington-Webb through the system and see what turns up.'

'Never heard of him. He's not part of the enquiry as far as I know, and by the way, the investigation is being run by Kent Police. That's where most of this shit went down, so it's their case.'

'What about the abduction? Rosie was taken from here. And then there's Tom, the kid at the garage. He must have been killed by the two Albanians who kidnapped Rosie.'

'Yeah, we have an investigation ongoing, but it's sort of shackled to the Kent case. Twelve dead bodies overshadow even Rosie's kidnap and the kid's death.'

'Twelve? By my calculation, there were eleven. Buckingham, plus seven of Jones's goons, a club member dressed in a silly red robe, with a broken bottle and a death wish. Then there was the skinny guy, and Jones's wife, Danielle.'

'There was one more, on a desk in the study. The post-mortem revealed a knife wound through his Adam's apple and out the back of his neck.'

'I forgot about him.'

'Don't worry, Natasha already told us what happened. Kent police are not pursuing it. They're recommending self-defence to the Crown Prosecution Service. Hopefully, they'll do the same in your case. Even though you made quite a splash over there, I doubt they'll bring charges under the circumstances. As Coulson said, they should write it off as self defence.'

Mason nodded and thought for a moment. 'The guy on the desk in the study.'

'What about him?'

'His name's Korab, he's Albanian.'

'We know. Natasha told us.'

'The other guy, the one who was with Korab when they kidnapped Rosie. His name's Artan, he's still out there.'

'Yeah, we know that, too. We've got a team looking for him.'

'How many in the team?'

'Two.'

Mason shook his head but said nothing.

'Rewind a minute,' Jim said. 'Who is this what's-his-name something-something Webb?'

'Stephen Harrington-Webb is Natasha's step-father, or he was a few years back until her mother divorced him.'

'How does he fit in?'

'Well, you know why Natasha's still here?'

'Yeah, she's been advised not to go home for a few weeks in case the traffickers come for her again. Apparently, it's happened before when girls have got away and gone home.'

'That's right, and that's why she's going to stay with Harrington-Webb for a while, so I just want to see what we know about him first. Especially after what she's been through. I don't want anything else bad happening to her.'

Jim took a moment before answering. 'I thought she was staying at your place with Rosie and Kathy, and you now that you're home.'

Mason said nothing.

Jim smirked. 'Am I missing something?'

Mason cleared his throat. 'Nothing happened. But Kathy picked up on some vibes. You know, women's intuition. Before I went into hospital, she wasn't too happy about Natasha being around. I mean, have you looked at Natasha? She's gorgeous. What wife wouldn't be wary?'

'So what worries you about the stepdad?'

'Not a lot. But Natasha's mum didn't trust him. She wouldn't let her stay there after they split up.'

'Has Natasha made allegations against him?'

'No, to the contrary. She said his interest in her seemed innocent, and he never said or did anything inappropriate.'

'So why the concern?'

Mason stared down at the floor for a long moment. Then raised his head. 'I don't know, Jim, just a feeling, that's all, a gut feeling. It's probably nothing, but I just want to be sure. She's a witness on your patch, so the checks can be done above board.'

Jim shook his head. 'I think we're wasting our time, but jot down his full name and date of birth, and I'll see what I can find out.'

'Thanks Jim, she doesn't know his date of birth but thinks he's around fifty and his birthday is in January. There can't be too many Stephen Harrington-Webbs born in January, living in Surrey, with a previous address in London. And it's Stephen with a ph.'

52

MASON

The next morning Mason was first to get up and hit the shower and go down for breakfast. As he finished his first cup of tea, Kathy and Rosie joined him at the kitchen table.

The boiler fired up a few feet away, and Mason glanced up to the ceiling, which was directly below the bathroom. 'Natasha must be up.'

Rosie nodded. 'She went into the bathroom as I came down.'

'I'm taking her to Surrey today,' he said.

'What time?' Kathy asked. Then she opened the fridge and took out a pot of natural yoghurt. She peeled off the top and spooned half of its contents into a bowl of muesli.

'It depends,' Mason said. 'I'm waiting for Jim to call.'

Right on cue, Mason's phone sprang to life and hovered across the wooden tabletop in an intermittent vibrating dance.

He plucked it from the table and swiped to answer. 'Hi Jim, what you got?'

'According to PNC, not a thing, he's clean. Not even a speeding ticket.'

'Natasha was right then. She said there'd be nothing to find.'

'I had Sharon run his name through social media and some databases.'

'I remember Sharon, she's a wizard with all that. If she can't find something, it doesn't exist. What did she get?'

'He's made a chunk of cash from company take-overs. He buys out companies in trouble at knock-down prices and strips out the assets. The last one involved a national chain of couriers. He bled the pension fund dry and sold what was left of the company for peanuts. According to social media, that one could come back to bite him soon. There are court actions against him for over two million, but even that's believed to be a fraction of what he's worth.'

'So, not a nice man, then?'

'Not if you're one of the pensioners he left in his wake. But that's not all. He's a big player in commercial property, mainly in and around London but he's been doing a lot of travelling recently to Prague, Madrid, Amsterdam, and even as far as Rio.'

'A man who enjoys travel and holidays or a man looking to do business in some of the world's best cities for the sex trade.'

'Can't blame him for choosing some of the wildest party capitals of the world.'

'I suppose not. But from what you've just told me about his business credentials, I can't say I'm likely to be a fan any time soon.'

'But legally at least, he's squeaky clean, so you can put your mind at rest as far as Natasha is concerned.'

'Yeah, it looks like my radar is off pitch. Must be the coma dulling my senses. But thanks Jim, I appreciate your help. And pass on my appreciation to Sharon.'

After the call, Mason stared at his phone, deep in thought. He hadn't expected Jim to find a criminal record linked to Stephen, and now it had been confirmed he should feel better than he did. But he still had that nagging feeling deep in the pit of his stomach. *Those three days in a coma must have really messed with my instincts.* He looked up to see Rosie staring at him across the table.

'Well, are you going to tell us what that was about?' she asked.

'It was nothing to worry about. Just Jim updating me, that's all.'

Kathy swallowed down the last of her muesli and put down her spoon. 'Well, are you going to update us then?'

Mason got up from the table and tucked his phone into his pocket. 'Nothing of interest. Just Jim running names through the system looking for anything of note.'

'And?' Kathy said.

'And nothing. Where are my car keys?'

Kathy opened the top draw on a pine chest next to the table and pulled out his keys. He took them, thanked her, and headed for the door. 'I'll just check the battery. It's been stood for three weeks.'

Mason slid into the driver's seat of his old Ford Mondeo and slotted the key into the ignition. With the fingers of his left hand crossed, he turned the key with his right and the engine fired on the first turn. He popped the bonnet catch and jumped out to check under the hood.

He heard a voice he recognised. 'Is everything okay?'

He raised his head to see Natasha walking towards him in tight black jeans, a white cotton camisole top, and white sports shoes. Her flowing black hair flicked in the gentle summer breeze. He took a moment to look at her, then to be discrete, he turned back to his maintenance.

'Just checking,' he said.

'I heard your phone ring. Any news yet?'

'Yes, it was Jim. Your ex-step-dad checks out. You were right. Apart from some dodgy business deals, he seems clean.'

'So you and my mum need to stop worrying.'

'I guess so. But I'll take you, anyway. I still want to meet him.'

'That's okay with me. Whenever you're ready.'

He dropped down the hood of his car and wiped his hands on an old rag. Then he took a moment to look at her again.

Natasha smiled. 'I'd better get my bag ready.'

'Bag?'

'Yes, while you were in hospital, I bought a few things. I couldn't keep wearing Rosie's clothes.'

'I suppose not,' Mason said. 'We can go after you've had breakfast. Did you get his post code?'

'Of course, when I spoke to him last night.'

'So he's expecting you?'

'Yes.'

They went back to the kitchen and Natasha prepared herself eggs, toast, and coffee. When she finished she said her goodbyes, twenty-minutes' worth, mainly while hugging Rosie and promising to keep in touch. The two girls had a strong connection after going through similar experiences.

Rosie's smiles and waves couldn't conceal her sadness at the sight of her newfound friend driving away.

Natasha waved back until Mason turned right at the end of the road and the two girls lost sight of each other. He drove in silence for a few miles, leaving Natasha with her thoughts. Then he turned his head and asked, 'Are you okay?'

Natasha took a moment then sniffed and said, 'I'm going to miss her.' Then she sniffed again and said, 'And you, and even Kathy.'

Mason glanced at her again. 'Kathy?'

'Yes, I don't blame her for the way she feels. She hid it well while you were in hospital. She made me feel welcome.'

'I'm glad to hear that. She's a good person, really. I wouldn't have been married to her for twenty years if she wasn't.'

Natasha nodded. 'I hope you can sort things out.'

Mason stayed quiet. Then reached over and pulled out the sat-nav from the glove box, stuck it to the windscreen, and plugged it in to the cigarette outlet. Then they both looked at each other and laughed.

53

MASON

Fifty minutes later, the sat-nav announced they had reached their destination. There was a sign that read: Welcome to East-Brook House. It was stamped onto a metal plate and slung on a chain between two posts ten feet above the entrance to a single lane access road. The gravel track led to a large period house set well back from the road, and as they drew near, it opened onto a wide circular drive with a flower bed and a small pointed stone monument in the centre.

In the middle of the flat fronted house, there were tall double doors in solid wood painted dark blue and adorned with what looked to be solid brass furniture. Mason counted six large square windows along the ground floor, all identical, and made up from several smaller square panes of glass. There were seven along the top floor, with the extra one directly above the entrance. The high-pitched roof had dormer windows, suggesting there were additional rooms in the attic. The front forecourt was low mainte-

339

nance, covered in stone chippings with border stones, and small lawns on each side.

As the Mondeo crunched to a halt in front of the double doors, Mason unfastened his seat belt and turned to look at Natasha. She did the same.

'Well, this is it,' he said.

She stared at him for a full a moment before leaning across and kissing him on the lips. He didn't push her away. Despite the age gap, and despite being married, and despite her being able to get any man she wanted, he couldn't resist.

She sat back in her seat and glanced over her shoulder at the house. There was no sign of Stephen, so she turned back to Mason.

'In another life we are together,' she said. 'In another life, you are not married, and there is nothing to keep us apart. In another life I have fallen in love with you.'

She opened the door and stepped out. She paused by the car for a moment, then bent down to make eye contact with him.

'No,' she said. 'In this life I have fallen in love with you.'

Then she closed the car door and walked to the blue double doors and rang the bell.

Mason stared out of the passenger window, his eyes focused on the most beautiful creature he'd ever seen, and for the first time in years he was speechless. His thoughts were interrupted when the left-hand door opened and a man stepped out onto the wide step. He hugged Natasha, and she hugged him back.

Mason stepped out and shouted across the roof of his car. 'Hello.'

The man looked up and shouted back, 'Hello.'

Mason joined them on the front step and shook hands with the man. 'I'm Mason Cooper, pleased to meet you.'

The man nodded. 'I've heard about you. I'm Stephen. Thank you for rescuing my Natasha.'

Mason wanted to say, *She's not your Natasha.* But instead just said, 'Don't mention it.'

Natasha smiled at Mason and took his hand. 'Come in for a coffee before you drive back.'

Mason knew what she was doing. She knew he wanted to meet Stephen before leaving her there, and that meant more than just shaking hands and a few pleasantries on the front doorstep. And part of him wanted to believe that she didn't want him to go just yet.

Stephen showed them into a huge kitchen at the end of a wide entrance hall. The units were gloss white above and below a black quartz worktop, and all on a white porcelain floor.

'Very nice,' Mason said as he glanced around. 'Your own design?'

'Unfortunately, I can't take the credit,' Stephen said. 'I was out of the country when it was done, so I left it in the capable hands of my interior designer.'

'Interior designer, I'm impressed.'

'Don't be,' Stephen said. 'Can I get you something to drink?'

'Just a coffee, thanks.'

'Where's the bathroom, Stephen?' Natasha asked. 'I would like to freshen up.'

'Take your bag to your bedroom, Natasha. It's the second door on the left at the top of the stairs. It has an ensuite.'

She thanked him and made her way to the stairs in the middle of the entrance hall.

Stephen filled a stainless-steel kettle from the tap and set out three cups he'd taken from an upper cupboard.

Mason studied him. He was tall, around six-feet-two, and slim. His brown hair was neatly trimmed and his face recently shaved. He wore a pale blue open-necked shirt with the cuffs turned back twice, and grey trousers with an immaculate front crease. His shoes looked like they cost more than Mason's last monthly salary, and a large diamond ring on his right hand must have cost more than the average family car. Elegant but flash. Mason thought.

'Do you work abroad a lot?' Mason asked.

Stephen poured the water into the cups and stirred in the coffee. 'I didn't say I was *working* out of the country.'

'Sorry, I just presumed.'

'That's okay, I was scouting for properties, so you could say I was working.'

'Did you find any?'

'Not on that particular visit but I did on others.'

'Anywhere nice?' Mason wasn't just making polite conversation. He was trying to glean any information he could about the man he was about to leave Natasha with. But it was also something of a habit. A consequence of eighteen years spent as a detective.

'Prague,' Stephen said.

'Anywhere else?'

'Rio and Madrid are possibilities. But then you know that, don't you?'

Mason said nothing.

Stephen said, 'You've done your homework. If you're as good as Natasha says you are, then you've checked me out. And that's why you're here now, isn't it? To check me out?'

Mason said nothing.

Stephen handed him a cup and smiled. 'Do you take milk and sugar?'

'Just milk.'

Stephen topped up Mason's cup from a milk jug and turned to look out of the kitchen window onto a large, neatly trimmed lawn surrounded by six-foot-high fences. Mason glanced out through the same window at the garden. Not as big as he'd expected from the size of the house, but he guessed that the gate in the opposite fence gave access to more land owned by the property.

'I care about Natasha.' Mason said.

Stephen turned back to face him. 'Who wouldn't? She's a beautiful young lady. Very few can match her beauty.'

'That's not the reason. She's a great girl. I would be proud if she were my daughter.'

'But she's not, is she?'

'No, and she's not yours either.' Mason said.

Stephen's face changed. The friendly expression evaporated, and he stood up tall. But just as he opened his mouth to speak, Mason's mobile rang.

'Excuse me,' Mason said. 'I need to take this, it might be linked to the investigations that are ongoing.'

Stephen nodded, 'Please do.'

54

MASON

Mason pulled out his phone and glanced at the display, but didn't recognise the number. He swiped to answer. 'Mason speaking.'

A man's voice on the other end said, 'Mason? Mason Cooper?'

'Yes, who's calling?'

The voice seemed familiar, but as he was searching his memory to match it to a face or a name, the caller said, 'It's Benny Grant from The Lady Blue Club. We spoke a few weeks ago.'

Mason said, 'Yes I remember.'

Grant said, 'I saw the news and was pleased to see you got your daughter back. How is she?'

'She's good Benny. Thanks for asking. Yeah it worked out in the end.'

Mason was sure he had figured out Benny Grant, and knew what kind of guy he was, and what kind he wasn't. And he wasn't the kind to ring for a chat just to pass the time of day. So he expected Grant to have a good reason to call, and he was right.

'You asked me to call you if I heard anything.'

'Yes, that's right.'

'Well, I heard something. And I guess I owe you for dealing with Buckingham and getting him off my back. So I thought you should know.'

'Know what?'

Mason looked over to Stephen and mimed, *Sorry*, as he pointed at his phone.

Stephen nodded.

Grant said, 'You took out a lot of those guys from what I heard, but you didn't get em all.'

'I know,' Mason said. 'We didn't get the top dog in the organisation, a Mr Scarlet. Nobody knows who he is yet.'

'I do, he's a businessman in the city, a property dealer, and he's put a contract out on you. One hundred grand. There's an Albanian leading the race to get you, and from what I hear, he's planning on making it a family affair. Do you know what that means?'

'I can guess,' Mason said.

'It means he won't stop at you, he wants your whole family.'

A chill ran down Mason's back as he listened to Grant talk. He knew it wasn't over yet, but hearing it from Grant made it even more real.

'How do you know this, Benny?'

'I can't divulge my sources, but they are reliable. The Albanian is called Artan, and the guy at the top is known as Mr Scarlet. I'm expecting to hear a name sometime today. I called in some favours to get it. When I hear, I'll text you with it.'

'I appreciate the warning, Benny, and yes, please let me know when you get the name.'

'I will, good luck, Cooper.'

'Thanks, Benny.'

Mason put his phone away and turned to Stephen. 'Sorry about that, I'm just waiting to hear some information about the top guy in the organisation that ran The Scarlet Club.'

'Are you expecting the information today?' Stephen asked.

'Yes, any minute.'

Just then, Mason's phone pinged with a message alert. He pulled out his phone and read the message on the screen. It was from Grant's number and it read, *First name Stephen, owns property all over London. Wait for last name.*

Mason tapped a reply, thanking Grant, then popped the phone back into his pocket. Stephen is a common name. Probably thousands of them in the country, and hundreds in London.

But that gut feeling was back.

He took a moment to think, then pulled out his wallet and took out the card with the red handwriting. He flipped it to the side that read Mr S. Then he took out his phone again and tapped the number on the card into it.

Stephen said, 'Any news?'

Mason said, 'Yes, I just got a first name.'

'Only a first name, that's not much help.'

'I've got a feeling I'm just about to discover who Mr Scarlet is.' He pressed call on his phone, then selected speaker and held the phone in front of him. Several small beeps were audible followed by a ring tone as Mason's phone made the connection with the number it was dialling. But after one ring, Mason's phone was drowned out by a phone ringing in Stephen's pocket. Stephen pulled it out and looked at the display.

Mason said. 'There's no need to answer that, it's me calling you.'

Stephen cancelled the call and the ringing stopped. He stared down at the floor for a moment, then opened a kitchen draw next to him and pulled out a semi-automatic pistol.

Mason smirked. 'Let me guess, a Beretta nine millimetre with a standard fifteen-round magazine. Am I right?'

'I'm impressed.'

'Don't be. How fast can you pull that trigger?'

'Why?'

'Because I reckon you can only pull it two or three times before I get to you.'

'That's enough, isn't it? Three bullets should do the trick.'

'It'll do the trick, eventually, but not before I grab a bread knife from that rack and slice open your windpipe.' Mason turned forty-five degrees. Smaller target and ready to move. 'You see, that phone call just ensured that you'll die before me.'

'How's that?'

'Because I was just told you've taken out a contract on me, and that the killer wants my family dead.'

'So what?'

'So when you threaten my family, you ensure that I'll have enough adrenalin surging through my veins to kill you no matter how many bullets you squeeze off before I get my hands on you.'

'Then we'll both die,' Stephen said.

'Maybe, but tell me first. What about Natasha, why did you ask her to come here?'

'Are you kidding me, you've seen her, she's stunning. I've wanted her since she was twelve years old, but I've been patient. I knew the day would come, eventually. And she's more beautiful now than when she lived with me. But let's not talk about her when she's not here.' He raised his chin and shouted, 'Artan, you can bring her down now.'

Mason looked over his shoulder and sighed when he saw the big Albanian coming towards him, holding Natasha by her hair. Artan stopped in the hall and grinned. 'I knew I'd get you eventually,' he said. Then he pushed Natasha into the kitchen towards Stephen.

She stared at Mason through wide eyes and said, 'I'm sorry.'

Artan took out his pistol and placed it on a table in the hallway. 'I won't be needing that.' Then he interlocked the fingers on both hands and flexed them, cracking his knuckles. The sound echoed down the hall.

Mason turned his stance. 'I'm ready when you are.'

The fight was brutal and lasted several minutes. It spilled from the kitchen into the hall and then into a large study. Though Mason had not fully recovered from his wounds, the adrenalin ensured he felt no pain. As both men stood opposite each other, bloodied and breathless, Artan made his final charge. Mason lowered his stance and drove his right fist into Artan's throat, stopping him instantly. As the big man gasped for breath, Mason drove a kick forward and upward into Artan's groin, dropping him to his knees.

Mason stared at him and thought how similar he looked to his brother in his final moments of life. He moved to Artan's side and drove a fatal blow with his knee into the big man's temple.

Artan toppled over and took his last breath.

Exhausted, Mason staggered back and rested on a desk opposite the study door. Stephen appeared in the doorway, pistol in one hand and a fist full of Natasha's hair in the other. The table where the Albanian had left his gun was just behind them.

Stephen said, 'You fought well, Cooper. It's a pity it was all in vain.'

Mason focused on Natasha. She grimaced as Stephen pulled her head back.

'Let her go, Stephen,' Mason said. 'Let her leave and I won't resist.'

Stephen laughed. 'Having seen how you handled the hardest man I've ever met and made him look ordinary, I have no doubt you could have done what you said in the kitchen. I think you could have killed me even with three bullets in you. But not now. Just look at you. You have nothing left, you're spent. Whereas I have it all. I have more money than I can spend, and now I have Natasha. And I can keep the Scarlet Club going. I just need a new manager now Jones is locked up. There'll always be a market for what we sell.'

Mason's heart jumped at the sound of Natasha's name.

'Let her go, Stephen, for just a minute. So she doesn't witness what you're about to do.'

Natasha said. 'Yes, Stephen, please let me go upstairs. I'll wait for you. I don't want to watch this.'

Stephen didn't move for a long moment as he appeared to think about what Natasha had said. Then he turned to look at her. 'You'll wait upstairs?'

'Yes I will,' she said. 'Why do think I came here? I wanted you, too.'

Stephen smiled at her and said, 'Okay, but if you try to run, I will kill you.'

'I know, Stephen. I won't run.'

He let go of her hair, and she looked up at him and smiled. Then she slowly turned and walked into the hall.

Stephen turned back to Mason. 'Can you guess what I'll be doing within a minute of killing you?'

Mason pushed himself up and stood unaided in front of the desk. In just a few days, he'd learnt enough about Natasha to know exactly what she was about to do, and he was right.

'Stephen,' Natasha said in a low, deliberate voice. 'Drop the gun or I will shoot you dead.'

Stephen glanced over his left shoulder. Natasha held Artan's pistol in an outstretched hand, pointing straight at Stephen's head.

'You couldn't do it, Natasha. You couldn't shoot me.'

'If you believe that you are more stupid than I thought you were. But then you were stupid enough, or arrogant enough, to believe I wanted you, weren't you? Drop the gun now, or I will kill you. You will be number three. Mason can tell you about the first two.'

Mason studied Natasha. Her right hand was trembling, but her stare was firmly locked onto Stephen. There was steel in her eyes.

Stephen was silent for a moment, and then he said, 'So what now?'

'Drop the gun and step into the hall. I will let you leave. I owe you that for being my stepdad. Or my ex-stepdad.'

Mason was surprised. This was not what he expected to hear. Why would she let him go?

Stephen remained silent for a long moment, then slowly he bent at the knees and dropped the Beretta on to the floor. Natasha backed up as he walked into the hall. He paused and look at her.

She pointed at the door. 'Get out.'

Stephen turned and left the house. Mason went to the window and watched him walk across the drive to a large brick garage. He watched the double door roll up, and he watched him get into a black Range Rover. Then he watched him drive up to the front doors and lower his window, and he heard him shout, 'Natasha, how is Katerina, how is your little sister?' Then he rolled up the window and drove away. As the Range Rover turned onto the main road, Mason looked at Natasha.

'Why did you let him go? You think you owe him that?'

Natasha tightened her lips and shook her head. 'I owe him a bullet in the back of the head after he tricked me to come here and was about to shoot you.'

'Then why?'

She looked at the gun in her hand. 'This bloody thing wouldn't shoot. I pulled the trigger as soon as I aimed it at him and before I spoke to him. But it's jammed. It wouldn't fire.'

Mason walked over to her. 'Let me see.'

She handed him the gun, another Beretta. He looked at it, smiled, and shook his head. 'The safety catch is on.'

'What?'

'The safety catch, right there.' He showed her the side of the gun and pushed the lever with his thumb 'Off and on, and off and on.' Then he flipped the gun to show her a similar lever on the other side.

Embarrassment flooded her face. Mason put his arms around her and hugged her to him. 'It's okay.'

His phone rang again.

MASON

Mason pulled out his phone and swiped to answer. It was Benny Grant again. 'Cooper, I just got more info.'

'Go ahead Benny.'

'The top guy is Stephen Harrington-Webb. As I said earlier, he's a London businessman but has fingers in many illegal pies.'

'Thanks Benny. I'm at his house now. Just had a run-in with him and his hitman, Artan.'

'And you're still alive? What happened?'

'Let's just say Artan certainly won't be collecting on that contract.'

'What about Harrington-Webb, Mr Scarlet?'

'He took off in his Range Rover.'

There was a moment's silence. Then Grant said, 'I think I know where he'll go.'

'Yeah?'

'His associate in the trafficking business is an Albanian, like Artan. His name is Malik.'

Mason took a breath. 'I know him. You got an address for him?'

'He's holed up in an old brickworks in Leicestershire. It's next to an old disused mine. The nearest village is Brookington, it's about four miles away. He's gathering help but not the type that lay bricks. He's pulling in guys from other crews in the city. That's how I know what's going on. He tried recruiting one of my guys who used to run with him a few years back, but pulled out when he learned about the trafficking side of their business. Your man might go there.'

Mason stayed silent. Mulling over what Grant had told him.

Grant said. 'What you gonna do?'

Mason said. 'Take a drive into the Leicestershire countryside. I hear it's nice this time of year.'

'You're gonna need firepower and back-up, they'll be locked and loaded.'

More silence.

Grant said, 'I can help with the firepower, but not the back-up. I have contacts if you want to buy. But my days rocking and rolling in a gun fight are over. I'm too old for that now. Just come into the club if you want to buy some hardware, and I can set you up with a meeting.'

'Thanks Benny. I might just do that.'

After the call, Mason told Natasha the details of his conversation with Grant and suggested they go to his club in London.

Natasha said. 'But we don't need any more guns, we've got these two.' She pointed to the Beretta in Mason's hand

and the other one on the floor that Stephen had dropped near Artan's body.

'I'm going to need more than these,' he said.

'You mean we are going to need more than these.'

'What?'

'You heard what Stephen said before he drove away. That wasn't polite conversation when he asked about my little sister. That was a threat.'

'I know that.'

'Then you should know this. Just as you would do anything to protect your daughter, I will do anything to protect my little sister. So I'm in this all the way. I won't be happy until I see him take his last breath.'

Mason took a long moment to think over what she had said. Then he bent down and picked up the Beretta from the floor and handed it to Natasha. 'I'm not going to argue with you. I've seen what you can do.'

Natasha showed just the hint of a smile.

Mason said, 'Now we know how the traffickers knew about your sister. It looks like this was a setup from the beginning, all the way back to that woman you met in Bucharest.'

'Of course, that's it. I remained friends with Stephen on Facebook. He must have seen that I was going to Romania to see family, so he got his contacts there to target me.'

Mason nodded, then went to the large oak desk situated in front of the window in the study and searched through paperwork, notebooks, and ledgers. There were lots of figures, lots of names, lots of telephone numbers, and hand-written notes. No doubt useful to investigators looking into Stephen Harrington-Webb, the businessman.

But to Mason, it was all meaningless. He sat back in the comfortable executive chair and sighed.

'What were you looking for?' Natasha asked.

'I don't know.' Mason said.

'Then how would you know if you'd found it?'

'I'd know.'

He glanced down into a woven straw waste paper bin that was empty apart from a few torn fragments of lined paper. He bent down and pulled out a couple of pieces and placed them on the desk. Then opened one of the notebooks on the desk in front of him. The paper matched. Nothing unusual about that. Most bins in most studies would have the same discarded note paper. But something made him retrieve the other fragments and lay them flat on the desktop. Then he spent several minutes sliding them around until they married up with the other pieces, and slowly, like a jigsaw puzzle, it all came together.

'What is it?' Natasha asked.

'Not sure yet, it looks like a list of some sort.'

He used his hand to flatten the paper fragments until he was able to read the words.

'It looks like a note to remind him to go shopping,' Mason said.

'Why rip it up then?'

'Because it's not a grocery list, and at the top of the page, it says for Malik. It's a reminder for six Beretta pistols, twenty-four fifteen-round magazines, and a thousand rounds. And there's more. It looks like four MP5's with twenty fifteen-round magazines.'

'What's an MP5?'

'It's a German made light-weight automatic rifle or

machine gun. It was made famous by the SAS back in 1980 when they took out terrorists with it in the Iranian Embassy siege in London. It's popular and very effective.'

'That is before my time,' she said.

'Yeah, I was only a kid when it happened, but I remember it well.'

'How do you know so much about the rifle?'

'A good friend and colleague of mine was a firearms instructor. I used to go to the range with him. They have just about every small arms weapon available, so I've played with most of them. And sometimes on training days we would get shown videos of different weapons used in crime and how devastating the injuries can be. It was to stop any of us from getting the idea that we could shield behind a car door if anyone shot at us. Something they do in the movies all the time, but in real life they'd be blown away. Virtually every firearm will shoot straight through a car door, and just about any other door for that matter.'

'Where would Stephen get weapons like that?'

'The Berettas are readily available in Europe for a price. The MP5s are a little harder to come by, but if you have the right contacts and enough money, there's not much you can't buy. What we need to be concerned about is whether they've taken delivery of this lot yet.'

Mason stood up, stepped over Artan's body, and walked into the hall. 'We should go, but I want to check around here first. I wonder if he has a basement like the one in Buckingham's house in Kent.'

He began searching along the wall below the stairs for a hidden door that might lead down to a basement. Natasha followed. As he studied the wooden panelling looking for gaps or joins, Natasha took hold of a small picture on the wall and turned it clockwise. There was a click and one of the six-foot high panels moved back an inch.

Mason pushed on the panel, and it opened, revealing a staircase leading down into blackness. He looked at Natasha.

'I saw it in a movie once,' she said. Then she grinned. 'But Stephen had the same method of entry to a cellar in his London house. I wasn't supposed to know about it, but I saw him open it once when he didn't know I was behind him. But I never got the courage to go down and see what was there.'

Mason shook his head, smiled, and fumbled inside the panel until he found a light switch. Then they made their way down the stairs. The basement was nothing like the Kent house. There was no sign of anybody having been kept down there and no torture equipment. It was just a concrete floor, bare brick walls, and storage boxes. The strip light on the ceiling gave off a stark light, but good enough for them to take a closer look at the box's contents. They were full of clothes, lamps, books, pots, and general household items, no doubt left boxed from Stephen's previous move.

He was about to give up when he glanced down and saw a thin strip of metal just visible under a few boxes. He pushed the boxes to one side and revealed a steel trapdoor in the concrete floor. It was about four-feet long and two-feet wide. There was a small cut-out in the middle of the nearest long edge, just big enough to put his hand through, and next to it was a keyhole. He tried to pull it open, but it was locked down.

He remembered seeing keys in a drawer of the desk in the study, so he ran back up and returned with two sets with about six or seven keys on each set, but from the shape of the keyhole, only two were a possible fit. They were heavy duty long metal keys, and the first one he tried opened the lock. He put his hand through the cut-out and pulled open the steel door, then swung it over through one hundred and eighty degrees until it rested flat on the concrete floor. Natasha gasped as she looked into the one-foot deep compartment.

Neatly laid out were four semi-automatic handguns, two pump action shotguns with shortened barrels, and two compact rifles which Mason recognised as MP5's, the same as in the note he had pieced together in the study. At one end of the pit there were several boxes of nine millimetre cartridges, twelve-gauge shotgun cartridges, and several magazines for the pistols and the MP5's. At the other end was a large black holdall bag, and next to it was a black tubular item that Mason guessed was a suppressor for the MP5s.

'That could be useful,' he said.

'Are these the weapons in the note?' Natasha asked.

'They could be, but my guess is these are Stephen's own supply, and the note is a separate order.'

Mason pulled out the four hand guns and confirmed they were the same Beretta nine millimetre pistols that Artan had carried and that Jones's men had used. He checked each one in turn and confirmed they were loaded and ready to go. He pulled out the holdall and placed the Berettas into it. Then he pulled out the MP5's and did the same. As he scooped up the magazines for the pistols and the rifles, Natasha took one of the Berettas out from the bag. She now had two.

'I'd better have another one of these,' she said.

Mason watched as she raised a Beretta and pointed it at the wall at the end of the basement. 'They are hard to aim, aren't they?' she said. 'Where's the safety catch again?'

Mason shook his head and took both pistols from her. 'I'm not sure you'll be able to handle the recoil if you fired one of these.'

'But I'm going with you so I need something.'

He reached into the pit and pulled out a shotgun. 'This is a pump-action shotgun. It holds eight cartridges, or nine if there's one in the chamber, and it fires one at a time.' He checked the chamber, making sure it was empty, then handed her the gun. 'You hold this end, point that end at the bad guy, and pull this trigger. If you're having fun, and want to do it again, you pump the slide to reload. Then you point at another bad guy and pull the trigger again. It's going to kick like hell, but at least you can hold it in both hands. Just keep it waist height to avoid it taking your head off when it recoils.'

He pulled out the second shotgun and demonstrated the action of pumping the gun, pointing, and firing. 'So, it's pull, point, and fire, pull, point and fire.'

She practiced a few times with the empty shotgun and seemed to prefer it to the pistols. 'Is there one of those safety catches on this?' she asked.

'Yes, there is.' He showed her its location on the top of the weapon, and how to push it off and on. 'Keep it on until you're ready to shoot and then slide it off with your thumb.'

She pumped the gun again and then looked at him and said, 'Let's do it.'

Mason smiled at her. 'Okay, take it easy, Rambo.'

Mason filled the bag and left the pit empty. Then they headed back upstairs. While he went out to put the holdall in the boot of his car, Natasha ran up to the bedroom to get her own bag. When she came out, she threw her bag onto the back seat and jumped into the front seat beside him.

Mason turned to her. 'Okay, let's go get em.'

56

MASON

It was early evening by the time they reached the village of Brookington. It had taken the best part of three hours to drive from Surrey around the slow moving M25 and up the M1 motorway. So they decided to get some food before completing the final four miles. They found a small village pub and parked in the spaces provided at the side. Theirs was the only car.

Mason had to duck his head as they walked under the old oak beam above the front door into the main bar area. More beams crossed the walls and ceiling, adding old world charm that was both structural and decorative.

They approached the bar, which carried on the old-world theme, with its polished mahogany, hand carved shelves, and low hanging lantern style lamp shades.

Mason guessed it must be over four hundred years old.

The barman looked like he'd just arrived in a time machine from around the year the place was built. He was short and stocky with grey hair turning white, and a matching beard worn longer than most. Mason placed him somewhere around seventy-five, and from the depth of the lines on his face, he guessed they had been seventy-five hard years.

The barman looked up and managed a broad smile. One that suggested they were his first customers of the day. 'Good evening, sir,' he said. 'What can I get you and your'—he hesitated as he studied Natasha–'your beautiful daughter.'

Mason smiled to himself. Even the pause for thought didn't prevent him from getting it wrong. But Mason didn't correct him. He'd rather the guy think she was his daughter than think she was being taken advantage of by an older man.

Mason ordered two local beers and some food, and they took their drinks over to a table in the corner. Natasha sat down on one of the wooden chairs, and he sat opposite her, facing the door. It was an old habit, more necessary now than ever before. He didn't want any nasty surprises. Especially with Malik and his crew only four miles away.

'How many men do think he has now?' Natasha asked.

'Hard to say. But even if he only managed to pull in one from each crew in the City, my guess is around seven to eight. Then there's the guys he already had with him. We could be facing around twelve fully armed men, including Malik and Stephen.'

'Six each,' Natasha said.

Mason grinned. 'I'm still hoping to talk you out of it. You could wait here for me and enjoy the local beer.'

'I'm done waiting in diners, or cars, or pubs. From now on I'm going to be right there by your side.'

Mason shrugged. 'Okay, it seems every time I leave you

on your own you manage to kill someone anyway, so you may as well be with me. And at least you're working your way up through the weapons. First an iron, then a kitchen knife, and next a pump-action shotgun. But that's still quite a leap.'

'I'll be okay. I don't know if you know this, but they were my first kills with an iron and a knife, so I think I did all right for a beginner. I think the shotgun will be easy in comparison.' Then she smirked at him and asked, 'What's the plan?'

'We go in there and blast them off the face of the earth. If the hired help decide to take off, we let them go. But Stephen and Malik must...' he paused and looked across the table at Natasha. 'All joking aside, they have to go down. For your sister's sake, for my family's sake, and for the sake of other innocent girls out there who don't even know they are future victims if those two survive.'

Natasha showed a more solemn face. 'I know, but seriously, us two against twelve?'

'We have the element of surprise. I'll reduce the odds pretty fast.'

'No, my point was, if there's only twelve of them, they have no chance.'

Mason laughed out loud.

A few minutes later a young woman wearing a white apron brought them their meals, and she brought the cutlery and salt and pepper, then retreated through the low narrow door into what must be the kitchen. They ate in silence, Mason planning and preparing mentally for what lay ahead.

When finished, he looked out of a nearby window. 'It's

going to be dark soon. We should take a look at the site. See what we're up against in terms of landscape, entry points, and such.'

Natasha agreed. 'Are we doing it tonight?'

'I'll make decisions once we've had a look. But I'm thinking along the lines of a little recognisance tonight and then moving first thing in the morning. That way I could use the suppressor and balance the numbers when they start to emerge.'

'That sounds like a plan. Where are we sleeping?'

Mason shrugged. 'Did you notice whether this place said anything about bed-and-breakfast on your way in?'

'Sorry, no.'

Mason got up and approached the barman, who was watching a comedy show on an old-fashioned television at one end of the bar. There were no other customers to keep him busy.

'Excuse me. Do you have accommodation here?'

'We used to. Got a couple of rooms up there, but since my wife passed away, God rest her soul, I haven't rented any. She used to do the breakfasts, you see. My kitchen girl lives ten miles away and only works in the evenings.'

'That's okay, can you recommend anywhere?'

'Nearest would be back in Corby, I suppose.' He rubbed his chin for a moment and said. 'Don't see why I couldn't let you have a room if you're not fussed about breakfast. It's got twin beds so you could push them apart. I could get my kitchen girl to prepare something for you and leave it on the bar.'

'You said you had two rooms'

'I do, but one is full of my wife's belongings. I couldn't bring myself to get rid of them yet.'

'Thank you, but we'll try Corby. And I'm sorry about your wife.'

The man just nodded.

Mason returned to Natasha and explained they would need to drive back to Corby after checking out the brickworks.

'I thought I heard him say he has a room.'

'You did, he has, but only one.'

'That's all we need, isn't it?'

Mason looked at her. 'I couldn't ask you to share a room. I mean it's the oldest trick in the book, isn't it? To come back over here and tell you that there's only one room.'

'It would be if it was a lie. How many rooms does he have available?'

'One.'

'So it's the truth and not a trick, is it?'

'Well no, but—'

'But nothing. Tell him we'll take it. That way we don't have a long drive back to that town and we're closer to where we want to be in the morning.'

'If you're sure.'

'I am, unless sharing a room with me would be too horrible for you.'

Mason laughed. 'I promise I will be on my best behaviour.'

She smirked. 'I can't make the same promise.'

Mason shook his head and smiled, then returned to the barman. He left a deposit, signed the book in the name of

Mark Carter, and told him they would be back within the hour. Then he returned to Natasha.

'I'm Mark Carter, so that makes you Miss Carter.'

As they walked back to their car she said, 'I would have preferred Miss Cooper, but Carter is Okay.'

It took twenty minutes and only two wrong turns to find the brickworks. They parked in a small lane one field away and Mason jumped out to scan the countryside. The approach road was open, with only low hedges lining the unlisted country lanes. But along the back of the site, there was a wooded area that appeared to stretch along the length of the perimeter wall.

He jumped back behind the wheel and drove off in search of the best place to park to enter the forest. Before the light had almost gone, he found the perfect little secluded spot. Probably well used by courting couples, as it was off the road and shielded from prying eyes by trees, bushes, and hedges.

'I'm going to go through the woods and take a look.' Mason said as he got out of the car. He opened the boot and took out one of the Beretta pistols and tucked it in the front of his belt, then pulled his jacket closed and fastened two buttons. Before he could close the boot, Natasha leaned in and pulled out another Beretta.

Mason shrugged and closed the boot lid. 'Let's go.'

'Wait,' Natasha said.

She placed the pistol onto the roof of the car, opened the back door and rummaged in her bag on the back seat and came out with a black, long-sleeve cotton shirt. She pulled and shimmied her white camisole top up and over her head and threw it into the bag, giving Mason a full view of her pink lacy bra. Then she pulled on the black, close fitting, stretch top with buttons that started just below her breasts. She fastened the first two, leaving just a glimpse of pink lace visible above. After changing from the white sports shoes into a pair of black, low-heeled ankle boots, she closed the back door, picked up the Beretta, and tucked it into her back pocket. 'Now I'm ready.'

57

MASON

They crossed the narrow lane and headed into the wooded area, where they found a well-worn path through the centre of the trees. They followed it for over a hundred yards, and Mason guessed they had another hundred to go.

Up ahead, a large shaggy dog walked into view towing a man, in a cloth cap and a green barber jacket, on a long fully extended lead.

Natasha turned to Mason and flung her arms around his neck and kissed him full on the lips. He responded in kind and they held the embrace until the man and dog had passed by and were out of sight.

When she stepped back, Mason drew a breath. 'Wow, I hope this is a popular dog walking path.'

'I presume you don't want anyone to see our faces. Especially if this place is going to be all over the news by tomorrow night.'

'You're right. Watch out for more walkers. In fact, we

should stop and do that every ten yards, just to be on the safe side.'

She laughed.

Another few minutes walking brought them to the edge of the forest and right up to the high brick perimeter wall of the brickworks. The eight-feet high wall was too tall to see over, so Mason looked around and found an old tree branch lying amongst the leaves that looked long enough and sturdy enough to use as a kind of ladder. He dragged it thirty feet and wedged it up against the wall. Then he climbed up and looked over the top. His view point was the rear of the site, and he found himself looking straight at a Black Range Rover parked at the back next to seven other cars. There were Fords, BMWs, and VWs.

There were several buildings clustered in the main compound ranging in size from a small outhouse to the main office building, which was brick built, two stories high, and large enough to house a dozen offices. Some had their lights turned on. Fifty yards away there was another, more industrial looking building, with a tall chimney dominating one end. It was probably three times bigger than the office block and had no doubt once housed the ovens, equipment, and machines used to run the site. Stacks of bricks, some over ten feet high, littered the rest of the site alongside piles of sand and aggregate.

He guessed the site originally belonged to the old mine and had been adapted as a brickworks after it closed, probably in the eighties when there was a purge on the mines. Payback for strikes that the politicians of the day believed were holding the employers and the government to ransom.

He'd seen enough. He was sure the Range Rover must belong to Stephen, and that the rest would belong to Malik and his men. The site was a dream for anyone wanting to move around covertly and would provide plenty of cover in a firefight.

He climbed back down and helped Natasha up the branch to have a look. 'It's good to get a view of the site so you can picture it in your mind tonight.'

She spent a minute looking over the wall at the layout and then climbed down. They made their way back to the car without encountering anymore dog walkers.

Back at the village pub in Brookington, Mason paid for the room in full and got the key from the Licensee. They followed the old rickety staircase from the corner of the bar up to a long, narrow landing. He found room two and unlocked the door. Natasha entered first, breathed in, and went straight to the window to open it. Mason glanced around. On one side of the short entrance hall was a small bathroom and on the other side a wardrobe with no door. Then the room widened to accommodate twin beds that were pushed together between small wooden tables supporting frilly lamps. The curtains were predominately white and covered in flowers and perfectly matched the wallpaper.

Mason said, 'The old guy told me he hasn't let the room since his wife died. I felt bad for him and thought it must have been recently. But looking at this room, she must have passed away twenty years ago or more.'

'It is a little dusty,' Natasha said, 'but it will do for one night. I've opened a window to let in some air from this century.'

She went into the bathroom and from the metallic squeaking sound, Mason guessed she had turned on the bath taps and flicked the lever for the shower, which was probably just a simple attachment running off the taps. The pipes banged and vibrated, and moaned and groaned, then he heard the trickle of water slowly picking up pressure. It was shut off just before Natasha came back into the bedroom.

'At least we have a shower.'

Mason had already stretched out on one of the beds, which he'd separated from the other by a few inches.

'You'd better push them back together,' she said. 'I don't want to fall down the gap.'

He smiled and swung his feet around onto the floor and sat up on the side of the bed, then switched on the bedside lamp. Natasha walked over and sat down next to him. She didn't speak. She just gazed into his eyes. He stared back, unable to take his eyes off her. She had little to no makeup on, her hair was tussled and falling partly over her face, and her lips were parted ever so slightly.

Their faces drifted nearer to each other, as if that same magnetic force was at work again. With her fingertip, she gently traced along his top lip and then back along his lower lip. Her touch was electric and sent his pulse racing.

'We are both adults,' she said. 'We have feelings for each other, so why resist? Why fight it?'

He turned his body square to her and cupped her face in his hands. 'You are so young, so beautiful. But we should stop right now. You think this is what you want, but you might regret it in the future, when you find that right person for you.'

She paused for a moment, then said, 'Who knows what I might feel in the future. I only know what I feel right now, and I'm more likely to regret what we don't do, than what we do.'

She leant forward and kissed his lips. He wrapped his arms around her and pulled her close. They fell back onto the bed entwined in each other's arms, their lips pressed together, breathing in each other's breath. Neither had the will-power or the desire to stop what they had started, and as they kissed and stroked each other, clothes were slowly unbuttoned and pulled off, until eventually they lay naked in each other's arms.

He gently rolled her onto her back and traced kisses down her neck, pausing while he teased her soft skin with the tip of his tongue, then continued down to her small, rounded breasts. She gave out little groans of pleasure as his tongue went lower and lower down her trembling body, teasing and caressing all the way. Then her body tensed and her back arched upwards off the bed as she had her first orgasm with him. As she breathed out, long and slow, he kissed his way back up her body to her lips, and slowly lowered himself down and entered her. They moved together on the single bed for what must have been close to an hour before lying in each other's arms, exhausted, but deeply satisfied.

They slept like that until the morning daylight came through the single window and Mason opened his eyes. They had forgotten to draw the curtains or set an alarm, but when he checked the time, it was right on six a.m. The exact time he had planned to get up and prepare for the day's events.

Slowly, he eased his arm from under Natasha's head, then leant over and kissed her shoulder. 'We need to move, it's six,' he said.

He rolled out of bed and went to the bathroom and took a shower. When he came out, Natasha went in. He pulled on the same blue jeans and the same black cotton tee-shirt he'd worn the day before. They were still fresh. The only sweating he'd done the previous night was after taking his clothes off.

While waiting for Natasha to shower and dress, Mason placed the black holdall on the bed and began checking each weapon in turn. He'd done this the day before, but as their lives would depend on these weapons, he would check them again. *You can never be too careful,* he thought as he started with the two MP5s, both loaded with fifteen-round magazines. He checked that the firing mechanism was set to single shot, as fifteen rounds wouldn't last long on automatic. He checked the Berettas, then the shotguns, and then he took out the suppressor. He held it to his eye and checked down the barrel, then returned it to the bag. He would fit it to the MP5 at the brickworks, otherwise the rifle would be too long for the holdall. Before putting everything back in the bag, he loaded eight rounds into each shotgun and checked the safety catches were in the on position.

Natasha came out of the bathroom smelling of flowers and perfume. She dressed in the same faded black skinny jeans, and the same black button up top that she'd worn the night before, but Mason couldn't see any glimpse of pink lace.

'No pink bra today?' he said.

She turned to him and pulled her top down slightly. 'No, black. If I'm going to war with those guys at the brickworks, I don't think they'll take me seriously in a pink bra.'

He raised an eyebrow. 'When you blow a hole in them with a twelve-gauge shotgun, I don't think they'll give a damn what colour bra you're wearing.'

She stopped and appeared to think about what he'd said. Then she shrugged and pulled on her flat leather ankle boots.

The bar area was silent and still. But just as the old man had promised, they found two plates of egg sandwiches on the bar-top next to a flask of hot coffee. They sat at the same table as the day before and ate breakfast.

'He kept his word,' Mason said.

'Not bad either,' Natasha said.

They finished eating, and Mason took a ten-pound note from his wallet and slipped it under the flask. 'For the kitchen girl.'

They let themselves out through the front door, pulling it shut and checking it was locked, before walking to their car. It was still the only one in the car park. Mason opened the boot and placed the holdall inside, then closed the lid and got in behind the wheel. He looked up through the windscreen at the sun trying to force its way through the light clouds.

'Not a bad day for it.'

Natasha looked out and nodded.

'You sure you want to do this?'

She turned her head to look at him. 'I have never been more sure about anything in my life.'

Mason nodded, then drove to the road and turned left. Towards the brickworks.

58

MASON

They parked in the same secluded spot as the night before.

Mason opened the boot and took out the black holdall bag. Then they crossed the road and retraced the route they'd taken the night before. The tree branch was where they'd left it, but Mason turned left at the wall and walked away from it.

'How are we going to get in?' Natasha asked.

'Not there, because we would be exposed when going over the wall. I saw last night that the best spot would be behind the small out-house. I estimated it to be about thirty yards along the wall.'

On the thirtieth stride, he stopped and put down the bag. He took a few steps back and then ran and jumped. He grabbed the top of the wall and pulled himself up to look over the top. Then he let go and dropped back down.

'Perfect,' he said. 'If we go over here, they won't see us.'

He began searching around the bushes and trees for another suitable branch but found nothing. So he left

Natasha with the bag and went to get the branch they'd used the previous night. As he arrived back, two loud bangs echoed through the trees.

Natasha gasped and ducked down. 'What was that?'

Mason looked back through the trees and shook his head. 'It's early morning, it's early summer, and we're in the countryside. My guess is somebody's out hunting foxes, pheasants, rabbits, or whatever. It sounded like it was a few fields away, so don't worry. It's not connected to us, or Malik and Stephen.'

'Do you think they will have heard it?'

'Maybe, but they'll probably think the same.'

He manoeuvred the branch into place and checked it was solid. Then he opened the holdall bag and took out two Berettas. He tucked one inside the back of his belt and the other down the front of his belt. He took out two Beretta magazines and pushed them into the back left-hand pocket of his jeans. Then he took out the MP5s and attached a strap to one of them before slinging it over his shoulder. He took two magazines for the rifle and pushed them into his back right-hand pocket. Next, he took the suppressor and fit it to the MP5 he was holding.

Finally, he went back into the bag and pulled out a shotgun and handed it to Natasha. 'Put some spare cartridges in your pockets,' he said.

She managed to squeeze three cartridges in each of the front pockets of her jeans. 'Six will have to do. My back pockets are too tight now.'

Mason glanced down at her and grinned.

She stood up and said. 'Okay, let's finish this.'

Mason nodded, then turned and climbed up the branch

to the top. He sat on the wall and waited for Natasha. She passed up the holdall and the shotgun and he placed them on the top of the wall. She climbed up and Mason lowered her down the other side behind the small building that was shielding them from the rest of the site. Once her feet were on the ground, he passed her the holdall, the MP5, and the shotgun, and then he lowered himself down to her.

He reached over and turned off the safety catch on the shotgun, took the MP5, and told her to stay behind the small brick built shed.

'I'll make my way over to the front of the office block where I can monitor the front door in the middle and the large factory type building fifty yards away. We need to balance the odds, so I'll use the silencer to take out as many as I can before all hell breaks loose. When it does, my guess is at least one of them may come through that door on the end of the block straight in front of you. It's only about thirty feet away, so all you have to do is point and shoot. The cartridges are large diameter buckshot so at that range you'll cut them in two. Are you okay with that?'

'If it helps me get nearer to that bastard, I'll be fine.'

'Okay, but don't get into a firefight with them. Just shoot and duck behind the building. Remember, it's pull, aim, and fire. You saw how I loaded the cartridges, so when you're empty use the cartridges in your pockets. I'll leave the holdall near the wall if you need more.'

'Got it,' she said.

Mason kissed her on the lips and then made his way to a chest high stack of bricks about forty feet in front of the main entrance to the offices. He checked his watch. It was fifteen minutes past seven. He waited.

As his watch showed seven-thirty, the front door on the office block opened and a man stepped outside. He was around forty years old, medium height and weight, with cropped black hair. He was wearing green combat pants tucked into heavy military style boots, a black tee-shirt, and a black cap. A pistol was just visible sticking up from the front of his belt. He stood with his back to the door and lit up a cigarette.

Mason ducked down behind the bricks and looked over to Natasha. She nodded as if to say she had seen him, then she moved back out of view of the man in case he looked to his left.

Mason flicked off the safety on the MP5, raised the suppressor over the top of the brick stack, and pointed it towards the man. With the rifle nestled into his right cheek, he closed his left eye and lined up the man in his sights. Then he adjusted his right hand and brought his first finger down onto the trigger.

He squeezed and watched the bullet rip into his victim's chest. The man fell back against the door, then staggered forward and collapsed face down in the dirt a few feet in front of the building.

Mason looked over to Natasha and held up a single finger and mimed one.

He turned back and waited.

Less than a minute later the door opened again, and another man, dressed like the first, walked out and froze as he looked down. He rushed to turn over the guy lying on the ground. Mason lined up the rifle on the second guy and waited for him to stand up, which he did within a few seconds of rolling over his friend and revealing the chest wound.

The second man was dead before he could raise the alarm. Mason glanced over to Natasha and held up two fingers. She nodded.

He turned back again and waited.

When the third guy came through the door and saw the two bodies in front of him, he shouted Malik's name and turned to run back inside.

Mason put two bullets into his back before the door closed. But now the third body was inside the building, so any element of surprise had gone. A few minutes later, a window opened on the upper floor and a rifle barrel poked out. It fanned left, then right, and then left again. Mason aimed six inches above the barrel and fired two shots. The rifle kicked up and disappeared back into the room.

Two more windows opened on the upper floor and shots rang out from what Mason guessed were MP5 rifles. They were firing on automatic and the bullets smashed into the brick stacks all around him. He ducked down away from the barrage. Then he heard a loud bang to his right and looked over to see Natasha step back behind the small brick building. She pumped the shotgun to reload and raised her right thumb in his direction. He glanced to the end of the office block nearest to her and saw a man lying on the ground and blood spattered up the wall behind him. They had taken out four, possibly five.

He waited with his rifle trained on the front of the building, but nothing moved. He hadn't seen Stephen or Malik, so it wasn't over yet.

He motioned to Natasha that he was going to approach

the block, then took one more visual sweep before running for the entrance.

As he stood in front of the door, he flicked the MP5 onto automatic. He had nine rounds left in the magazine, so he brought his hand around and checked the spare magazines were still in his back pocket. Then he slowly inched the door open to look inside. He heard footsteps on the floor above. Someone was moving about. Maybe running from office to office and from front to back. They would have no way of knowing how many they were facing.

Mason slipped inside the door and as he moved forward to get view up the wide staircase, a figure flashed across the landing above, firing down as he ran.

Mason tracked the figure and fired off his remaining rounds in an automatic burst but doubted he had hit his target.

He removed the suppressor and discarded the empty rifle in a tall waste bin. Then he swung the second rifle around in front of him and reattached the suppressor. It could still be useful if the firefight moved outside, because although audible, it would be harder for his enemy to determine his position.

While crossing the hall to the stairs, he glanced to his left along the corridor that ran the full length of the block. The door at the end was wide open. It was at the opposite end to Natasha, so she couldn't have seen anyone leaving by that exit.

He turned back to the stairs just as a man ran down, firing an automatic rifle wildly from the hip. Mason knelt down, took aim, and fired three shots. The man fell down the remaining stairs and lay still at Mason's feet. There were three holes in his chest. Mason looked up and listened for a full two minutes. There was just silence. He made his way along the hall to the open door at the end and looked across to the factory. It was the obvious place Stephen and Malik would run to if they had left the offices.

There was plenty of cover between the two buildings, so after scanning the foreground, Mason made a dash for the first stack of bricks. He waited a moment and then ran to the next stack. He was now only twenty yards away, but he would be an easy target when he crossed the last stretch of open ground to the factory entrance.

There was only one way to find out if they were watching and waiting for him, and that was to make the run. He flicked this rifle to automatic and set off with it raised to his shoulder, ready to locate anything that moved in front of him.

To his surprise and relief, he reached the factory wall, next to the open roller shutter door, without resistance. But that was to change as soon as he set foot inside. Bullets ricochetted off the walls all around him as he dived for cover behind oil drums and piles of broken bricks.

Inside the factory, there were large conveyer belts crisscrossing each other. There were low dividing walls, no doubt built for health and safety reasons to funnel non-essential workers away from moving machinery. There were small brick offices scattered around that had probably been used by workers to escape the heat of the ovens, and there was the machinery used to drive the conveyer belts set on concrete foundation blocks. There were ramps to different levels and steel staircases leading up to gantries and an upper floor at one end.

Mason moved around, firing back whenever he was fired upon. He ejected his empty magazine and replaced it with one from his back pocket. A sound above alerted him to someone on a gantry twenty feet above him. He dived to the ground and emptied his rifle at the figure firing at him. Sparks flew in all directions as his bullets ricochetted off the iron walk way. But as the last bullet left his rifle, the man above fell back over the railing and crashed to the ground, dead.

Mason ejected the second magazine and slotted home the last one from his back pocket. Then he changed his position again and continued to exchange fire with several targets in various positions around the factory's main area. He counted two more casualties before his rifle was empty. He brought his hand around to his right-hand pocket for another magazine, but there weren't any more. So he discarded the MP5 and pulled both pistols from his belt. He'd only ever fired with his left hand occasionally at the shooting range, and although competent, he was no marksman with it.

He moved forward up a short ramp onto a higher level. A door swung shut up ahead. He moved towards it, one pistol pointed at the door, and the other outstretched behind him, ready for any attacks from the rear.

When he reached the door, he swung it open and stepped back out of the line of sight. He expected to hear shots, but it was silent. He peeped around the door frame into a large open plan storage area that had shelving and piles of bags that appeared to contain sand or cement, and there were more low dividing walls to maintain clear walkways.

There was enough cover to hide a dozen men if necessary, so it was impossible to know how many were still alive. He brought the Berettas up in front of him and ran inside, both guns blazing as targets became visible. He dropped another of Malik's men before finding himself facing the two men he'd come to kill.

Stephen was about thirty feet to his right diagonal, with a pistol pointed in his direction, and Malik was roughly the same distance to his left, also with a pistol aimed at him. Mason held both arms outstretched in front of him, a Beretta pointed at each of them. The three of them stood in a triangle, all guns raised and ready to kill.

Stephen gave out a forced laugh and said, 'You are good, Cooper. Better than I thought. But now there are two of us with you in our sights. You won't win this one. We only have one target, you have two.'

'Then I'll have to decide which one of you I take with me. If I take you, Stephen, The Scarlet Club dies with you, and many girls will be saved from rape, torture and death. But if I take you, Malik, I will have kept the promise I made to you the first time we spoke on Victor's phone. I told you then I'd find you and kill you.'

Malik said, 'Then you have a difficult choice to make.'

A voice spoke from behind Mason. It was Natasha. Calm and deliberate. 'Keep your promise, Mason. I hate people who break their promises.'

She walked forward and stood fifteen feet to Mason's right, her shotgun raised and pointed at Stephen.

'Natasha,' Stephen said. 'You couldn't shoot me yesterday. What makes you think you can shoot me today?'

'Can a girl not change her mind,' Natasha said.

'Of course, but why would you when you know how I feel about you?'

'Because yesterday you reminded me, that as long as you are breathing, my little sister is in danger. You see, when you spoke her name, you made your last mistake.'

Mason saw the change in Stephen's eyes. The arrogance had been replaced by apprehension and maybe fear. He must have seen the determination in Natasha's eyes and now knew she wanted him dead. Mason lined him up in his sights. He would have to kill him before he shot Natasha. But as he began to squeeze the trigger, a shotgun blast reverberated around the factory, and Stephen took the full force of nine steel balls as they tore into his chest.

Mason turned, lined up both Berettas on Malik, and fired six shots from each alternately. As each round thumped into Malik's head, neck, and chest, he jolted and staggered back, blood spraying into the air. Then he crashed to the ground and lay still.

Mason walked forward, keeping both men in view, but as he closed the gap, he lowered the Berettas. It was over in seconds, and it was clear that neither Stephen nor Malik would ever be a threat again.

Natasha walked forward, and as she stood over Stephen's lifeless body, she pumped the shotgun, aimed, and fired. 'Pull, aim, fire,' she said, in a trancelike state. Then she dropped the gun on the ground and turned to Mason.

'Now Katerina is safe and my family can go home.'

Mason walked over and put his arms around her. 'Yes, it's over, Natasha. It's over.'

59

MASON

Mason picked up the shotgun and the two ejected cartridge casings. 'Follow me, Natasha.'

He made his way around the site, collecting both MP5s and the empty shotgun cartridges near to the small outbuilding. He placed them all into the holdall bag and said, 'Let's get out of here. If anyone heard those automatic rifles, they'll know we weren't shooting rabbits.'

'Why did you pick up the empty cartridges?'

'I loaded the shotgun, my fingerprints and DNA will be on them.'

'What about the cartridges from your pistols?'

'I didn't load the magazines, so they'll probably have Stephen's DNA on them.' He paused. 'That's given me an idea.'

He went back to the factory where he found an old rag on the floor and used it to wipe Natasha's shotgun and the two MP5s, including the magazines, clean of any prints. He bent down and wrapped Malik's right hand around the shotgun stock and then around the trigger mechanism, and his left hand around the wooden slide before discarding the weapon on the ground a few feet in front of him. He did the same with one of the MP5s. Then, he walked over to Stephen and after wiping the Berettas he had used to shoot Malik, including their magazines, he imprinted Stephen's prints on them and dropped them next to his body. He picked up Stephen's Beretta and placed it in the holdall.

Then he said, 'Now we can go.'

As they left the factory, he discarded the second MP5 on the ground near to one of the dead men after using the same method of transferring the man's prints onto the weapon.

'Now it looks like they all killed each other, and even if they work out someone else was involved, they'll probably think it was another one of the gang.'

'Clever,' Natasha said.

They left the site through the main gates and walked around the perimeter wall to the forest and then back along the track to their car. Neither spoke for several miles of motorway as they were both lost in their own thoughts. Thirty miles later, Mason pulled off the M1 motorway and parked in a service station car park.

After a moment, he turned to Natasha. 'You need to leave now, today, while you still can.'

She looked at him but said nothing.

'They may never link those deaths in the brickworks to the Scarlet Club, or to us, or to what happened last month in Kent, but it's safer for you to leave now, just in case.'

Two hours later they arrived at Heathrow airport, and after parking, Mason walked with Natasha to the departure terminals. They found the right desk and he waited while Natasha checked in to her 2.50pm flight to Chisinau Airport in Moldova. Then he walked with her to the security gate.

He had bought her ticket using his phone while parked in the motorway carpark, and they had arrived at the airport just in time for her flight.

As they reached the security gate, they stopped and hugged each other.

'You know I'll never forget you, don't you?' Natasha said, with tears filling her eyes.

'I should hope not,' Mason said. 'I certainly won't forget you. But please keep in touch. You've promised Rosie you would, and remember, you hate people who break their promises.'

As tears trickled down her cheeks, she smiled. 'I don't want to go.'

He nodded. 'And I don't want you to.'

She looked up at him. 'I know I have to, but it doesn't make it any easier.'

Mason cupped her face in his hands. 'Some young man out there is going to be the luckiest guy in the world.'

Natasha reached up and kissed his lips. Then she pursed her lips and nodded. 'Yeah, well, if you can't even take out a simple gang of traffickers on your own, without the help of a girl, what good are you to anyone?'

With tears streaming down her face, she turned and walked through the security barriers and out of sight.

As Mason turned and walked away, he had a feeling deep down inside that one day, he would see her again.

BOOK THREE - AVAILABLE NOW

INNOCENT GIRLS
Powerful, gritty, dark, and disturbing.

When Natasha Caraman's twelve-year-old sister, Katerina, vanishes from a local beauty spot she remembers the threats made against her family and fears the worst.

Natasha knows first hand how evil the criminal gangs that trade in girls can be. But she is about to discover new depths to their depravity. And they are about to find out that she is no longer a helpless victim.

As she cuts a swathe across Europe, and right through their organisation, she realises she will need help, and there is only one man she can trust.

Meanwhile, can young Katerina thaw the icy cold heart of the gangs most prolific kidnapper and avoid every victim's fate?

A fast paced thriller, battling the dark side, and dispensing justice, Natasha Caraman and Mason Cooper style.

Available from Amazon

See Author's message, next.

AUTHOR'S NOTE

Thank you for reading book Two in the Mason Cooper Thriller Series. The novella, TAKING NATASHA (Book 1) is a short prequel and is free to download (in some Amazon stores) or buy in paperback from Amazon.

INNOCENT GIRLS - Book 3, is available now.

GET NEWS OF NEW RELEASES

It only takes a minute to leave your email address for updates on future book releases and other items you may find interesting. Your data will not be shared with any third parties, and I will not bombard you with emails.

Sign-up at **terencemitford.com**

I am always happy to hear from readers and will personally respond to all correspondence, so feel free to contact me at :-

Terence@terencemitford.com

Website: terencemitford.com

ABOUT THE AUTHOR

Terence Mitford is a retired UK police sergeant with 30 years service, and for a time he was in charge of a department dealing with serious sexual offences, domestic violence, and child abuse. It was a period in his career that heightened his awareness of what happens in the shadows of society, behind closed doors, and away from public scrutiny, and it was a period when he encountered the darkest side of human nature.

For many years, he was a dedicated martial arts practitioner and then a police self defence instructor which, in addition to the countless situations he encountered, helps when writing the adrenalin filled action scenes.

He has many books in the pipeline, so doesn't expect to run out of ideas anytime soon.

Made in the USA
Columbia, SC
08 August 2022

64873649R00240